A LOVER'S QUESTION

She savored the moment, letting her hands glide over the powerful muscles of his shoulders, and wander down to let her fingers curl into his springy chest hairs. Zane had claimed his ownership of her body. Now Deborah was claiming her right to his. Her touch produced a shudder that quivered through him. The circle of his arms grew smaller as he molded her more tightly against him and pressed his mouth to her cheekbone.

"Do you know what you are doing to me?" Zane breathed the sensual question into her ear.

from "Difficult Decision"

Yes, I Do

JANET DAILEY

ZEBRA BOOKS
Kensington Publishing Corp.

www.kensingtonbooks.com

ZEBRA BOOKS are published by

Kensington Publishing Corp.
119 West 40th Street
New York, NY 10018

All Kensington titles, imprints, and distributed lines are available at
special quantity discounts for bulk purchases for sales promotion, pre-
miums, fund-raising, educational, or institutional use.

Special book excerpts or customized printings can also be created to fit
specific needs. For details, write or phone the office of the Kensington
Sales Manager: Attn.: Sales Department. Kensington Publishing Corp.,
119 West 40th Street, New York, NY 10018. Phone: 1-800-221-2647.

Zebra and the Z logo Reg. U.S. Pat. & TM Off.

ISBN-13: 978-1-4201-4446-8
ISBN-10: 1-4201-4446-4

ISBN-13: 978-1-4201-0626-8 (eBook)
ISBN-10: 1-4201-0626-0 (eBook)

First Printing: July 2008
10 9 8 7 6 5 4

Printed in the United States of America

Contents

ENEMY IN CAMP

Chapter One

The taxi went as fast as the traffic on the boulevard of Jefferson Avenue would allow. Ahead rose the gleaming structure of the Renaissance Center in downtown Detroit. The seventy-story cylindrical tower of the Plaza Hotel dominated the four sister towers that surrounded it like ladies-in-waiting. The monolith of modern architecture overlooked the Detroit River, the Canadian province of Ontario on its opposite shore, and to the northeast, Lake St. Clair.

The driver slowed the cab at a red light near the entrance driveway to the Renaissance Center and glanced in the rearview mirror at his female passenger. "We're almost there, miss," he announced and noticed her glance at the delicate gold watch on her wrist. "I told you we'd make it in no time flat."

"Yes, you did." The smile Victoria Beaumont gave him was polite, and nothing of her inner impatience showed in her expression.

The cabbie liked the sound of her voice. Calm and well educated. Not that she had talked to him much. Other than confiding that she was late for a lunch date at the Renaissance Center and asking him to please hurry, she'd been pretty quiet and he'd done nearly all the talking.

"I wouldn't worry about him bein' upset. As soon as he sees you he'll forget that you're late." There was no doubt in the cab driver's mind that she was meeting a man for lunch.

He silently wished he was ten years younger, forty pounds lighter, and had all his hair. The heap of up-scale shopping bags and dress boxes on the seat beside her indicated his pretty passenger was kind of high-maintenance, but the cabbie would be willing to overlook that.

"I'm not so sure," Victoria replied, choosing not to ask why he assumed she was meeting a man.

"If he don't, then he don't know a good thing when he sees it," the cab driver insisted and unabashedly studied her profile in his mirror.

Her skin looked smooth and soft to him, with a light tan even though it was only May. She had nice cheekbones, and a perfect nose, not straight and not too short. Her mouth was sensational, soft and shiny with lipgloss. It was obvious to him that she was something special.

"Are you a model?" he asked.

"No." Victoria didn't volunteer the information that she was a member of the idle rich—okay, her family had money but they were never idle. Her mother, for one, had an appointment calendar filled with charity meetings, country club functions, tennis dates, and a variety of parties. Victoria hadn't strayed too far from her mom's example.

"You sure got the looks for it," the cabbie replied. "I oughta know. I get all kinds of passengers in my cab from hookers—pardon my French—to housewives. But you're different. You got class, you know? Hope I'm not talking too much."

"No, it's okay." Victoria thought there might be a compliment in there somewhere, but it was a struggle not to laugh. Her eyes were dancing with it, though, and she looked out the window so he wouldn't think she was laughing at him.

"It ain't just the way you smell," he assured her, having been enveloped in the sensual cloud of her expensive perfume since she had entered his cab. "It's the color of your hair. On any other woman it'd probably be light brown, but on you it looks blond. What color do you call it?"

"I don't know." Victoria had never had to label it before. It couldn't really be considered brown but it lacked the golden quality of true blond. "Honey-colored, I guess."

"Yeah," the driver agreed after a moment's hesitation. "And there's the way you got it fixed, too. When my wife goes to a beauty shop, she either comes out lookin' like a poodle or else like she's had her hair starched. Even though your hair ain't long it looks, uh, sorta windswept. Is that the right word?"

"It'll do," Victoria murmured. The cabbie was so engrossed in her reflection she had to call his attention to the traffic. "Um, the light's about to turn green."

"Right," he answered quickly, like he'd been paying attention all along.

When the traffic ahead of him moved out of the way, he turned the cab into the drive and stopped at one of the entrances of the center. He got out of the cab and walked around to the rear passenger door to help Victoria, assisting her with a gallantry that was more touching than amusing.

"Thank you." Victoria added a generous tip to the fare.

"You're welcome." He began hauling out her shopping bags and dress boxes from the rear seat. "You want some help with this?"

"I think I can manage." It took some maneuvering to slip her fingers through all the plastic handles, but she succeeded with help from the cab driver. "What time is it?"

"Half past one. And you tell that guy if he's upset with you for bein' late, there's plenty of other fellas that'd be happy to be in his shoes."

"Right." This time there was nothing distracted about the smile lighting her face.

The driver started toward the entrance door to open it for her—the doorman was nowhere in sight—and stopped. "What color are your eyes?"

Hmm. His interest in her was getting to be a little too much. Victoria kept her reply to one word. "Gray."

An audible breath of amazement came from his throat. "I never knew anybody with gray eyes before." It was said to himself as he moved to hold the hotel door for her. "If you ever need a cab again, miss, you just call up my company and ask for Joe Kopacek. That's a Czech name."

"I'll remember, Mr. Kopacek," Victoria promised with a faint nod. Enough was enough. She wasn't going to do anything of the kind.

Inside the entrance, Victoria was confronted by a labyrinth of corridors connecting a multistoried shopping center. No matter how many times she came here, she still had trouble finding her way around. Fortunately a security guard was standing by a wall.

"Excuse me, which way is the restaurant?" she asked.

"Which restaurant?" He grinned at her question. "I think there are fourteen in this complex."

"Aarghh." She couldn't help the muffled exclamation of irritation. Victoria just didn't remember the specific one, so she opted for the place they usually ended up at when they were downtown. "The hotel has a terrace-type café, doesn't it? Near the elevators?"

"Yup." The guard pointed to the corridor on Victoria's right. "Go that way and keep to your left. You can't miss it."

"Thank you."

Victoria followed his directions and arrived at the open center of the complex. It was an ultramodern area of curving, rising buttresses of concrete, its blockiness softened by big potted plants and trees. Crisscrossing walkways and escalators connected one side to the other and one level to the next. At a bottom level was the restaurant Victoria wanted. It looked like a sidewalk café, except that it was in the center of the complex and cordoned off from the rest of the lobby.

Making her way to the restaurant entrance of bamboo screens, Victoria glanced at the tables as the hostess approached. "How many, please?"

"I'm meeting someone here," Victoria explained. She caught sight of a familiar brown-haired woman seated alone at one of the tables with her back to the entrance. "There she is."

With a brief smile at the hostess, she made her way through the tables, the bags and boxes in her hands slowing her down. She didn't want to bump into anyone, seated or not. When she reached the table where the woman was sitting, Victoria stopped and began piling her stuff in an empty chair.

"Hi, Mom. Did you give up on me?" Victoria greeted her with a cheerful but slightly guilty smile. "Sorry. I lost track of the time."

"As long as that was all you lost," Lena Beaumont announced with a dryly indulgent look at the overflowing chair. "Shop until you drop, hmm?"

Victoria simply laughed at that and sat next to her mother. "Looks like I missed Dad." She glanced at the empty coffee cup and crumpled napkin at the place setting opposite her.

"Yes, he had an appointment and couldn't wait."

The waitress appeared to give Victoria a menu and offer her coffee. "No, thank you. Iced tea, please," she requested and began to study the lunch offerings. "What did you and Dad have?"

"I had a club sandwich and your father had soup and broiled fish."

"Healthy choices for him," Victoria said absentmindedly.

"We are at that age." There was a subdued gleam in her mother's gray eyes, which were very much the same color as Victoria's, although the passing years had given them a warm wisdom.

"Mmm." The reply was noncommittal. When the waitress returned Victoria closed the menu and ordered. "Spinach salad with very little dressing—low calorie if you have it."

"Yes, we do." The waitress collected the menu before moving away.

"You have more willpower than I do, Tory." Her mother sighed. "You should loan me some of yours so

I can get rid of this extra fifteen pounds I'm carrying around."

"On you it looks good," Victoria insisted. They were the same height and the same approximate build. Despite the extra weight, her mother still had great, very feminine curves. No one would ever accuse her of being heavy.

"Spoken like a diplomatic daughter." Lena Beaumont laughed.

"On the subject of looking good, wait until you see the clothes I found." With a flick of her long fingers, Victoria gestured toward the bags and boxes piled in the chair near her.

"What did you do, buy a whole new summer wardrobe? I know you 'don't have a thing to wear,'" her mother teased.

"That's not so far from the truth." Victoria felt compelled to defend herself. "Yes, I have tons of clothes, but most of them are from my college days. Ta da! I am twenty-three! It's time I began dressing like it."

"Twenty-three? Oh, that's very old."

Victoria refused to rise to the bait. "You know exactly what I mean. Anyway, all of it's in really good condition but it's not 'me' anymore. Adrianne was mentioning the other day that the secondhand clothes shop needed donations, so I thought I'd clean out my closet on their behalf."

"That's an excellent idea," her mother said.

"I thought so." Victoria paused, seeing for the first time the drink glass with an olive on the bottom that sat where her father had been. "What's this? A martini lunch? That isn't like Dad."

"He was celebrating."

"What?" Victoria lifted a finely arched brow, not

remembering anything significant about this particular day in May.

"He persuaded Dirk Ramsey to spend a couple of weeks with us at Mackinac Island this June," Lena Beaumont explained.

"He what?" Victoria's astonishment bordered on incredulity. "Why on earth is that something to celebrate? And why would he want to persuade that sniping, vicious . . ." Victoria couldn't find adjectives vile enough to describe the political journalist whose syndicated column appeared in all the major US newspapers and online.

"Keep your voice down, Tory." Her mother's voice held a note of reproof.

"I don't care who knows what I think of Dirk Ramsey. He makes a living out of shredding reputations and careers." Victoria lowered her volume, but not the venom of her tone. "Look at the innuendos he put in his column about Dad! Or maybe lies is a better word."

"There was just enough truth in what Dirk wrote to make it not really worth denying," Lena reminded her.

"That's precisely my point. Dirk Ramsey spins things just to stir up controversy. He's never even really talked to Dad—I guess they were introduced at one point, though. For what it's worth!" Victoria flared up. "Which didn't keep Dirk from saying something about Dad being, quote-unquote, a puppeteer who pulls the strings in the governor's mansion. Or hinting that Dad's sense of civic responsibility is motivated by greed. And he's even insinuated that Dad's interest in national affairs is an attempt to get inside the Oval Office or get appointed to the Supreme Court! It's totally ridiculous, Mom!"

"Tory—"

"And it's sickening, too. That man thinks he can get away with anything."

"Tory, you're old enough to be aware that your father is very influential," her mother began in a reasoning tone.

But Victoria didn't feel like being reasoned with. Her eyes were the turbulent gray of storm clouds rolling in from the Great Lakes. "Well, of course. His legal firm has a national reputation by now. When Dad was actively practicing law he was one of the best attorneys in Michigan. And I do understand since he's become politically involved that he's going to get a lot of public scrutiny. I don't object to that. I do object to some stranger acting like Dad has something to hide or there are skeletons in his closet or whatever."

"That's precisely your father's point." Lena Beaumont paused and held up a silencing forefinger as the waitress arrived with Victoria's salad and freshened her mother's cup of coffee. Victoria kept quiet while the waitress was there, but it was a simmering quiet.

"What's 'precisely' his point?" she demanded when the waitress had gone, attacking the salad with a vengeance.

"That Dirk Ramsey doesn't know him," her mother explained. "Your father has always made it a point to be open with the press. On several occasions he's gone out of his way to cultivate their respect. The last thing he wants or needs is to feud with a famous journalist like Dirk Ramsey."

"Journalist—he doesn't deserve the term. He's a muckraker," Victoria snapped. "I wouldn't call him famous. Notorious is more appropriate."

"It doesn't matter whether you consider him

famous or notorious. Whatever Dirk Ramsey prints or says, people pay attention to it," Lena Beaumont continued.

"In my opinion Dad should sue him." Victoria stabbed at a dark green spinach leaf with her fork.

"Ever heard of the First Amendment?"

"Yes, Mom. Congress shall make no law abridging the freedom of the press. But I'm entitled to my opinion too."

"Of course you are."

Victoria kept on fighting with her spinach and didn't reply.

"Keep in mind," her mother added, "that it isn't possible to attack one reporter without others leaping to his defense. Instead of having one person against him, your father would have them all," was the dry retort.

"So if you can't beat them, join them. Is that his plan?" Victoria knew she sounded sarcastic and didn't care.

Until Dirk Ramsey began making sly references to her father in his column, Victoria had never even read it. After reading two daily doses of his interpretations of half-truths, she refused to look at it again. Once she'd heard Dirk introduced on some national television show and immediately switched channels. One glimpse of his arrogant but handsome face was all the convincing she needed that he was only seeking his own glory.

"Essentially, it is," her mother agreed. "Dirk Ramsey doesn't know your father. He's barely exchanged ten words with him. So Dad contacted him and suggested they become better acquainted. He invited him to spend two weeks with us at Mackinac Island for that purpose and Mr. Ramsey accepted."

"What? That's just crazy!" Victoria set her fork down to confront her mother.

"It's perfectly reasonable. Once Dirk Ramsey gets to know your father, he'll see for himself that Charles is exactly who he says he is."

"And if he doesn't get that, what then?" Victoria challenged.

"Then it won't be because your father failed to try to change his mind." She sipped at her coffee with a calmness that Victoria had so often envied and tried to emulate.

"Dad can't be serious." Victoria shook her head, her wavy hair brushing her neck. "He could accomplish the same thing by having dinner with the guy or playing golf or tennis with him."

"No, he couldn't." Lena Beaumont dismissed that suggestion with a wave of her hand. "Dirk Ramsey would suspect that your father was putting up a facade. But nobody can maintain a facade for two weeks, day in and day out."

"Wait a minute." Victoria straightened, eyeing her mother with suspicion. "When you said Dad invited Ramsey to Mackinac Island, you didn't mean that he would be staying with us—at our summer home? He will be staying at a hotel, won't he?"

"Of course not," her mother laughed. "He will be our guest, and treated just like anyone else we invite."

"That's even worse!" she declared. "It's like inviting your enemy into camp to inspect your defenses!"

"You are exaggerating, Tory." Her mother sighed with some amusement.

"I'm not. If you don't see it, Dad should," she insisted. "No matter what happens, Ramsey will get it all twisted."

"It's up to all of us to persuade him that he formed a misconception," Lena reasoned.

"You can't be serious, Mom," Victoria replied with obvious disgust. "And hey, what about Penny? You know the stage she's in," she said, referring to her six-teen-year-old sister. "She knows everything. She's always talking back and sassing. Can you imagine the kind of impression she'll give Ramsey?"

"Penny wants to be treated like an adult. So, we'll sit down and discuss this with her. And make it clear that she's expected to behave." Lena Beaumont refused to be as pessimistic as her older daughter.

"With our luck, Penny will meet some green-jeans radical and tie herself to a tree when the gardener shows up to prune it," Victoria muttered.

"You pulled stunts like that," her mother reminded with a definite sparkle in her eyes.

"Please don't remind me." The heightened color in Victoria's cheeks had nothing to do with the tint of blusher.

"Let's see. If I recall correctly, you were accusing your father of—I don't remember exactly how your sign was worded—but it was something to do with making too much money and thus depriving the poor. At the same time, you were trying to persuade him to raise your allowance." Lena paused, a smiling frown dominating her expression. "What was the name of the boy who instigated that rebellion?"

"I don't remember his name. Everyone called him by his nickname, Lightning." In spite of herself Victoria felt a smile teasing at the corners of her mouth.

"Whatever happened to him?"

"I think he went into corporate law. Go figure."

"Hmm."

"I can just guess how Ramsey will make hay out of that silly incident." She heard the impatient sound her mother made. "Mom, please listen. If Dirk Ramsey accepted Dad's invitation, you can bet he wasn't motivated by a desire to make any of us Beaumonts look good. He'll be gathering more ammunition for another attack. I'm sure he jumped at the opportunity to unearth any skeleton in the closet, and if he can't find one he'll invent it," Victoria declared, snapping a rye cracker in half.

"You are prejudging him, Tory," her mother pointed out. "That's exactly what you're accusing him of doing."

"Maybe so." She was really trying not to get angrier. "Didn't I hear that he said we are awful snobs or something like that? Too good to mingle with the rest of the world?"

Her mother didn't confirm it or deny it.

"Dad is just the opposite. But it sure describes Dirk Ramsey accurately."

"Oh, settle down, Tory," her mother reproved. "You need to keep an open mind about this."

"I prefer to keep my eyes open," she retorted. "I don't think I'm better than anyone else."

"No, but—"

"Okay, I had a lot of advantages because of you and Dad, but you brought me up with good Midwestern values all the same. I wasn't allowed to take what we had for granted, and I really did understand the meaning of hard work and all that. You made sure my head was on straight."

"I know that, dear." Lena appeared amused by the defensive speech, which only irritated Victoria.

"The last thing I'm going to do is advertise my virtue, though. I'm not going to make myself a target," she finished.

"Are you through? Should I applaud?" her mother teased.

"In another minute you're going to get this salad in your lap if you keep that up," Victoria threatened and pushed the plate away. "I'm not hungry."

"You're taking all this too seriously. You shouldn't let someone like Dirk Ramsey upset you."

"Right. Good old Dirk Ramsey." A silver light danced wickedly in her gray eyes. "Who stands for trust, justice, and the American way. So what's wrong with this picture?" she asked rhetorically.

"A lot!" Her mother laughed ruefully. "Dirk Ramsey is just going to be another guest who'll spend a couple of weeks with us—nothing more."

"I'll never believe that," Victoria stated, her mouth tightening. "Dad has invited an enemy into our midst. And I'm going on the basis that to be forewarned is to be forearmed." She picked up her iced-tea glass and swirled the ice cubes. "When will our 'guest' be descending on us? In June, you said?"

"He'll arrive the second weekend in June, whatever that date is, and in time for the Lilac Festival," she explained. "You and I and Penny will fly up the middle of next week to open the house. Your father will join us that weekend."

"At least we'll have some peace and quiet before the enemy arrives," Victoria muttered and sipped at her tea.

"Did you see Mrs. Ogden?" She was an elderly

woman that Victoria regularly visited as a volunteer for the shut-ins.

Victoria eyed her youthful-looking mother over the rim of the glass. "Changing the subject, Mom?"

"Yes," was the emphatic response.

Victoria had to laugh.

Chapter Two

The June sun had moved higher in the sky and now glared in Victoria's eyes. She flipped down the sunglasses resting on the top of her hair to the bridge of her nose so she could keep on reading the novel in her hand. Her skin glistened from a liberal application of sunscreen. The skimpy blue bikini she had on made it necessary. Victoria rarely wore this one in public, just to avoid the inevitable comments from guys. But it was fine for sunning on the private terrace of their Mackinac Island home.

It was an old, solid-looking house, built of brick, stucco, and wood in the traditional Tudor style popular in the twenties. The terrace was reached by a breezeway porch accessible from the living room of the house by sliding glass doors or from the front entry porch by means of a pair of iron gates. Directly behind Victoria was a garage, built in anticipation of cars being brought to the island, something that hadn't happened. Local transportation was limited to horse and buggy, bicycles or walking, and the occasional electric cart for handymen. There was an airstrip where small planes landed, but as there was no bridge to the mainland, boat service ferried most of the island visitors to and from the island.

Few people ever objected to the absence of cars, since it was part of the island's charm. Those who did bemoan the fact were usually those with blisters on their heels. Everyone else simply enjoyed the leisurely pace of life on the island. The garage of the Beaumont summer home was a storage shed for lawn tools and bicycles.

The sliding glass doors connecting the breezeway and terrace to the living room were opened. Glancing sidways, Victoria saw Josie Largent, the Beaumont's French-speaking housekeeper. But it was the tall, frosty glass on the tray that made Victoria straighten in the lounge chair and push the thin straps of her bikini into place on her shoulders.

"Lemonade! Josie, you are an angel!" she declared. "Thanks—I mean, *merci*."

"I thought you would be thirsty from all this sun," the housekeeper replied in French. Her English was flawless, but she rarely used it. Victoria suspected the housekeeper spoke French just to keep everyone on their toes. For Victoria it had meant her French courses in school had been a snap, since she'd conversed with Josie in French from the time she was a child.

Josie held the tray out to her so Victoria could take the glass. Her shrewd hazel eyes swept the bareness of Victoria's body, then flicked in the direction of the early afternoon sun.

"Do not stay in the sun too long or you will look like a lobster," she admonished, still in French. "And be careful of those sunglasses or you will have rings around your eyes like a raccoon."

"*Oui, mais je ne suis pas l'enfant.*" Victoria sighed the protest that she wasn't a child, although she smiled affectionately when she did.

"*Non?*" The haughty one-word challenge was Josie's only response as she pivoted and walked under the shade of the breezeway to the glass doors. After working for the family for twenty years, Josie just wasn't one to mince her words in any language.

Shaking her head, Victoria took a swallow of the tart, cold liquid. Josie always managed to have the last word in any discussion. At times it was an irritating trait, but no one really minded. She was a member of the family, practically a second mother to Victoria and her sister, and much sterner with them than their parents were. Holding her glass, Victoria leaned back in the cushioned lounger and tried to find her place on the page of the book.

"There you are, Tory! I'm going to use your ten-speed. My bike has a flat tire."

The greeting and announcement came out in a rush as Penny Beaumont burst onto the terrace. A silken curtain of long, pale blond hair hung almost to her waist, and she wore denim shorts and a red T-shirt. Super-slim, she was nonetheless irritated by the fact that she didn't have killer curves like Victoria. She was sixteen and anxious to look it. Bouncing forward, she spied the glass Victoria held.

"Is that lemonade?"

Water had condensed on the sides of the glass. It was too wet to hang onto, and it slipped out of Victoria's fingers when Penny took it from her and guzzled it.

"What happened to 'May I have a drink please'?" It was probably pointless, but Victoria attempted to remind her sister of her manners.

Penny shrugged. "You would have said that I could, so I saved all that time and breath. Ahh. That was good." She returned the glass of lemonade to Victoria.

"Thank you—you're welcome, Penny," Victoria mocked.

"I hate my name."

"So you use your real one."

"No way. Penelope is worse." She made a face as she rested a hip against the edge of the redwood table. "I decided from now on I'm going to use my middle name. Laurel sounds cool, don't you think?"

"Oh, yes," Victoria agreed, trying desperately not to smile. She remembered, not so many years ago, when she had disliked her own name. Now she did, but she was grateful that she had never been tagged with the nickname of Vicky. "And though you didn't exactly ask my permission, yes, you may use my bike. Where are you going?"

"I'm meeting Tracy." Penny referred to one of her friends. "Then we're cycling to the dock to watch the people."

"There must be boys on the ferry," Victoria teased.

"Uh, yeah," Penny grinned. "There usually are. You should come along. You might find someone."

"I'm not exactly on the shelf at twenty-three," Victoria said and settled more comfortably on the lounger. Then she added, "Let him find me."

Penny clicked her tongue. "You aren't supposed to wait for your ship to come in. You are supposed to swim out to meet it."

"You swim. I'll sun," she replied.

"Suit yourself." Penny shrugged and moved in the direction of the garage. "But you're not getting any younger."

"Thanks for pointing that out," Victoria murmured to herself. But she didn't care. Just the thought of being a teenager made her shudder. "Have fun boy watching, Penny."

"Laurel! The name is Laurel," was the quick retort.

"Have fun . . . Laurel." Victoria stressed it with faint mockery.

Returning her attention to the open book in her hand, she half listened to the sounds of her younger sister wheeling the bike out of the garage. In a few minutes she was pedaling away from the house, and once again Victoria was alone on the terrace—but not for long. She'd barely read the next paragraph when she heard her father calling for her.

"Tory? Where are you?" His voice came from inside the house.

"Out here, Dad!" she called back and set the book face down on her lap, sighing a little at the interruption.

Sliding open the glass door, Charles Beaumont stepped into the breezeway. Although fifty-five years old, he was still a good-looking man. His hair had turned a distinguished iron gray and begun to thin slightly at the temples. Age had thickened his waistline, but he looked fit and healthy. There was a contented light in his blue eyes.

"What's up?" She smiled at the sight of him.

"Were you planning on going anywhere this afternoon?" He returned her smile with equal warmth.

"The only plan I have today is to get some sun and finish this book." She lifted the open novel on her lap. "Why?"

"Your mother and I are off to play a couple of games of tennis," he explained. "Dirk Ramsey said he would arrive sometime late this afternoon or early evening. We should be back by four o'clock, but in case he comes before we return, would you explain where we are and show him which room he'll be in? You know, make him comfortable."

"Can't Josie do the honors?"

"No."

Her father didn't offer any more explanation than that and Victoria somehow knew better than to ask. But she didn't have to like it.

"No problem," she said. "Can I show him the fabulous collection of family skeletons, too? Or maybe I'll unearth Penny's diary and offer it to him."

"Victoria." He murmured her name with a sigh that said they had been over all this, which they had—many times.

"Oh, don't worry," she said in a brittle voice. "I'll be the soul of politeness."

"That almost worries me more than if you told him off," her father replied dryly.

"Don't tempt me," Victoria murmured and opened the book to resume her reading.

Her father turned to leave. "We'll be back by four."

"Don't be late if you can help it," she called.

He just smiled and waved. "Hold the fort while we're gone."

Victoria watched him disappear into the house, her gray eyes dark and turbulent. "How can I hold the fort when I'm supposed to let the enemy in?" she added. But he was too far away to hear, she guessed. He didn't respond.

A few minutes later, the clip-clop of hooves sounded the arrival of the horse-drawn taxi and the departure of her parents. The mere mention of Dirk Ramsey disturbed Victoria's concentration. She had to read the page she was on twice before she finally began following the novel's plot.

An hour later she moved out of the sun into the shade of the breezeway. She tended to tan even with sunblock on and Victoria chose not to flirt with the danger of a sunburn. Besides, the glare of the white pages of the book had begun to hurt her eyes despite the sunglasses she wore. By now Victoria was too engrossed in the characters to put it down.

She was two chapters from the end when she heard the horse and carriage stop in front of the house. She glanced once toward the sun, but couldn't judge the time by its angle. Victoria felt a fleeting sense of relief that her parents were back and she wouldn't have to bother with entertaining Dirk Ramsey, since he hadn't arrived. Then her concentration was back on the pages of the novel.

The horse pulling the carriage trotted away from the house at about the same time that Victoria heard the doorbell ring. It jolted along her nerve ends like an electric shock. She looked to the sliding glass doors, her eyes wary with suspicion. Within seconds, Josie appeared and stepped onto the breezeway to announce the arrival of M'sieu Ramsey.

"Oh, no," Victoria protested in a moan, rolling her eyes heavenward. She closed the book with a snap and swung her bare legs to the stone floor. "What time is it?"

Josie told her in French.

"Only three o'clock!" she exclaimed in a mixture of anger and exasperation. "Damn him!"

"*Mais, mademoiselle*—"

"Dammit, Josie, speak English!" Victoria flared. She didn't want to waste time translating the housekeeper's sentences in her head. There were too many things to think about. Number one was the fact that she hadn't bothered to bring a coverup onto the terrace with her. "Where is he now?" she demanded.

"In the foyer," the housekeeper replied.

"Show him to the library," she said with quick decision. An impish part of her wanted to meet Dirk Ramsey dressed exactly as she was—which was scandalously—and play the decadent daughter he probably expected her to be.

Victoria didn't doubt that she could carry it off, but . . . there was her father to consider. He might see the humor in her act, but she doubted that he would be amused.

"I'll use the rear service stairs to slip upstairs to my room and change." Victoria rose from the lounger and motioned Josie into the house. "Please go and please don't speak French to him. The last thing we need is for him to spread the news that the Beaumonts have a French maid. They'll start imagining a babe in a ruffled short skirt instead of—" Victoria shut up just in time. She loved Josie just the way she was, homely though Josie was, and the last thing she wanted to do was hurt her feelings.

"But—" Josie started to protest.

"Go! *Vite!*" Victoria waved her inside. "Let me know when he's in the library so I can slip in through the living room without being seen."

"*Oui.*" The snapping affirmative held a trace of sarcasm, because the housekeeper hadn't been permitted the last word.

While she waited interminable minutes for Josie to return, Victoria paced back and forth in front of the sliding doors. She wouldn't have time to shower away the sunblock or the sweat on her skin. She'd have to be content with a quick wash and lots of cologne. What to wear? It had to be something simple and understated. That halter sundress she'd just bought, Victoria decided. It was a demure blue color. She could dress it up a little with chunky bracelets and pendant earrings. Costume jewelry. Dirk was undoubtedly expecting them all to be dripping with diamonds and sitting in gem-encrusted furniture.

With her every move planned and thought out beforehand, Victoria didn't waste time when Josie returned to signal that the coast was clear. She slipped soundlessly through the living room and darted up the rear stairs, down the narrow hall to the second floor of the main staircase and the bedrooms. In less than ten minutes, she had washed, changed into the dress, slipped on the jewelry, and run a brush through her hair.

This time Victoria used the curving staircase. The grandfather clock in the corner niche of the staircase chimed a quarter past the hour of three. At the bottom of the steps her glance slid over the leather luggage on the floor. Turning, Victoria walked swiftly to the library door and paused to take a breath. One thing prep school had taught her was shatterproof composure. Victoria knew it was going to be tested. For her father's sake she was going to be pleasant. Even if it killed her.

Opening the door slowly, she walked into the room. "Hello. Sorry you had to wait."

The man standing at the bay window turned. Victoria had her first real look at him and realized that the photo that appeared with his print and online columns didn't do him justice. And he was taller than he'd appeared to be on TV. Over six feet and really built, he was just plain hot. His hair was as black as a moonless night and cut in a carelessly natural style. The kind that suggested it had recently been tousled by feminine fingers. Broad shoulders. Long legs. Blatantly masculine.

Uh-oh. He just didn't look like someone who spent hours at a keyboard. The darkness of his eyes reminded Victoria of a pool that didn't reveal the dangers beneath the surface. There was a cool arrogance to his look. Victoria felt her temper simmering. His dark gaze slowly inspected her from head to toe. She couldn't have felt more stripped and exposed if she had walked in wearing the skimpy bikini she'd just had on.

A sheer thirst for revenge made her return the insolent appraisal. Her gaze ran over the white shirt with its sleeves rolled partway up his forearms and the worn jeans that showed off the muscularity of his legs. When she looked at his face there was something faintly taunting in his eyes, as if he was challenging her to admit she liked what she saw.

"You must be Victoria Beaumont." His voice was deep and resonant.

That well-taught poise came to her rescue, forcing a throaty laugh. "Is that good or bad?" she said and walked forward, offering her hand to him. Victoria knew she would dearly love to rake her long fingernails over his strong jaw, but she also knew she wouldn't do it. "Welcome to Mackinac Island."

"Thanks. Interesting place so far."

"We weren't expecting you until later in the day so I have to apologize for my parents not being here. They're off playing tennis and won't be back until four."

"Oh. Well, I am early. Hope I haven't inconvenienced you." He, too, was mouthing polite phrases that he didn't mean.

Even the clasp of his hand in greeting was cool, yet firm. At the contact, something quivered along her nerves—a sexual response that Victoria hadn't expected. She had thought her active dislike of a man would override his obvious male attraction. That wasn't the case. She smoothly withdrew her hand from his strong fingers.

"Not at all, " she assured him. "I guess this is your first visit to Mackinac Island." Up close she noticed there was a ruthless quality to his smile.

"Yes." He seemed amused by the way she stuck with safe topics. "I had a pretty good view of it from the air before we landed."

"Oh, you flew?" Victoria attempted an interested smile.

"That's generally the way you see something from the air, isn't it?"

Duh. She'd asked a really stupid question. No doubt he'd made a mental note of that.

"Oh right. I almost forgot that you have a way with words." She widened her gray eyes with obviously false innocence. "I'll have to watch what I say."

"My, my. I don't understand how you could have forgotten my profession." His amusement wasn't pleasant.

Victoria turned away. If she hadn't, she might have been tempted to slap him. "My father's always entertaining friends, clients, associates, just about anybody." She put light stress on the last word, just in case Dirk Ramsey thought he was a big deal. "I can't keep everyone straight." She flashed him an over-the-shoulder look, knowing she sounded like some spoiled socialite and not caring. "I'm pretty busy, even up here."

His dark eyes narrowed fractionally as if he was trying to judge how much of what he saw was real and how much was an act. A corner of his mouth twitched, a vague signal that he'd made his decision, whatever it was.

"Really?" he asked with a quirk of an eyebrow. "You changed out of your bikini in record time. Or are you wearing it beneath that dress?"

Victoria faced him with astonishment, trying to mask it. "How did you know that?" She smiled but it didn't reach her eyes. What was he, a peeping Tom? Josie would have brained him with a flowerpot if she'd caught him at it.

"All I got was a glimpse," Dirk Ramsey conceded. "But the sight of a delectable female lazing about with a few triangular patches for clothing would have attracted any man's gaze."

"Then you saw me," she murmured stiffly.

"Those gates didn't exactly block my view." His gaze flicked her with a knowing regard for what was beneath the dress.

Victoria filed the information away for future use. "Then you understand why I didn't greet you right away. I wouldn't want to be accused of showing off," she countered smoothly.

"I wouldn't mind if you did." He lessened the distance between them, his dark eyes holding her look.

"Could we talk about something else?" Victoria tried to retain a pleasant tone although all her senses were becoming increasingly wary of his nearness.

"Maybe I should be on my guard." Dirk continued to

regard her, his voice thoughtful. "I could be tempted to go down the wrong road."

"What are you talking about?"

"Ah—do you mind if I say something corny?"

"No." *Mind if I put it on my Facebook page if you do?* Her parents wouldn't see it, only her friends would. And it would serve Dirk Ramsey right.

"You're the road. Complete with dangerous curves and"—his dark eyes moved over her upper body—"soft shoulders."

Just his look made a sensual shiver travel over her skin. Victoria felt almost as if he'd touched her but the sensation vanished as quickly as it had come. Again the fathomless dark eyes were roaming over her face. She was expressionless. On the outside. Victoria knew that inside she was all hot reaction.

"I don't know why you should need to be on your guard," she lied, since she fully intended to keep a very safe distance from him. "I just happened to be here and that's why I came down." She kept her voice light and vaguely amused, but it was an effort. "You happened to arrive early. In another hour, my parents would have welcomed you instead of me. You and I probably wouldn't have met until dinner."

"True," he agreed, but on a skeptical note.

Victoria wanted the subject changed—and quickly. She didn't trust herself to continue to assure him that he was welcome in this house.

"Did our housekeeper offer you anything? There's cold lemonade," she suggested like a dutiful hostess.

"I prefer coffee, if you'll have some with me," Dirk countered.

Hot coffee when she was already steaming? "Of course," Victoria agreed and walked to the door. "Josie?"

The housekeeper was in the hallway practically before Victoria called her name. Victoria didn't even have to step out of the doorway.

"*Oui?*" the housekeeper responded.

"*Deux café au lait avec sucre.*" Her request was automatically issued in French.

"*Café noir pour moi.*" Dirk Ramsey refused milk and sugar for his coffee in flawless French.

Victoria pivoted in surprise and recovered immediately. "Good accent. You speak French well, Mr. Ramsey."

"Why is it that your compliment gives me the impression of an accusation?" he asked wryly.

Remembering the housekeeper, Victoria glanced over her shoulder to find Josie still standing in the hall. "That's all, Josie."

The housekeeper nodded and left before Victoria responded to his question. "I can't imagine why you would think that."

"Maybe because you regard me as uncouth and unprincipled, and generally a little beneath you," he suggested.

She hadn't realized her dislike was so apparent. "Really?" Victoria laughed a shade maliciously. "My, my. Aren't you sensitive. I thought journalists could take what they dish out. Guess not."

"I don't think I dished out anything." Thick, spiky lashes came down to hood his look. "You're a gorgeous girl, if you don't mind my saying so. Close to perfection. But yeah, I am a reporter. Forgive me if I keep looking for what's wrong."

"As in, what's wrong with this picture. Found any flaws?" She had to bite her tongue to keep from mentioning a few of his.

"Only that air of superiority when you addressed your housekeeper in French."

"She's from Quebec," Victoria said. "And I've been talking with Josie in French since I was a toddler. So perhaps I can be forgiven for that," she suggested with cloying sweetness.

"She's the treasured family retainer, I take it," he mocked.

Up yours. She almost said it out loud. Victoria turned swiftly to distract herself. "So, what did you plan to do during your stay?"

Dirk only shrugged, as if he was waiting for her to make a suggestion.

"The island's kind of quiet." Feeling a little desperate, she gestured at the bookshelves. "But we've got thousands of books."

"So I see. A private library, no less," he commented.

Touchy as she was feeling, his remark sounded like a condemnation.

Victoria was about to say something truly snotty when Josie knocked at the library door and entered with the coffee. The timing was excellent because Victoria feared she would have lost her temper otherwise.

Chapter Three

The look in those black eyes was making Victoria increasingly uncomfortable. There were no more odd comments from Dirk Ramsey while they drank their coffee, but Victoria knew that when she'd exhausted her supply of safe small talk, she would have to find something else to occupy him.

Maybe he could take a bracing and unexpected jump in the lake. The thought made her smile. But— oh, well—a guided tour of the house was probably safer. "Would you like to see your room?" she suggested at last. "I'm sure you'll want to unpack and settle in before dinner."

"Sounds like a good idea," he agreed smoothly.

Yet Victoria had the distinct impression that he knew how eager she was to escape his company. It was becoming more and more difficult to keep a rein on her temper. Unless she was mistaken, he seemed not only to know it but was actually tickled by it.

Rising from the leather-cushioned chair, Victoria set her cup on the tray and walked to the door. Dirk

Ramsey was there first to open it for her, his show of manners all too obvious.

"I'll get my luggage," he announced when they reached the foyer. His suitcases weren't sitting where they had been. He arched a questioning eyebrow at Victoria. "Someone carried them upstairs already."

"It must have been Josie." Victoria started up the stairs.

"They were heavy," Dirk replied with a suggestion of protest.

"Josie's strong," she assured him. That was true enough. And it wasn't unusual for the housekeeper to help with things like that

He started up the stairs behind her. "She comes from good peasant stock, huh?"

Victoria hesitated on the stairs, wishing she could kick backward like a donkey and send him flying. The image of him plonked unexpectedly on his butt made her smile. Her reply was light. "I don't think my parents checked her bloodlines before they hired her twenty-some years ago."

"An oversight, no doubt."

Her long nails dug into the sensitive palms of her hands. Victoria laughed. It was either that or shriek at him. "You have a great sense of humor, by the way."

"I do?" He eyed her with suspicion.

"Oh, yes. I read a couple of your columns. They were absolutely hilarious!" she declared. "You really should write sitcoms or something. I think you'd be really good at it."

"You thought they were funny?" Dirk repeated. His dry tone indicated he didn't believe her.

"Especially when you said all that nonsense about my father. It was priceless." Victoria flashed him a wide smile and continued up the steps. "Okay, moving right along—the guest bedroom has its own private bath and a small sitting area. I hope you find it comfortable." Victoria felt more like locking him in the attic at the moment.

At the head of the stairs she turned right at the landing and walked to the bedroom door. She entered the room ahead of Dirk Ramsey, sidestepping the luggage stacked inside.

It was a simple room with dormer windows letting in light. The walnut bed was covered with a tangerine-colored spread. The same color was repeated in the plaid material of a stuffed armchair and in the curtains at the windows. A small desk and chair sat beneath one of the windows.

Crossing the room Victoria opened a door. "Here's your bathroom." She indicated another set of doors. "There are the closets with plenty of hangers for your clothes." She continued her sweep of the room. "Of course, you have a dresser, too." Finally she stopped by the bed. "I doubt if you'll need them, but there are extra blankets on the top shelf of the closet."

All the while she had been showing him the room, Dirk Ramsey had remained just inside the door. Now that she was finished he made no response and bent instead to his luggage. He picked up a gray metal case and carried it to the desk where he opened it.

"My laptop seems to have survived the trip," he murmured.

"You're on vacation, aren't you?" Victoria sat on the bed, putting her hands behind her and leaning on them. "Are you planning to work while you're here?"

"I'm always working." Dirk slanted her a smile as he closed the case. "But to answer your question, theoretically, yes, I am on vacation. If I find enough material I'll do a couple of columns while I'm here. I like to stay ahead of my deadlines."

"I just bet you will. After all, with your imagination it doesn't take much." Victoria gave him a wide-eyed look. "All you need is a few facts and you can invent the rest. Or exaggerate whatever you like."

When he turned to move leisurely across the room to where she was sitting, Victoria thought she saw his tongue running along the inside of his cheek. She had the impression her not-so-innocent jab had irritated him just a little, and she was glad.

"How do you like the room?" she inquired to fill the suddenly tense silence.

"Very nice." But his dark eyes never let their attention wander from her face. When he stopped he was towering at the foot of the bed, his arms crossed over the muscled width of his chest.

"What?" she said, looking up at him.

"Just thinking that you look very natural sitting on that bed," Dirk observed. "I should have brought someone along to keep me warm at night so I don't have to use those blankets in the closet."

Indignation burned her face. Victoria didn't waste any time pushing off the bed. All the while she was mentally counting to ten and beyond. She had succeeded in holding her temper to this point. Victoria didn't want to ruin it all by losing it now. "I'm sure my dad would have said yes." His idle comment was as disturbing as the thought of being nestled against his naked, male chest. "He wants to get on your good side. I can't imagine why," Victoria finally managed to add.

The open door presented an escape route and Victoria ordered her legs to take it. Averting her gaze from his compelling face she moved away from the bed, taking the short, straight-line route to the door. It meant walking past him, but she didn't expect Dirk to stop her.

He didn't.

Still, when she was level with him, she thought about it. The scenario played itself out in her mind in about two seconds, like the good part in a romance novel. She almost felt like she was reading one.

Dirk's arm came out to cross in front of her and hook a hand on the side of her waist. Victoria took an instant step backward to avoid the hard biceps that had flexed against her breasts. His hand stayed on her waist, his fingers firm in their spreading clasp. His touch started miniature tremors in her that confused her.

"Stay with me." His voice was low. Victoria lifted her gaze to his incredibly handsome face. Immediately she felt drawn by the mysterious blackness of his eyes. The dangerous enchantment made her heart beat faster. "I was fantasizing about how enjoyable it would be to sleep with you. I guess I shouldn't say that."

Victoria shook her head to get rid of the irrational fantasy. Where had that come from? A dangerous temptation seemed to charge the air. But she wasn't about to flirt with the enemy, especially when she wasn't thinking clearly and unable to combat his potent weaponry.

"If you'll excuse me." Victoria glanced pointedly at him with haughty disdain, although that was far from the mixed-up emotions quivering inside.

"Sure."

He moved away but the look on his face still really annoyed her. Victoria's agitation quickly turned to anger. It was evident in every controlled line of her body as she moved to the door. His low chuckle when she carefully closed it behind her, rather than slam it as her temper wanted her to do, made her clench her teeth. She would have stormed down the stairs except the high heels of her sandals forced her to go at a slower pace. When she reached the foyer Josie appeared and asked a question in French, but Victoria's mind was seething too furiously to translate it.

"Oh, speak English!" she exclaimed. "I'm sorry, Josie," she apologized in the next instant. "It's not you. I just—stayed in the sun too long or something."

"Is everything all right?" Josie repeated her question.

"I have a headache," Victoria said.

The housekeeper eyed her shrewdly. "Ah. And is the name of the headache Dirk?"

"You got it." Victoria had to smile at the way Josie pronounced it. Deerk.

"What is wrong? Isn't the room to his liking?" the housekeeper questioned sharply.

"The room is to his liking all right. It's Deerk—I mean, Dirk who isn't to my liking."

"Do you wish—"

"I wish to have him out of here," Victoria said with a sigh.

"Mr. Ramsey is your father's guest," Josie reminded her.

"And I mean to take that up with Dad the minute he returns." She turned away to enter the living room.

It seemed she had to wait forever for that eventuality. The ticking of the grandfather clock in the stairwell seemed impossibly slow. With each minute, Victoria's resentment of Dirk Ramsey got stronger. When her parents did return it was close to being out of control.

The carefree sound of their laughing voices as they entered the house only made it worse. And she really did have a headache by now. Her hands were clenched, although she told herself she was overreacting.

Carrying their tennis rackets they strolled into the living room. their hands linked together. Her mother looked good in her tennis whites, a radiant flush to her cheeks as she looked into the smiling face of the man at her side. The clock chimed four times to mark the hour.

"It's about time you came back," Victoria declared in a tight voice.

"Hello, Tory." Her father turned his smile to her. "Did you finish your book?"

"No. I was interrupted by Dirk Ramsey. He decided to come early." She placed sarcastic emphasis on the last word.

"He's here already?" Surprise replaced the smiling expression on Charles Beaumont's features. "Shoot! When did he arrive?"

"About an hour ago," Victoria informed him.

"I hope you made him welcome and explained why your mother and I weren't here."

Letting go of his wife's hand, he walked over and set his tennis racket on the sofa in front of the large stone fireplace.

Her mother followed him. "Is he in his room now?"

"Yes, he's in his room, and yes, I made him welcome." Victoria was trying very hard not to unleash her temper on them. "I explained where you were. Although I got the feeling that he thought you weren't here on purpose."

"Huh?" Her father frowned. "I'm not following you, honey."

Victoria squared herself to face him. "Ramsey said something idiotic about having to be on his guard," she said icily. "As if I was this big temptation, thrown in front of him or something. He really pissed me off."

Charles Beaumont gave an annoyingly hearty laugh. "You must have been very charming, Tory. Congratulations. I have to hand it to you."

"Don't!" she erupted angrily. "If you let that man stay in this house for two weeks, I'm moving out! I really don't need the aggravation."

"Victoria," her mother began in an attempt to soothe her.

It didn't work. "Don't 'Victoria' me. I mean it!" she snapped. "Dirk Ramsey is such a jerk."

"What do you mean?" her father asked.

"I'm not sure where to begin," she said heatedly. "He comes across as arrogant, for starters. And conceited. Did I mention self-important? No? Well, he's that and—"

"Ssh, Tory, that's enough." Her father raised a silencing hand.

"Don't you shush me! I've had to bite my tongue so many times it's sore!" Victoria declared in stormy protest. "You're wasting your time having that man here. Dirk Ramsey!" She was on a roll. "I bet Dirk isn't even his real name. It's probably a nickname that he's earned from stabbing people in the back!"

"Nope," a voice drawled behind her.

Victoria whirled around and saw the subject of her tirade standing in the living room arch. Dirk had a hand thrust negligently in the pocket of his dark slacks.

"Dirk is my real name."

"It fits," she retorted. It was too late to pretend now.

Victoria could tell by his hard expression that he'd heard everything she had said about him. She felt like a fool. And worse.

"Tory, Mr. Ramsey is a guest in our home." She heard what her father didn't say. *Hold your tongue.*

But Victoria let fly. "Really? Too bad that Mr. Ramsey is a pain in the—"

"Victoria!" Her mother's shocked voice cut across the sentence.

A smile of insolent amusement slanted the handsomely cut mouth. "She's entitled to her opinion." Dirk laughed.

"Hey, you are not my friend!" she retorted. "So don't pretend to be!"

"Victoria, you will apologize at once!" her father demanded in cold anger.

"No need for that. She doesn't have to apologize." Dirk moved into the room. "I think I startled her when I arrived—she was reading, I understand. As welcoming committees go, she did good." He stopped in front of her, his dark enigmatic eyes studying the pride and temper animating her classic features.

Her father came up behind her and put an arm on her shoulders. "Nice of you to be nice about it. But I'm afraid my daughter is—"

"Is commendably loyal to you," Dirk interrupted him to complete the sentence, his gaze finally swinging from Victoria to her father. "No need to apologize for that, either, sir."

Sir. Oh please. She favored Dirk with a blistering glare, but he ignored it or seemed to.

"You should be proud that she feels so protective and defensive of you," Dirk said.

"It's generous of you to be so understanding.

Thank you." Charles Beaumont offered his hand and Dirk shook it firmly.

"Getting better acquainted is why I'm here," he said. "Not many parents inspire such fierce loyalty." He winked at Victoria. "Duly noted by me." Releasing her father's hand, Dirk returned his attention to Victoria who was still eyeing him with hostility. "Now that we've cleared the air and everything's out in the open, I think we can observe a truce for the rest of my stay."

"With you, I'm sure it will be an armed truce, Mr. Ramsey," Victoria responded to his challenge, not his friendly tone.

"Call me Dirk. And I'm not going to forget what you said about me being a backstabber. It was really pretty funny." He smiled lazily and offered his hand to her. "And I'll call you Victoria and think of the queen. Maybe I'll remember to be properly humble in your presence."

She placed her hand in his and gave him an arching smile. "You do that . . . Dirk." And she stabbed him with his name.

Instead of shaking her hand, he gripped her fingers and bent over it. When Victoria realized his intention she automatically tightened her fingers to withdraw her hand from his descending mouth.

Oh no. So not suave. So not what she wanted. But it was too late to avoid the warm lips that pressed themselves to the back of her hand in a continental gesture that was meant to really get her goat. The brief kiss ignited a liquid fire that coursed through her veins.

As he straightened, there was a devilish blackness to his eyes. When he released her hand it was all Victoria could do to keep from rubbing the place where his lips had been, wanting to erase their imprint and the tingling sensation that remained.

She did the next best thing by mocking the gesture. "Aren't you gallant. Where did you pick up that move?" she taunted.

"Watching Errol Flynn movies," Dirk responded in the same vein. Then he was speaking to her father. "You haven't introduced me to your wife, by the way. And I promise I won't do that to her."

"Oh—I beg your pardon." Her father seemed a little bewildered but he reached out to draw his wife forward. "Lena, allow me to officially introduce Errol—I mean Dirk. Dirk Ramsey. "

"I'm sorry. This is a little awkward. I just bet Victoria has a headache," her mother said as she shook his hand.

If you only knew, Victoria thought with despair.

"I hope not. " Dirk smiled and Victoria saw how devastatingly good-looking he could be when he was being friendly, not fake-friendly. "I'm pleased to meet you at last, Mrs. Beaumont. I've often heard you described as your husband's most valuable asset. I think that's accurate."

"Thank you." Her mother accepted the compliment with genuine modesty. "I do hope you'll enjoy these next two weeks with us. Anything you need, just ask. Fresh towels. Political strategy. Anything."

"Thanks." He laughed but just for an instant his gaze flicked to Victoria as if she had something to add to that.

But her mother claimed his attention again. "Would you excuse me while I go change?" She glanced at her husband. "Why don't you fix Dirk a drink? I don't think it's too early for a cocktail. Dinner isn't far away."

"Good idea, dear," he agreed as she smiled and moved toward the foyer. "What would you like, Dirk? A martini?"

"I don't drink, thank you. Fix one for yourself if you like," he insisted.

"Don't tell me you don't possess any vices." Victoria couldn't resist.

"One or two." His gaze ran over her for a fraction of a second and no more—just long enough to let her know what he meant.

For a moment she felt out of her league. "Excuse me. I have a book to finish." She considered her retreat to her previous stronghold a strategic move.

The breezeway didn't offer total seclusion, though. And the book just didn't hold her interest. The voices of the two men in the living room drifted through the glass doors to distract her attention. Victoria found herself listening to their apparently friendly discussion. She envied her father's ability to respond so naturally and without any defensiveness to the questions Dirk put to him. The questions were casual, containing nothing controversial, and his tone indicated an appropriate interest in the answers.

The glass door to the breezeway slid open. "Would it bother you if we joined you, Tory?" her father asked. "It's too nice out here to stay inside."

"No, not at all." Her sigh revealed only a little of her dismay, or so she hoped. She kept the book propped in front of her so she wouldn't be expected to say anything.

Her gaze wandered from its pages when Dirk walked by her, but he seemed indifferent to her presence. She was glad, she told herself.

"Do you play tennis, Dirk?" her father asked.

"Yes, when I can find a partner, which isn't always easy when I'm away from home."

"You do quite a bit of lecturing, don't you?" her father asked. That was something Victoria hadn't known. She was aware how lucrative that sideline could be for well-known pundits.

"Yes," Dirk admitted, but no more than that.

Charles Beaumont didn't pursue the topic and returned instead to the first. "We'll play some tennis tomorrow. Mixed doubles. Tory plays a good game. She can be your partner."

"Thanks for volunteering me, Dad," she said a little edgily. "Maybe I have other plans."

Her father grinned. "But you don't, do you?" When no reply was immediately forthcoming, he laughed. "That's what I thought."

"I think she's worried about the word 'partner'. That relationship requires cooperation," Dirk pointed out. "She doesn't want to be accused of siding with the enemy."

"But we have an armed truce, remember?" Victoria offered with a honeyed smile.

"I remember," he assured her. "I was wondering if you did." The long, lazy look he gave her was subtly seductive. She felt it tugging at her breath, trying to steal it and almost succeeding. Her sister, Penny, chose that moment to return and distract everyone's attention.

"My youngest," Charles said as Penny stepped off the ten-speed bike and parked it alongside the garage on the terrace. Her waist-length blond hair swung freely when she walked toward them. Her blue eyes focused on Dirk with open speculation and interest. "Dirk, I'd like you to meet my daughter—"

"Laurel," Penny quickly supplied. At the raised eyebrow from her father, she explained. "My name is actually Penelope, but my friends call me Laurel."

"I'm pleased to meet you, Laurel." He shook her hand, holding it a little longer than Victoria thought was necessary.

"You must be Dirk Ramsey." There was a dopey look in Penny's blue eyes. "You're much better looking in person than your photos."

"Aw, shucks. Thanks, Laurel." Dirk gave the susceptible teenager a dazzling smile. Victoria could almost see Penny melting. There wasn't any way she could protect her sister against Dirk's brand of sexual magnetism, she thought. Victoria wasn't at all sure she could do that for herself.

Chapter Four

Victoria was Dirk Ramsey's doubles tennis partner the following afternoon. They lost the first match, mostly because of her lack of concentration. It wasn't easy to ignore the athletic man sharing the court with her. Or his mighty serve. Or how good he looked in shorts. Or anything about him, especially the conflicting emotions he generated.

Each time the resonant timbre of his voice called for the ball or absently complimented her on a good serve or a good return, her attention was diverted from the blistering pace of the game. She was more conscious of where Dirk was on the court than where the ball was.

It wasn't until the middle of the second match that she began to play with her usual skill and concentration, subconsciously accepting him as her teammate and letting her constant awareness of his position on the court become an advantage rather than a distraction. They began scoring more points than they lost, until they were even. Victoria became caught up in the exhilaration of competing.

When her overhead smash scored the match point, she forgot everything but the elation of winning. Her parents came up to the net to acknowledge their loss and Victoria went forward to accept their congratulations with Dirk at her side. She glanced at him with a winded smile that shared the victory, almost wishing for his very masculine arm to curve around the back of her waist. The contact would be pleasantly exciting rather than annoying, she thought.

"Great game, Tory." Her mother reached across the net to shake her hand. "You, too, Dirk."

"That last point was a dandy, Tory," her father declared a little out of breath. "You put the ball at my feet. I didn't have a chance to get my racket on it. And remind me never to play singles with your partner. He'd wipe me off the court." He laughed and shook hands with Dirk who had shifted his racket to the hand Victoria had fantasized being on her waist.

"I doubt if it would ever be easy to beat you, Chuck," Dirk insisted.

A light gleamed in her father's eye as he gently mocked, "Courting my favor?"

A low yet hearty laugh came from Dirk. It turned Victoria's head, lifting it so she could see his face beneath the white visor she wore. Her senses quivered, on red alert all of a sudden, completely attuned to the body of the man beside her.

The white of his shirt contrasted sharply with his skin, which shone like polished bronze with honest sweat. That coiled the dark curling hairs visible at the vee of his open-collared polo and intensified the warm, earthy smell of him that stimulated her already quickly beating heart. If only, if only . . .

She imagined making easy contact with him, even

resting her hand on his solid chest, rising and falling in a comfortable rhythm despite the exertion of the tennis match.

Her lips felt dry and Victoria pressed them together to moisten them with her tongue. She could taste the salty tang of her own sweat and felt the dampness of her hair curling against the sides of her face. As if feeling her eyes on him, Dirk turned his head to look down at her upturned face.

The heady male smile remained grooved into his cheeks, but the laughing glint in his coal-black eyes took on another dimension. His gaze shifted to dwell on the moistness of her lips. The sensual impact of his look struck Victoria hard and made her legs feel wobbly. In an instant she realized that she had let herself get drawn in by his dangerously handsome looks and potent charm.

With a quick turn of her head she broke free of the spell, feeling more out of breath than when the match had ended. "Let's call it quits for today and play the tiebreaker some other time," Victoria suggested.

"I second that," her mother agreed.

And then . . . his hand did touch the back of her waist. There was nothing restrictive in it. All Victoria had to do was simply turn and walk away. She did, moving parallel with the net to the end pole and walking around it to the gate in the court fence. Naturally Dirk followed but so did her parents.

Before leaving the court, they picked up the protective covers for their rackets and the tote bags that held the cans of balls. Outside the gate the quartet continued to the benches where they stopped as if by mutual consent.

As Victoria unzipped her bag and took out a hand

towel, she couldn't make up her mind whether it was by accident or design that she and Dirk were separated from her parents by several feet. She rubbed her face dry and tried to ignore him.

"Your father plays a great game," Dirk commented, tipping his head back to wipe the sweat from his throat.

Victoria flashed him a wary look. "And he doesn't cheat, either."

His hand halted the towel at the base of his throat as he turned to level his gaze at her. "I don't recall ever suggesting that he did."

"Didn't you once say something like that? I seem to remember that you did. Hey, I hope I'm wrong," she retorted in a low undertone.

His eyes remained harshly black, not lightened by humor although his mouth twisted into a smile. "We are supposed to be observing a truce."

"An armed truce," Victoria reminded him, and flipped her visor off to jam it in the tote bag.

"Hello, Dirk." Penny sidled up instead of going at her usual madcap pace. In fact, Victoria thought her sister must be up to something. She had the impression her little sister had matured overnight.

"Hello, Laurel." Dirk returned the greeting with a gentleness that was indulgent, as if he knew what was happening to the girl. Victoria knew, too. Penny was in the throes of puppy love.

"I saw you playing and stopped to watch," Penny said to explain her presence. "You have a wicked backhand. Maybe you could give me some pointers sometime."

"How about right now?" Dirk suggested.

"I—" Penny's delight nearly bubbled over into

teenage exuberance, but she checked it just in time. "I'd like that."

"Let's get the court before someone else takes it." He took his racket out of its cover.

"May I borrow yours, Tory?" Penny asked.

"Sure." Victoria shrugged, knowing her younger sister would never understand a refusal—or accept it. She watched the pair take the court and observed Dirk instructing Penny how to position herself, step into the swing and follow through. It was amazing how Penny, who was such a quick learner, was so slow to catch on.

"I see Dirk is teaching Penny the finer points of a two-handed backhand," her father remarked, coming to stand beside Victoria and watch.

Victoria turned away. "Like she needs lessons," she said in disgust. "She's had, what, a thousand hours of instruction at the country club?"

"Oh, come on. She's young and feeling flirty," her mother reasoned.

"What's his excuse?" Victoria challenged, slicing a glance at the tall, dark man on the court. "He's experienced enough to know what she's doing." In Victoria's opinion, Penny was making a fool of herself, and she didn't like the idea of Dirk Ramsey laughing at any of her family.

"He's being kind," her mother insisted.

"Kind? That isn't an adjective I would associate with him," she retorted. "Found out any more about his agenda, Dad? Or him?"

"Not much," he admitted, pursing his lips together in a considering expression. "I know he came up the hard way."

"The hard way, huh?" Victoria was skeptical. "With

his looks I can't imagine that anything was ever hard for him."

"With his looks," her mother inserted, "I imagine it was difficult for people to take him seriously as a journalist."

"I'm sure you're right, Lena," her father agreed.

Victoria didn't agree, but rather than argue she excused herself to go for a walk just in case her legs cramped up. But it was really to let off steam.

At dinner that evening, Penny appeared at the table with her long blond hair swept on top of her head. Victoria recognized the gold hooped earrings her sister was wearing as her own, obviously swiped from her jewelry case. Her baby sister was attempting to look worldly even though she lacked the experience to carry it off.

Aware that it was all done for Dirk's benefit, both Victoria and her parents were careful not to comment on Penny's sudden burst of sophistication. Only Victoria was close enough to hear Dirk voice his reaction to the new Penny.

"You look pretty, Penny. And with your hair up, very young. And vulnerable."

"Vulnerable?" Penny asked. "Is that good or bad?"

"Neither," Dirk said. "It's just a description." And it was accurate, even though it was the exact opposite of the effect that Penny was trying to achieve. And Penny wouldn't have believed it from anyone else.

Dirk took the sting out of his comment by adding, "And I feel very old in comparison." It was the twinge of regret in his look and voice that made the difference, and soothed Penny's hurt feelings.

Victoria's reaction to his comment was mixed. On the one hand, she was glad he had been truthful and had not let Penny think she looked older. Yet she resented him, too, for paying that much attention to Penny's feelings. Or Penny herself, for that matter.

Breakfast wasn't served at a set time in the Beaumont household, especially when they were vacationing on the island. Whenever anyone came downstairs in the morning there was cereal, fruit, toast, and juice in the kitchen. Victoria ate her toast and coffee alone in the breakfast nook partitioned from the kitchen by a decorative iron screen. Everyone else, with the exception of Penny who was still in bed, had already eaten.

When she'd finished, she stopped by the library where her father was reading and her mother was catching up on bills and family correspondence. Lena Beaumont still believed in handwritten letters and didn't use e-mail very often. Her father glanced at her over his reading glasses.

"Good morning, Tory," he greeted her.

"Hi. I'm going into town this morning for some shampoo and stuff. Is there anything you want me to pick up for you, Mom?" she asked.

"Not that I can think of, no," her mother replied after a second's pause.

"Have you phoned for a taxi or were you planning to walk?" The inquiry came from her father. The smile on his face said he had already guessed her answer.

"Would you call one for me?" Victoria grinned. "I'm

going upstairs for my purse. I'll probably have lunch in town, so if I'm not back by noon don't wait for me."

"All right," her mother agreed.

Ascending the stairs Victoria took her time. Unless there was a taxi in the immediate vicinity of their summer home, it would be several minutes before one arrived since it was literally dependent on horse-power. In her room, she paused in front of the vanity mirror to adjust the collar of her sleeveless lavender dress. At the last minute, she added a narrow belt to make a waistline.

Her bedroom faced the front of the house directly above the library. The bay window that jutted out from the room below was repeated in her bedroom. The lower half of one window was raised to let in the heavy scent of lilacs blooming in the front of the house. A pair of birds chattered noisily outside the window, nearly drowning out the sound of trotting hooves approaching the house.

Slipping the strap of her purse over her shoulder Victoria hurried out of the bedroom to the second-floor landing. At the same moment Dirk came out of his bedroom.

Good manners dictated that she couldn't ignore him, so she tossed him a casual, "Good morning." Victoria would have left it at that, but she wasn't given the chance.

"Is that your taxi pulling up outside the house?" Dirk asked.

"Yes." She paused with a hand on the railing of the stairs. "I'm on my way into town. Why?"

Dirk stopped near her, dressed in jeans and a nice, oyster-gray shirt. "Would you mind if I came along with you?"

Irritated because she couldn't think of an adequate reason to refuse him, Victoria asked, "Nothing else to do?"

"Not really." His tone echoed hers. "I spent the morning sharpening my pen so I could dip it in poison ink. But making up stuff about innocent people gets kinda boring."

"I bet it does."

He noted her cool expression with a lazy look. "Anyway, I need more material. May I ride with you?"

Victoria took a deep breath and let it out in a long, exasperated sound. "Of course."

"Don't sound too overjoyed or I might get the wrong idea," he mocked.

"I wish that was true," she murmured and started down the stairs. It didn't require a sixth sense to know that her leisurely, peaceful morning in town had just been shot down by the enemy.

Her father was in the entryway when Victoria rounded the curve of the staircase. "Your taxi is waiting." When he caught sight of the man behind her, he asked, "Are you going with Tory?"

"Yes," Dirk answered without elaboration.

Her father didn't seem unduly surprised by it. "It's a beautiful morning. We'll see you when you come back." He continued on to the library.

Crossing the foyer Victoria walked to the front door. Dirk reached in front of her to open it. She inclined her head in a haughty acknowledgment of his courtesy and avoided that mocking light she knew would be in his gaze. There wasn't really any reason for her to be so stiff and formal, but she figured it was her only protection.

The main entrance of the house was recessed under

the timbered roof that connected the breezeway to the garage. The horse-drawn taxi waited for them by the stone walk. Dirk helped her into the rubber-wheeled buggy, then climbed in to sit beside her. Victoria didn't remember the seats being so narrow. After asking the driver to take them to the harbor, she adjusted the side of her dress so it wouldn't reveal so much thigh.

With a flick of his whip and the urging click of his tongue, the driver had the horse leaning into its harness. The buggy started forward with a slight lurch before the horse settled into a steady trot.

The silence was more than Victoria could tolerate. It made her too conscious of the muscled arm and shoulder so near hers. She moved her purse onto her lap so it wouldn't be poking her in the side and let her fingers fidget with the metal clasp.

"What are your first impressions of Mackinac Island?" Her gray eyes slid him a sideways look of feigned interest.

"It has a certain nostalgic appeal. It's an escape into the past." His encompassing glance included the bobbing head of the horse pulling the buggy, and the green trees rising out of the rocky ground.

"Well, at least our pollution problems are limited to horse droppings and the occasional gum wrapper," Victoria admitted with a wry smile.

"How long have you been coming here?" Dirk asked.

"We've spent at least a month here every summer since I was five," she replied. The question brought back a lot of childhood memories of idyllic days on the island. "I loved the horses," Victoria recalled. "When I was seven one of my friends had her own pony and cart. I begged my father to let me have one, too, but he convinced me it wasn't fair to the pony since it would be lonely all the months I was gone."

"It must be tough to be the daughter of rich parents," he said, a corner of his mouth quirking.

Her bristling response was automatic. "It has its drawbacks."

"Such as?"

"Such as enduring the company of rude reporters."

Dirk chuckled. "I think the lady is trying to put me down."

"Wherever did you get that idea?" she murmured with cool innocence.

"Where did you go to college? Bryn Mawr? Vassar?"

"What makes you think I didn't go to Ann Arbor?" Victoria countered.

"Did you?" He arched a skeptical brow.

"As a matter of fact I didn't," she fairly snapped out the admission. "But I don't doubt that you already know which university I attended. More than likely you researched the background of everyone in the family, including me. I'm sure you know all my vital statistics."

"No, not all," Dirk denied that, a flirtatious light glinting in his dark eyes. "But I think I could make a guess, considering how much of you I saw in that swimsuit." His gaze made a slow sweep of her now. "Do you want to know what I think your measurements are?"

"Not particularly." She frowned as her fingers tightened protectively on the small shield of her purse.

Dirk leaned forward and asked the driver to stop for a minute. His request caught Victoria off guard, confusing her as to his motive. He stepped out and walked to a lilac bush growing close to the road. Snapping off a cluster, he returned to the buggy and dropped the richly scented flowers in her lap as he climbed back in.

"What's this for?" Victoria wondered if it was supposed to be some kind of peace offering. She had no desire to make peace with him.

"You seem to be having trouble finding something to do with your hands," Dirk replied as the buggy lurched forward again. "I thought you could play with the flower instead of your purse. At the rate you're going the clasp will be broken before we reach the harbor."

Even as he made his explanation Victoria discovered her nervous fingers were already twirling the stem of the lilacs, spreading their light but intoxicating scent in all directions. She forced her hand to hold it still.

"Maybe if I put my arm back here, you'll feel more relaxed." He rested his arm along the back of the buggy seat. Her shoulder was no longer rubbing against it, but she could feel her hair brushing his sleeve. If anything, the suggestion of having his arm around her was even more sensual—and troubling. He probably knew it, but Victoria would never admit it. "What do you do, Victoria?"

"Do? By that, do you mean am I gainfully employed?" She bridled at the question and forced a measure of calm into her answer. "The answer is no, I don't work at anything where I get a salary. I'm involved in arranging many charity benefits and I do a lot of volunteer work at the hospital and with the elderly. I keep busy."

"All that education going to waste," he murmured in subtle condemnation.

"Education is never wasted," she said with heat.

"I'm doing something that is both worthwhile and needed. If I had told you that I worked as an administrative assistant or a teacher, you probably would have pointed out that someone else needed the job and its salary more than I did. Either way you would have found fault."

"You're probably right," Dirk conceded, eyeing her with a considering look.

"I know I am." Victoria stared straight ahead, her jaw clenched in an effort to check her growing anger.

"Let's move on."

"Does that mean it's time for more obnoxious questions?" she said even more heatedly.

"I can come up with some, sure. If that's what you want."

Steamed, she didn't reply.

"Okay. Unmarried, no engagement ring, no guy friends, no lover—at least I haven't seen any evidence of one. You're a beautiful woman, Victoria, so what's the matter? Training to become a nun?" He was deliberately baiting her and sitting back with amusement to watch the result.

"No! At the moment I don't happen to be dating anyone and I'm not looking. As yet I haven't found a man I want to spend a whole day with or a whole night, let alone the rest of my life."

"Whoa!" he said, holding up his hands. The horse twitched its ears. "I wasn't going to go that far."

Victoria snorted. "Sooner or later you would."

He conceded the point with a nod. "Okay, rant on. I'm listening."

Feeling like she'd escaped from her parents' house made her bold. And, Victoria told herself, she really didn't care what she said to him or what he thought. It was a nice day for a rant.

"I do want to get married someday."

"Hurrah."

"But it isn't like a dress that you throw away when you get tired of it. When I get married it's going to be for keeps. I know it would get great buzz if I had a bunch of crazy affairs, but that's not me!" She glared at him. "I don't care if you consider me a freak."

"A rare bird, maybe. But I wouldn't say a freak." There was quiet contemplation in the steady regard of his eyes, but his reaction otherwise was unreadable.

Victoria had had enough of being on the sharp end of his pointed questions. It was time he had a taste of his own treatment.

"What about you? What makes you tick?" she challenged. "Tell me about your life!"

"Just your typical hard-luck-kid-growing-up-in-the-streets story with his sick mother in a dingy apartment," Dirk shrugged but with a harsh bite to his self-mockery. "I always worked. Sometimes the job was legal, sometimes it wasn't. Vacation to me only meant that I didn't have to go to school. I had to work at two full-time jobs to make it through city college, so I never had time to study to make the grades that might earn me a scholarship. But I got into a university and took all the courses I could on journalism, speech, and television. Eventually I got my degree."

"Then what?" Victoria prompted and refused to let herself feel any pity for him.

"I couldn't get a job. I ended up interning on a weekly newspaper in a little burg outside Washington, D.C. When I wasn't doing layouts or bugging the advertisers or taking want ads, I wrote articles that I started submitting to the editorial pages of big newspapers. That was the beginning of my column. So you see"— Dirk glanced at her, a sardonic expression on his face— "my life story is very boring. What about yours?"

Boring? It sounded like a determined struggle to Victoria, a struggle by a tenacious fighter. But she doubted that he would take her seriously if she said that.

"Mine is just as simple. I was born with a silver spoon in my mouth and I've been collecting them ever since," she retorted.

Unexpectedly, Dirk laughed. Equally unexpectedly, Victoria found herself joining in.

Chapter Five

The horse-drawn taxi stopped at the curb by the white-fronted buildings that marked the commercial district of Mackinac Island. Dirk climbed out of the buggy first and turned to help Victoria down. She reached for his hands, but they circled her waist instead to lift her out of the buggy. Clutching the spray of lilac in one hand, Victoria gripped the flexed muscles of his upper arms for balance.

When he slowly set her on the ground, she ended up sliding the last couple of inches against his chest with his hands deliberately forcing her that close. The contact with his hard, lean body had her pulse beating wildly. Victoria quickly pushed some distance between them and thanked the driver. She hurried onto the covered sidewalk by the storefronts.

"Are you late for something?" Dirk seemed very aware of her haste.

Victoria summoned up her composure to come to her rescue. "No, I . . ." She glanced to the street just as a carriage filled with tourists pulled away from the ticket office, the fringe on its top swinging with the rhythm of the trotting horses. "I was just getting out of the way of the tour carriage."

"Oh." It was a disbelieving sound, but Dirk didn't pursue her lie. "Where shall I meet you?" He joined her on the sidewalk, drawing her to one side so they would be out of the pedestrians' way.

"There's no need for that," Victoria insisted with an offhand shrug. "Whenever I'm through with my shopping I'll make my own way home. I don't expect you to wait for me."

"But I might not make my way back." He tipped his dark head to one side. The prospect appeared to amuse him.

"This is an island. How could you get lost?" she laughed.

"I'm not taking any chances. Where should I meet you?" Dirk persisted.

Victoria hesitated for an instant, then gave in. "Eleven-thirty at the Grand Hotel," she said and immediately started to walk away.

"Where is that?" he asked.

"You can't miss it. It has the longest front porch in the world," she called over her shoulder.

Before she looked to the front again, she saw his half salute of acknowledgment. Victoria didn't have much shopping to do. A stop at a drugstore took care of everything on her list—shampoo, polish remover, and cotton balls. She wandered along the sidewalk, looking in windows and entering a few places to say hello to shop owners she had known since childhood.

When eleven-thirty drew near Victoria found her steps turning eagerly toward the Grand Hotel. She deliberately slowed them. She would seem as giddy as Penny if she wasn't careful. But she had no control over the way her heart somersaulted when she saw Dirk leaning against one of the pillars of the endless white porch. She immediately looked away to pretend an interest in the bright yellow and red carpet of the flower beds. Her hand trailed along the railing that lined the sidewalk on the opposite side of the street from the hotel. She crossed the street at the hotel's main entrance and climbed the steps to the famous porch. Dirk was there, having traversed its porch to meet her.

"Did you get your shopping done?" His dark eyes glanced at the single package in her hand.

"Yes, I did."

"Are your parents expecting us back for lunch?" Since his question didn't have a simple answer, Victoria hesitated and Dirk immediately guessed. "Obviously they aren't. So, why don't we have lunch before going back?"

Victoria was on the verge of refusing when she heard herself agreeing. "But only if we go dutch," she said.

"I wasn't going to buy your lunch. I was going to let you buy mine." His big smile made really sexy grooves in his cheeks.

"Oh, you were?" Victoria laughed, not certain whether she should take him seriously.

"Why not? You can afford it," he replied. "Although I was kidding. But I am just a poor writer."

"As if," she chided. "Your column is syndicated in practically every major newspaper in the country. You're a very successful writer."

"Maybe, by most people's standards," Dirk qualified. "Let me put it this way. You probably spend more money on clothes than I live on during the period of a year. My bank balance is a few decimal places shy of your father's."

"What's he got to do with it? You're not competing with him, I hope," she said. "If your goal is to make a lot of money, you're in the wrong profession."

Dirk shrugged, looking a little uncomfortable. "I have a lot of ambitions. Not all of them have been realized yet. Yeah, one of them is financial security, but it doesn't take as much money to satisfy me as it takes for you." His smile was aloof.

The remark roused Victoria's ire. "If you think I'm going to spend the rest of my time over lunch apologizing for the fact that I happened to be born into a wealthy family, then let's cancel it now," she informed him icily.

A flicker of genuine amusement entered his dark eyes. "Don't go all cool and highbred on me, Victoria. I thought we had progressed past that point," he murmured.

But she wasn't so easily soothed. "My parents were rich, and your parents were poor—" she began.

"And never the twain shall meet . . . except over lunch." Dirk offered his arm to her, challenging her with his smile. "Shall we?" At Victoria's hesitation Dirk took her hand and slipped it on the inside of his left arm, spreading her fingers over his forearm with: "I believe that's the way it's done."

Men just didn't get more annoying. Victoria started to pull her hand free. His right hand closed around her fingers and pressed them to his arm with considerable strength. "You are touchy about all that, aren't you?"

Victoria was surprised to find that both his voice and his look were soothing. Kind of . . . velvety. "Considering some of the things you say, is that so surprising?"

"I have a big mouth sometimes."

His expression of disguised amusement was actually kind of cute. Plus he was right about that. His honesty was awfully male. She could hear her much-too-responsive heart thudding loudly against her ribs.

"I can control it if I put food in it. Scout's honor." He raised his fingers in the three-fingered pledge.

"Were you a Boy Scout?" Somehow she doubted it.

"As a matter of fact," Dirk paused deliberately, a cynical look in his dark eyes, "no."

"That's what I thought," Victoria muttered.

"Anyway, I can make or fake civilized conversation with the best of them." A low chuckle came from his throat. "Come on." Without allowing her any more protests, Dirk escorted her inside the hotel to the restaurant.

When they were shown to a table, heads turned, especially the female ones. Victoria could understand the effect Dirk had on women. After all, she knew he couldn't be trusted and here she was sitting down to eat with him anyway.

Dirk kept his word and their conversation over lunch was focused on impersonal topics. In spite of that Victoria found herself analyzing his every sentence for a double meaning. She tried to be pleasant, but could never manage to entirely lower her guard and be natural.

Both of them refused dessert in favor of coffee. Victoria sipped at hers, holding the cup in both her hands and swirling the coffee to cool it. "Where did you learn to speak French?" she asked. "In college?"

"No." Dirk set his cup down and returned her curious look with an amused one. "About ten years ago, there was a French girl who lived in the same building as I did. She had only recently emigrated and knew very little English. I could understand when she was saying 'no,' but I wanted to be sure I knew when she was saying 'yes.' Between a French dictionary, a phrase book, and Jeanne, I learned French."

"Where is Jeanne now?" Victoria put her cup down because her hands suddenly felt a little shaky at the thought of saying 'yes' to him. She tried to sound nonchalant and undisturbed.

"I think she married a plumber." Dirk started to reach a hand into his shirt pocket, then paused. "Oops. Almost forgot that I gave up smoking."

"Good thing you did," she said. "Were you in love with her?" she asked.

"Do you want an honest answer to that?" Hs dark eyes were bright with challenge.

"Yes." Victoria blinked, not understanding the reason for that question.

"Because I don't want to be accused of being crude," Dirk explained it. "No, I wasn't in love with her. I just enjoyed going to bed with her."

A flash fire of heat spread over her skin, but Victoria refused to let him see that his bluntness in any way disconcerted her, or that his unexpected answer bothered her.

"Then you obviously learned when she said 'yes,'" she murmured.

"Obviously," Dirk agreed dryly. His gaze narrowed slightly to glide over her face. "With you it would be more difficult to figure out. I would have to get over a class barrier instead of a language barrier."

Victoria caught at the breath she was taking. "You

seem to be determined to see me as a snob." She let the breath escape in anger.

"Uh-oh. And I promised a civilized conversation, didn't I?" he said with mock regret.

"I didn't really expect you to keep your word," she returned with icy calm.

"I was fantasizing again, trying to decide what it would take to persuade you to say yes." Dirk shrugged, his eyes not leaving her face, observing her every reaction.

"You have an overactive imagination," Victoria countered.

"I believe you've hinted at that before." He seemed completely unconcerned.

"It deserves repeating, Dirk."

"It's your fault."

"Mine?" Victoria repeated with wide-eyed indignation.

"Yeah. Either you shouldn't be so beautiful or else you should give up that touch-me-not attitude. It's an irresistible challenge."

What the hell could she say to that? Victoria searched her mind for a suitably scathing retort and drew a blank.

"Victoria!" At the sound of her name, she turned to see a tall, statuesque woman of indeterminate age approaching the table. She recognized Daphne Bourns, a contemporary of her mother's. "It's been so long since I saw you last. Your mother stopped by last week to let us know you all had arrived on the island. How are you?"

"Fine, thank you, Mrs. Bourns."

The sophisticated brunette faked a wince. "Oh, call me Daphne," she said. "You make me sound as old as your mother." Which she was, although she looked closer to Dirk's age.

"Daphne, you look great. That's just not an issue," Victoria responded diplomatically.

"Okay, thanks," the woman laughed and looked pointedly at Victoria's companion. "Aren't you going to introduce me to this gorgeous hunk of man, Victoria? Or must I do it myself?"

With a sideways glance, Victoria saw that Dirk was standing in polite deference to the woman's presence. His expression was neutral.

"Of course. Daphne, this is Dirk Ramsey who is . . . visiting us." Victoria chose not to identify his profession. It was unlikely that Daphne knew his name since she rarely read anything but the lifestyle section of a newspaper and she didn't go online except to shop. "This is Daphne Bourns, a friend of the family."

"It's a pleasure, Mrs. Bourns." Dirk acknowledged the introduction with a nod, the width of the table precluding a handshake.

"Ooh, the pleasure's all mine," Daphne Bourns cooed. "Are you here getting acquainted with the family, Mr. Ramsey?"

"You could say that," he conceded with an amused twitch of his mouth.

The brunette turned to Victoria. "I had heard you had a guest. The island grapevine at work again," she explained her source in a laughing tone. "My, but you keep things to yourself, Victoria. No one has even hinted that you had someone like this in the wings."

It was clear that Daphne took Dirk for Victoria's boyfriend and assumed that his visit indicated the seriousness of their supposed romance. She probably suspected there was an engagement announcement in the offing.

"I think you misunderstood," Victoria said quickly. "Dirk's a reporter, so this isn't strictly a social visit."

"Oh." Daphne's gaze made a quick reassessment of Dirk. "I can't imagine it's all work and no play. You don't look a bit dull."

"I try to keep myself entertained," Dirk replied in a dry tone.

"How long will you be staying?" Daphne asked.

"I plan to be here two weeks." Something about his tone seemed to say that he might change his mind.

"Marvelous!" the brunette exclaimed in a husky voice. "Then you can come to my party Saturday night. It's formal but it's fun. My little contribution to the lilac festivities." She directed her next sentence to Victoria. "Be sure to bring him, won't you, Victoria?"

"Of course." She smiled politely. If Daphne's party this year was like the previous ones, Dirk's opinion of her and her family as high-class snobs would be reinforced. Their lifestyle on the island was usually casual, but Daphne always insisted on throwing a very formal bash. Her reason was that she wanted an excuse to dress up, and it probably was that simple.

"It's very nice of you to include me," Dirk murmured.

The waitress paused at their table to leave the check. Dirk stopped her, glanced at the total, and placed the amount plus a healthy tip on the metal tray before giving it back to the waitress.

"Nice?" Daphne repeated the word, a knowing gleam in her brown eyes. "I'm making sure my party is a success. We need new blood, mwahahah. And a new man is always welcome." With an infinitesimal shrug of her shoulders she gave them both a stretchy smile. "Well. I'm having lunch with some friends. If I'd seen you earlier, you could have joined us. Perhaps you could have coffee with us?"

"Another time, perhaps," Victoria refused, trying to conceal the irritation gnawing at her poise. "We have to be going."

"That's a pity," Daphne said with a faint sigh. "Then I'll see you both Saturday, if not before. Take care."

"It was a pleasure meeting you, Mrs. Bourns," Dirk offered.

"No, no. Call me Daphne." With a little wave of her hand she walked from the table.

"Divorced?" Dirk's hand was at the back of her chair to assist her when Victoria pushed from the table. She didn't want dear old Daphne to think she'd been lying about leaving.

"No. She claims to be very happily married. But her daughter's single." There was a slight edge to her voice. It wasn't like her to be catty and Victoria didn't understand it.

"Is she like her mother?" His hand was at the back of her waist as Dirk guided her through the cluster of tables to the exit. His voice sounded only mildly interested.

"Shelly is more introverted," Victoria replied, again with an edge.

"I don't imagine that Mrs. Bourns is eager to share the spotlight," Dirk commented. They walked to the area in front of the hotel where they could find a horse-drawn taxi. "How old is her daughter? Your age?"

"No, she is—nineteen." Victoria had to think for a second.

Daphne Bourns adored her daughter, but she also overshadowed her and wasn't aware of it. It was something Dirk had known instinctively. Inwardly Victoria had to agree with Dirk's observation that Daphne unconsciously competed with her daughter for attention. It was odd, though, that his guess had been so accurate on such short acquaintance.

After hiring a cab, Dirk helped her into the buggy seat and climbed in beside her. As the taxi pulled away from the curb Victoria opened her purse, counted out some money and offered it to Dirk.

Raising his eyebrows he gave her a sharply questioning look. "What's the purpose of that?"

"For my lunch." When he didn't take it she forced it into the palm of his hand.

"That isn't necessary." He held the bills between his middle and forefinger and offered them to her.

"I believe it is," Victoria insisted with a proud tilt to her chin as she stared straight ahead and ignored the money he held out to her. "The agreement was we would each pay for our own."

"I didn't make any agreement if you recall," he replied lazily. "Buying your lunch won't break me."

"I'm sure it was an investment, one that's bound to pay you enormous dividends. Daphne was impressed when you picked up the check, but that was the idea, right?" Victoria shot him a cool look.

"What?" His disbelieving voice was low and controlled.

"Maybe you missed your calling," she suggested haughtily. "You would make a great accessory for a real rich bitch. Every hostess would simply drool to have you accept an invitation to her party."

Dirk took her purse before Victoria could stop him

and slipped the money inside. Snapping it closed he gave it back, his jaw clenched in hard anger.

"If I wanted to do that, I would be writing a gossip column or something. Just in case you haven't read me, I deal with issues of corruption, energy, and crime." For all the glittering fire in his look, his voice was level and infuriatingly calm. "I fully intended to buy your lunch all along, and you will do me the courtesy of accepting."

It was impossible not to believe that he meant every word he had said. Victoria realized that she had wanted to think the worst, a discovery that didn't make her feel very proud.

"All right. I—I'm sorry. I shouldn't have said that," she admitted with grudging reluctance.

"Guess not. But you did." Dirk stretched out his arm along the back of the buggy seat.

For nearly a block neither of them spoke. The only sounds were the clip-clopping of the horse's hooves, the creaking of the buggy, and the whir of the wheels rolling over the road. A breeze stirred to life by their motion fanned the hair around her face. Victoria grew uncomfortable with the silence and half turned in her seat to face Dirk.

"You have to admit that your past behavior wouldn't exactly inspire me to trust you," Victoria justified. "Look at the way you attacked my father on the basis of circumstantial evidence without really ever knowing him."

"All evidence is circumstantial. As the daughter of a lawyer you should know that."

Victoria was silent. Actually she hadn't.

"It's the eyewitness accounts that never quite add

up and they're more open to interpretation. You should know that too."

"Don't lecture me, Dirk."

He shrugged. "Sorry. But it's kinda fun. If only because it gets you mad."

"Are you going to tell me I'm beautiful when I'm angry? I swear, Dirk Ramsey, I will push you out of this carriage if you do."

"Hey, I have a point to make and I'm going to make it." He smirked.

She really could push him out. Not a problem. But she was curious as to what he was going to say next.

"When I look at you," Dirk went on, "I see Italian shoes, a dress that probably boasts a London label" —after his gaze had lazily skimmed the expensive material, he leaned slightly closer—"and I catch the fragrance of French perfume. On the surface you appear to be a walking advertisement for foreign goods, except . . ." Dirk paused and a magical, warm look entered his eyes that Victoria found dangerously fascinating. His hand shaped itself to the back of her neck, the contact so pleasurable that she didn't want to move away. "Those lips are very American."

His firm grip prevented Victoria from drawing back from the steady approach of his mouth. As it came closer, her lashes automatically lowered. A breathless weakness fluttered through her at the easy possession of his kiss. Leisurely, his mouth explored the soft curves of her lips, demanding no more than her acquiescence. It was a heady investigation that teased her into wanting something more. But Dirk didn't give in as he moved away and untangled his fingers from the tawny silk of her hair. Victoria blinked once and looked away from his knowing regard.

She summoned the poise that was her defense. "And how do American lips compare with French?"

His mouth quirked at her cool question. "A little inexperienced but their passion is much more genuine."

"You would know." Victoria let a little of her annoyance creep into the retort.

"That's right." His tone was teasing. "They call you Tory, don't they?"

"My parents do, and some of my closest friends," she admitted. Her phrasing was deliberately designed to exclude him from that select group.

"I'm sure you know that English conservatives are called Tories. I wonder if you'd qualify," Dirk mused. "But you do seem liberal about some things."

"I usually don't discuss politics. Make that never with reporters," Victoria countered smoothly.

"Gotcha," he said with an easy laugh. "You know more than one way to backstab. It's effective."

Victoria despaired of ever finding a way to penetrate that Teflon exterior of his. He always seemed so totally in command of every situation, and she always felt outmaneuvered. With a barely concealed sigh Victoria turned her head to view the scenery the buggy was passing.

"This is a beautiful island," Dirk remarked.

Again, Victoria was shaken by the impression he was diverting the conversation to a safer topic because he knew she couldn't cope with anything sexual, even as a joke. And it was true.

"Yes. And historic as all get out." Victoria accepted the new topic and elaborated on it. "There are lots and lots of places to see."

"I noticed the old fort when we flew in."

"Built by the British during the American Revolution

and used again by them during the War of 1812." She was beginning to sound ridiculously like a tour guide and immediately stopped talking.

"Can I persuade you to take me on a tour of the island some day while I'm here?" He eyed her as if he had been reading her mind.

"You would learn more if you took the official State Park carriage tour," Victoria said.

"No, thanks. What if I end up with a guide who resembled the horses?"

"I wouldn't feel sorry for you," she said tartly.

"Well, I prefer you. You're very easy on the eyes, even if you do play games with me," Dirk replied.

"I find it hard to believe that it really bothers you." She had a little trouble breathing normally after that provocative comment.

"You get to me, Victoria." When she didn't respond, he gave her a mocking look. "Isn't that what you wanted to hear?"

"Not particularly." She shook her head, trying to rid herself of the sensual tension in the atmosphere.

The trees thinned out as the horse-drawn taxi turned into the driveway that curved in front of the two-story stucco and brick home trimmed in dark wood. It had been a short ride, but Victoria was relieved it was almost over.

"Here's your package." Dirk handed her the bag she'd wedged between them on the seat, a paper barrier that really hadn't protected her very well from his unsettling presence.

"Thank you." She took it as the buggy stopped in front.

Dirk stepped out first to help her down. Remembering the last time, Victoria kept her arms rigidly straight to maintain a distance. Her feet touched the ground a foot from where he was standing.

Dirk paid the driver and held up a silencing hand when she began to protest. "No arguments."

"Or else?" She felt compelled to challenge him, not aware that the driver was smiling at their exchange as he clicked to his horse.

"Or else I really will believe you're one of those spoiled rich girls who always wants her way," he replied.

Anything would have been preferable to that comment. Now she didn't dare argue, which had been his aim all along. Simmering behind a mask of composure, Victoria walked to the sheltered roof of the entryway.

Before she reached the door, the iron gate to the breezeway and terrace swung open with a rasping protest of metal. Penny strolled through, pretending to be surprised when she saw Dirk and Victoria.

"Hey. You made it back, I see." She smiled brightly and Victoria knew her sister wasn't addressing her.

"Safe and sound," Dirk agreed with a hint of a different kind of amusement in his smile.

"Dad wanted to see you, something about fishing, I think." Penny passed the message on to Dirk with an air of importance. Victoria decided that explained why her younger sister was dressed in bellbottoms and a white tank—and why a sailor hat in white cotton was perched atop her blond head. Could Penny *be* any more obvious?

"Thanks." Dirk opened the front door and held it for Victoria.

"Oh, Tory, can I talk to you for a minute?" Penny asked with feigned nonchalance.

Taking an affirmative answer for granted, she turned and walked back through the open gates to the breezeway. Victoria followed.

"What is it you want, Penny?" She had a pretty good idea.

"I want to borrow your red windbreaker."

"Going fishing?" Victoria couldn't help teasing just a little.

"Yes, Dad asked me to go with them . . . him," she corrected, instantly on the defensive. Just as quickly Penny changed to attack. "Honestly, Tory, I don't know whatever possessed you to invite Dirk along with you this morning."

"I didn't invite him, he invited himself." Victoria made that point clear.

"Either way you shouldn't have stayed gone all morning," Penny retorted. "Someone should remind you that Dirk is here because he wants to talk with Dad."

"I think I'm more aware of the reason for his visit than you are." Victoria found her younger sister's criticism annoying, to say the least.

"If you are, then you shouldn't be monopolizing Dirk's time. I realize you must be desperate for attention, but—" Penny was giving a very good imitation of adult disdain.

"Listen, little girl," Victoria interrupted her. "You can just knock it off right now. Dirk Ramsey is the last man I want any attention from. And before you make a total fool of yourself, keep in mind that he's twice your age."

She saw the tears spring into Penny's eyes and the veneer of adulthood shatter. Victoria immediately regretted that she had been so harsh and angry, but it was too late. Whirling away on a choked sob, Penny dashed into the house with her long hair trailing like a blond cloud behind her.

"Great. Now he has us fighting over him," Victoria murmured and bit at her lower lip.

Chapter Six

Everyone went fishing except Victoria. Her mother tried to persuade her to come with them, but Victoria was adamant in her refusal. Her reason was twofold. The tension of the morning with Dirk had upset her, and Penny would undoubtedly think she was competing for Dirk's attention. Josie sent the fishing party off with a basket of sandwiches, snacks, and cold drinks in case they were late returning.

It was late in the evening before they trooped into the kitchen with their catch. Victoria was there helping Josie with the night's meal so it would be ready within minutes of the fishing party's return. She looked up from the relish tray she was preparing when the boisterous group entered. Her glance ricocheted off Dirk's lazy smile and took in her parents and sister.

"Did you have a good time?" Victoria asked pleasantly, although their happy, flushed faces revealed the answer.

"The best!" Penny declared and sent a sideways glance at Dirk.

"Josie, I heard you wishing the other day for some really fresh fish. Here you are!" Charles Beaumont proudly deposited their catch in the sink. "How is that?"

The housekeeper exclaimed over them as if she had discovered a treasure. Victoria looked in the sink at the fish and added her praise of their size to Josie's, then returned to the side counter to finish the relish tray. Dirk leaned against the counter near where she was working and Victoria became conscious of how small the horseshoe-shaped kitchen suddenly seemed.

"Mmm, stuffed olives, my favorite." Dirk reached to take a half dozen from the tray.

"Quit stealing." She started to tap at his hand with the side of the fork she held, but he was already out of striking distance.

"Am I?" He popped an olive between her lips, his fingers lingering on the lower curve after her teeth automatically bit into the olive. "You're eating them, too, so that makes you equally guilty."

"No, it doesn't." Victoria wished he would move away and go scale the fish. That plaid shirt and his worn jeans gave him an earthy look that was vital and raw. A lake breeze had rumpled his raven hair and Victoria felt an urge to smooth it into place.

"You look very domestic." His intonation implied that looks were deceiving.

"I'm not lost in a kitchen," she retorted. She stopped trying to field his remarks and began asking questions of her own. "How many fish did *you* catch?"

"Only two," Dirk answered and popped another olive into his mouth. "I'm not much of a fisherman." It didn't sound as though it bothered him.

Penny walked over in time to catch his reply. "You may not have caught the most, Dirk, but you caught the biggest." She came to his defense immediately.

"So I did." The warm look he gave Penny ignited a spark of anger in Victoria. He had no right to encourage Penny's infatuation.

Taking the sailor hat off her head, Penny rose on tiptoe to place it on top of Dirk's dark hair. "I crown you King of the Fishermen!" she declared. "And Mackinac Island!"

"Only Mackinac? But I want to rule the world, " Dirk said with gentle mockery.

"Okay," Penny agreed, a shade breathlessly and Victoria wanted to scream. Her baby sister's adoration and relentless flirting was getting out of hand. It seemed innocent enough, but Victoria knew how willing a teenager was to believe what she wanted to believe. *King of Mackinac Island, my*—Victoria didn't finish the rude thought, just seethed at the way Penny was practically ready to worship the ground Dirk walked on. At least he kept a little distance from his not-so-secret admirer.

She had to say something or burst. "Where did a street kid like you learn to fish, Dirk?" Victoria asked.

"I didn't, not as a kid," he replied. "In fact, I was twenty-six before I ever had a fishing pole in my hands. The owner of the weekly newspaper I worked for took me fishing one weekend."

"What did you catch?" Penny tipped her head back to look at him even more admiringly.

"A few tree limbs and sunken logs—it took me a while to get the knack of casting." Dirk smiled. "Eventually I think I caught one fish, but maybe not."

Victoria shot a glance at her parents. It appeared

they didn't see anything wrong with Dirk being adored by their teenaged daughter. But if she stayed there another minute, Victoria knew she was going to throw olives at Dirk and yank Penny's hair. She picked up the relish tray and walked into the dining room. She dawdled at the table, precisely arranging the place settings of silverware.

"The table looks nice," her mother remarked as she emerged from the kitchen. "I can always tell when you set the table, Tory."

"Thank you," she said acidly. "I taught myself. Very useful skill, isn't it? Sometimes I wonder what my very expensive education was good for."

"Tory, I've never heard you sound so bitter." Lena Beaumont frowned at her in surprise.

"I'm sorry, Mom." Victoria ran her fingers through her hair. "Pay no attention to me. Our *guest* has just made me touchy about certain things."

"Dirk?" Her mother sounded skeptical.

Had her mother defected to the enemy, too? Victoria wasn't in the mood to argue her case, so she simply shook her head and forced a smile to her mouth. "I'm probably imagining things." She shrugged. "Forget what I said, okay?"

Her mother hesitated, then accepted the explanation. "Would you mind helping Josie in the kitchen for a few more minutes? I have to go wash this fish stuff off my hands and change."

"I don't mind." Victoria agreed even though it meant going back in the kitchen where Dirk was, and where she didn't want to be.

As her mother left, Victoria walked to the kitchen door and collided with Dirk who was just coming out. His reaction was instantaneous, grabbing her shoul-

ders when she bumped into him. The steadying grip
of his hands only added to her confusion. When she
lifted her gaze, Victoria saw Penny's cap still on top of
his head and was immediately filled with annoyance.
If that was the right word.

"Would the king let me by?" Her voice was chilling,
but her gray eyes were blazing.

His gaze narrowed on her for a long second. "Being
a king doesn't suit me. You can wear the crown. You
enjoy looking down on people." As he released her he
took the hat from his head and put it on hers, then
walked around her and out of the room.

Victoria stared after him, her throat tight with some
unknown emotion. Turning, she pushed open the
kitchen door and walked through. The cap slipped
and she whisked it off, tossing it to Penny.

"Take care of that," Victoria ordered. "And you'd
better get cleaned up. Don't think you're going to sit
at the dinner table smelling like fish, because you
aren't."

Penny bristled at the barrage of tactless orders.
"You are *so* not the boss of me, you know! I'm not a
child, so don't try to order me around."

"Someone has to. Mom and Dad won't. Shut up
and go wash," she said.

"I'll go when I'm ready," Penny answered defiantly.
"You don't give the orders around here."

"No, I do," Josie interceded between the quarrel-
ing pair. "This is my kitchen and *I* am telling you to
go. *Vite!*"

Penny didn't dispute Josie's authority, although she
showed her displeasure by storming out of the room.
Victoria watched her go.

"What a brat," she declared and walked to the stove.

She lifted lids on the pots without noticing the contents and let them clatter back into place. "Did you notice the way she tries to hang all over Dirk? And the way she worships him is just obnoxious."

"*Je . . .*" Josie started to reply in French, then appeared to realize that Victoria's mood was not conducive to translation. "I think you might be wishing he paid attention only to you."

"Oh, no, I don't."

"You should open your eyes, Victoria, before he decides to open them for you," the housekeeper warned.

"I get what's going on," Victoria assured her.

"Then why pretend that you weren't a little jealous of your sister?" Josie countered with a tiny smile edging the corners of her mouth.

"There isn't any point in discussing this with you. You don't understand," she declared in exasperation.

When she sat down to the table fifteen minutes later, Victoria didn't have any appetite for the food she had helped prepare. She excused herself as soon as she decently could and went up to her room.

After a long sleep and a meager breakfast, Victoria discovered that she felt just as unsettled and restless as she had the previous night. The obvious solution was to burn up the nervous energy that was keeping her on edge. She changed out of the baggy pants and shapeless top she'd put on when she'd gotten up, and into a pair of brief white shorts and a blue knit top.

Downstairs, she exited the house through the sliding door to the breezeway and walked directly to the garage. Her bicycle was parked in front of the automatic door. Victoria flipped the switch that would raise it. There was a faint whir as it lifted. When it was up Victoria walked to her bike.

"Hey there. I thought I heard the garage door opening," Dirk said as he wandered into view. "Going for a ride?"

"I'm taking my bike out. I need some exercise." She took hold of the handlebars to wheel it outside.

"Sounds like a good idea. You wouldn't have another bike I could use? I'll ride with you."

"Only Penny's, and it has a flat tire," Victoria was glad to say. But that was something he could fix. "Besides, the frame is way too small for you," she added. "Tough luck. Sorry."

"What's this?" Dirk spied something in the garage and went to investigate it. "Holy cow. A bicycle built for two. I've never ridden one of these things," he declared in a bemused voice.

"It's Mom and Dad's. I don't think they've ridden it since last summer. It might be broken." Victoria hoped so. "Takes practice to ride a tandem."

"I can ride anything. I had an old motorcycle when I was seventeen. Cheap wheels." The glitter in his dark eyes laughed at her attempt to put him down. "It ran mostly on leg power. Sometimes I had to scoot that sucker." He pushed the kickstand back and guided the two-seater bike out of the garage. All the tires were inflated and nothing seemed to be wrong with the chains. "What do you say?" Dirk glanced at her. "Are you game for a ride on this?"

There was a definite challenge in his question, but it was the eagerness in his look that Victoria responded to. He really had never ridden a bicycle built for two and he wanted to find out what it was like.

"All right," she agreed, "as long as you promise not to start singing 'Daisy, Daisy, give me your answer true.'"

"You have my word," he chuckled, "even though I was going to. How about if I hum it?"

In spite of herself Victoria found she was laughing right along with him. "I don't care," she declared and wheeled her bicycle back into the garage.

"Do you want the front seat or the rear?" Dirk asked.

"You take the front," she said and turned so he wouldn't see the impish light in her gray eyes.

At first the bike was unwieldy until they adjusted to their mutual weight and different cycling rhythm and balanced themselves accordingly. They were both laughing as they wobbled the first few feet, threatening to crash any second, but the coordination eventually came.

"No backseat driving allowed," Dirk reminded her when they were safely underway.

"I wouldn't dream of it," Victoria assured him, that gleam still in her eyes.

She had already discovered that it wasn't wise to concentrate too much on the scenery they were riding past. When she did, she tended to try to turn the fake pair of handlebars, which invariably threw them off balance. It was better to spend most of her time looking straight ahead, which meant looking at the back of Dirk's head and the breadth of his shoulders. Victoria didn't really mind that. In fact, it was interesting to watch the play of the muscles in his shoulders and back beneath the thin cotton of his shirt, and to notice the changing shades of his black hair in different light. It was blue black in the sunshine and coal black in the shadows of the trees.

They hadn't gone far when the road began to make a gradual rise. It was a gentle slope, not at all steep. Carefully Victoria lifted her feet off the pedals and rested them on the crossbar, letting Dirk do all the work to get them up the small hill. Before they reached the top he was standing in the pedals.

"It didn't look this steep, did it?" he said to her, his breathing only slightly labored.

"No, it certainly didn't," Victoria agreed, hardly able to keep the laughter out of her voice.

Dirk must have caught a hint of it, because he looked back and saw she wasn't helping him pedal up the incline. By then they had reached the top and he sat down on the seat.

"No wonder." Shaking his head, he applied the brakes and slowed the bike to a stop. "You got a free ride, huh? And let me do all the work?" He half turned to look at her, an amused scowl on his face.

"I couldn't resist." Victoria couldn't really defend herself and she was trying hard to keep the laughter from bubbling through.

"You think it's funny?" he challenged. "Maybe it is. I'll have to find out for myself." Dirk stepped away from the bike and it nearly slipped to the ground before Victoria could right it. "We're going to change places so you can chauffeur me for awhile."

"Come on. It was just a joke," she coaxed.

"I know, but it's my turn to laugh." After setting up the kickstand to support the bike, Dirk hooked an arm around her waist and lifted her up and over the crossbars of the bike. Her cries of protest were lost in the giggles she couldn't stop. In the end, she was set on the front seat and Dirk climbed onto the rear.

"I'll never make it." Victoria glanced over her

shoulder in a last plea. She had laughed so hard that she could hardly breathe.

"Try," Dirk ordered.

From the top of the hill the road sloped down. All Victoria had to do the first few hundred feet was to let the bike coast. With their combined weights they soon picked up speed. When the road leveled out it wasn't long before Victoria had to rely on pedal power. She really did try. The bike slowed to a crawl and she finally had to stop to catch her breath.

"It isn't fair," she panted. "You weigh a ton."

"What do you think you are? Thistledown?" He chuckled. "You read too many romances." But his feet moved to his set of pedals to help when they did start out again.

"Do you want to change places or shall I do the steering?" Victoria asked after she'd gotten her breath.

"No, you can drive."

"My, but you are a trusting soul," she mocked.

"I don't know that I would trust you with my soul," Dirk replied softly. "You might get careless with it. But I will trust you to steer the bike."

Victoria put a foot on the pedal in preparation for starting out while the other foot remained on the ground for balance. She glanced over her shoulder to meet the steady, dark gaze.

"Whatever happens, happens to me first, is that the theory?" she chided with an unmistakable sparkle of laughter in her gray eyes.

"You guessed it, honey." His mouth curved into a half smile.

The endearment was casual enough, but her senses responded to it with anything but indifference, excited by the caressing timbre of his voice. Her pulse fluttered in her chest, briefly interfering with her breath, as Victoria faced the front again and pushed off to start pedaling.

During the continuing ride, Victoria stayed totally aware of the man behind her. It was exhilarating, something Victoria couldn't explain and tried to rationalize away as a result of the invigorating exercise.

The rocky ground offered a grass-tufted clearing to the right of the road. When Victoria saw it she pointed to it. "Let's stop there for a breather."

"Why not?"

At his offhand agreement, Victoria guided the bike to the edge of the road. When the front wheel bumped into the uneven ground she braked and stepped off to balance the bike's unwieldy length. With Dirk's help she wheeled it off the road and leaned it against a tree.

In the center of the clearing, a breeze was cooling the sun-warmed air. Slightly warmed herself by the exertion and the morning sun, Victoria moved toward the center and lifted the hair away from her neck to let the breeze dry her skin.

"Just a minute." Dirk's voice made her pause. "You have a thread hanging."

"Where?" Victoria stopped and tried to twist around to look behind her, a virtually impossible task.

"I'll get it," he volunteered and started to crouch behind her.

Victoria couldn't see the thread, but all of a sudden she could feel it dangling from the hem of her shorts, just barely brushing the back of her thigh. The discovery of its location and his offer to deal with it made her blush.

"Uh, never mind," she said hurriedly and tried to turn away.

"You can't even see it," Dirk chided while his hand clasped her hip to prevent her from moving out of his reach. "Stand still."

Struggling would only turn a slightly embarrassing situation into a humiliating one, so Victoria obeyed his command rather than display an exaggerated modesty. It wasn't easy to stand motionless under the firm touch of his hands. They seemed to burn as Dirk twisted the thread around his forefinger, a knuckle digging into the bare skin on the back of her thigh. On the surface his action was impersonal, but underneath there was an implied intimacy. With a quick tug his hand pressed against her rounded flesh and the thread snapped. A riptide of heat coursed over her flesh.

"There you are." Dirk straightened and held out the white thread for her inspection.

Victoria couldn't meet his smiling glance. "Thank you." The words were as stiff as her posture.

When she took an escaping step forward, his hand settled on her waist while he kept pace. Dirk tipped his head to one side in an inquiring angle, his dark eyes running over her profile.

"What's the matter?" His tone was curious.

As if he didn't know. "Nothing," she insisted.

By lengthening his stride, Dirk moved a half a step ahead of her and stopped to block her way. When she tried to go around him, his hand moved to capture her chin and lift it so he could see the expression she was trying to avoid showing him.

"I do believe you're embarrassed."

Victoria couldn't lift her gaze higher than his

neck. She was fully aware of the hot color that flushed her cheeks. Her discomfort wasn't improved by his closeness.

"There's no need to be." His hand glided from the curve of her waist to her butt, lessening the distance between them to inches. The ease of his sensual caress trembled through Victoria although she tried desperately not to show he was getting to her. Big time.

"I'm already familiar with every curve and muscle back there," Dirk murmured. "I've been watching it on that bike for long enough."

The breath Victoria tried to take never got farther than her throat, lodging there at his provocative comment. Her gaze rushed up to become trapped in the enveloping sexuality of his. At the catapulting leap of her pulse, a flurry of sensations left her defenseless. When his mouth claimed her lips, Victoria was launched into a heady plane where only desire existed. She responded hungrily to his devouring kiss.

His hand moved in a long, leisurely caress from her chin, down her throat, across her shoulder, and around her back. Its persuasiveness brought her against his length, her soft curves imprinted by hard, male contours, from the muscled wall of his chest next to her breasts to the oak-solid trunks of his legs scraping the bareness of hers.

His masterful kiss was incredibly erotic and Victoria felt something wonderful taking over her. Under the languid domination of his mouth, she was dazzled by the slow-burning flames that grew ever more consuming. Her arms had encircled him. Her hands were reveling in the feel of the flexing muscles in his shoulders and back.

I want him.

But an inner voice was arguing with that. Victoria knew if she listened to it, it would spoil the delicious joy she was experiencing. So she ignored everything but the dangerous pleasure of the moment. Trembling with a blissful weakness, Victoria had to cling to him for support. Beneath her cheek, she could hear the hard thud of his heart. He broke off the kiss and she felt bereft.

His warm breath stirred the hair on her forehead and she inhaled his intoxicating, earthy smell. When his hand cupped the side of her face, Victoria didn't resist that either. Those few minutes had given her time to conceal the wild excitement his embrace had caused. Victoria had to understand the reason why Dirk had initiated it.

"Why did you kiss me?" While his hand slowly caressed her cheek and jaw and the little hollow below her ear, his thumb traced the outline of her lips, feeling the warmth and moistness that remained from his kiss.

"For a lot of reasons," Dirk replied with a husky pitch to his voice. "Number one, because you're a beautiful woman. I had to feel the softness of your body and mouth. Had to."

Victoria needed something more complicated than that. It was too close to her own very basic reaction and therefore, the elemental attraction became too dangerous a premise to accept. Besides, his exploring thumb had parted her lips in a way that was too blatantly sensuous. Withdrawing her arms from around him, Victoria reached up to pull his hand from her face.

"And the other reasons?" she prompted as the male

hand she had been holding reversed the possession to hold her hand within its grip. "I have to know, Dirk."

His mouth quirked briefly before he bent his head to press her fingertips against his lips and look at her through his thick lashes. "To prove what I already suspected. You're not cool at all. You're pure passion. You just haven't accepted that yet." There was something very seductive in his veiled but steady regard.

Her heart began beating at triple speed, instinctively knowing that Dirk could expertly teach her everything she needed to know. With a fluttering of panic, Victoria freed her hand and stepped away. Folding her arms in front of her she walked to the center of the clearing. Apprehensively, she sneaked a backward glance at Dirk to see if he was following. He had moved generally in her direction, but he had stopped on a stretch of grass-carpeted earth to lower his muscled frame to the ground. Victoria felt a twinge of regret and hated herself for it.

"There's plenty of room." Dirk indicated the wide patch of grass to his left. "Why don't you join me?"

Chapter Seven

Victoria was tempted, but the knowing glint in his eyes revealed that he was expecting her to say yes.

"No." With a quick shake of her head, she refused. The length of rough green earth reminded her too much of a blanket on the ground. Dirk continued to watch her, waiting for an explanation. She didn't want to admit that she just wasn't ready to get horizontal, so she chose a much more mundane excuse. "I don't want grass stains on my white shorts. They might not come out."

"Is that all that's stopping you?" Dirk said it as a statement despite its question form.

His reply puzzled her, but not as much as what he did next: unbutton his shirt. Her gray eyes widened as his bronze torso began to be revealed.

"What are you doing?" The faint tremor in her voice exposed her own susceptibility to the sight of so much masculine flesh, and nice, feathery, dark chest hair.

Dirk was bare-chested by now, his muscles rippling in the sunlight. He spread the shirt on the ground beside him. "You can sit on this and you won't have to worry about grass stains."

"B-but—" Victoria searched helplessly for another reason, stunned by his action, while trying to maintain her poise.

"Isn't that chivalrous enough for you?" he said. "A real gallant would spread his cape over a mud puddle. Sorry, no cape. And no mud puddle. So the shirt and grass will have to do."

"Your shirt will end up with grass stains." There had to be a way to wiggle out of this increasingly treacherous situation.

"I bought it on sale. Besides, a highborn lady like yourself shouldn't be concerned with a lowly servant's clothes." He was deliberately taunting her.

Victoria guessed that Dirk expected her to refuse his shirt and sit on the grass beside him to prove she wasn't a spoiled snob. She intended to show him that she wasn't so easily maneuvered. Her mouth curved into a smile.

"You know, you're right," she declared. "Why should I worry about your shirt?" She walked over and sat down squarely in the middle of it, wiggling to rub the cotton material into the grass and guarantee a stain.

"You little brat." Instead of being angry, Dirk chuckled with open amusement at her audacity.

"You said it," Victoria reminded him. "Better your shirt than my shorts." She leaned back on her hands, challenging him with a look.

"You don't think you are going to get away with it, do you?" Dirk turned to face her. Suddenly what distance there had been between them vanished. A wall of bronze flesh loomed beside her.

Victoria regretted the desire for retaliation that had

brought her low. Literally. An uneasiness kept her there, followed immediately by a quivering awareness of how fantastic it had felt to be in his arms.

"Oh geez, I'm sorry," she said suddenly. "It's just that—oh, you made me angry when you said those ridiculous things about me. I really don't care about sitting on your shirt."

She would have moved to pull it out from beneath her, but his hand took hold of her thigh.

"No, you don't," Dirk warned. "The damage is done. Now you are going to sit there."

"It's your fault." Victoria's voice wasn't as steady as she wanted it to sound.

"No, it's your fault," he countered and leaned toward her, "for teasing me with one kiss and walking away."

"I wasn't teasing." With the hand on her thigh she couldn't scoot away, so Victoria attempted to escape his continuing approach by leaning farther and farther backward.

"I'm relieved to hear that." His dark eyes mocked her as he followed her down.

When his mouth was inches from hers, tantalizing her with sensual promise, Victoria whispered, "I don't want this to happen."

"Liar," Dirk murmured and let his mouth do the rest of the convincing.

She tried to summon some resistance, but his mouth claimed hers with a sensual, leisurely thoroughness. His overwhelming potency made her deliciously weak. Fingers that had wound into the blades of grass released the green tufts to hesitantly seek the warm skin over the muscled expanse of his shoulders and back. He claimed her lips, explored her mouth and rekindled the hot fires that had consumed her only moments before.

The pleasureable weight of him eased to one side as he forced an arm under her to mold her to his will. Victoria shifted to more easily accommodate his arm and enjoy the searing fire of his kiss. His free hand had left her hip and was exploring her waist. Dirk moved down to her throat, nibbling at the highly sensitive skin at the hollow.

Her breaths were little more than sighing gasps of pleasure. Victoria bit her lip to try to keep her sensual responses within reason. It didn't work. This wasn't about reason. This was about passion.

When his fingers slipped under the cotton of her T-shirt, her hand slid along his hair-roughened arm in an effort to stop this new, even more intimate exploration of his hand. Her effort was puny at best, and she quivered all over with excitement at his caressing touch.

As if sensing this inner resistance, Dirk's mouth returned to her lips to claim them again. When he found her teeth in possession of her lower lip, he let his tongue trace the outline, teasing until her mouth was turning to find his. While her senses had been occupied with the tormenting nearness of his mouth, his hand had moved upward to cup her breast and tease the peak into hardness beneath the silken material of her bra. A sweet, consuming ache began . . . and became more intense. Victoria stiffened.

"Let go." His caresses were as seductive as his voice. "Let go, Tory. Just be mine."

The temptation to yield was strong, but Victoria twisted away. "No," she choked out.

"Why not?"

Fear took the place of the passion she wanted to deny. And fear did the talking. "Because all you want is me."

"Damn straight," he growled.

"Meaning you want Charles Beaumont's daughter. And wouldn't that be a story . . . am I right? But you aren't going to get it."

When he lifted his head to glare at her in surprise, Victoria took advantage of his action to roll from beneath him and onto her feet.

"Do you actually believe what you just said?" Dirk demanded, rising to stand behind her.

"Do you deny that it's true?" she retorted without looking at him.

"It would make a hell of a story, but—I can't believe you said that!" he snapped and bent to whip his shirt from the ground. "You're crazy, you know that? Or I am. Or we both are. What's the French for insanity for two?"

"*Folie à deux,*" she whispered.

Victoria watched him buttoning his shirt. She couldn't tell by his expression whether that barely contained anger had been genuine or faked. Dirk glanced up and caught her wary look. Tucking his shirt into his pants, he walked over to her.

"You don't seem to have much confidence in yourself as a woman. Why, Tory?" His dark gaze pinned her.

"Don't call me that." She avoided his question. "It's a name reserved for my family and very close friends."

"You and I just got pretty damn close. So what am I?" His gaze raked her up and down. "Not good enough, huh?" His strong white teeth were biting out the words.

"No!" Victoria angrily denied that. "I'm talking

about what you do for a living." She lowered her voice
to a more normal level. "I don't trust you. The closer
you get the more scared I feel."

His mouth quirked, grooves slashing deeply at the
corner. "That's actually smart. Could be the smartest
thing you've ever said to me, in fact."

"Thanks. I guess." Victoria resorted to sharpness,
having no other defense against him. His candor un-
dermined her wariness.

"You don't have to thank me for that," he mocked.
"But I want you to remember what you just said." His
hand reached out to hold the back of her neck and
bring her to him. His mouth bruised her lips in a hard,
searing kiss. It ended with the same abruptness, but his
face was only inches from hers, his dark gaze intensify-
ing her confusion. "Let's get back on the bike, okay?
Exercise is a better way to handle sexual frustration
than talking." Not waiting for a reply, Dirk turned and
guided her to the tree where they had left the bicycle.
"Only this time I'll take the front seat. I think I have a
better idea where we're going than you do."

Victoria opened her mouth to protest, but Dirk had
already turned away. No longer able to see his expression, she couldn't be sure his comment had been as
ambiguous as she had interpreted it.

"Are you ready?" When he glanced over his shoulder his look was bland and unreadable.

Was she imagining the double meaning? Her
thoughts were going in circles that didn't stop and
didn't make sense. Victoria shook away the mental
confusion and walked to the rear of the bike.

As she swung a leg over the crossbars, Dirk half
turned to ask, "Is something else bothering you?"

"Just you," she answered shortly without lifting her gaze from the handlebars.

"At least you're honest." He pushed the tandem forward to walk it to the road.

There was no conversation during the long ride back and she let him do most of the hardest work. This relationship, brief as it had been, was spinning faster than the wheels of this damned bike. At first she had actively disliked him. If asked whether she regarded him as an enemy her answer would have been an unequivocal yes. Now, when he had almost breached her defenses, Victoria found that she didn't resent him for it. There was a part of her that was sorry she'd put a stop to it. Her flimsy accusation made her cringe inside.

The smear of yellowish-green grass stain on the back of his shirt taunted Victoria. The thin material hid the taut flesh her hands had so eagerly caressed. She wished she hadn't said what she'd said. Dirk wasn't the enemy. She'd let her fear run away with her.

At the Beaumont house Victoria got off the bike as soon as Dirk braked it to a stop. Eager to escape his unnerving company, she was in a hurry to put the bike away, but Dirk took his time wheeling it into the garage.

"Kind of makes you crazy, doesn't it?" He tossed out the non sequitur with deceptive casualness.

"What does?" In spite of a little voice insisting that she didn't want to know the answer, Victoria asked the anticipated question.

"To . . . like someone that you were determined to dislike." Dirk hesitated deliberately. Was he trying to imply that the attraction was stronger than the word indicated?

"I really wouldn't know," she lied and hurriedly left the garage to let him maneuver the tandem into its rightful place.

Oh, great. In the breezeway she was confronted by her younger sister. Jealousy was behind the disdainful look Penny gave her, and only Victoria understood just how jealous her little sister would be if she knew everything.

"A bicycle built for two? Really, Tory, how juvenile can you get?" Penny declared contemptuously.

"Don't look at me." Victoria attempted a cool defense. "It was Dirk's idea, not mine."

Surprise mixed with chagrin in her sister's expression. Victoria took advantage of the speechless moment to slip inside the house and upstairs to her room.

Shifting the tennis racket to her other hand, Victoria pushed open the front door and walked inside. It had been unusually hot and sticky on the tennis court that afternoon. Foremost on her mind was a desire for a cold drink and cool shower. Her sneakers barely made any sound as she crossed the foyer, ignoring the stairs and making a beeline to the door to the kitchen area. Pausing, Victoria was struck by the silence of the house. It was strange. Even the kitchen was empty when she entered it. She looked curiously around, then walked to the refrigerator to take out the pitcher of lemonade. As she filled a tall glass from the cupboard, out of the corner of her eye she saw the housekeeper entering the kitchen.

"Hello, Josie."

"*Mon Dieu!*" The woman nearly dropped the bundle of neatly folded towels stacked in her arms.

"Did you think I was a ghost?" Victoria laughed and took a refreshing sip of the lemonade. "Where is everybody?"

The housekeeper was obviously suffering from shock since she lapsed into English to answer curtly, "I have more important things to do than keep track of the comings and goings of this family."

"Sorry I asked," Victoria murmured with an exaggerated lift of an eyebrow. "It's late, though. Usually everyone's home by now."

The comment made the housekeeper glance at the wall clock. By her dismayed expression Victoria guessed that Josie hadn't realized what time it was. There was a sudden haste to her footsteps as she crossed the kitchen and unceremoniously forced the folded bath towels into Victoria's arms.

"I have to begin dinner," she explained. "Take these towels to M'sieu Ramsey's room."

Victoria hesitated, but it was a reasonable request since she was on her way upstairs to shower and change. She took another swallow of the lemonade before setting the glass down to arrange the towels in their previously neat order.

"I'll come back for my tennis racket," Victoria promised and received a nodded acknowledgment.

Leaving the kitchen, she climbed the stairs to the second floor. As she neared the top, Victoria heard the light tap-tap-tapping of a laptop keyboard coming from Dirk's room. She paused at the head of the stairs. Her family might be gone, but Dirk obviously wasn't. Nibbling at her lower lip, she wavered . . . and crossed the little distance to his door, holding the towels in front of her like a shield.

When she knocked, the typing stopped. So did her

heart. The scrape of a chair leg was followed by foot-steps crossing the room to the door. She mentally braced herself and fixed a composed expression on her face as the door was opened. The preoccupied light left his dark eyes the instant Dirk saw her. His gaze took on a velvet quality, stroking her as he surveyed her length and the bareness of her legs beneath the short white tennis skirt.

"Not going to drop them and run? This is my temporary lair, you know."

"Josie asked me to bring you some clean towels." Victoria didn't want to explain the reason for her presence. She would have preferred to throw the towels at him, but that would mean getting all emotional. No repeats of that scene, she told herself silently. Dirk stepped out of the doorway so she could enter. He motioned in the direction of the bathroom.

"Hotels don't hire chambermaids who look like you," Dirk remarked. "Great uniform."

"Ha ha." As she walked briskly past him toward the door to the private bath, her gaze was drawn to the laptop on the narrow desk and its glowing screen. She was consumed with intense curiosity to find out what he was writing. Another article about her father? She couldn't read it and felt a little guilty for wanting to.

Dirk followed her as far as the door to the bathroom and leaned against the frame. "I take it you've been playing tennis."

"Yes, with some friends." Victoria arranged two sets of the towels on the brass racks and knelt to store the rest in the cupboard.

"We still haven't played that tiebreaker with your parents, have we?" he remembered. "We should set that up for tomorrow."

"I can't. I have other plans." She didn't know what those other plans were, but she would think of something. Straightening, she walked toward the doorway, arching an eyebrow in an unspoken request for Dirk to move.

With a nod, he made a ninety-degree pivot to allow her past. "I noticed that you've been awfully busy these last couple of days," Dirk said. "I guess I could ask the daughter of—what was your friend's name? Mrs. Bourns? She'd partner me in a match with your parents."

"I'm sure Shelly would like that!" Victoria snapped, then halted to glare at him. "Wait a minute. You haven't met her, have you?"

He shook his head. "No. But she's only a phone call away."

"You aren't that desperate," Victoria informed him.

"You sure?" he mocked. "I can't just fool around online, you know."

"Don't be disgusting." There was a wretched tightness in her throat.

He shot her a look she couldn't really read. "Do you know you almost sound jealous, Tory?"

"Yeah, well, I'm not," she said. "Personally, I couldn't care less who you play tennis with. Mrs. Bourns will make sure that everything you do ends up on the grapevine."

"Of course," he murmured dryly. "Gossip makes the world go round."

In agitation, Victoria turned away and took two steps. It was purely by accident that she had happened to move in the direction of the desk and the laptop. The white screen and its rows of typed lines beckoned for her attention.

"I see you haven't been spending all your time looking up things on Wikipedia," she remarked. "You obviously managed to do some writing."

Before she could read it, Dirk was there to cover the screen with the thick volume of a dictionary which he stood on its side. "No snooping."

"You act as if you have something to hide," Victoria said. Following an impulse she knew was wrong, she reached to move the book. "What are you writing?"

His fingers closed around her wrist to stop her. "I don't let anybody read any of my material until I'm finished."

"Afraid of what I'll see?" She strained to twist her wrist free of his hold without success.

"Could be." Dirk shrugged noncommittally.

"What's the subject?" Victoria was sure that it had to do with her father.

"Maybe my imagination is running rampant again," he suggested with a wink.

"I wouldn't be at all surprised," she retorted.

"What do you suppose happens when two people who always got what they wanted are unexpectedly thrown together?" he mused, exerting just enough pressure on her arm to bring her a few inches closer.

"I really wouldn't know." She heard the breathless catch in her voice, but couldn't do anything about it.

"Two people like us," Dirk continued. His free hand curved around her waist to keep her inside the circle of his arm. He seemed indifferent to her attempt to keep a small space wedged between them with her arms on his chest.

"What do you mean?"

"You were always given what you wanted, and I always fought for what I wanted."

"Get to the point," she said softly.

"Okay." He released her wrist to let both of his arms gather her in, trapping her hands between them. "The solution would be to join sides, so we could both want the same thing."

He held her fast. To be in the sensuous clasp of his arms—and alone within a bedroom that was his, at least for now—was an incredible feeling. The lower half of her body was firmly shaped to his length, her hips pressed against something resolutely male. Victoria felt weak all over again.

"Will you please let me go?" Her voice was low and it shook a little.

"No, I don't think so." Dirk smiled and lowered his head.

She turned her head away, but he was satisfied to let his mouth trail over the curve of her neck, pausing to nibble sensually at an earlobe along the way. Shivers of pure delight danced over her skin and sent tremors through her entire body. Dirk was in no hurry to find her mouth, letting his lips tease and tantalize every inch of her neck, ear, and cheek. All the while his caressing hands were roaming her back and hips, stirring raw needs and confusing her thoughts.

"Kiss me." His husky order came when Victoria's resistance was at its lowest ebb.

The sensual firmness of his mouth was only inches from her own. With masterful ease he had tuned her senses to his desire. Her lips parted even before they felt the warm contact of his. While she strained to respond to the demanding ardor of his kiss, her hands glided around his neck to thread her fingers through his thick hair.

Dizzying waves of sensation rocked her until Victoria

had to lean against him to keep her balance. The scorching fires ignited by his hard kiss swept through her. Dirk shifted her slightly in his arms, the driving force of his mouth tilting her head back onto the curve of his shoulder. His hands had slipped beneath the knit top of her tennis outfit and explored the pliant softness of her flesh. The ever-growing intimacy of his caress drove Victoria to the edge of her ability to say no. But she had to.

After all was said and done, she hardly knew him . . . didn't trust him . . . but oh, how she wanted him. "Dirk, stop," she breathed against his mouth, feeling the heat of his breath mingling with hers.

"Why?" He took a fraction of a second to answer as he let his mouth move over her lips, tracing their outline with his.

The half kiss was devastating to her train of thought. It was several seconds before Victoria could come up with a reason. "It's late. Josie is fixing dinner."

"I have the only thing I'm hungry for right here." His teeth made tiny love bites on her lower lip. Her own sensual appetite grew more intense.

Victoria tried once more. "She knows I went up to shower and change," she whispered. "I can't go back downstairs all sweaty and flushed. She's not stupid, Dirk. She'll figure it out in a second."

"We'll shower together. You wash me and I'll wash you." His hand slid from her rib cage to the center of her spine as he crushed her to his chest and covered her mouth in a searing kiss.

Chapter Eight

In the downstairs foyer the front door slammed.
Someone came rushing up the stairs, taking the steps
two at a time. Locked in a pair of arms she never
wanted to leave, Victoria was only half-aware of the
sounds intruding on the raw bliss of the moment.

"Dirk!" Penny's voice broke through the golden
haze like a glaring white light. "Are you there? I don't
hear the laptop." Her voice and half-running footsteps approached the guest room. "Have you finished
the . . ." She stopped in mid-sentence as her footsteps
halted.

Until that second Victoria had forgotten Dirk's bedroom door wasn't closed. Tearing her lips from his,
she just stared at her sister's stricken face. Penny stood
stock-still in the doorway, the pain of disbelief obvious
in her suddenly brimming eyes. As if indifferent to
the interruption, Dirk continued to nuzzle Victoria's
cheek. His arms were locked even tighter around her
to prevent her from escaping his embrace.

"Did you want something, Laurel?" Dirk asked without ever glancing at the doorway.

"How could you?" Penny accused with a choked sob. "She's so stuck up and prissy . . ." There would have been more, but she couldn't hold back the tears. With a muffled cry she turned and fled to her room.

"Penny!" Victoria called after her and struggled to get loose. "You heard her coming," she accused Dirk. "Why didn't you remember the door was open? She shouldn't see us like this—it's just not right."

Dirk continued to hold her with one strong arm while he captured her face and held it still. His knowing eyes studied her flushed face and her lips, swollen and soft from his kisses.

"I didn't mean for that to happen. What's the difference? She would have taken one look at you and guessed that we'd been fooling around."

"But she didn't have to *see*," Victoria protested.

"It's better that she did," he insisted, "I don't want her misunderstanding anything. I only want one of Charles Beaumont's daughters. The grown-up one."

"Even so."

"It just happened," Dirk conceded with a careless shrug. "Finding out this way is tough, but it's more effective than trying to explain."

"Well, I have to say something to her," Victoria declared angrily. "Let me go. I have to talk to her and try to make her understand."

"Now?" He sighed reluctantly and let his gaze linger on her mouth.

"Yes, now!" Victoria wasn't about to be sidetracked by more of his lovemaking.

His arm loosened to let her go and Victoria didn't give him a chance to change his mind as she hurried out of the room into the second floor foyer. At her sister's bedroom door she stopped. From inside the room she could hear Penny weeping uncontrollably. So much for that teenaged infatuation. Victoria tried the door, but it was locked.

Glancing over her shoulder she saw Dirk leaning against the frame of his door, watching her. There wasn't much that he could do at the moment, but Victoria did think he was being a little unkind, even callous. However, the situation was incredibly awkward for all three of them. She couldn't exactly fault him for not knowing how to deal with a lovestruck teenager.

With an abrupt turn she walked to her bedroom. She and Penny shared an adjoining bathroom. Since those doors could only be locked from inside the bathroom, it was unlikely that her younger sister had even given them a thought. She hurried to the door and the knob turned easily in her hand. Her sister's muffled sobs grew louder as Victoria crossed the fluffy carpet to the other connecting door.

When she opened it she saw Penny sprawled across the bed on her stomach, her face buried in a squashy stuffed elephant. Her blond hair tumbled over her shoulders and arms as her young body heaved with wracking sobs.

Victoria felt a wave of sympathetic anguish. Penny was at an age when feelings could be hurt so easily, and a few moments ago they had been just plain stomped on. Victoria moved toward the bed, awash in guilt because of the unwitting part she had played.

"Penny, I'm sorry," she murmured.

A blotched, tear-drenched face was lifted from the furry hide of the stuffed toy. "Go away!" Penny pushed the long strands of hair from the corner of her mouth, choking on the sobs that wouldn't stop. "I don't want you here!"

"I didn't mean to hurt you, Penny." Victoria knew the words were inadequate, but she wanted to comfort her young sister somehow. "It's the last thing I would do intentionally."

"You don't care!" Penny accused. "Neither do I, because I hate you! I hate you!" Those words hurt, even though they were issued in the heat of the moment. Unable to stop the tears, Penny hid her face again in the toy elephant.

"Penny—" Victoria tried again.

"Go away!" Penny hurled the elephant in her direction, then wrapped her arms around a stuffed giraffe, part of the menagerie of toy animals that adorned the room, and hugged it tightly, shielding her face behind its slim neck.

Her aim was poor and the elephant missed Victoria by a foot. It was a second before she realized that she hadn't heard it hit the floor behind her. She turned and Dirk was standing inside the room, holding the stuffed animal he'd caught.

"What are you doing here?" she hissed under her breath, "Penny doesn't want to see you."

"I don't doubt that," he said. "I just wanted to add my apology to yours."

"I'm staying," she insisted, continuing to speak in the low undertone as he had done.

Tossing the elephant in the corner, Dirk looked at Penny. "I'm sorry," he said, looking shamefaced. He mad a rueful face at Victoria. "This has to be between sisters and it has to be private," he stated.

She nodded but gave him a little shove that moved him in the general direction of the door, away from the girl on the bed whose sobs had drowned out their muted conversation.

Victoria walked to the bed and sat on the edge of it. Her hand reached out to stroke the back of Penny's head.

"Hey, golden girl," she murmured softly.

Penny's muffled reply was a hurt, "How could you?"

"I think I know how you feel. Talk to me, okay?" Victoria gently urged her sobbing sister to turn on her side.

Victoria watched Penny look up. Her sister's chin quivered, then her arms were reaching out and Victoria gathered her into a comforting circle. The stuffed animals were forsaken in favor of crying on a sisterly shoulder. Victoria felt better that at least she was able to comfort her. Penny had clearly had a huge crush on Dirk.

That came on fast, she thought worriedly. But then Dirk tended to get an instinctive and very strong response from the female of the species, no matter what age they were. "Want a tissue?" Victoria asked softly.

Penny nodded and Victoria pulled one out of a decorative box and handed it to her. Penny blew her nose, which meant the crying part was over. Victoria found such irony in the situation. But the embarrassment part wasn't. She didn't know whether Penny wanted their mother and father to know one thing about this—and Victoria didn't either.

She bit at her lip before she asked, "Penny?"

There was a long pause before her sister managed a husky answer. "Yes?"

Now what? "W-will you be coming down for dinner?" Two sets of footsteps began climbing the stairs. Victoria recognized the sound. Her parents. How often had she heard them climb the stairs? For sure, more than once after she'd flung herself heart-broken on her bed, wailing loudly.

"Dinner's almost ready," her dad called. His heavier tread moved away, but her mother came to the door.

An eyebrow arched quickly as Lena Beaumont sent Victoria a sharply questioning look. "What's the matter with Penny?"

"Nothing much." Nervously Victoria brushed a strand of hair away from her forehead. "She was upset, and I've been talking to her."

"Guess what," Penelope said dully. "I had a stupid crush on Dirk. I am such an idiot. But it's over."

Her mother looked askance at both of them.

"Hmm," she said lightly, knowing better than to dwell too much on emotions where a teenager was concerned. "I thought that was Victoria who had the crush."

"Mom!" the sisters said in unison.

"I'm sorry," her mother said. "But am I wrong in thinking this is something you two don't really want to talk about with me?"

"No," Victoria replied quietly.

"Okay, then. I'm going to leave you to it." Her face was thoughtful. "Sometimes I wish Penny had an older brother who could tell her how awkward it is from the guy's point of view."

"Well, she doesn't," Victoria said. "She has me. And I'm doing the best I can." She still felt guilty for not having thought of the possibility of Penny seeing her and Dirk, but she had been swept up in the heat of that moment and not thinking at all.

"True," her mother agreed, then smiled at Victoria. "You were always so much more self-reliant than Penny. And not as boy crazy."

"Just . . . shut . . . *up!*" Penelope dragged the words out. "Dirk isn't a boy. He's a man," she said dramatically. "I don't know what I was thinking, Mom, all right? It just happened. Right now I need to finish crying. If nobody minds."

"You're entitled," Victoria said. "We've all been there. It takes a while to feel better, but you will. And other than that, I don't know everything, Penny. No matter what Mom says."

She stroked Penny's arm, thinking about what it would have been like for her to have had a big brother. Might have helped to have someone in the family near her own age to rely on beside herself. It hadn't taken Victoria long to learn the art of camouflage to hide her own vulnerable feelings. Her appearance of self-reliance was mainly a pose to avoid excessive exposure to hurt. "We'll be downstairs in a little while. Or I will."

"So will we," her mother promised, eyeing Victoria closely as she went out the way she'd come in. She had heard the serious note in Victoria's otherwise offhand reply and was reassessing the older daughter she thought she knew so well.

In the kitchen the housekeeper was hurrying about, trying to make up for the time that had slipped away. Victoria volunteered her help and Josie sent her into the dining room to set the table. She was positioning the water goblets around the place settings when Penny walked into the room. Her eyes were still puffy from crying and her cheeks had a freshly washed glow, but she seemed calmer.

"Tory, I didn't mean those things I said to you. I'm sorry," Penny apologized.

"I know you didn't," Victoria assured her with a quick smile.

"I guess I'd figured out that you and Dirk were, you know." Her younger sister smiled, self-consciously without saying what *you know* actually meant. "Anyway, I did daydream about him. But it didn't mean anything."

"Well, it still had to be weird for you to see us hugging and smooching."

"Yeah. It was."

"You were hurt and wanted to hurt back. I know what it's like."

"I'm sorry. I really didn't know what I was thinking—about Dirk, I mean. Probably it was like when I swipe one of your sweaters—what's yours is mine if I want it bad enough," Penny added quickly. "But not him. That's not going to happen."

"It's a sister thing, huh?"

"Yeah. Thanks for listening. I feel better, I guess." Penny shrugged with vague embarrassment.

"I'm sorry too," Victoria offered. Penny was confused, and Victoria couldn't exactly blame her. The whole household had been upside-down since Dirk's arrival in some indefinable way, although their routines were pretty much the same.

"Want some help?" Penny volunteered.

"Uh . . . no," Victoria refused with a shake of her head. "Josie has everything in hand and I'm almost finished here."

"Okay." Penny nodded and turned to wander aimlessly out of the room.

Sighing, Victoria finished setting out the water goblets and returned to the kitchen for the condiments. She hoped her reply hadn't sounded like rejection;

she hadn't meant it to. It wasn't until Penny had left the dining room that it occurred to Victoria that her sister might have wanted an excuse to stay and talk some more. As she reentered the dining room carrying the twin sets of salt and pepper shakers, Dirk walked in. While she tried to maintain an outward show of composure, her nerves were on edge.

"How's Penny doing?" he inquired.

"Fine. She was here a minute ago." Victoria set a pair of salt and pepper shakers at one end of the table and had to walk to the opposite end with the remaining pair, which brought her close to where Dirk was standing.

"Did she talk to you?"

Feeling his narrowed look, Victoria didn't meet it. "Yes, and she took back everything she said and apologized. So we're both off the hook. But I don't think we should ever do that again."

Dirk swore under his breath, his lips compressing into a thin line.

"What are you so upset about?" Victoria asked.

"Look, so we got caught in a clinch. That's not the end of the world, is it?"

"No. And nowadays it's not like it's shocking. But it's still not something I want to have happen again."

"It didn't just happen. We wanted it to happen, Victoria."

"Mmm."

Her non-reply didn't satisfy him. "Back into your shell, huh?"

"Yes. I need it. Things are getting a little out of control."

"Victoria, please—"

She didn't want to meet the sensual fire in his dark

eyes, although she could swear his gaze made her feel warmer. Stay cool, she told herself. And don't talk too much. You'll only encourage him.

"Josie needs my help in the kitchen, if you don't mind." She glanced again at him. Dirk was just standing there. She shrugged and returned to the kitchen and relative privacy.

After dinner, Josie refused her help in washing up and shooed her out of the kitchen into the living room where the others were having coffee. A cushion on the sofa beside Penny was vacant and Victoria immediately took it. It wasn't exactly ideal since she was facing Dirk, seated in an armchair. His hard gaze probed every time it rested on her until she felt like a pincushion. Victoria didn't taste the coffee she drank, but it kept her from participating in the conversation.

"What's your opinion about the energy situation, Tory?" Dirk unexpectedly directed his question at her. "We were just discussing biofuels."

"I don't know enough about them to discuss the issue," she said.

"Just asking your opinion," he said, his eyebrow quirking.

She hesitated a fraction of a second, covering it by placing her cup on its saucer. "Well, I have heard my father say—"

Dirk never allowed her to complete the sentence.

"Come on, Victoria. You have a college education. You can think for yourself."

"You're right about that. And if you want to know what I'm thinking right now, it's that you're incredibly rude!" Victoria flared in retaliation.

"Tory," her mother murmured.

"She's right, though," Dirk insisted. "I could have been more tactful. Sorry, everybody."

Penny frowned. "Why are you two fighting?"

"We aren't fighting." Victoria controlled her temper with an effort. She set her cup and saucer on the coffee table. "Would you excuse me? I have to decide what to wear to Mrs. Bourns's party."

"It's difficult to fight when your opponent keeps running, Penny," Dirk observed.

As Victoria flashed him a silvery glare, she picked up on the look her parents exchanged. Admittedly she was running, but it was preferable to being cornered. She escaped into the foyer and ascended the stairs to her bedroom.

Within seconds Penny was knocking at her door. "What's the matter, Tory? Why did you leave?"

"I told you, I have to think about what I'm going to wear to the party tomorrow," Victoria repeated. The excuse was valid, but it was a task she could have easily accomplished the next morning.

"Why are you so angry with Dirk?" Penny persisted.

"He was rude."

"But I thought you and he were—"

"Well, you thought wrong!" Victoria interrupted sharply and Penny drew back to frown at her. "I'm sorry, I didn't mean to snap."

"He makes you nervous, doesn't he?" Penny studied her older sister. "And that's not all. Are you scared, Tory?" Penny guessed.

Victoria opened her mouth to vigorously deny it, but thought better of it at the last second. "I don't want to talk about it. Would you mind? I'd . . . like to be alone."

Her sister hesitated, then shrugged. "Sure." She backed up toward the door. "I'll be in my room if you change your mind."

"Thanks."

When Penny left Victoria sat on the edge of her bed and stared at the floor. The truth was that she wished she was downstairs with Dirk. Just the two of them. He had her so mixed up that she didn't know what she wanted anymore, unless it was the peace she had known before he had entered her life.

His remark about her college education did sting, though. She hadn't done much with it, that was for sure. And playing dress-up at silly parties wasn't exactly how she wanted to spend the rest of her life. Or even the rest of her time during their Mackinac Island stay.

Draping an embroidered shawl around her shoulders, Victoria adjusted the long fringes to hang straight against the cinnamon-colored material of her dress. Since the party was formal, she'd done her hair in a sophisticated coil that emphasized the classic perfection of her features. Satisfied with the results the mirror reflected, she crossed her bedroom to the door. As she stepped into the upstairs foyer, Dirk came out of his room. His gaze swept over her appearance, not missing a single detail.

"You'll dazzle them," he said. "The party gives you a excuse to parade your diamonds, doesn't it?"

The diamond-studded earrings happened to be the only jewelry she was wearing. They had been a gift from her parents on her twenty-first birthday. She treasured them because of their sentimental value, not for what they were worth. It was typical of Dirk to stress the latter.

In an effort to return the barbed compliment, Victoria gave him a raking look. Resplendent in black tie, Dirk wore the formal attire with casual ease. Instead of looking more civilized, he looked more dangerous.

"You look fabulous too," she remarked. "You're lucky. Rented tuxedos generally don't fit that well."

That jab made him chuckle. "Still trying to put me in my place, huh?" Dirk mocked. "Would you like to pretend I'm your chauffeur? I understand heiresses often have affairs with their drivers."

"You've seen too many movies," she retorted.

He only shrugged. "By the way, the tux happens to be my own. It comes in handy when I have to lecture at a formal dinner," he explained, a self-satisfied light glinting in his dark eyes. "Good thing I brought it along. Too bad I had to disappoint you by not renting one."

"I'm not disappointed," Victoria replied coolly. "Since we seem to be explaining things, the earrings were a birthday present from my parents."

"I didn't think they came from a boyfriend."

"Why not?" she demanded.

"At the moment I can't imagine you being that seriously involved with someone."

"There's a lot you don't know about me," Victoria murmured tightly.

"Really? Then I'll have to find out more," Dirk warned and offered her his arm. "I believe they're waiting for us downstairs. I heard the carriage drive up just before I came out."

She let her hand rest on the black material of his sleeve as they descended the stairs together. Her parents were waiting in the foyer along with Penny and a girlfriend Penny had asked to keep her company while they attended the party.

Since the horse-drawn cab was already outside, the goodbyes were hurried. Within minutes Victoria was seated beside Dirk in the carriage. A purpling twilight was spreading across the sky, the first star winking down at them.

"It's going to be a lovely night," her mother remarked.

"Yes, it is," Dirk agreed and shifted to curve a possessive arm around Victoria's shoulders. She stiffened, then forced herself to relax.

Chapter Nine

By the standards of previous parties given by Daphne Bourns, this one was small. There were about twenty couples. While it was less crowded, it didn't seem less noisy. The minute they walked in they were swept into the tide of the event.

Daphne attempted to introduce Dirk around, but her obligation as hostess soon called her away, and Victoria's father finished the task. Dirk's arm remained firmly around her waist, taking her with him to whatever group her father wanted him to meet. Other than stating he was a guest and identifying him as a journalist to those who didn't recognize the name Dirk Ramsey, her father didn't offer any more. But she had a feeling that the determined way he kept her beside him was going to spark a lot of gossip.

A uniformed caterer finally caught up with them toward the end of the introductions and offered them a glass of champagne from the silver tray he carried. Dirk refused, but Victoria took a glass. She sipped the bubbly wine as a substitute for talking, offering a smile or a nod in acknowledgment of the conversation buzzing around her. Under those conditions it didn't take long to empty the glass. A second caterer was there with a towel-wrapped bottle of champagne to fill it.

"Do you plan on getting drunk?" Dirk inquired, bending his head slightly toward her in an attitude that suggested intimate conversation to any onlookers, of which there were many.

"Wouldn't it meet with your approval if I did?" she said over the rim of the glass.

"It might make you a little more friendly," he conceded, "but, no, I wouldn't approve."

"Friendly, ha!" Victoria drank half of what was in the shallow glass, nearly choking on the tickling bubbles. "Why don't you join me instead of criticizing all the time?"

"I prefer to get drunk on the sight of you." His gaze ran over her face with caressing thoroughness.

Her heart beat hard against her ribs as she tried to mock his comment. "What a line. It really does sound like an old Hollywood movie."

"I always thought it did, too," Dirk agreed softly. "But after meeting you I've changed my mind."

"You don't expect me to believe that," she taunted.

"Why not? Writers get drunk on metaphors."

"Oh, please."

He thought for a moment before he spoke again. "You remind me of liquor with your whiskey-colored hair and the clouded ice of your eyes. A fine, very expensive whiskey from an exclusive distillery," he continued with a glinting light in his dark eyes. "The first contact with you leaves the impression of something tall and cool, but one taste and you burn all the way down, Tory."

"Is there a legal limit for metaphor intoxication? If there is, you're over it. And ripe for rehab, pal." She looked away from his compelling male features.

"I meant every word."

"Uh-huh. Sure you did." She was beginning to feel warm all over, but she forced a cool smile onto her lips.

"Anyway, you make me act like I'm under the influence," Dirk said ruefully. "Which is fine. But it's the lingering hangovers that I have trouble with."

His provocative insinuations were becoming more than she could handle. Across the room, Victoria spied a familiar face and immediately grasped at her chance to escape.

"Hey, there's someone I went to college with. Imagine that."

"Female?"

"Yes, Dirk. Excuse me." She tried to move swiftly away.

"I'll come with you. I'd like to meet her," he stated.

"I'd rather you didn't," Victoria protested.

At that moment her father came to her rescue. "Dirk, would you come over here a minute?" he called to him from an adjoining group. "There's a fella here I'd like you to meet."

When Dirk hesitated, triumph glittered in her gray eyes. "Go. Could be a story there for your column."

Her father glanced at her with a teasing smile. "Stop monopolizing the man, Tory."

As if. It was entirely the other way around. "I wouldn't dream of it," she murmured tightly and nodded to Dirk before she weaved her way through the guests to the brunette she had seen minutes ago. A sixth sense told her Dirk hadn't followed. Before regret could set in, she was being greeted by her old classmate.

"Tory! It's been ages!"

"How are you, Racine?" She hugged the slender brunette. "I didn't know you were going to be here."

"Paul and I just came up for the weekend. We're leaving Sunday." Racine Dalbert glanced across the room, her brown eyes shining in quiet speculation. "Who is that hot guy you were with?"

"Dirk Ramsey, a guest of my father's," Victoria replied.

"He looked more like your guest," her friend teased. "Gawd, he's a handsome devil!"

"Is that any way for a bride of less than a year to talk?"

"If Paul can look at a beautiful woman, I'm certainly going to give men like your friend the eye," Racine declared.

Victoria changed the subject. "I heard you bought a new house. Have you redecorated it yet?"

"I've tried," Racine admitted with an exaggerated look of woe.

"What's it like? How many rooms?"

Victoria sipped her champagne while Racine Dalbert began a lengthy description of her new home and the changes she had made. The conversation naturally led to the adjustments, mostly humorous, of married life. Dodging the occasional question Racine directed at her, Victoria kept her college friend talking. The champagne glass was emptied, but the caterer came around with a new tray and Victoria exchanged her glass for a full one.

She was about to sip from it when it was taken out of her hand and offered to the brunette. There had been no warning of Dirk's approach until she saw him beside her. Her heart thumped wildly in reaction.

"Would you take this?" He put the glass into Racine's hand. "Thank you. Excuse us, won't you?"

When the hand at her waist attempted to guide her away, Victoria resisted. "Dirk, this is my friend Racey. Racey Dalbert . . . Dirk Ramsey."

"Racey?" His eyebrow arched in questioning amusement.

"Short for Racine," the brunette explained with a throaty laugh. "My mother's last name before she was married. When I was single, I got called Racey. It was considered a description." She flirted openly and without embarrassment. "This is the first time I've regretted being out of circulation."

"Racey," he repeated and eyed Victoria. "What did they call you? Connie? For Miss Conservative?"

"How did you guess?" Racine laughed in surprise. "She isn't really, of course. I mean—"

"I know." A lazy smile played around the corners of his mouth. "It was a pleasure meeting you."

"I'll talk to you later," Victoria promised, unable to ignore the pressure of his arm guiding her away.

"What a pair the two of you must have been," Dirk murmured when they were out of the brunette's hearing. "The tortoise and the hare."

"Racine was the hare," she replied thinly.

"And you were the snapping turtle," he finished.

That was actually funny, but not particularly flattering. "Where are you taking me?" she demanded. Her question was answered before she had finished asking it. Dirk stopped in a dimly lit alcove of the room that was being used for dancing. He turned her easily into his arms and molded her close to his length.

"This is where I've been wanting you all evening." Dirk curved both of her hands around his neck and let his own slide down her arms, momentarily tangling his fingers in the loose weave of her shawl before they slid beneath to spread over her spine.

"Is it?" She felt weak, but she couldn't blame it on the champagne she had consumed. It was caused by his swaying hips and the seductive pressure of his legs brushing against her thighs as they moved to the slow tempo of the music.

"You know it is." His dark head bent to nuzzle the hair near her temple.

That was too much. Victoria fought back the rising excitement in her body. Her breath was coming much too shallowly, so she took deeper ones to steady her nervousness. The action filled her sense with the sensually male fragrance of his cologne and his own unique scent. One disturbance was being traded for another of equal potency.

She lifted her head, seeking to dispel the intimacy with conversation. "Why haven't you ever married?"

"That's a hell of a question for a clinch," he grumbled. But something made him answer it. "Hasn't happened, that's all. And I have no plans to get married for several years yet, not until after I become more established in my profession and can cut down on the traveling. Why?"

She couldn't meet his level gaze so she looked over his shoulder and shrugged indifferently. "Racine asked me and I didn't know the answer." She fingered the smooth collar of his jacket. "What happens if you fall in love before that time is up?" Victoria realized that she was intensely interested in his answers and tried not to show it.

"Did Racine arouse all this curiosity about my love life?"

"Of course," she lied.

"To answer your question, it would all depend on the woman I loved, wouldn't it?" Dirk countered.

Something in his tone made her glance at him. His gaze seemed to go deep inside her. Victoria couldn't risk that kind of penetrating scrutiny, so she looked away again.

"I imagine it would," she agreed diffidently.

"What would happen if you fell in love with a guy who didn't have money?" he challenged.

Her first reaction was a startled laugh. "What?"

"Is that so impossible?" Dirk questioned. "I suppose it's unlikely since you only hang out with people like this."

He meant the present company—which, fortunately, was out of earshot. "I wouldn't judge a man by the money he has or the lack of it," Victoria defended. "If I loved him I wouldn't care if he was rich or poor or middle-class."

"Everybody imagines their ideal mate. What's on your list?"

It was a question that made Victoria think. "He would be intelligent, have a sense of humor, and be gentle and strong." She hesitated, then added, "Most of all, he would love me."

"Anything else?" Dirk prompted. "What about his looks?"

"Do you mean—would he be tall, dark, and handsome?" That phrase really did describe him, she realized as she flashed him a look through the sweep of her lashes. She succumbed to the urge to prick his arrogant conceit. "Oh, I don't care what he looks like.

Handsome is as handsome does and all that. It doesn't mean much. Look at you."

His nostrils flared in a sharp breath of anger. "Are you trying to pick a fight?" Dirk accused, unconsciously tightening the circle of his arms to remind her who was stronger.

She blinked innocently. "Why would I do that?"

His mouth thinned into grimness as he suddenly released her to take hold of her wrist. "Let's get some air," he stated and pulled her along with him to a side door.

Too startled to protest, Victoria let herself be taken along. Once outside he released her arm and just studied her for a while. Then he shook his head and stared into the star-strewn sky. He seemed to have forgotten she was there.

"I think I'll go back inside," she murmured and started to turn away.

"Oh, no, you don't!" His hand snaked out to seize her arm and pull her back, "You aren't going anywhere."

"But—"

Dirk sighed, as if he'd held back too much for too long. With a muffled groan he crushed her to him, burying his face in her hair. "Don't you realize what you're doing to me?" he muttered. "I've been one big ache since I met you."

The passion in his voice was so raw that Victoria couldn't believe she had aroused it. She attempted to protest. "No."

"Yes!" he growled and took care of her unwillingness as best he knew how. He kissed her.

His mouth moved against her lips with harsh demand as he pressed into her, as if seeking to absorb her body into his own. Victoria was lost to the scorching rush of emotion that swept through her. The exquisite pain of his fierce embrace tingled through every nerve end. While his hands began moving over her body his mouth followed the soft curves of her face.

The urgency of his need was contagious and her hands moved around his neck. The tumult within her body was a glorious thing, dazzling and brilliant. She arched ever closer to him. Her unconditional surrender removed the pent-up anger from his caresses. They were just as demanding, but more deliberate. She felt him take a shuddering breath.

"I want you, Tory," Dirk mouthed the words against her cheek. "I need you."

"Yes." Her voice echoed the husky pitch of his, and she was rewarded with a hard, short kiss. His hand slipped between them to cup her breast. It seemed to swell at his touch, straining against the material that confined it. Her heart felt as if it would burst.

Voices and laughter from inside filtered into the night. They both seemed to realize at the same time that anyone walking out the door would see them. By silent mutual consent, a small space opened between them as Dirk removed his hand from her breast to let his fingers caress her cheek and neck. The smoldering desire in his dark eyes kept the flames inside her burning hotly.

"Isn't there any place we can have some privacy?" he asked thickly.

"I don't know where." She shook her head in a rueful negative.

"God, what I wouldn't give for a car right now!" A smile twitched at his mouth. "What did couples do in the horse and buggy days? It would be hard to make love in a carriage."

"I suppose that's what enclosed carriages were for . . . and barns and haylofts," Victoria whispered.

"Where's the nearest barn?" He brushed his mouth against her lips and pulled away as if unable to be content with just a kiss.

"I have no idea."

"Have you had enough of this party?" he demanded. When she nodded he folded her hand inside the clasp of his. "Then let's get out of here."

"We'd better tell my parents," she reminded him.

"Don't you think they'll guess what's up if we disappear?" He sighed. "Okay. We'll tell them."

When they returned inside Victoria saw her parents standing together on the edge of a group. They worked their way through the throng of guests to the side of the older couple.

"There you are." Her mother smiled and glanced at the two of them in speculation.

"We're going to take off," Victoria explained.

"We'll come with you," her father said. "Your mother and I were just looking for an excuse to go, but we didn't feel right about leaving the two of you in the lurch." Without giving anyone an opportunity to speak he held up a hand. "You wait here and I'll call a carriage."

Victoria caught the flicker of irritation in Dirk's expression, but it was the only indication he gave that he wasn't pleased by the turn of events. Her mother sent her a veiled look of apology.

"Let's find Daphne, shall we?" Lena Beaumont suggested.

By the time they had convinced their hostess that

they had truly enjoyed the party, the carriage had arrived to take them home. While her father kept up an easy flow of conversation during the ride, her mother seemed to be the only one who noticed that neither Dirk nor Victoria were contributing much. His arm was around her shoulder, absently massaging her in a sensual way. Victoria cast a sideways glance at him. How long had she known Dirk? A week? She shivered.

"Cold?" he murmured.

"A little." At least, her feet were, an age-old symptom of second thoughts.

But Dirk took her literally and nestled her more closely against his side. It didn't seem to help, not as much as Victoria thought it would. The carriage stopped in front of the main entrance to the house and Dirk helped her out. When her parents started toward the door Victoria would have followed, but Dirk held her back.

"We'll be in soon," he told them calmly.

"What?" Her father gave him a blank look before sudden understanding dawned. "Oh, of course. Good night."

"Good night," Victoria responded as Dirk was already guiding her toward the iron gates to the breezeway.

Without speaking he escorted her through them. All the while she kept remembering his statement that he had no plans for getting married for several years yet. So what was he offering her in the meantime? An affair? Of what duration? For as long as he stayed with them? Or maybe he'd stop in to see her whenever he was in the vicinity? Could she be satisfied with such a casual commitment?

Not likely.

Some of the spreading numbness inside her must have crept into her lips because they were coolly unresponsive when he turned her into his arms and covered them with his own. His mouth moved persuasively against them. Her lips softened, but not all that much, nowhere near the degree of her previous yielding to him. Dirk lifted his head, a gathering frown darkening his expression.

"What's the matter?"

"I don't know. I . . ." How could she tell him without setting herself up for heartache and hurt? "I think I'd better go inside."

"Victoria?" He caught her shoulders and stared incredulously into her face. "At the party, you wanted this."

"Yes, I know," she admitted.

"And now you don't?"

"I'm not sure."

"Hell. First you're hot, then you're cold!" Dirk released her with a sudden move. "How do you turn it on and off like water faucets? Will you tell me? I would really like to know. Because it doesn't work that way with me."

Maybe his anger was justified, but it didn't make it sting any less. "Maybe I just want to know where I stand," Victoria said.

"What does that mean?" he demanded. "Do you expect me to get down on my knees and beg for the privilege of wooing you? By the way, I don't happen to have a crystal slipper handy, princess."

"Oh, shut up!"

"What gives? And who does the giving and who

does the taking, Victoria? Maybe that's something that I should know, too."

She stared at him wordlessly, a terrible pain shattering through her body. There wasn't anything she could say, so she pivoted toward the sliding glass doors. Again Dirk caught at her arm, but Victoria wouldn't turn around, aware of the tears filling her eyes. He didn't make her face him.

"Just what the hell do you expect from me?" he declared.

Victoria had to fight to get the word out of her taut throat, but she finally succeeded. "Nothing."

He let her go and she glided across the stone floor to the living room entrance. Once inside the house, she didn't stop until she had climbed the stairs to her room. She undressed in the dark and fumbled in the closet to hang up her dress. Yanking the bobby pins from her hair, she found the physical pain a welcome counterbalance to the emotional anguish tearing her apart inside. Victoria brushed her hair until her scalp hurt before finally going in search of her nightgown. She couldn't find it, not in the dark.

The sound of footsteps mounting the stairs froze her beside the dresser. She didn't make a sound to draw Dirk's attention to her bedroom. Yet his quiet tread approached her door. The knob turned and the door was pushed open. Victoria was unaware that she was framed by the moonlight streaming in through the window. She was only conscious of the male shadow that loomed in her doorway.

"I'll scream," she threatened in a voice that was lower than a whisper.

If he had said one word to her she probably would have raced into his arms. Instead, his shadow receded and the door swung closed. Rejection rooted her to the floor as Victoria listened to him walk to his room. Silently, she walked to her door and turned the lock. Forgetting the nightgown she hadn't found, she went to her bed and crawled under the covers where she cried silently.

Chapter Ten

Victoria spent long, sleepless hours trying to decide whether she had made a mistake. She couldn't make up her mind whether her decision had been right or wrong. Either way, she was convinced she would have experienced the same anguish and doubt.

As a result, she woke up feeling more wretched than she had the night before. A glance in the mirror while she was brushing her teeth revealed that she looked worse than she felt. It took a series of cold water compresses to fade the redness in her eyes and dissolve their puffiness. Heavy makeup hid the rest of the damage from her tossing and turning.

Dressed in a pair of red jeans and a striped top, Victoria was about to leave her room when she heard a carriage stop in front of the house. She glanced out the window as the driver alighted from his seat. Briefly she wondered where her parents were going this morning as she walked out the door.

From the top of the stairs she could see everyone gathered in the foyer below, her parents, Penny, and the housekeeper. Was everyone leaving? She frowned and started down the steps. Then she saw the luggage stacked beside the door and Dirk shaking hands with her father.

"What's going on?" Her sharp question drew everyone's gaze, including Dirk's. His expression looked as grim as she felt. When she looked into his dark eyes she had the sensation of falling into a black, bottomless well. At the same time it felt as if her heart was plummeting all the way to her toes.

Penny dashed to the bottom of the stairs to meet her. "Dirk's leaving. Won't you tell him he doesn't have to go?" Her confused blue eyes sent a silent appeal for Victoria's support.

Even though the luggage by the door had given her the first clue, to actually hear someone say the thing she had guessed was overwhelming. Victoria felt stunned.

Her gaze swung back to Dirk. "I thought you were planning to stay another week."

"We all did," her mother agreed. "But he's convinced that he has to leave and we simply haven't been able to talk him out of it."

"I've really enjoyed your hospitality, Lena." Dirk smiled, but without warmth. "And thanks, Charles, for everything. But I've outstayed my welcome. Haven't I?" The last was issued as a direct challenge to Victoria.

"Have you ever heard such nonsense?" her mother declared, but her eyes were questioning Victoria, asking her the cause.

There was a knock at the door and Victoria was saved from responding. Dirk was the closest to the door. He opened it and Victoria glimpsed the carriage driver standing outside. Dirk sliced a glance at Victoria before speaking to the man.

"I'll be with you in a minute," he said and the driver

nodded before moving out of sight. Dirk didn't close
the door as he turned to face the others in the foyer.
"I'd like to speak to Victoria for a few minutes. Alone,
if you don't mind."

"Of course not," her father agreed and quietly shep-
herded the others into the living room.

When they were alone Dirk looked at her expec-
tantly and waited. "Were you going to leave without
saying goodbye?" she demanded in weak defense.

"Penny said you were awake, that you'd be down as
soon as you were dressed." Which wasn't really an
answer.

"What if I hadn't come down? The carriage had already arrived when I left my room." It hurt to think he
would have left without attempting to see her, and she
was very vulnerable this morning.

"I would have sent Penny upstairs to tell you I was
leaving," Dirk replied.

"Everyone expects you to stay another week."

"What would it accomplish?" he challenged, tipping
his head back to eye her.

It was meant as a personal question, but Victoria
chose to misinterpret it. "The reason for your visit was
to get to know my father. Isn't that what you hoped to
accomplish?"

"I know the reason that I came. You were a surprise,
though. A very pleasant one." He darted an impatient
look toward the living room and reached for her
hand to draw her behind him out the door. When it
was closed, he turned around to face her. "Is there any
reason why I should stay another week, Tory?"

She hesitated and moved closer to the wood tim-
bers that framed the front door. "We never did play
that tennis game to break the tie with my parents,"

she reminded, him nervously. "And you haven't taken a tour of the island. Fort Mackinac is really fascinating, and the view's great from those limestone cliffs that overlook the harbor and the Straits of Mackinac. And there's the governor's mansion—it's open to the public."

"Victoria." He cut across her silly chattering, his jaw hardening.

"Excuse me, sir," the carriage driver interrupted him. "Are you ready to leave?"

"Not yet," Dirk said, "Sorry to keep you waiting. Be right there." He took a deep breath. "I have some luggage inside the door." He pushed the door open. "You might as well load it in the carriage for me."

"Yes, sir." The man moved from the horse's head and walked across the stone entry to the door. Victoria watched him lug the suitcases, carrying them all in one trip. When he loaded them in the carriage Dirk's departure seemed suddenly very final.

"You really are leaving," she murmured.

"I can have him unload that luggage," Dirk replied.

"Are you going to?" Victoria held her breath.

"Do you want me to stay?" he asked instead. She couldn't answer that. It would be much too revealing. Dirk became impatient with her silence. "A simple yes or no will do."

"I don't know!" she flared in agitation.

"Look, I don't know what you want from me." His gaze felt like black steel cutting into her. "One minute you're practically inviting me into your bed and in the next you're trying to keep me at a respectful distance. I am not going to stay around here and wait for you to make up your mind, Victoria."

"I never asked you to. You don't understand," Victoria protested.

"Why don't you try to explain?" Dirk said.

She wanted to wail but she controlled her voice. "I don't know you."

"What is it that you want to know?" His hands were lifted palms upward in a beseeching gesture that reflected his exasperation. "I'm male, thirty-four years old, single, a reporter. I like children and a good joke. I used to smoke, but I don't anymore and I don't drink. I play tennis, football, chess, handball, and a couple of other sports. As far as I know I'm in good health. Maybe you want to check my teeth. Shall I send you my dental records? Sorry I can't supply you with a family tree, but I've never been too concerned about my lineage."

"I don't care about that!" She winced inwardly at his unsubtle digs.

"Then you'll have to be more specific in your request," he countered, not letting up.

"Are you ready yet, sir?" It was the driver again.

Dirk pivoted to glare at him. "Hold your horses!" Immediately he released a long sigh. "Sorry, I wasn't trying to be funny. I'll be there in a minute." He turned back to Victoria. "Well?"

"You can't give me an ultimatum like this," she protested. "I need more time."

"How much time? Another week?"

"I don't know." She shrugged impatiently.

"What then? Two weeks? A month? A year? How long is it going to take for you to decide?" he demanded.

"I can't narrow it down like that!"

"If you can't, then I guess you've answered my

question. I've taken my quota of cold showers, Victoria." The anger was gone from his voice, leaving it hard and flat. "And I'm not going to lie awake any more nights thinking about you in the bedroom across the hall. So I guess this is goodbye."

"You don't have to go." There were hot tears stinging the back of her eyes.

Just for an instant Victoria glimpsed a flicker of regret in his gaze. Then his hands were firmly taking her shoulders and drawing her toward him. Automatically her head tipped back to meet his descending mouth. His kiss was warm and fiercely gentle. Victoria couldn't believe that Dirk could kiss her like this, with so much sensual hunger, and then leave. Her arms wound around his neck as she arched on her tiptoes to deepen the kiss.

His hands slid over her shoulders to press her close to his length and the hard male shape of him that was so familiar and also so exciting. Just for a minute the erotic mood threatened to consume them both . . . then Dirk was reaching up to pull her arms from around his neck and set her away.

"All you have to do is ask me to stay," he told her.

She stared at him helplessly, a lump in her throat. With a wry smile, Dirk turned away and walked to the carriage. She stood where he had left her, not really believing he would leave. He motioned to the driver who clicked to the horse and tapped his whip on its rump. Dirk was rubbing the back of his neck in a weary gesture as the carriage moved away from the curb. Victoria waited for him to look back at her, but he never did. Some vital part was wrenched from her soul and went with him. She stayed by the door until he was out of sight.

"Dirk, don't go," she said in a voice barely above a whisper, but of course he didn't hear her. An icy shudder wracked her body and she hugged her arms around her.

The front door burst open and Penny came flying out. "Couldn't you make him stay?" she moaned.

"No." Her chin quivered and her eyes became filled with tears.

"Did you ask him?" Penny demanded.

"No," Victoria admitted and turned to walk into the house.

"Has Dirk gone?" her mother inquired when she entered the foyer. Victoria managed a faint nod of affirmation. Her heart silently echoed her mother's sigh of regret. "Your father and I were just going to have our breakfast. Why don't you join us, Tory?"

She shook her head and walked blindly to the stairs, her vision blurred by welling tears. "I'm not hungry." Victoria knew the choked tightness of her voice was a betrayal, but she couldn't hide it.

The tears slithered down her cheeks as she climbed the stairs to her room. She sat on the edge of her bed and rocked slowly back and forth, letting the tears fall unchecked.

"If you're crying because he's gone, why didn't you ask him to stay?" Penny frowned, standing in the doorway.

"I just couldn't," she managed.

"Why?" Her sister was plainly confused.

Lena Beaumont entered the room. "Tory, are you all right?" She walked to the bed and sat down beside Victoria, putting a comforting arm around her shoulder.

"Yes." The nod of assurance wavered.

"She's crying because Dirk left but she wouldn't ask him to stay," Penny explained.

"Did you want him to stay?" her mother asked.

Victoria lifted her shoulders in an uncertain shrug. "I don't know," she whispered.

"Are you in love with him?"

"I've barely known him a week," she reminded her mother with a tearful laugh.

"Love isn't measured by time, dear. A woman can be married to a man for twenty years and never know him at all. It's just something that happens or doesn't," Lena reasoned.

"How can I be sure?" Victoria shook her head in confusion.

"Love is something you have to take on faith. There are no certainties," her mother murmured. "Does Dirk love you?"

"I don't know. God, I'm getting tired of saying that. I wish there was something I did know for sure." She wiped at the river of tears swamping her cheeks. "He told me he didn't want to get married for several years yet. So . . . yes, he cared, but—" She couldn't finish it.

"Are you going to see him again?" Penny asked.

Again Victoria shrugged. "He said goodbye, so I don't suppose I will."

"But he might," her sister offered hopefully. "You said that he cared about you. If he does, then he'll see you again."

"He said he would stay if I asked him, but I didn't ask," Victoria explained.

"Why?" It was her mother who asked this time.

"Because I don't know if he wanted to stay because I'm Charles Beaumont's daughter or because he cared about me. It's something I don't think you understand, Mom," she said tightly.

"I do," Penny spoke up. "Millie van Bolten used to be my best friend. Do you know why? Because we have this house on Mackinac Island. That's the only reason she always wanted to come over. To get out of Detroit in the summer."

"Friends aren't always what you think." Victoria exchanged a sad smile with her sister.

"Who needs Millie van Bolten?" Penny shrugged.

"Who needs Dirk Ramsey?" Victoria echoed her sister's careless remark, but she knew the two didn't compare. Maybe she'd only known him a week, but it would be a long time before she got over him.

Chapter Eleven

The city street was lined with aging brick buildings and their cobweb of rusty fire escapes, and sets of concrete steps leading from the sidewalk to the individual entrances. Victoria parked her car at the curb, slipping the strap of her purse over her shoulder before reaching for the bag of groceries on the passenger seat.

When she stepped out of the car a blustery autumn wind whipped a torn sheet of old newspaper against her leg, then chased it down the street. Locking the door, she shut it and walked around the hood to the cracked cement walk with tufts of brown grass growing through the fissures. The sky was leaden and depressing, its dull gray color doing nothing to brighten the row of apartment buildings.

Carrying the grocery bag in front of her, Victoria started toward the building in the center of the block. It was easy to tell from the others since it was the only one with a handrail on the concrete steps.

"Hey there, Queenie! Whatcha doin'?" A young male voice hailed her from across the street.

A half smile was already curving her mouth when she turned. "Hi, Rick," she greeted the lanky kid jogging across the street toward her. Another boy was with him but Victoria didn't know him. She smiled at him anyway.

"Long time no see," Rick declared, stopping in front of her. His hand flicked out to touch the grocery bag. "Ya goin' to Granny's house?"

"Yes, I'm running a little late, though. Mrs. Ogden has probably given up on me." She sighed.

"Who's Mrs. Ogden?" the other boy asked.

"Ah, you know her. The old lady that lives downstairs from me," Rick informed him impatiently. "Queenie, this is my friend Fred. Fred, this is Queenie. She brings food and stuff 'cause Granny's too crippled to leave the apartment."

"Hello, Fred." Victoria acknowledged the introduction with a nod.

"Hiya," he mumbled, eyeing her uncertainly, but she was used to being regarded with suspicion in this neighborhood.

"Shouldn't you boys be in school?" She frowned as she happened to glance at her watch and noticed it was still very early in the afternoon.

"Naw, we got expelled," Rick replied in a faintly bragging tone.

"Yeah, by the big man hisself," his friend added.

"What kind of trouble did you get into now?" Victoria asked, since it wasn't the first time.

"The big man, he conducted hisself a little illegal search and seizure," Rick explained. He could speak excellent English, but when he was with his friends he talked tough.

"Yeah, and when he happen to find a knife like this

one"—the boy named Fred proudly flashed a switch-blade—"he expelled us."

"I thought you said he took yours," Victoria said to Rick.

"He took a box cutter last time." Rick eased a knife like Fred's from his pocket and snapped it open. "So we upgraded." He shrugged, then eyed his friend and laughed.

"Gotta carry protection." Fred laughed.

"What you get is trouble," Victoria replied.

"You got yourself trouble," Rick said, gesturing at her with his knife. "I don't remember you bein' so skinny. How come you work so hard when you don't have to?"

"To keep from being bored," she answered, rather than admit it was to keep her mind occupied with something other than thoughts of Dirk Ramsey. Yet the volunteer work that gave her lonely life some meaning hadn't helped her appetite or let her fall asleep any quicker at night. Which was the longest part of any day.

"Man! If I had that car"—Fred pointed to hers—"I sure wouldn't be bored."

"Ain't that the truth." Rick began cleaning under his fingernails with the pointed end of the switch-blade knife.

"I'd better get up to Mrs. Ogden's before this milk starts to sour," she said.

"Me and Fred'll go along with you. We got some punks that moved onto the block. They ain't learned their manners yet," Rick explained.

"I'd like the company," she agreed.

Brakes squealed as a shiny black sports car swerved to a stop at the curb near them. Shock drained the color from her face when she saw Dirk step quickly out of the car and come swiftly around the hood to the sidewalk.

"What are you doing here, Dirk?" she asked in disbelief. Not a word from him in three months—to have him show up on this particular street was stretching coincidence too far.

"I was in town so I called your parents to say hello." Other than a brief, assessing look at her wan face, his gaze hadn't left the two young men eyeing him so warily. "Your mother mentioned that she had expected you back an hour ago. When she gave me this address I realized why she sounded worried."

"As you can see, I'm all right." Victoria frowned, feeling a twinge of rejection in his attitude. He didn't appear interested at all in seeing her again. He'd only come to soothe her mother's needless fears.

He slipped a hand under her elbow. "Just the same, you're coming with me."

"No, I'm not." She shrugged her arm out of his grasp and took a step away.

"I don't want to argue with you, Tory," Dirk said flatly.

"The lady don't have to go with you if she don't want to," Rick inserted. "She's got business here."

"You butt out," Dirk warned.

"Hey! Maybe he don't know we know how to use these knives." Fred laughed.

"Maybe he's worried about gettin' that handsome face of his cut up," Rick joined in.

"Don't try it, guys." Every nerve was alert. Victoria saw the ruthless line of Dirk's mouth and knew he meant it.

"Is that, like, a threat or something?" Fred took a step backward in mock fear.

"Maybe we should do a little threatening of our own, huh?" Rick waved his blade around.

Victoria had known Rick for almost three years. She could tell by the mischievous look in his eyes that he was only teasing. Her concern was for the embarrassment he was causing himself with such juvenile behavior. Rick make a move with his knife toward Dirk, but it was a swing that was intended to be short of its mark.

Instead of stepping backward to dodge the sharp blade, Dirk stepped in behind it and grabbed the boy's wrist, twisting it behind his back and hooking an elbow around Rick's throat all in one motion. The knife clattered to the pavement. Rick clawed at the muscled arm.

"Hey man! You gonna break my neck!" he protested hoarsely.

"Let him go, Dirk," Victoria added her pleas to the boy's. "He didn't mean any harm."

"We was just screwin' around," Fred insisted, folding his knife closed and backing off.

When Dirk released the boy he pushed him forward to sprawl on the sidewalk. Watching both of them carefully, he reached down and picked up the knife that had fallen. He snapped it shut, but held it for another instant.

"On my street, you never flashed a knife unless you were going to use it. You'd better keep that in mind the next time, man," Dirk advised and tossed the closed knife to Rick. He sliced a glance at Victoria. "Are you ready to come with me?"

"I have to take these groceries up to Mrs. Ogden's."

She lives in that middle building," she said, a little bewildered by how fast all that had happened.

"Okay, then I'm coming with you." His hand slid under her elbow again as he took a step then paused to glance at the kids sidling away from him. "Is this your block?"

"Yeah," Rick admitted with defiance as he rubbed his arm and flexed it.

Dirk took a bill from his pocket and handed it to him. "Watch my car. I don't want to come back and find the tires slashed."

The boy grinned. "You got it!"

"All right. Now let's go." He ushered her forward to the set of steps with the handrail. He glanced at the street number painted above the row of mailboxes. "One of your father's former clients owns this building, isn't that right? I seem to remember the address when I did some background work on him."

"Yes, he does," Victoria retorted defensively. "You'll find that all the electrical wiring is new. The plumbing works as well as the furnace."

"I know." There was a lazy curve to his mouth that told her he'd already verified that several months ago. "So who's the punk? One of your secret admirers?"

"Do you mean Rick? He lives in the building. Since I've started stopping by to see Mrs. Ogden, we've become friends," she explained. "He really wasn't going to hurt you."

"He didn't look very friendly when I drove up." Dirk opened the main door to the building and held it for her.

"Did you think they were assaulting me?" The possibility just occurred to her.

"Two kids that age stopping a beautiful woman on

a sidewalk just to show her their knives isn't that common," he reminded her dryly. "Which floor is your friend on?"

"The second one," she answered. "That is what Rick was doing—showing me his knife," she elaborated. "They were expelled from school for carrying them. Nothing new for those two."

As she led the way up the steps, Victoria realized that they were both behaving as if it hadn't been three months since they'd last seen each other. Yet there was a new feeling present that she hadn't known before: the sensation of being protected.

Several weeks ago she had accepted the fact that she was in love with him, but since he'd made no effort to get in touch with her she had decided it was one-sided. Seeing him again was reinforcing the emotion and giving her a thread of hope that it wasn't unrequited. Suddenly she had an attack of nerves.

"How . . . have you been?" She darted him a guarded look and noticed there were more hard lines cut into his features and the hollows under his cheekbones seemed leaner.

His gaze touched her briefly, but he didn't answer the question. "Which apartment is hers?"

"The second one on the right." She stood to one side while he knocked on it.

"Who is it?" Mrs. Ogden's aging voice cracked in demand.

"It's me, Victoria," she answered.

The whir of a motorized wheelchair being propelled forward filtered into the narrow hallway. Then there was some fumbling with the locks before the knob turned and the door was swung inward.

"I'm sorry I'm late, but Mrs. Jackson wasn't well," Victoria explained.

But the woman waved her explanation aside with a gnarled hand. "Who is this young man?" Although her voice cracked occasionally and her fingers were crippled with arthritis, her blue eyes sparkled with a unexpected youthfulness. Her hair was snow-white and her flawless complexion had always reminded Victoria of bone china.

"This is Dirk Ramsey, a friend of mine," she said. "Dirk, this is Mrs. Ogden."

The woman added to her own introduction, "A very old lady who was afraid she was going to wait an eternity before she finally met Victoria's young man."

"It's my pleasure, Mrs. Ogden." Dirk bowed slightly as he bent to shake her hand.

"Oh, he's very handsome, Victoria." She smiled.

"Yes, he is," she agreed, wondering if she should have contradicted the impression Mrs. Ogden had formed about Dirk's relationship to her.

"Do you know that is the first time Victoria has ever admitted that I was handsome?" Dirk observed with a glinting look at her. "I'm going to have to come with Victoria to visit you more often, Mrs. Ogden."

"I would like that." The woman beamed under his smile. His charm knew no age limit, it seemed.

"I'll put the groceries away for you," Victoria murmured and turned toward the cubbyhole room that served as a kitchen in the small apartment.

"Let Dirk put them away. It's good practice for a man," Mrs. Ogden instructed.

"Oh, I . . ." Victoria started to protest, certain he would never agree to it, but Dirk had already reached out and was taking the bag of groceries out of her arms.

"I don't mind," he murmured, leaving her a little disconcerted as he carried the groceries into the kitchen.

"Come with me, Victoria." Mrs. Ogden pivoted her chair and guided it to the open space by the window where she usually stationed herself during the day. "I have something for you."

A little confused, Victoria glanced toward the kitchen, wondering whether Dirk would put the supplies where the woman could easily find them. She would have to double-check before she left. She followed the woman across the room. Mrs. Ogden was trying to unfasten the looped clasp of her wicker sewing basket, a great big thing that was crammed with projects and sewing materials.

"Let me open that for you," Victoria offered and kneeled down to help.

She had always marveled that the woman had continued to sew, a task that had to be difficult as well as painful considering the gnarled stiffness of her fingers, but Mrs. Ogden insisted that sewing had kept her hands fairly nimble, besides bringing her enjoyment during the long, lonely hours in the apartment.

"Do you see that bundle near the bottom wrapped in tissue?" The woman pointed. "Would you hand it to me?"

"Of course." The thin paper crackled as Victoria slipped it out from beneath the skeins of yarn and half-finished doilies. She placed it on the woman's lap, and waited while Mrs. Ogden began to painstakingly unwrap it.

"I started crocheting this two days after you visited me for the first time. That was nearly three years ago, remember?"

"Yes, I certainly do." Victoria nodded.

"Every girl should have a fancy tablecloth when she gets married, or so my mother claimed." Mrs. Ogden winked. "So I started making this for you, but I fully expected you to be married before I finished. Your timing is excellent, because I only completed it last week."

"You made this for me?" Victoria repeated with a questioning frown. Even as she said it, the last layer of tissue paper was carefully folded away to reveal the tiny, precise stitches of the exuberant rose design on the crocheted tablecloth.

"Yes, it's for you," Mrs. Ogden confirmed and lifted the tablecloth free of the paper to hand it to her.

Victoria held it gently, fingering the delicate threads that formed the intricate pattern. When she thought of the time, the labor, the pain it had cost the woman to crochet this for her, she was overwhelmed. Tears sprang to her eyes as she glanced at the gnarled hand on the armrest of the wheelchair. Bending, she kissed the crippled fingers, then pressed her cheek against them.

"Thank you," she whispered and felt the light, stroking caress of Mrs. Ogden's other hand on her hair. "I'll invite you to my first dinner party," Victoria promised as she lifted her head to gaze into the sparkling blue eyes.

"Gracious, no!" Mrs. Ogden laughed. "I'll knock something over with these awkward hands of mine and stain it."

"Your hands aren't awkward," Victoria insisted, spreading her smooth and supple hand over the bony fingers on the armrest. "Hands that could create something as beautiful as this could never be awkward."

"That is a lovely thing to say. Thank you, Victoria."

There was a flicker of movement out of the corner of her eye. Victoria turned her head slightly to see Dirk standing in the arched opening to the tiny kitchen. His look was gently questioning. Self-consciously, she wiped the tracks of tears from her cheeks and straightened, carefully holding the hand-made tablecloth.

"Mrs. Ogden made this for me," she explained.

He moved forward to touch the slender threads hooked closely together to make the rose motifs. His gaze skimmed her overly bright gray eyes, then slid to the woman in the chair.

"It's lovely work, Mrs. Ogden. No wonder Victoria is so proud." It wasn't a patronizing statement, issued to be polite. Dirk sounded as if he truly meant every single word he said. Victoria wanted to hug him.

"I don't have any children of my own to do these things for," the woman murmured with a trace of poignancy. "Both of my sons were killed in Vietnam. They had no children. So I don't have any grandchildren except the ones I adopt, like Victoria."

"Why don't you let me fix you some coffee?" Victoria suggested.

"No, thanks. It'll just give me the fidgets. And I'm sure you and your young man would like to be alone. I know how that is. I'm just pleased you brought him along so I could meet him." There was a glimmer of tears in the woman's eyes, but she determinedly blinked them away. "You two run along."

"I would like to have a cup of coffee with you, Mrs. Ogden," Dirk insisted.

"Liar," she teased gruffly. "You'd like to have that girl beside you all to yourself. Come see me another time."

"We can't fool you, can we?" Dirk smiled.

"No, you can't! Now, shoo! Both of you!" She waved them out of the apartment.

"Just let me check to be certain Dirk put everything where you can reach it," Victoria insisted and pressed the cloth into his hands as she hurried into the kitchen. Surprisingly, everything was exactly where it belonged. When she came back in, Dirk had rewrapped the tablecloth in the protective tissue paper and he handed it back to her. Before leaving she bent and kissed the woman on the cheek. "Thank you again."

"I'll talk to you tomorrow." Mrs. Ogden smiled.

In the hallway Dirk waited for her as she closed the door. "Does she call you?" he asked.

"Actually, I call her. I or another woman phones every day to be certain she's all right and that there isn't anything that she needs," Victoria explained. "And she's signed up for the city's visiting nurse service, so her health is seen to."

"Good idea."

"When I first started visiting her I tried to persuade her to move out. But she's lived in this building practically all of her life. It's her home. I'm just grateful that she has a front apartment so she can see out."

Dirk paused at the bottom of the stairs and looked up the dark stairwell. "My mother wouldn't move out of our old apartment building, either. She died there. Unfortunately she didn't have anyone to check on her every day and keep her company—not even me, although I came when I could," he admitted with a bitter twist of his mouth.

"You weren't living there?"

"No, I was going to college and working." He shrugged and reached in front of her to open the door. "It was a long time ago." Her hand smoothed the tissue paper that covered the tablecloth and Dirk noticed the action. "You like that, don't you?"

"Yes." Victoria expected him to mock her sentimentality, but he simply gave her a gentle look that melted her wariness. "It's actually a wedding gift."

"I know." His hand rested lightly on the back of her waist as they walked down the concrete steps to the sidewalk.

"I didn't have the heart to correct her when she thought you and I were getting married," she apologized.

"Neither did I." Dirk looked straight ahead toward his car and the boys waiting beside it. "We'll work it out later." As they neared his car he asked them, "Do either of you have a current driver's license?"

"I do," Rick said and pulled a fat wallet on a chain out of his back pocket to show him.

Dirk wrote something on a slip of paper and handed it to Rick along with a set of car keys. "Take my car to this address, and no joyriding," he warned.

"Do you mean it?" Rick eyed him suspiciously. "The car ain't hot, is it?"

"Yes, I mean it, and no, it isn't stolen. Now get going."

Rick let out a whoop and raced around to the driver's door. "Can Fred come along?"

"You just remember what I said about no joyriding, and I don't care who rides with you as long as the car is in the same condition it's in now," Dirk replied.

"Aren't you taking a chance to trust them with your car?" Victoria murmured.

"If you were safe with them, I think my car is. You and I are going for a little drive. We have some things to talk about." He held out his hand for the keys to her car and Victoria gave them to him, a tiny sparkle of excitement in the look she gave him.

Chapter Twelve

Hope was in her heart as Dirk slid behind the wheel and started the car. There seemed to be so few subjects that he would want to talk to her about, but Victoria contained her curiosity until he identified the topic. He waited until he had driven away from the curb and into city traffic.

"I lied to you," he stated.

"When? About what?" The startled questions sprang from her.

"When I said I happened to be in town and called your parents to be polite. That was a lie. I canceled in the middle of a lecture tour to fly here. And I didn't call to talk to your parents—I wanted to speak to you."

"Why?" She held her breath, crossing her fingers beneath the cover of the tissue paper.

"Because I've had all the sleepless nights I can stand. We've got to work out a compromise." Dirk kept his gaze fixed on the traffic, a muscle working in his jaw. "I don't know how long it's going to take for you to get to know me better, but I think I can understand some of your hesitation."

"I'm glad because—"

"No, hear me out," he interrupted. "When we're married—I mean if you say yes—sorry, am I rushing this?"

"Yes."

"Okay. I'll try not to rush. And I will take questions afterward."

"You'd better," she said, aflutter with nervousness and expectation.

"I asked your father to recommend a lawyer to write a prenuptial agreement. If you kick me to the curb I don't get anything."

"What?"

"If anything else happens—if we marry and things don't work out, I mean—I still don't get anything. You're never going to believe I love you otherwise. And I'm paying for the prenup, by the way. Isn't it romantic?"

After a while, he answered his own question, because she obviously wasn't going to. Victoria was speechless with surprise.

"Well, it is, Victoria. In a practical way. There was no getting around the difference between us and we'd gotten stuck there. Totally stuck. You have to admit it."

She only nodded, a little numbly.

"I've always been able to take care of myself. And I know you don't want to be dependent on your parents. So we'll get by."

"We'll do better than that, I think," she murmured.

"Well, yeah. I was talking worst-case scenario. But I'll parlay my national column into a best-selling book. Or sell out and write a celebrity bio or something. Or the story of a great dog." He grinned at her. "It's been done."

"But—"

"Marriage isn't like floating around on a big pink cloud forever after, Victoria. Takes work. Takes commitment."

"Then I want nothing to do with it," she said. That got his attention. He sat bolt upright.

"Okay, I know you know I'm kidding." He relaxed after he looked at her. "Think we can make it on our own?"

Victoria thought it over, *really* thought it over. In fact, she made him wait a while. But her answer was brief. "Sure, if we're together."

"You're an optimist."

"Dirk, you're a lunatic. I mean that in the nicest possible way."

"What's the difference?" he said at last.

"Not a lot sometimes," she admitted. "You have to be a little crazy to believe in love."

"And you have to be an optimist to make it last."

"Yeah," she said slowly. "I think you're probably right about that. Not that I have any actual experience, but that would be my guess too."

"Okay," Dirk said with relief. "We are on the same page about that. Anyway, I did what I did because I didn't want you to ever think that I have any interest in your money."

An incredulous joy trembled through her. Not only did he want to marry her, he was putting his money—or lack of money—where his mouth was. It was more than she had hoped for, more than she had dared to dream.

"Unless you want the fanfare of a big wedding, I

would just as soon get married in a chapel. I'm not asking you to elope, though. I have a feeling you want a real wedding. You're a traditional kind of girl. My kind of girl." He nodded with satisfaction. "And I want you to be the one and only Mrs. Dirk Ramsey ever. How does that sound to you?"

"Dirk, would you stop the car?" Her voice wavered on a breathless note of sheer happiness.

"Not yet." He continued to talk. "I'll have to cut down on my traveling, but I've found a house in the country convenient to Washington, D.C. It needs some fixing up, but I think we can do it. There won't be any housekeeper, not for a while anyway. You can continue to call Mrs. Ogden and visit her. Maybe she'd like to come out to the country if we can get van service." He drummed his fingers on the steering wheel. "Fresh air. Flowers. Yeah, it'd do the old lady good. Have I left anything out?" he murmured, as if to himself.

"I hope I'm going to have a baby," Victoria said.

"What?" His head jerked around to stare at her. "You and I never got that far."

"Watch where you're going," she warned.

Dirk had to slam on the brakes and swerve into the next lane to avoid the car turning in front of them. A horn blared and brakes squealed behind them.

"What possessed you to say such a thing?" he demanded, taking a deep breath.

"You seemed to have everything else planned, but you didn't mention anything about children. I'd like to have one or two." A tiny smile tugged at the corners of her mouth. "Have you picked out my ring? I hope it's something simple. I'm not much for flashy jewelry."

"Wait a minute. What are you saying?" Suddenly he was the one who was uncertain.

"I think we were talking about getting married, weren't we?" she teased. "There's a parking spot over there." She pointed to a meter by the curb two car lengths ahead of them.

Dirk quickly maneuvered the car into the parking place and switched off the motor. As he turned in the seat to face her, Victoria had the impression he was leaning toward her even though he hadn't moved.

"You want to marry me . . . with no arguments?"

"That's right," she agreed. Before she finished the movement that took her toward him, Dirk was reaching out to gather her into his arms.

The hunger that had been bottled up from long months apart was appeased in a long, aching kiss. It was followed by at least twenty smaller ones. Victoria felt the violent shudder that ran through his body, and understood its cause.

"I thought I'd lost you," she whispered. "Everything happened so fast. I was so scared, so unsure. I thought love was something that had to grow, not just suddenly explode on the horizon one day."

"Nobody ever tied me up in knots the way you did," Dirk insisted. "I never gave you a chance to think. So, yeah, I had a few things to learn. Like patience. I had to leave you to find out I couldn't live without you. I don't want to live without you."

"You said marriage wasn't part of your plans," Victoria reminded him.

"I said that it hadn't been part of my plans, but my plans were revised on the day I saw you. You weren't what I assumed at first—just another gorgeous rich girl, pampered, spoiled—okay, you were gorgeous. Are gorgeous."

He kissed her again for even longer.

"Mmm. But you were a really good person, through and through. If I needed any proof of that, you gave it to me today. Crying over a tablecloth some old woman made."

"It's the love, the caring that she crocheted in every stitch," Victoria attempted to explain.

"You don't have to tell me." He laughed softly and kissed her yet again.

"Dirk, have you checked to find out how long it will take to get a license and a minister?"

"Not yet, but you'd better believe it's the first thing I'm going to do," he promised. "I'm not going to give you a chance to change your mind."

"I'm not going to. When that carriage disappeared I finally realized that I loved you," she admitted.

"Why didn't you write? Or call? Or e me?" he groaned and stroked her hair.

"I didn't think you loved me."

His mouth found hers to do whatever convincing still needed to be done.

DIFFICULT
DECISION

Chapter One

The door to the inner office swung open and another job applicant walked out. The look on the man's face said he didn't know how the interview had turned out, but there was relief in his resigned expression. Deborah Holland felt all her muscles tensing as the administrative assistant gave the man a cool smile of dismissal and glanced at the next name on her list. There were three applicants sitting in the outer office, including Deborah. The names hadn't been called in the order of their arrival so she had no idea who would be interviewed next.

The intercom buzzed, a signal that the next applicant was to be sent in. The assistant looked up, smiling that distant smile of hers. "Ms. Drummond, you may go in now."

Deborah watched the woman on the sofa next to her rise to walk across the room to the solid oak door. She studied her competition, looking under her lashes at the efficient-looking woman in her mid-forties. At least this wasn't the kind of company that tried to get away with age discrimination. But it was impossible to figure who had what advantage. Concealing a sigh, Deborah reached in the outer pocket of her purse for a plastic box of tiny mints. The man in the chair next to the sofa sat up when he heard the lid of the box pop open under her fingernail, but he settled back down, adjusting his glasses.

She put a mint in her mouth. "An evil habit," she said around it.

"Yeah?" He shrugged and smiled. "Evil isn't what it used to be. Smoking's a lot worse."

"True." She sucked discreetly on the little mint, her only outward sign of stress. But they were all feeling it.

"Enjoy it. Even a mint can be a great tranquilizer for the nerves when you're waiting. My name's Bob Campbell, by the way."

She nodded, reassured by his friendliness, considering he was also her competition. In his late thirties, by her guess, she had a feeling he was probably highly qualified for the position. His quiet manner and strong features gave the impression that he was both dependable and experienced.

Your basic nice guy. They were getting harder and harder to find these days. Oh, well. No matter who got the job, there would be no occasion for them to meet again. Deborah had never really liked idle flirtation, even though she was only twenty-six. Whatever. There was no reason to begin now. Especially here.

"Nice to meet you," she said politely, but didn't introduce herself. Nice guy or not, she intended to do everything she could to beat him out of this job. It seemed hypocritical to respond to his friendly overtures, even if his only intention was to pass the time.

The assistant behind the desk began typing. The next couple of minutes were dominated by the noise of her keyboard and the occasional click of her mouse. Deborah leaned forward to pick up a magazine, although she really didn't want to read. There was a natural, fluid grace to her movement.

"This will be my third interview," Bob Campbell volunteered the information. "How about you?"

"Yes." Her hand automatically inched the hem of her royal blue skirt down to cover her knees. "I've been called back a few times."

"They've screened a lot of applicants for this job. I guess we should consider ourselves honored we're still in the running, now that the field has been narrowed down to five."

"Guess so." *Still in the running* wasn't going to pay the rent. Deborah flicked through the magazine. As far as she was concerned, her attitude was realistic. If others, including Bob Campbell, felt honored by getting this far—well, they were entitled to their opinion. It meant nothing to her. Being one of five was not a consolation unless she was the one who aced the final interview and landed the job.

"Anyway, I wish you luck," he said and eyed her through the thick lenses of his glasses. The opening of the connecting door distracted him, for which Deborah was grateful. The woman who had entered the private office only minutes before exited the room without so much as a glance at the other occupants. She shook her head and looked sad, as if she'd blown it somehow.

"That was quick," Bob Campbell murmured sotto voce to Deborah. "It looks like the field is down to four."

Deborah cast a speculative glance at the departing

applicant and silently agreed with his conclusion. The buzz of the intercom was getting on her nerves.

"You may go in, Ms Holland." The assistant didn't even look at her, just went on typing.

Deborah's heart skipped a couple of beats in a row, but her inner vulnerability was well armored with her iron poise. Straightening from the sofa with apparent calm, Deborah ignored the nervous sensation in her stomach. Job interviews were always confidence-destroying experiences, but she didn't have to let it show.

Bob Campbell gave her an encouraging smile. "Good luck," he said. Hearing that from her competition made her more nervous but Deborah thought it was a nice thing for him to do.

Entering the private office, Deborah closed the door quietly behind her. Her footsteps made no sound on the plush, thick carpeting in an autumn shade. Nice. Everything she saw was nice—and expensive. She walked to the oak desk. The man seated behind it was studying her résumé. He didn't look up when she approached, but she didn't doubt for a minute that he was aware of her presence.

Silently she waited for him to acknowledge her, taking the opportunity to study the man who might be her next employer. When she had been called back after the first interview, Deborah had attempted to find out more about him online and elsewhere. She had garnered little information beyond his name and vital statistics: Z. Wilding, thirty-eight, married, no children. Since he'd assumed control of LaCosta Enterprises twelve years ago, the firm had grown into a successful conglomerate, which said something for the aggressiveness and ability of the man who ran it. But Deborah hadn't been able to learn much beyond that. He stayed well in the background, an invisible power behind a corporate facade.

Yet the broad-shouldered man before her would never be regarded as a nonentity. Deborah found herself wondering how he had managed to remain behind the scenes. What she saw of his craggy features and the suggestion of height in his muscular build indicated an ultra-male kind of guy. The luster of his jet-black hair was only emphasized by its unruly tendencies. Its darkness and the sun-bronzed look of him in general added to his attractiveness. His looks alone would command attention; his influential position would demand it. So why had she been able to find out so little about him on Google and in the business magazines?

This was the age of the corporate rock star. Some CEOs were just about that well-known and singled out by paparazzi too. Not Z. Wilding. Z as in . . . zero information. And zero gossip. It was strange when she thought about it.

With the ease of someone who was accustomed to people waiting for his attention, he lifted his head to look at her. Deborah found herself gazing into a pair of shattering blue eyes and a face that seemed almost literally chiseled. The features were relentlessly hard, almost ruthless. His dark, ice-blue eyes were emotionless in their inspection of her. From her memory bank, Deborah recalled a college lecture on the theory that blue-eyed people tended to be more calculating and less influenced by emotion, capable of putting aside personal feelings in favor of abstract reasoning. Supposedly a predominant number of male and female astronauts, pilots, and race car drivers were blue-eyed, and blessed with a so-called inherent ability for detached analysis. Although how anyone could describe a race car driver as a rational being was beyond her.

Detached, emotionless, calculating—chilly words but they did describe the man who was now assessing her. His indifferent blue gaze noted her hair, which was smoothed back in a businesslike bun at the nape of her neck, swept disinterestedly over the curves beneath the classic simplicity of her suit, and returned to peruse the résumé in his hand.

Not once was there a flicker of male admiration for her. Hmm. Deborah hadn't reached the age of twenty-six without being made aware about a hundred times a day that men thought she was cute. His lack of interest stung her ego a bit. Of course, she would have been offended if he'd commented on her looks. It was irritating to discover that his reaction would have bothered her either way.

"Have a seat, Ms. Holland." His low-pitched voice vibrated to her, leaving Deborah with the impression that she had been hovering over his desk like some tongue-tied teenager. Which wasn't true at all. She'd shown calm and patience.

"Thank you, Mr. Wilding." She let her voice register a courteously polite tone and sat in the straight-back chair positioned to one side of his desk.

Again there was a long pause while he reviewed her application and the remarks noted by her previous interviewers. Deborah wondered if he was deliberately making her wait to make her nervous. She was nervous, but she was pretty sure it didn't show.

"You have a B.A in business administration." The sharp blue eyes glanced at her for confirmation.

"That's right."

"But your last position was with a travel agency." Before she could acknowledge that, he leaned back in his chair with a ripple of unseen muscle. Deborah prided herself on judging men the way men judged women. Underneath all that corporate correctness, this guy was really built.

"Let me fill in the rest," he was saying. "You had a wide range of duties and responsibilities with that company, worked on their website and with customer service apps. You obtained a good deal of experience in many fields."

Okay, he'd actually read it. So far, so good.

"Yes. And I traveled extensively in the past six years, taking tours to Europe, the Orient, the Caribbean and South America. Later, I was also responsible for booking tours and arranging accommodations. Through that I became involved in the accounting side and ultimately became more involved in the management side. And then I got to work with the online services, which was and is the fastest growing sector of the company." Deborah briefly mentioned the various assignments, knowing the details of each position were spelled out in her résumé.

He didn't look impressed, or even particularly interested in learning more about her previous position. "Were you informed of your results on the database management tests that were conducted the day of your first interview?"

"No, I wasn't told my scores." They hadn't concerned her since Deborah was aware she was proficient with most office software and programming.

"They were the highest of everyone tested." He imparted the information without making it into a compliment.

"That's great," she murmured. She hoped she accepted the news without too much smugness. The tests had been unfamiliar and they didn't come from a textbook. She'd been required to think a lot of things through and even debug some common programs. It had all been designed to simulate working conditions and not a classroom.

There was a deceptively lazy lowering of his lashes as his eyes narrowed on her. "Your application states that you voluntarily resigned from the travel agency. Why?"

She took a deep breath before she answered. "It wasn't a mom-and-pop place, but it is a family-owned company. All the executive positions were held by family members so there was no room for advancement. I stated my reason in the application."

"The truth please, Ms. Holland." His voice was dangerously soft.

"That is the truth, Mr. Wilding." Deborah felt herself bristling at his implication that she was lying, and firmly willed herself to remain calm.

A dark brow arched with skepticism that annoyed her. The expensive fabric of his suit was tested as he reached for another folder on his desk. He set it in front of her. Its tab bore her name.

"We did more than check your references, Ms. Holland. We ran a thorough investigation of you. *If* you are offered the position as my personal assistant, you will have privileged access to a lot of confidential material. I have to know that you are someone who is reliable and trustworthy." He studied her coldly.

Deborah sat up ramrod straight and returned his stare. Don't be a wuss, she reminded herself. Wusses don't win.

"You were engaged to Adam Carter, son and heir

apparent of the family and the company. That engagement was broken. My guess is that your reasons for leaving were personal and had nothing to do with the lack of advancement potential."

"That's not correct." Her hazel eyes smoldered with resentment but she managed to keep the anger out of her voice. "My engagement was broken a year and a half ago, after I realized that marrying Adam would be a mistake . . . for both of us. It was a personal decision that didn't affect our business relationship."

"I see."

She forged on. "In the past few months I realized I had gone as far as I could go with the company. Higher positions would always be filled by family." Her teeth were on edge as she met his calm look. "If my reasons had been personal, Mr. Wilding, I would have stated that. I certainly wouldn't be ashamed of it or attempt to hide it."

The majority of her explanation was true. She omitted the fact that the most serious blow in her broken engagement had been to her pride, rather than her heart. Her relationship with Adam had grown out of companionship, business involvement, friendship—a solid foundation, in Deborah's opinion, and not particularly passionate. She had looked the other way when Adam flirted with other women, accepting it as part of his nature. Okay, she'd accepted it until the day she returned early from a meeting and entered her private office to find Adam scrambling off the couch while a red-faced, bleached-blond tour guide hastily tried to button her blouse.

At the time Deborah had swallowed her sense of outrage and calmly handed Adam the diamond engagement ring, suggesting that neither of them was ready to get married. She had even smiled politely at the blonde and told her to stop at the restroom to repair her smudged makeup. The whole company hadn't needed to know what'd happened.

The episode was chalked up to experience. Like every other young woman who threw away her dog-eared copies of *Modern Bride*, Deborah had healed and her heart had been toughened against future romantic flights of fantasy. That's how she could sit across the desk from someone as sexually attractive as the dark-haired man who faced her and not let her imagination run wild.

"Tell me something about your goals, Ms. Holland." The sideways tilt of his head and the narrowed eyes implied challenge.

"To make the fullest use of my education," Deborah responded without hesitation, sure of herself and her answer. "More specifically, to become a corporate executive."

Her answer seemed to amuse him. "How is a position as my personal assistant going to help you achieve that?"

Deborah suddenly had a picture of herself making coffee all day and fielding constant demands. Yikes. But if she had to, she would. "As the position was explained, I see it providing me with a broad base of knowledge and experience. Your corporate structure will teach me a lot about organization and the inner workings of a giant firm. Time To Travel was not on the level of LaCosta. And I'm ambitious."

Which was a quality she saw no reason to be ashamed of.

"Are you? Ambition can be the counterbalance for an unhappy personal life," he remarked and rubbed a hand across his mouth while he considered her coldly.

"That's an interesting theory. My mother always regarded ambition as a means of developing one's potential," Deborah replied, rather than defend the state of her personal life.

His gaze slid from her to the résumé. "Twenty-six. You seem really mature for that age. But I guess you didn't know you don't have to put your age on a resume."

It was his attitude rather than his questions that Deborah found so strange. Her previous interviews had been grilling, but here she was being subjected to the third degree. He hadn't asked a specific question yet about her qualifications for this job. He was discussing her as a person and Deborah was finding it an uncomfortable experience.

"I've been earning money since I was eleven. Little jobs around the neighborhood—the usual suburban stuff. I've been on my own since I was seventeen," she said in explanation.

His gaze briefly flicked to the unopened folder lying on the desk in front of her, the folder carrying the report of his firm's investigation of her. "What about your parents? Are they living?"

Deborah resisted the impulse to ask him why he was bothering with these questions when he knew they really weren't relevant. "My father died when I was eleven. My mother recently got her GED and enrolled in night courses. At the moment she works as a hotel maid."

Her voice sounded calm, but she was raging inside. She had struggled to get where she was and she wasn't about to feel ashamed of her background. The clothes she wore were good, and she'd paid cash for them. No credit cards, no hand-me-downs from relatives who were better off. Money from her savings had provided her mother with a long-postponed opportunity for an education that had previously been denied her. Deborah was proud of all that she had accomplished. The great and powerful Z, whatever the initial stood for and whoever he was, couldn't make her feel small.

A light glinted in his blue eyes as if he was secretly amused by her obvious pride, but otherwise, no emotion registered on the hard features. What a poker face. His lack of expression was unnerving. It heightened the sensation of danger that played along her nerve ends.

"Any brothers or sisters?"

"Two brothers, both in the air force. My sister was married a month ago. All of them are younger than I am."

"Oh. That wedding—" The word seemed to have triggered a train of thought he didn't share with her. "Did it have something to do with your quitting your last job?"

"I explained my reason for resigning," Deborah reminded him stiffly. "But my sister's wedding did contribute to the timing."

This was not going well. He wasn't what she expected at all. She swore inwardly, because she needed this job. Truthfully, Deborah had felt with her experience and skills she wouldn't have much difficulty in finding a new and challenging job. Instead, she had found herself losing out because she was overqualified, or else her prospective employers appeared more interested in her looks than her ability. She certainly couldn't accuse Mr. Z. Wilding of that.

"And you haven't found another position yet?"

"I'm not so desperate for work that I have to take the first job that's offered me." But her savings account was quickly becoming depleted. Soon she wouldn't be able to be that choosy.

"A personal assistant has to be completely available for a certain number of hours every day—it's not a job where you can wander around and shop at lunch time. And you will have to work late. Are you up for that?"

Okay, she got it. He was looking for what Adam had been looking for. Deborah's hazel eyes widened in indignant anger.

"Within reason." The question was typical of those put to her by men whose interests were more sexual than professional. "I think I've covered my qualifications for the position." Her sharp voice attempted to put him in his place, but that was a lost cause.

He was a dinosaur. *Executivus rex.* She guessed that he ate poor little helpless assistants for breakfast.

"I actually wasn't asking about your love life, Ms. Holland." His low voice carried the ring of steel, without altering its unemotional pitch. "If that was what you were implying. The question is a legitimate one from my viewpoint. The position really is demanding. There are no set hours. You could work from dawn to midnight some days. I have a grueling schedule that involves a lot of travel. On occasions, you will be required to accompany me with almost no advance notice. So it's important that any other, ah, obligations don't conflict with the demands of the job."

"And your demands come first," she murmured sweetly, seeing his point but resenting his selfish attitude.

"Yes, they do," he agreed with a smile. "Which is the reason I'm prepared to pay a competitive salary, and it's high. And it's also why I'm being so selective. I can't buy a person's loyalty but I can buy his or her time. If it's knowledge and experience you are seeking, Ms. Holland, I can give you both."

Something shivered down her spine. Despite the coldness of the sensation, it heated her flesh. For a fleeting instant, Deborah thought he was referring to sexual knowledge and experience, but there was nothing in his expression or tone to give her that impression. She banished the thought quickly.

"I understand, Mr. Wilding," she said calmly.

"Good. Someone from my office will be in touch with you soon to inform you of my decision." Abruptly he dismissed her, setting her résumé aside and reaching for the next one.

Deborah sat in stunned silence. Then her natural aggressiveness asserted itself. "How soon, Mr. Wilding? I do have another two offers on the table," she lied, "and I don't want to postpone my decision about which to accept because I'm waiting to consider yours."

Put that in your pipe and smoke it, she thought. Not for anything would she sound overeager for the job, even if it meant losing it.

He looked up from the résumé with narrowed eyes. "I have no idea but I'm not going to rush it. I have to take the chance that you might not be available, don't I?"

Deborah took a deep breath and held it, checking

her surge of anger. "Perhaps you could tell me at least how I stack up against my competition?"

At the verb "stack," his gaze seemed to run instinctively over her figure. Despite the vague suggestiveness of it, his attitude was totally impersonal.

"You're outstanding, based on your skills, education, and experience alone. However—" He paused and the qualifying word stole the satisfaction his initial statement gave her.

Then he sat back in his chair, eyeing her with cold disapproval. "Do you always talk back to potential employers?"

"You asked me questions and I answered as honestly as I could. I don't consider it talking back. I prefer to call it speaking out." Her fingers gripped the clasp of her purse, but she kept her response even, betraying none of her inner agitation. "If you want someone who does whatever you say, just because they're scared of you, please withdraw my application from your consideration. I think before I do anything else, regardless of how much money I'm paid. If you want a robot, then you don't want me."

His gaze fixed on her eyes. "Interesting. Well, thanks for coming in, Ms. Holland. As I said, someone from my office will be in touch with you soon." This time the dismissal was final.

Gathering what remained of her poise, Deborah walked across the length of the room, past the empty desk that divided the room, to the door. Her chance of landing this job hovered between slim and none as far as she was concerned. With a sour-grapes attitude, she tried to convince herself it was just as well. Z. Wilding was probably a tyrant. Deborah briefly wondered what the Z. stood for besides zero. Zenophobic, probably.

In the outer office, Bob Campbell glanced up when she walked in. He scanned her expression through the thick lenses of his glasses. For the first time, Deborah didn't see him as competition. His faint smile warmed her after the arctic atmosphere of her interview.

"How did it go?"

She lifted her shoulders in a shrug and continued to the door as the intercom buzzed. "Okay, I guess." This time, her mouth curved in a wry smile. "Good luck." He would need it. Anyone coming in contact with Z. Wilding would need it.

Stepping into the wide corridor of the office building, Deborah paused to glance at the door. It was marked "Private" with no other identification of its occupant. The building itself didn't carry a name, either outside or on its entrance doors, only a street number. The holding company of LaCosta Enterprises kept a very low profile, as did its owner, Z. Wilding. It would have been a fascinating experience to be a part of it, to learn what really went on behind the scenes. She hadn't been excluded from consideration yet.

A wishful sigh slipped out as Deborah turned to walk down the long corridor. Outside the building she stopped to put on her sunglasses to shade the glare of the bright Connecticut sun. Her sporty Honda was parked in the lot. The sleek, black and silver model had been a present to herself two months after she had broken her engagement to Adam Carter. She had to find a job soon or the finance company would repossess it. There was enough in her savings to make this month's payment, but next month . . .

The interior of the car was hot and stuffy from sitting in the sun. The upholstery burned the back of her legs as she slid behind the wheel and pressed the window button. A gentle sea breeze breathed fresh air into the stagnant interior.

Closing the door, Deborah fastened her seatbelt and started the motor. As she backed out of the parking lot and drove forward onto the city streets of Hartford, she paid no attention to the cars buzzing around her. The Honda zipped through the traffic while its competent driver pulled the bobby pins from her long auburn hair and shook it free so the wind rushing through the open windows could blow her blues away.

At the apartment complex, Deborah parked her car in the spot reserved for her. She didn't linger in the spring warmth of the afternoon, but hurried up the outside stairs to the second-story entrance of her studio place.

The combination living room, dining room and kitchen were decorated in soothing light blues with an accenting array of potted plants. New carpet covered the floor in the living area, giving way to white tile streaked with gray and blue in the kitchen. Chrome and glass end tables flanked the sofa upholstered in a harmonizing shade. Two chairs complemented the sofa in solid shades of light and dark blue. Semiabstract paintings of sea and sky in chrome frames adorned the white walls. It was a cool and breezy atmosphere, reflecting her taste and spirit.

Deborah slipped out of her high heels and wiggled her nylon-stockinged toes in the plush carpet. The door to the bedroom invited a change of clothes, but she walked to the refrigerator instead. A gallon jar of iced tea sat on the lower shelf. She set it, and a tray of ice cubes from the freezer section, on the blue

Formica top of the kitchen counter. She paused to take the receiver of the wall phone from its hook and punched in the number of the employment agency to report the results of her interview.

While it rang, she hunched her shoulder to hold the receiver to her ear, leaving her hands free to open the white-painted cupboard door and remove a glass.

"Mrs. Freeman, please," Deborah requested when the receptionist answered. Two ice cubes clattered into the glass as she was connected with the woman. Deborah juggled the telephone for a moment. "I wanted to let you know that I had my interview."

"How did it go?" The female voice sounded as if she expected the answer to be positive.

"Not too well. Z. Wilding is a piece of work." She overrode her rancor with nonchalance. "I hope you have some other job interviews lined up for me." Balancing the phone on her shoulder again, Deborah filled the glass with the cold tea from the gallon jug.

"Not at the moment." The private employment agent sounded briefly troubled before she forced a brightness into her tone. "But I'm sure we'll find something for you. I'll just have to check my files."

"Of course," Deborah responded dryly. She exchanged a few more courteous phrases with the woman before the conversation ended. As she turned away from the counter, she replaced the receiver on its wall hook and took a sip of her cold drink. The telephone instantly rang. Deborah answered it with a cool, "Hello."

"I didn't know whether you would be home yet or not." Her mother's voice came over light, bright, and cheery. "I was going to wait until this evening and call before I left for class to find out how your interview went."

"A disaster, if you really want to know." Deborah sighed.

"Oh." The one word reflected the disappointment her mom must be feeling. That made two of them. "What happened, Deb?"

"I have the feeling that if I was your son instead of your daughter, I'd be hired now. There's nothing wrong with my qualifications or my experience, except that Mr. Wilding"—she spoke his name with mocking emphasis—"is actually looking for a robot."

"What was he like?" Her mother quietly changed the subject.

"Arrogant. About as emotional as a stone." Deborah took another swallow of her cold drink.

"He isn't the only pebble on the beach."

Deborah groaned at her mother's attempted joke. "Please." She shook her head wryly. "At the moment his job is the only one in sight. The economy's tanking, in case you haven't heard."

"I don't watch CNN. You do."

"Yeah, well, in this case, there is a light at the end of the tunnel, but it happens to be a train. He said I would be contacted soon about his decision, but . . ." Deborah left the sentence unfinished. "So, how is my college-girl mother?"

"Scared to death that she's going to flunk her tests. I'm not sure I should have let you talk me into these night courses."

There was so much hesitancy and lack of confidence in her mother's voice that Deborah wanted to sigh in frustration. "Don't talk like that. You are very intelligent. You just never had a chance to use it.

You're not going to be a hotel maid all your life. Not if I have anything to do with it."

"I'm not ashamed of it."

"Neither am I," Deborah said, hoping her voice wasn't cracking. "But look at the way you pushed me to make something of myself. It's my turn to push you."

"In that case you can drive over here this weekend and help me study for the final semester exams," was the answering challenge.

"To tell you the truth, Mom, if I don't get a job soon I won't be able to afford the gas to drive from Hartford to New Haven." Deborah had to admit her growing financial dilemma.

"Is it that bad?" Her mother sounded worried.

"I'll find work," she assured her mother quickly. "It's just I wanted that personal assistant gig so badly. I've never done it but the pay is fantastic and a lot of my living expenses would be covered. I can start saving again."

"The power of compound interest," her mother said, as if she didn't quite understand the phrase but had heard it a lot. "You keep telling me about it."

"It's for real. And, Mom, every other offer is like nothing in comparison. I just have to stop being so picky."

"If you need the money, I'll return that check you sent me this month. Art mailed me some money. I can get by—"

"You keep that, Mom. If I needed it, I wouldn't have sent it." She immediately seized on the mention of her brother's name to change the subject. "Did Art mention when he'll get some leave? Guess you got a letter from him. I didn't."

The rest of the conversation became focused on the

family; money and finances had no more part in their discussion. Her mother fretted about the long-distance charges and said goodbye, before the conversation with Deborah became too expensive.

"Relax and enjoy your free time," her mother offered in parting.

"Yes, I thought I'd change and go down to the pool," Deborah admitted.

"And don't give up hope about that job. That Mr. Wilding might have a change of heart."

"From granite to marble."

"Deborah." Her mother's tone was kind.

"I know. I need a good dose of optimism. Bye, Mom. Love you."

"Love you too, honey."

The employment agency had exhausted its supply of job openings that would suit Deborah's qualifications. She didn't have a single interview the rest of the week. On Friday morning she looked at job postings online for a couple of fruitless hours and went to buy some New York newspapers, already considering the possibility of moving out of the Hartford area to find work. She was unlocking the door to her apartment when she heard her phone ringing inside. Naturally the key stuck. A few inventive curses aided in getting it free and she rushed to answer the phone.

"Ms. Deborah Holland, please," a female voice requested.

"Speaking." Part of the thick newspaper slipped from her hand and skittered to the floor.

"Please hold while I connect you to Mr. Wilding."

An eyebrow shot up in surprise. The man himself

was calling her to deliver the bad news. Deborah hadn't expected that. As a matter of fact, she hadn't expected any notification about the position until late next week.

A line clicked. "Ms. Holland."

It was strange how immediately familiar his voice sounded, commanding and cool. Or was icy a better word? "Yes, sir." She hoped she sounded equally un-emotional.

"Can you report to my office Monday morning at seven a.m.?"

"Seven—oh." It took a second for the implication of his statement to sink in. "This means you are offer-ing me the job."

"I wouldn't waste my time or yours asking you to come to my office on Monday if I intended to offer the position to someone else." His dry tone was indif-ferent.

Her backbone stiffened at his response. "Do I have time to consider the offer before deciding whether to accept it?"

"You've had plenty of time to decide whether or not you want the position, providing it was offered to you, Ms. Holland." His tone held little patience. "If you haven't made up your mind by now, then you aren't the person for the job." He paused, and Deborah couldn't think of a single response. "Do you want it or shall I call someone else?"

"I want it, Mr. Wilding," she admitted through her teeth, gritting them until they ached.

"Monday morning then. Seven o'clock."

"I'll—" The call ended. She heard only the hum of the dial tone in her ear.

Deborah glared at the receiver for a frozen instant

before slamming it back on its cradle. The newspapers rustled noisily under her feet. There was no need to study the out-of-town classified advertisements. She had work—the position she wanted, but she didn't feel any desire to celebrate.

Bending down, she picked up the newspaper and jammed it in the wastebasket, then walked to her green and blue bedroom to choose her wardrobe for the week ahead. Deborah had no illusions about her new job. Challenging might not be a strong enough word to describe it. And she had no doubt that she would soon find a better word. Z. Wilding would see to that.

Chapter Two

Demanding. That was a much better description. After one full week on the job and part of a second, Deborah had found the correct adjective. From daylight to dusk she had lived, breathed, and thought LaCosta Enterprises. She had learned, in short order, that her employer tolerated no excuses, not even ignorance. If she didn't know something, someone or someplace, he expected her to find out. Therefore, besides the long hours she put in on the job, Deborah lugged home stockholders' reports, printouts, corporate analyses of the various firms under the LaCosta banner, résumés of all the corporate executives to familiarize herself with their names and backgrounds, and projections for expansion.

Her duties were many and varied, ranging from making coffee in the hidden office alcove or acting as chauffeur to taking notes at various meetings and conferences. Depending on the confidentiality of the contents, Deborah typed them up and created a computer filing system for all the information, just for him. Even the administrative assistant, Mrs. Haines, in the outer office, didn't have access to it.

All interoffice and corporate communications were screened by Deborah, and she determined what was important and what wasn't. Financial reports, cost sheets, profit-and-loss statements, and project estimates were all required to have her opinion attached to them before they were given to him. Half the time Deborah was working in the dark with only rudimentary knowledge of the company or item discussed. When her ignorance surfaced, her employer was quick to point it out—bluntly.

One thing Deborah had learned: the Z stood for Zane. The only person she had ever heard address her employer by his given name was Tom Brookshire. He was a quiet, nondescript man with brown hair and eyes, and about the same age as Zane Wilding. If Tom had a title, she hadn't discovered it. She had the feeling the two men were longtime friends, not that Zane Wilding ever acted friendly toward anyone. Tom seemed to be his adviser, consultant and right arm. She had the impression he was an attorney, but she hadn't the vaguest idea where his office was located—in the building or elsewhere. Tom just materialized whenever Zane Wilding had need of him. At times it was uncanny.

The columns of figures on the spreadsheet blurred. Deborah paused to rub her eyes tiredly before attempting to find her place and continue rechecking the number totals with the calculator she pulled up on her computer screen. The door to the inner office where she and her employer had their desks swung open. Deborah glanced up. Only Tom Brookshire entered this private office without being announced or knocking. But it was a petite blonde who walked in. Deborah was too stunned to do more than glance at the dark-haired man behind the large desk.

Zane Wilding looked up too when the door opened, his piercing blue eyes narrowing on the woman who entered. Unfolding his length from the chair, he stood. Was it her imagination or had she seen a nerve twitch in the hardened line of his jaw? Deborah wondered about it.

"What are you doing here, Sylvia?"

Not seeming to notice the absence of warmth in his greeting, the fragile-looking blonde walked to his desk. There was a haunting delicacy to her profile, Deborah saw. For all the sophistication and elegance of her clothes and hairstyle, the woman had an aura of sensitivity.

"I rode into town with Madelaine and Frank. I thought I would surprise you and give you an opportunity to take your wife to lunch," she announced in a melodic voice.

Wife? More like a waif. It seemed impossible that this fragile being was married to Zane Wilding. Deborah felt instant pity. Seeing the two of them together was almost too strange to put into words. Zane Wilding dominated her with his height and muscled leanness. His rugged countenance revealed no emotions at all.

"You should have called to let me know you were coming." He walked around the desk to loom over her. "I have a business lunch today. It's important."

Deborah's hazel eyes widened at his statement. She had checked his appointment calendar not an hour ago. He had no such engagement. As a matter of fact, he had no meetings until two in the afternoon.

"Oh." The blonde's disappointment was a touching expression. "I suppose it'll be one of those long, boring affairs." The wistfulness of her tone hinted that she was saying the words before he did.

"Yes." There wasn't the slightest trace of apology or regret on his face. Strong, male fingers gripped her small-boned elbow to turn the woman from his desk. His intention was obviously to escort her from the room.

But as his wife was turned she saw Deborah seated behind the smaller desk. There was a odd loveliness in her sad smile. Deborah was struck by the ivory pallor of the blonde's complexion. She was as pale as if she'd been locked away for several years.

"Is this your new assistant, Zane? You never mentioned that she was so beautiful," she said without malice or jealousy.

His blue gaze froze for an instant on Deborah's features. "I hadn't noticed." Which was an ego-shattering comment, since Deborah was convinced it was true.

When Zane Wilding showed no inclination to introduce them, Deborah took the initiative. "I'm Deborah Holland."

Limp fingers clasped the hand Deborah extended as the blonde responded, "I'm Sylvia Wilding." Everything about his wife was so feminine and dainty that Deborah felt like an amazon in comparison.

As the hand was withdrawn, Sylvia Wilding tipped her head sideways to look up to her husband. "You never were attracted to redheads, were you?"

"No, I never have been." There was an underlying tone of impatience in his attitude. Deborah could feel it charging the atmosphere.

His reply was barely out when the door opened and

Tom Brookshire walked in. His alert gaze quickly took in the situation as he strode forward, a gentle smile spreading across his face. Out of the corner of her eye Deborah saw the hand signal Zane Wilding made behind his wife's back, indicating he wanted Tom to take his wife from the room.

"Sylvia. This is a surprise." Tom Brookshire sounded genuinely glad to see her. With a natural ease he bent to kiss the blonde's pale cheek. That display of affection was more than she had received from her husband. "When did you arrive?"

"Just this minute. How are you, Tom? It seems like ages since I saw you last." There was a trace of even more sadness in her smile.

"I'm afraid it has been," he admitted and held both of her hands in his. "You're looking well and pretty as ever. What brings you to the city?"

That was another piece of information Deborah hadn't known—where Zane and his wife lived. Obviously it wasn't here in Hartford. Where? She wondered about that too.

"Nothing special. I thought I'd stop and have lunch with Zane," Sylvia began.

"She didn't know I had other plans," Zane inserted and the faint emphasis in his voice seemed to prompt a reply from the other man.

"I'm free for lunch. Since Zane can't take you, why don't we sneak away together?" Tom suggested.

"I . . . I'd like that," she agreed after a poignant hesitation.

Tom offered her his arm in a show of gallantry. "Shall we?"

Sylvia Wilding curved a hand inside his arm and paused to glance at Deborah. "It was nice meeting you."

"My pleasure, Mrs. Wilding." Deborah was aware that compassion put added warmth in her response.

As the couple walked from the office, she sliced an accusing look at her employer, seething at the way he had so coldly palmed off his wife. As if feeling the pricking of the poison darts Deborah was mentally throwing at him, the electric blue of his gaze moved calmly to her.

"If you haven't finished checking those figures, Deborah, I suggest you get busy instead of standing around doing nothing."

"Yes, sir," she snapped out, venting some of her anger through sarcasm, but it had no visible effect on him. His skin was much too thick.

The inner office line buzzed on her desk. Returning to her seat in the swivel chair, Deborah punched the lighted button and answered the phone. "Deborah Holland."

"This is Mrs. Haines," the administrative assistant in the outer office identified herself. "I'm leaving for lunch now and I wanted you to know that all incoming calls are being switched through your phone."

"Thank you. Have a good lunch."

"Be back in an hour," the older woman promised and hung up.

Only when Mrs. Haines was away from her desk was Deborah responsible for screening the incoming calls for Zane Wilding. The majority of the time she was free from interruptions like that. Her employer returned calls but rarely accepted any, which necessitated a lot of message taking.

Deborah glanced at the fact sheet she was checking and sighed. It was unlikely she would finish it until after Mrs. Haines returned. Minimizing the spreadsheet into a rectangular button at the bottom of her screen, she started entering more figures into the onscreen calculator. With a click of the mouse, she made a tiny mark beside each number as she punched it up.

The phone rang halfway through the painstaking task. Deborah let it ring a second time before picking up the receiver. "Mr. Wilding's desk, Deborah Holland speaking."

"This is Simpson Armbruster. Is Mr. Wilding in, please?" The male voice sounded elderly. The name was not one that Deborah remembered hearing mentioned before.

She shot a questioning glance at her employer. Zane Wilding had lifted his head from the report he was reading, his expression an impenetrable mask.

"One moment, Mr. Armbruster." She pressed the hold button, but Zane was already shaking his head to refuse the call. Deborah reconnected the blinking line. "I'm sorry, sir. Mr. Wilding is on another line. May I take a message or have him return your call?" Deborah requested. It hadn't taken her long to invent a variety of excuses why her employer was refusing calls.

Mr. Armbruster asked that his call be returned and Deborah jotted down the number where he could be reached. When she hung up the phone, a sunbrowned hand was reaching to tear off the sheet of paper with the number. Deborah hadn't realized Zane was anywhere in the vicinity of her desk until that moment, the thick carpet muffling the sound of his approaching footsteps.

He was standing directly behind her chair. There

was an edge of blue steel in the look he gave her. "Did he say why he had called?"

"No. Just asked you to call him back at your convenience." Everything was always at *his* convenience, she thought, getting a crick in her neck from looking up into Zane's face with its powerful jawline and slanted cheekbones. Out of sheer frustration with her low position on the office totem pole—he was most definitely at the top—she added, "Your wife seemed to be a very nice woman . . . very beautiful."

The steely quality in his blue gaze grew sharper. "I'll return Armbruster's call from the pool." Pushing back the cuffs of his white shirt and dark jacket sleeve, he glanced at the gold Rolex on his wrist. "I'll be back at one-thirty."

If he'd said flat out that he wasn't interested in any personal comments from her, Zane Wilding couldn't have made his meaning more clear. As he walked away from her desk toward the door, Deborah studied his lithe way of moving.

There was so much about him that was sexy. The barely tamed thickness of his black hair looked feather soft at times. His stature dominated most people he came in contact with and he had the powerfully tapered build of a swimmer, broad muscled shoulders and chest with a flat stomach and slim hips. On the average of three days a week he took a long lunch hour and went to a swimming pool at an exclusive nearby gym to exercise, Deborah had learned. That explained his excellent physical condition in spite of the hours spent behind the desk.

He radiated so much damn virility that Deborah had to wonder why she had gained the impression of unfulfillment from his wife. A woman as feminine as

Sylvia was a perfect match for a man as masculine as Zane Wilding. But his chiseled mouth had stayed firm—he'd made no attempt to kiss his wife, not even give her a chaste peck. Deborah remembered that she had never seen him flirt with anyone, ever, let alone her. Somehow she found it difficult to reconcile his attitude of iron celibacy to the male lust that she suspected was behind that corporate correctness of his.

Taking a firm grip on her wandering thoughts, Deborah dismissed her half-baked speculation about her employer's love life. Who he slept with—or didn't sleep with—wasn't her concern. Zane Wilding would be the first one to tell her so.

After a month, Deborah's life settled into a routine. Unfortunately, the only thing routine about her job was the lack of a set routine, other than work, work, work. Her duties weren't restricted to the office. Four times she had attended business dinners with her employer where she was required to take mental notes of the discussion and transcribe a general account of the meeting into a report that she submitted to Zane Wilding the next afternoon. Fortunately, after these late night dinners she wasn't required to be in the office until noon the next day, but she usually spent the free mornings jotting down her recollections of the previous night's conversations so they could be organized into yet another report when she reached the office.

There were two out-of-town trips in the first month, one to New York and the other to Los Angeles. The first time Tom Brookshire had flown with them, but the second time it was only Deborah and her employer. If it had been anyone other than Zane Wilding, Deborah would have been wary of spending two or three nights in the same hotel as her boss. But she could have had three eyes and one leg for all the notice Zane Wilding paid to her. Everything was strictly business.

In all the long hours they'd spent together, he had never made any comment that could be construed as friendly or personal. All that came out of his mouth were orders, commands, or requests. On rare occasions he opened a door for her or held a chair, but Deborah could count those times on her fingers. They were the only occasions that he revealed he was aware of the fact she was a member of the opposite sex.

Once or twice her female side wanted to rebel at his indifferent treatment of her, but Deborah always quelled the revolt. Theirs was a business relationship—employer and employee. It wouldn't be wise to complicate it, she realized.

The job was living up to her expectations of learning all about the many and varied facets of a large corporation. Whatever her opinion was of Zane Wilding as a human being, Deborah had no reservations about his skill as a businessman. His experience and natural acumen were beyond hers. He seemed born to command. She doubted that there were many men who could sit silently through an entire meeting and still be totally in charge of all that was discussed—as he was doing now.

He insisted that she not use a laptop in meetings because he didn't. Zane Wilding was a believer in the power of eye contact. He also made it clear that people talked more freely when they didn't think they were being electronically recorded. He didn't say so in so

many words, but she got the impression that a woman
with a pencil and pad of paper was essentially invisible
in a corporate world that was still very much male-
dominated.

She glanced absently from her notepad and her
jotted record of the discussion to the strong, lean hands
on her right. They were male hands with squared, clean-
cut nails and fine dark hair curling at the wrists from beneath white shirt cuffs. Beneath the tanned skin was the
tensile strength of carbon-fiber wrapped around steel.
Definitely hands that held the reins of a multibillion-
dollar conglomerate.

Thumbing to the next page of the report, he lifted
a hand to rub a knuckle against the hard line of his
mouth in aloof concentration. Deborah found herself
wondering how often the inherent mastery in his
touch was directed into a caress. She had never met a
man who exhibited less need for human contact than
Zane Wilding did.

One of the double doors to the large conference
room was opened a crack. Deborah saw Mrs. Haines
peer hesitantly in. The interruption drew a glance of
censure from Zane. As unobtrusively as possible, Deborah rose from her chair and walked quietly to the
door.

"What is it?" she whispered.

The older woman wore an apologetic, yet agitated
look. "Mrs. Wilding's on the phone."

"Which line?"

"Two."

"Thank you, Mrs. Haines." Deborah smiled firmly
and closed the door.

Before the meeting had begun, Zane Wilding had
left strict orders to hold all calls. With that indelibly

imprinted in her mind, Deborah walked to the phone on the small table in the corner of the room. She pushed the button to connect the second line and picked up the receiver. "Mrs. Wilding? This is Deborah Holland." She kept her voice low so as not to intrude on the discussion going on behind her at the long table.

"I don't want to talk to you! I asked to speak to Zane. Where is he?" The strident female voice slurred most of the words. Deborah heard nothing that reminded her of the soft-spoken blonde she had met in the office in the voice of the agitated woman on the line.

"I'm sorry. He's in conference right now. Let me have him call you back in an hour," Deborah suggested.

"Conference! He isn't in any conference. You're lying to me!"

"Please, Mrs. Wilding—"

"You damned little bitch!" It was becoming more and more apparent that Sylvia Wilding was drunk. "He's with you right now, isn't he? What's he doing? Making love to you? Is he kissing you and fondling you? You cheap little slut, I bet you think it's funny to be talking to me while he's holding you in his arms."

The flurry of jealous accusations momentarily shocked Deborah. "Mr. Wilding is chairing a corporate meeting." The denial came out in a breathless rush of indignation.

"Hah! I know him. I know what he likes. Do you like all that naked muscle against your skin? I'll bet you want to have his baby."

"Please—" There didn't seem to be anything she could say to stop this torrent of suggestive questions.

"I want to speak to Zane! You put him on the phone this instant!"

"Who's that?" The harsh demand came from Zane Wilding.

Clamping a hand over the mouthpiece of the receiver, Deborah half turned to answer him. "It's your wife."

But the hand covering the mouthpiece didn't stop the stream of abusive and obscene language that echoed into the room. And all those vile, sexually explicit comments were directed at Deborah. The red stain of embarrassment heated her face as all eyes focused directly on her.

Anger blazed in Zane Wilding's eyes. Deborah sensed the suppressed violence as he uncoiled himself from the chair and crossed the room to yank the receiver from her hand.

"I'm here, Sylvia. This is Zane. Everything's all right now. Settle down," he ordered.

At the same instant that he spoke, Tom Brookshire was rising from his chair and quietly ushering the other men from the room. No one questioned his reason. Deborah was conscious of the executive staff leaving, but she was rooted to the floor, still in shock from the foul things Sylvia Wilding had said to her. Deborah waited for Zane to defend her and refute all the accusations.

As Zane became aware of her continued presence beside him, he turned and gestured to Tom to take her out of the room. His look was cold when it glanced off her, his eyes the deep arctic blue of a glacier. Deborah was stunned by his attitude.

As Tom took hold of her arm to lead her away, she heard Zane say to his wife, "Don't be ridiculous. I have never refused to take a call from you. If anyone claims I did, they're lying. Where is Madelaine?" Ignoring Deborah's outraged look at the implication in his words that labeled her a liar, Zane covered the receiver again and issued a sharp order to Tom, "She says she doesn't know where Madelaine is. Try the other estate number. If you can't get anybody, patch Armbruster into this line for a conference call."

"Right." Tom didn't take any notice of Deborah's stiffness as he escorted her from the conference room. Outside, Mrs. Haines had commandeered another assistant's desk and was using the phone. She looked up anxiously when Tom stopped at her chair.

"I can't get any answer at the other number," she informed him.

"Keep trying." His fingers remained firmly on Deborah's elbow as he walked to an adjoining desk. "Take a coffee break," he told the young woman seated there and glanced at her coworkers in the room trying not to show their interest in what was happening. In a louder voice Tom ordered, "Everyone take a twenty-minute break."

As the cubicles and workstations emptied out, Deborah muttered angrily beneath her breath, "I've never been so humiliated in my life! She had no reason to speak to me like that. Everyone in the conference room heard what she said."

Tom's mouth slanted in a wry smile. "Sooner or later everyone in the company will begin speculating about whether you and Zane are having an affair. Sylvia just put the thought in their minds that much quicker." He picked up the telephone and tapped out a number on the push buttons.

Tom's reply didn't do anything to cool the heat in her

cheeks. "They can speculate all they like and it still won't be true. That arrogant—" Deborah checked the word that trembled on the edge of her tongue. "He practically called me a liar, when he had made it clear that he wanted all calls held while he was in that meeting."

"All calls don't include ones from his wife. They are put through to him, regardless," Tom informed her.

"No one told me that," she retorted.

"That's unfortunate," he admitted, then turned his attention to the receiver in his hand. "Yes, Armbruster. Sylvia's on another line. Hold on while I patch you through." After a hurried consultation with someone who understood the complex phone system, Tom made the connection between the two lines and hung up his receiver. The tense lines of concern that etched the corners of his mouth went away as he sighed and turned his attention back to Deborah. "Don't take the things Sylvia said to you too personally."

"Too personally?" Her scoffing laugh was harsh. "Is there another way to take them? I don't think she said anything that wasn't obscene."

"Yes. . ." Tom paused to take a deep breath, an action that seemed weary. "Sylvia can't be held responsible for what she does or says."

"If you mean simply because she was drunk, I should ignore—"

"Sylvia is an alcoholic," Tom interrupted. "And she's addicted to prescription drugs. And there are other things going on as well."

"I didn't know." Deborah frowned. "I didn't guess. When she was in the office—"

"She happened to be sober that time." He sat his lanky frame on the edge of the desk, hooking a leg over the corner. "Zane doesn't talk about it, but I'm not telling you anything that isn't common knowledge among the other members of his private staff. Since you're now a part of the team you might as well know, too."

"I see," she murmured, her feeling of outrage slowly dissolving.

"I've known Sylvia almost as long as I've known Zane. She was never very stable, emotionally speaking. Her moods fluctuated from very high to very low. After Ethan drowned, she fell apart."

"Ethan? Who is Ethan?"

"Their son. He was only four years old. Sylvia was in a doctor's care for several months after his death. She blamed herself for the accident. He was out playing by the river and fell into the water. Sylvia had been reading not far away while he played. She heard the splash, but by the time she reached the riverbank he'd gone under. She was hysterical when Zane finally found her wading along the river searching for Ethan's body. That was fourteen years ago."

"But hasn't anyone tried to—" Deborah stopped, aware that she might be asking questions that weren't any of her business.

"I don't know how many times Zane has persuaded her to go into rehab, but it's been a revolving door. She rarely lasts longer than a month before she goes on another binge. Obviously that's what happened today. Sometimes she just cries and other times she makes a lot of wild accusations. There have been occasions when she gets drunk and doesn't say a word for days, just walks around in a stupor. It's pitiful, really."

"Yes, I can see that." Deborah nodded.

The conference room door opened and Zane stepped out. He glanced around the empty and virtually silent workstation area, before his grim look stopped on Tom.

"Have somebody bring in a fresh pot of coffee and tell the others we'll resume the meeting in fifteen minutes," he ordered. His hard gaze had a laser sharpness to it, Deborah thought. "Come in here, please."

Uncertainty flickered across her expression as she glanced at Tom, but he was already straightening from the desk to carry out Zane's request. Deborah had no idea what she had done to spark his obvious displeasure, but she wasn't about to let him intimidate her with his glowering expression. Carrying herself with determined poise, Deborah walked past Zane into the empty conference room and left him to close the door behind her.

"Would you explain to me what the hell you were trying to prove by refusing that phone call?" With hardly a break in stride, he made his tight-lipped demand and swept past her to the chair at the head of the long conference table.

"What I was trying to prove?" Her temper ignited and she tried to bank the heat of her anger. "I was following the instructions you left to hold all calls. I wasn't aware that the restriction didn't include your wife!"

"Now you are. I don't want a repeat of this incident," he snapped and picked up the opened report lying on the table.

"Believe me, I don't either!" Deborah flared.

His gaze lifted from the papers to study her face. "Are you expecting an apology for what happened?"

There was a foreboding quality to the softly spoken question.

"I don't think it would be asking too much," she retorted.

"If I began apologizing for every time my wife went crazy, I would be doing it the rest of my life. Now that you're aware of how far Sylvia can go and how unpredictable she is, you have a choice of either dealing with an occasional outburst or leaving the company," he said with indifference.

"Just like that," she breathed in enraged astonishment.

"I'm not about to stroke your ego, Ms. Holland. If you can't take a few insults from a drunk, I have no use for you. You'd better learn to roll with the punches, even the low blows, or you'll never make it in this organization. Make up your mind. You either stay or you go. I only have room in my life for one paranoid female."

"You really are a piece of work, aren't you?"

"What?"

Pressing her lips into a thin line, Deborah turned on her heel and walked to the corner table where she had left her pencil and notepad beside the phone. With these in hand, she returned to the chair she had occupied on Zane Wilding's left and sat down. Through her actions, she gave him her decision. His expressionless blue eyes took note of the fact, but he made no comment.

Chapter Three

"Wow, it's humid out tonight." The sophisticated brown-haired woman leaned closer to the long mirror and fluffed powder on her shiny nose and cheeks. A huge diamond cocktail ring on her finger caught fire in the artificial light.

"Yes, it is." Deborah was seated on one of the pink velvet-covered stools in the restroom of the exclusive restaurant. She took her time freshening her lipstick as her hazel eyes took in the well-groomed reflection of Babe Darrow, wife of a venture capitalist. He was vacationing in Florida, hence the flying business trip to Tampa to meet with him.

"I tried to convince Bianca that it would be much too warm to dine on the lanai this evening." The woman's glance strayed to her daughter standing next to her, brushing her long chestnut curls. "But she thought it would be so romantic. Fabulous setting, but I feel so sticky now."

"Yes." Deborah blotted her lips with a tissue.

What had started out to as a business dinner to persuade Foster Darrow to back a large land development project for LaCosta Enterprises had rapidly become a social event. Instead of it being a quiet dinner between the financier and Zane with Deborah and Babe Darrow sitting on the sidelines, the man had brought their nineteen-year-old daughter along. She was a beautiful girl with glossy chestnut hair and golden tanned skin. Within minutes after being introduced to Zane she had made her interest in him quite obvious. At virtually the same instant, Zane had excused himself to find out what was delaying Tom Brookshire.

To Deborah's knowledge there had been no mention of Tom's being included in the evening's discussion. Fifteen minutes later, Tom had joined them and immediately began using his quiet charm on the daughter, distracting her attention from Zane. It hadn't taken Deborah long to realize that her employer was using Tom as a buffer to keep the starstruck young girl at bay.

She felt sorry for Bianca Darrow, but part of her understood the attraction the girl felt for the aloof, dark man. His remoteness and air of indifference toward the opposite sex challenged every woman to be the one he noticed. Couple that with his severely handsome looks and obvious virility and it made a very potent combination.

"I don't know how many times I've told Foster that I hate Florida in July. The climate is so tropical that it's oppressive in the summer," Babe declared.

"Tonight is an exception," Deborah said. "Usually the Gulf breezes keep it from becoming too steamy."

"Deborah, have you lived here long?" The faintly brittle question came from Bianca Darrow.

"I live in Connecticut."

"How long have you worked for Zane?" A pair of

youthful but heavily made-up eyes swept over Deborah's reflection, as if assessing her competition.

Her copper-tipped lashes made a pretty good screen for her response to the girl's once-over. Deborah could have told Bianca that there was nothing to worry about as far as she was concerned. If Deborah really had been a robot, Zane Wilding couldn't have shown less interest in her personal life. He didn't even recognize that she had one.

But the distantly polite smiles Bianca Darrow had received tonight were more than Deborah had seen in all the time she had been working for Zane Wilding. For sure, not one had ever been directed at her.

"I've been working for Zane Wilding for a little over three months now," Deborah answered and absently smoothed her dark copper hair at the sides, checking to be sure no wisp had escaped the sleek coil at the nape of her neck.

"Did you know him before?" The young brunette wandered over to stand behind Deborah.

"No." Deborah noticed how pale her skin was getting. The long working hours that sometimes included the weekends had deprived her of free time to spend lazing in the Connecticut summer sun. Compared to Bianca Darrow, she looked too pale, especially considering the copper shade of her hair.

"It's a shame about his wife," Bianca commented, more or less out of nowhere. "What happened was so sad. Do you know her?"

"I met her once," Deborah admitted and offered no more than that.

"From all I've heard, she's a substance abuser. In and out of rehab. Or so says my source. Sylvia Wilding is a sick, sick woman," Babe Darrow said.

Deborah had suspected the venture capitalist's wife loved to gossip and wondered how she could get out of this conversation.

"It can't be a happy marriage," Babe stated the obvious. "I'm surprised he hasn't divorced her after all this time."

"Sometimes people take their vows seriously. You know, in sickness and in health." Deborah slipped the tube of lipstick into her small purse. Truthfully, she didn't know what his feelings were toward his wife, or even if he had any.

"No one would blame him if he divorced her and tried to find happiness with someone else," Bianca said with a dreamy look in her brown eyes.

"No one would blame him," Deborah agreed dryly. "But I don't think Mr. Wilding would be concerned if they did."

"Has Zane ever indicated to you that he was considering a divorce?" the girl asked.

"Hey, I'm only an assistant. He doesn't discuss his personal affairs with me." Deborah wanted to emphasize her point that her relationship to Zane Wilding involved only business.

The girl turned to her mother. "I don't think he lets it show, but I'm sure Zane is really lonely."

If he was, Deborah thought to herself, it was by choice. There were probably a lot of gorgeous young things like Bianca Darrow, who were eager to console him, and women closer to his own age as well. Maybe he had a mistress or two hidden away, although Deborah didn't know when he ever found the time to see them. Her own social life had dwindled to practically nonexistent since she had gone to work for him.

Glancing at her reflection in the full-length mirror,

Deborah ran an adjusting hand around the neckline of her white silk blouse. It was discreetly scooped to show off the cameo necklace resting near the hollow of her throat. Her pleated skirt almost touched the floor, belted at the waist to accent its close fit. Deborah never dressed to draw attention to herself, but the simple styles always succeeded in bringing out her natural assets rather than downplaying them.

"It must be wonderful to work so closely with Zane," Bianca remarked with a trace of envy.

"It's challenging." Deborah altered the meaning without disagreeing with the young woman. *She* knew what a hard taskmaster her employer was. But in Bianca Darrow's rose-colored view, he was a very romantic figure. The girl would never get what Deborah was even talking about if she gave her opinion of the driving, emotionless side she dealt with every day. "Okay. I look as good as I'm going to. Shall we rejoin the others in the lounge?"

"We should, yes." Mrs. Darrow's laugh was shrill. "Of course, Foster is used to waiting for me, but I imagine Zane is an impatient man."

Deborah didn't comment on that as she led the way out of the ladies' room to the dimly lighted lounge. A small band was playing a slow number for a handful of couples on the dance floor. At their approach, the three men rose courteously to seat them. Deborah walked around the table to take the chair between her employer and the financier. It was her usual position at most informal meetings, permitting her to take mental notes of what Zane Wilding said and the response he received. She doubted that there would be much business discussion this evening, though.

In a strictly polite gesture, Zane Wilding pulled her

chair away from the small circular table. Her responding smile was equally automatic, with no more meaning than his action. As she moved to the front of the
chair and lifted her long skirt out of the way, he inclined his head slightly toward her.

"I already ordered you an after-dinner liqueur."

"Oh. Thanks."

"Is Drambuie acceptable?" he asked in a low tone.

"Yes." She paused to answer him, turning her head
to look at him when she did.

"Listen to that music, Zane." Bianca Darrow had
walked to the chair on the other side of Zane, a position
that put her between him and Tom Brookshire. There
was an effusive, happy note in her voice. "Doesn't it
make you want to dance?" Her question was really just
begging for an invitation.

Indifferent to the young woman's obvious attempts
to get Zane interested, Deborah started to sit down. A
strong, male hand clamped her wrist to stop the
movement. Startled by the knowledge the hand belonged to Zane Wilding, her questioning eyes darted
to his shadowy face. His next words surprised her even
more than the unexpectedness of his touch.

"As a matter of fact, it does," he said to Bianca's
remark. "I just asked Deborah to have this dance with
me. Please excuse us." The last comment was directed
to everyone at the table.

Concealing her astonishment and ignorance of any
invitation, Deborah managed to close her mouth
before she was led away from the table to the dance
floor. Just as Tom had been used as a buffer, her presence conveniently kept the young woman at a distance.
Deborah didn't think for one minute that Zane Wilding was doing it because he couldn't deal with Bianca

Darrow's sweet little crush on him. She suspected that he wanted to avoid any rude confrontation that might offend the girl's father. It was a rare show of diplomacy from a man who was accustomed to bluntly speaking his mind. She saw the flash of jealousy in Bianca's look as Zane guided her to the dance floor.

An odd feeling of self-consciousness attacked Deborah when he shifted his hold on her wrist and placed a hand on the curve of her waist. The other couples dancing to the slow music were almost melted together, but at least six inches separated Deborah from the muscular build of her partner. His steps followed a basic pattern that was easy to follow, although the hand at her waist made sure of it by firmly directing her movements to match his.

Deborah wasn't sure which was more unnerving— being held so firmly at a distance as Zane was doing now, or being held close to the hard male body inches from her own. Either way, the situation made her feel on edge. The warmth in the strong fingers clasping hers brought a tightness to her throat. Her gaze focused itself on an imaginary point on his right shoulder, rather than lift the few inches necessary to study his face at close quarters.

Just the same, she was conscious of his strong chin on a level somewhere near her forehead, and the chiseled contours of his mouth above that. The clean, real-man fragrance of his shaving cologne dominated her sense of smell.

The music and the intimacy of dancing together were making her reaction to his nearness much too physical. Deborah realized that she was on dangerous ground. She had to say something and get them back on a business footing again.

"This hasn't been a very productive evening, has it?" she remarked in what she hoped was a calm voice.

"No. It's been a waste of time, if you want a more accurate description." His low-pitched voice triggered pleasant vibrations through her bones, despite the grimness of his tone.

Fighting that reaction, Deborah quipped, "Well, not totally wasted. The food was good."

She lifted her gaze a few inches and saw his mouth quirk at her statement. It was the closest she had ever come to receiving a smile from Mr. Tall, Dark, and Taciturn. Of course, the flicker of amusement never reached the steel-blue depths of his eyes. Deborah was convinced nothing ever did.

His impersonal gaze briefly moved over her. "Didn't you wear that two weeks ago when we had dinner with the president of the architectural firm?"

That was an interesting revelation. He actually noticed what she wore? Her pleasure shone in her clear eyes. "Yes, I did."

Immediately his blue gaze narrowed. "I suppose you don't have that many evening gowns, which is why you have to keep wearing the same things over and over."

Deborah realized that she had mistakenly interpreted his first remark as a compliment. "No, I don't," she replied stiffly. "My glamour get-ups consist of one dress, one pantsuit, another evening gown, and this. None of them is very extravagant, but then I'm not taking part in a fashion parade. I have other things to spend my money on besides evening clothes to entertain your business associates." A look like lightning flashed in her eyes, crackling with her temper.

"Is that all? That can be fixed." His tone indicated

an impatience that he had to be bothered with such a minor detail.

"Actually, it can, and fast," she said. "Just give me a raise and free time while the shops are open. I'd be happy to correct the situation." Deborah was practically steaming, resenting his criticism of her limited wardrobe.

"Are you complaining about your salary and long hours?" A black eyebrow lifted in challenge.

"You're the one who is complaining—about my evening wear. If it's a big deal to you, I was offering a remedy." She gave him a saccharine smile.

"I see." There was a glint in his eye that suspiciously resembled amusement.

Deborah looked away, preferring his frigid courtesy to silent, mocking laughter. Her gaze touched on other dancing couples, entwined in each other's arms. The distance between them made her feel conspicuous. Not that she wanted to rest her head on that chest of living stone, because she didn't have feelings like that for him. But she was aware that the firm warmth of the hand at her back and the fingers curved around her own communicated something very much at odds with his attitude of chilly indifference. She stifled that knowledge, not knowing where it might lead.

"Too bad you aren't as quick to praise as you are to criticize," she said tightly, looking anywhere but at her employer. Who did he think he was, anyway? His carved face was close enough to slap. Or kiss. "Because it seems impossible to satisfy you."

"Lighten up, Deborah. If you do something that doesn't satisfy me, I'll let you know." Dry humor lurked in his low voice.

She met his gaze again. "Which is precisely my point. A person is just as eager to find out when she does something right as she is to know when she's wrong."

"So you want me to say you've done an excellent job so far."

"No, I don't want you to say it," she muttered. "I want you to mean it. Praise is worth nothing when it's prompted."

"I'm surprised you know that," he murmured in a superior tone.

Deborah gritted her teeth. "I knew working for you was going to be an experience, but I didn't realize it was going to be a lesson in male arrogance."

The arm at her waist tightened to turn her away from a couple that would have danced blindly into them. Briefly Deborah felt the contact of his muscled thigh. It was a jolting reminder of the lean, hard length of a man in his prime. After that, she kept her mouth closed rather than have Zane Wilding think she was making a move on him. When the song ended, she escaped the unnerving indifference of his arms and turned to walk back to the table. But he was right behind her.

His low, bland voice made her jump. "Unprompted, I have to say that your silence was refreshing."

Deborah flashed him a glance over her shoulder and met his eyes. "Say whatever you want. You're the boss." Satisfied that she'd had the last word, she fixed a calm expression on her face and continued to the table where the others waited for them.

Ignoring the speculative looks from the financier and his wife, and the jealousy in their daughter's eyes, Deborah walked to her chair. Zane Wilding was there to pull it out for her and she caught the curious look Tom Brookshire gave him.

"Thanks for the dance, Deborah." The glinting light in his blue eyes was challenging and hard.

A sharp retort trembled on her lips. She wanted to say that she hadn't been given the opportunity to refuse, but she bit it back and nodded with faked courtesy. While he took the chair beside her, Deborah reached for her drink to cover her tense unease.

"You looked great out there on the dance floor, Debbie," Darrow remarked. "Can I call you Debbie?"

"Okay." She glanced at the financier over the rim of her glass. "And thanks. I guess you didn't notice how many times I stepped on the big guy's toes." *Figuratively, at least,* she thought, and glanced across the table at Tom Brookshire, who looked like he wanted to laugh out loud.

But no one pursued her comment as Bianca Darrow spoke to draw Zane Wilding's attention to her and away from Deborah. Not once during the course of the evening did he ask either Babe or Bianca Darrow to dance. Deborah expected them to be offended, but except for the jealous looks Bianca kept casting her way, neither woman seemed insulted by the lack of an invitation.

The financier asked Deborah to dance once, after he dutifully danced first with his wife and later, their daughter. On the floor he confessed to Deborah that he loved to polka, just loved it.

Oh, no. The corniest, sweatiest dance on the planet. Was that the reason he kept pumping her arm while they danced to a slow tune? It was probably an unconscious effort to speed up the tempo of the song. Whatever his reason, her arm practically ached by the time the song ended. At the table Deborah kept her mouth firmly shut most of the time, not speaking unless a remark was addressed specifically to her. Having stuck her foot in her mouth once that evening, she had no intention of repeating it. Besides, if Zane Wilding found her silence refreshing, she decided he could freeze in it.

When Tom led her onto the dance floor near the end of the evening, he commented on her subdued behavior. "You're awfully quiet tonight, Deborah."

"Don't you find my silence refreshing?" The caustic challenge was out before she could stop it.

Automatically his gaze shifted to Zane Wilding seated at the table. He didn't need to be told who had prompted that remark.

"I'm sorry, Tom," Deborah apologized right away. "I had no reason to snap at you."

"But you've been snapping at him," he guessed with a slight smile.

"He was complaining that I wear the same evening clothes all the time. Working eighteen hours a day, seven days a week for him," Deborah exaggerated in anger, "when do I have time to buy anything new? I don't like being unfairly criticized and I told him so." Tom's eyes flicked to the dark copper sheen of her hair. Deborah noticed it and simmered. "Please don't blame my temper on red hair. My sister has fiery red hair and she's as timid as a church mouse. I've always been independent and outspoken."

"I didn't say a word." Tom drew his head back.

It was just the right attitude to cool her down some. "I snapped again, didn't I?" She smiled ruefully and sighed.

"Don't worry about it." He dismissed her need to

apologize. His calmness in the face of her stormy resentment toward their mutual employer had a stabilizing effect and eased her out of her silent, bristling mood.

It took the curse off the evening, in fact, which ended on a peaceful note. But it was part of Tom's job to smooth the feathers his boss might have ruffled. Deborah had realized that a long time ago.

Because of the late flight back to Connecticut, Deborah wasn't required to come into the office until ten the next morning. Passing through the outer office, she tossed a "good morning" to the efficient, prim assistant guarding the door to the private domain of her employer. Zane Wilding was on the phone when she walked in. His gaze took note of the fact as she continued toward her desk.

Cupping a hand over the mouthpiece, he glanced at her. "What are your measurements?"

"Huh?" The question stopped her dead. "I—beg your pardon?" The phrase tumbled out in an astonished breath.

"Your measurements—what are they?" he repeated curtly.

Deborah stiffened. "I don't see that it's any of your business."

His mouth thinned into an exasperated line. Removing his hand, he spoke into the phone. "Hold on a sec." He punched the red hold button and lifted his head to study her. "I'm talking to a personal shopper. She's going to have evening clothes sent to your apartment— you get to pick and choose, and send back whatever you don't like. On me. I could guess at your size, but it would be much simpler if you gave me your measurements, your height and your weight."

His sweeping gaze mentally stripped off what she had on, and assessed her figure. Self-consciousness flamed her skin at his thorough inspection. Despite the analytical quality of his look, that intense virility of his added undercurrents of sexual interest.

"It isn't necessary for you to arrange anything," Deborah huffily refused his offer. "I'll take care of my wardrobe myself."

"As you pointed out, both your time and your money are limited," he replied, "and so is my patience. I entertain business clients in the evening and we both have to look good. Like I just said, I'm paying for this. Think of it as a perk. Or a reward. Or, I don't know, a uniform? Anyway, you need some new things that I deem necessary. Is that clear?"

"Perfectly," she agreed rigidly.

"Then tell me your measurements." It was an order, a demand, but not a request.

Struggling to keep her poise, Deborah responded. "I'm five foot seven, 125 pounds, and the tape says 35-25-36. Will that do?"

Without a flicker of an eye, Zane Wilding repeated the numbers over the phone and added, "She has dark auburn hair and hazel eyes. I'll trust you to make the appropriate choices, including accessories. She'll return what she doesn't like. Send the bill to my attention." When the conversation was ended, he hung up. Deborah was still standing in the center of the room. He took a closer look at her face. "I don't think we stayed in Florida long enough. You could use some sun."

She realized his criticism of her appearance wasn't

over yet. "When would you suggest I do that? I spend just about every daylight hour inside these four walls." Her question had an edge.

But he was unscathed by her sharpness. "Well, too much sun isn't good. Try a full-spectrum lamp, though. It's supposed to cheer people up." He began shifting the newspapers stacked in front of him to resume his morning reading of the big national dailies and the *Wall Street Journal.* He preferred real papers to their online versions because, as he'd explained, there were no idiotic pop-up ads to distract him.

"Is that what you do?" She took in the sun-bronzed features and their disgustingly healthy color.

"I have in the past," he admitted, giving her a considering look. "You can use the pool at my gym if you want to during your lunch hour. Just ask. The exercise would probably do you good."

At that moment, Deborah fervently wished they were both at the swimming pool so she could have the pleasure of pushing him in. Instead, she kept a rein on her temper and walked to her desk without responding to his suggestion. The problem was that he was so often absolutely right in his judgments and solutions. For some mysterious reason, it infuriated Deborah.

It was dark by the time she left the office that day and drove to her apartment. Her neighbor must have signed for the delivery and got her key from the building manager. Dress boxes were stacked on her carpet, bearing the scrolled name of a well-known and very exclusive fashion shop in the city. Deborah stared at them resentfully for a minute, then kicked off her shoes and began opening them.

By the time she had finished, mounds of protective tissue paper were piled on the floor and an array of evening gowns and cocktail dresses adorned the sofa. The understated simplicity of the clothes had a subdued elegance that looked expensive. All the colors were designed to complement her unusual combination of auburn hair and hazel eyes. The accessories ran from designer shoes to scarves and evening shawls.

Deborah could find fault with only one choice. A scarlet cocktail dress with threads of silver was just too flamboyant a combination with her red hair. That she set aside to be returned to the store. After trying on three and discovering they were a perfect fit, she didn't bother with the other dozen that remained.

Her clothes closet hadn't been filled before. Now she found herself taking things out to make room for the expensive gowns. The task meant rearranging and cleaning out all the drawers of her bedroom bureau in order to find a place to put the clothes she had taken out of the closet. It was nearly midnight before her apartment was restored to some semblance of order and she was able to tumble into her bed and fall into an exhausted sleep.

As usual, when she arrived at the office early the next morning, Zane Wilding was already there. Deborah informed him that the evening dresses had been delivered and that she was returning one. She kept her tone businesslike and skipped thank-yous he would have dismissed anyway. She argued with herself that to feel gratitude was wrong. After all, he had been the one who was dissatisfied with her appearance.

The following week there was another late-evening business dinner that she was required to attend. Deborah wore one of the new gowns, a simple yet sophisticated design fashioned in silver lamé. It was a killer look with her coloring. Tom Brookshire was quick to tell her how great she looked, but there wasn't a single remark from Zane Wilding about her appearance. If it hadn't been for a cursory, sweeping glance from those arctic-blue eyes, Deborah might have thought he hadn't noticed the new dress. It was an effort to smother her irritation with him, but she eventually succeeded. Sort of, anyway.

Chapter Four

Deborah wasn't sure what had wakened her, but it hadn't been the buzz of the alarm clock on the bedside table. She stretched lazily and yawned before glancing at the clock's face. The glowing numbers said half-past seven. She jumped out of bed in panic, grabbing for the clock. Damn it! She'd set for p.m., not a.m. and the buzzer hadn't gone off.

"Damn, damn, damn," she swore softly as she raced for the bathroom.

Some inner sense had warned her subconscious of the lateness of the hour and wakened her anyway. But she wouldn't have time for any breakfast, not even a cup of instant coffee. She had under thirty minutes to dress and drive to the office, which usually took an hour.

Zizzing an electric toothbrush over her teeth, Deborah promised them a better cleaning that night. She slapped on some lipstick and ran a brush through her hair. There wasn't time to pin it up so she let the waving curls tumble around her shoulders. Pulling a shapeless, ocher-colored dress over her head, she grabbed a belt from the closet and a pair of shoes. As she hurried out her apartment door, she was fastening the belt while juggling her purse, shoes, and the amended report for the business meeting scheduled promptly for nine that morning.

The traffic that September day was heavy. Usually she left early enough to miss the rush, but this time she was caught in the middle of people on their way to work and parents driving their children to school. The frustration of having to poke along when every part of her screamed to hurry worked on her nerves. Her fingers drummed on the steering wheel.

The traffic light at the intersection just ahead of her changed to yellow. Deborah considered trying to speed through the caution light before it changed to red, but it was a school crossing, so she stopped. It was an interminable wait for the green light. Her gaze kept darting impatiently to the light meant for the crossing traffic. Finally it turned to yellow, which meant only a matter of seconds before her lane of traffic would be good to go.

Anticipating the change to green, Deborah shifted her bare foot from the brake to the accelerator to get a head start on the traffic around her. The light had just changed as the hood of her small car poked into the intersection. She didn't see the car that raced to beat the light on the opposite side. She wasn't aware of any danger until she heard the squeal of car brakes and a blaring horn.

Pure instinct made her wrench the steering wheel to angle away from the sound. As the other car skidded sideways into her door, she raised an arm to ward off the shattering glass of her car window. The impact hurtled her sideways to the passenger seat where her shoes, purse and the report lay. Her car seemed to make a slow spin before coming to a rocking stop in the intersection.

Dazed and only half-sure of what had happened, Deborah sat up. There was a funny smattering of red on her dress and she wondered where it had come from. Then she noticed there was a lot of it on her left arm. It seemed to be oozing out of her skin. The fingers of her right hand touched the warm, wet liquid and came away stained. Blood? She didn't feel any pain.

Car doors began slamming. A stranger stuck his head in the window. "Are you all right, lady?" He saw the blood on her arm and ducked his head out to shout to someone. "This one is hurt, too!"

Too? It was a split second before Deborah realized he was referring to the driver of the other car. It prodded her out of the numbed disassociation with reality. The glass from her broken car window must have cut her arm, but the injury wasn't bothering her so it couldn't be too bad. She transferred her concern to the driver of the other car and tried to open her door.

The same stranger said, "The door is bashed in. You'll have to get out on the other side."

Deborah scooted across the seat to the passenger door. It opened easily at her touch. The items on the seat spilled onto the pavement. Someone helped her pick them up. She remembered thanking the person and worrying about the blood that had dripped from her arm onto the report.

Looking around, she saw the car that had careened off the side of hers. It had rammed into the front of a third car stopped at the light. It was the occupants of the third car who were hurt, not the driver who had run the stoplight. She could hear the distant moans of pain. They were almost instantly drowned out by the wail of police sirens, followed by an ambulance.

When they arrived on the scene, Deborah was caught in a rush of confusion. Everyone was talking at once, the police asking questions and everyone, including her, answering them. An ambulance attendant was administering first aid to stem the flow of blood from the cut in her arm, and making his own inquiries. The intersection was blocked and horns were blaring with impatience. Policemen were blowing their whistles and directing traffic to a limited degree.

The next thing Deborah knew, she was being ushered into an ambulance and a policeman was handing her shoes, purse, and report to her. One of the more seriously injured victims was being slid into the ambulance on a stretcher.

As the rear doors closed, Deborah heard herself ask, "What time is it?"

"A little after eight, miss," an EMT guy replied.

She glanced at the report on her lap and remembered why she had it. "I have to get to the office. I'm late for work."

"You're going to be later yet." He smiled sympathetically. "That cut needs to be looked at. Your boss will understand."

"You don't know my boss," Deborah murmured. She could just imagine Zane Wilding's reaction to the accident. He would probably accuse her of being an incompetent driver.

At the hospital one of the ambulance attendants ushered her through the emergency entrance while the other two brought in the second victim. Inside, an admitting nurse guided her to one of the treatment rooms where Deborah was subjected to more questions, this time about her medical history, allergies, medication, et cetera. Her answers were jotted down on an admittance form.

"The ER doctor will be in directly." The nurse started to leave the small cubicle.

"Excuse me, but I'm late for work. How long will it be?" Deborah wanted to know. "I have a nine o'clock meeting and my boss needs that report." At the moment it was sitting on a straight-backed chair in the room, along with her purse and shoes.

"I'm sorry, Ms. Holland, but I don't know. It won't be long, I promise," the nurse assured her. "I'm positive you'll be able to leave as soon as the doctor examines you and sees to that injury."

"But—" Deborah paused in her protest, searching for the words to convince the nurse of the importance of the papers she had in her possession.

"Why don't I call your office and explain the reason for your delay?" the nurse suggested helpfully.

"Yes. Ask for Mr. Wilding, Zane Wilding." She felt slightly relieved by the offer. "He'll probably want to send someone over for these reports rather than wait."

"I'll call him right away," the nurse promised and left.

The minutes dragged while Deborah waited for the doctor to appear. The shock had worn off and her arm had begun to throb. She was sitting on the treatment table, her nylon-stockinged feet dangling over the edge, when she realized she still hadn't put on her shoes. Just as she slid off the table to remedy that, the doctor entered the room along with a nurse.

"Don't tell me my patient is planning to run away," he joked with a pleasant smile.

"I was just going to put on my shoes. I was in such a

rush when I left for work this morning, I forgot," Deborah explained, feeling a little ridiculous as she did.

"I wouldn't bother with them now"—he consulted the chart the nurse handed him before he added— "Ms. Holland. Have a seat while I take a look at your arm." He motioned toward the treatment table.

Favoring her left arm, Deborah inched her way onto the table again with as much grace as possible. The doctor unwrapped the temporary bandage that had been applied at the scene of the accident. Blood from the wound had already begun to dry on her skin.

"Messy, isn't it?" He grinned. "But I'll bet it isn't as bad as it looks." No comment seemed to be expected from Deborah and she made none.

The nurse brought him some towelettes and a bowl filled with a disinfecting solution. Deborah watched as he began cleaning the excess blood from her skin. There were several small cuts, but only one major laceration on the inside of her arm. The flow of blood had been reduced to a slow seepage.

"It's going to require a few stitches," he informed her. "First, we'd better make sure there aren't any glass splinters in there."

Working with professional efficiency, he probed the cut. Deborah winced several times, biting at her lower lip to check the gasps of pain. When the stitching was all done and the injury once again bandaged, the doctor leaned back.

"Any other aches or pains I can treat?" he asked in a half-joking manner. "You didn't hit your head, twist your back?"

"No. Nothing." Deborah shook her head. The movement started a shower of tiny slivers of glass that had been caught in her thick hair.

"You were lucky. You know that, don't you?" the doctor remarked. "If you hadn't lifted your arm, that broken glass would have cut your face more than it did." Glancing at the nurse, he ordered, "Bring me that bowl of antiseptic."

"My face?" She was suddenly conscious of a vague stinging sensation along her left cheek.

"Don't worry," he smiled. "It's just a few tiny nicks. The skin has barely been pricked. They'll be all gone in a couple of days."

His gentle, capable hands swabbed the pinpoints on her cheek. "How is the driver of the third car?" she asked.

"A broken leg, I understand." The nurse was the one who answered her question.

As the doctor finished, a movement in the doorway drew Deborah's gaze. "Zane," she breathed in astonishment, unaware she had used his given name. He entered the treatment room, making it seem smaller than it already was. Something flickered in his shattering blue eyes, but the glimpse was too fleeting for Deborah to identify it.

"Are you a relative?" the doctor was asking in his pleasant voice.

"No, I'm her employer."

"This is Mr. Wilding, doctor." Deborah would have introduced them but she couldn't remember the doctor's name or whether he had told her. Her initial shock at seeing Zane was receding, but her confusion hadn't. "What are you doing here?"

"The hospital called and told me about the accident."

If he had intended to say more than that, Deborah didn't give him a chance. "Of course, the meeting," she remembered. "Is it nine o'clock yet? The report is on that chair behind you. The first pages are a little smeared with blood. They should be retyped, but—"

"Her face, will it be scarred?" Even as Zane asked the question, interrupting her hastily prepared speech, his strong fingers were closing on her chin and turning her head so he could examine the left side of her face for himself.

The doctor was filling out paperwork and didn't object to what Zane was doing. His touch stopped her heartbeat before it went racing into a snare-drum roll. One of his fingers was on the pulse in her neck and Deborah wondered if he had felt her reaction to the unexpected contact. It made her feel hot and slightly giddy. She was relieved when the doctor finished with the clipboard and set it down.

"No. Those little cuts will go away in a day or two," the doctor assured him. "She did have a bad laceration on her left arm, but we've stitched that up. It'll give her pain for a few days, but I'm sure it will heal perfectly. She will have a scar from that."

A nerve twitched in his hard, lean jaw as his hand fell away from her chin. Deborah had trouble trying to breathe normally again. Zane appeared upset about something. If it wasn't because she was late for work, then she didn't know why.

"Is she free to leave now?" he demanded of the doctor.

"Yes. Here are a couple of prescriptions, one for an antibiotic to ward off any possible infection and the other is for a mild painkiller if it's needed." The doctor rose from his stool after handing two slips of paper to Zane, and smiled at Deborah. "Take care of yourself, Ms. Holland. Stop by the desk on your way out and the nurse will give you an appointment to have the stitches removed."

"Thank you." She returned his smile.

"Are these your things?" Zane turned to the chair behind him as the doctor and nurse left the treatment room.

"Yes." His efficiency and his serious expression disconcerted Deborah. "The accident wasn't my fault," she asserted just in case an accusation was forthcoming. "The other driver ran a red—"

"Yes, I know," he interrupted, picking up her shoes. "I've already received a full report from the police."

She reached to take her shoes from him, but he was already bending to slip them onto her feet. "I'll do that," she protested in a surge of self-consciousness. But a hand was already cupping her heel and sliding her foot into a shoe. The contact was oddly intimate, not at all resembling the impersonal touch of a shoe salesman.

"You're no Cinderella," he remarked in a dry, flat voice. "You managed to hang on to both your shoes."

That begged for a retort. "And you sure as hell are no Prince Charming."

As he straightened, an odd smile slanted his mouth. "Now you sound like yourself, Deborah."

Before she could guess his intentions, his hands were spanning the sides of her rib cage to lift her off the table, setting her feet on the floor. A crazy weakness attacked her legs. Deborah wavered unsteadily against him for an instant, aware of his hard strength and an elusive, masculine scent that clung to his skin. Then he was stepping away, blue eyes revealing nothing of his thoughts. Was it her imagination or had he held her a fraction of a second longer than was necessary? And why was she disappointed that his hands were no longer against her flesh?

Deborah gave herself a mental shake. This was all insane. Where were these silly, romantic notions coming from? Zane Wilding was a married man. She didn't want to become tangled in that kind of nowhere situation. Plus, despite his rugged good looks and all the money he had to play with, she didn't actually like him as a person. He was too hard and insensitive, totally lacking in compassion and gentleness. Deborah decided that the accident had simply knocked her a little more off balance than she had realized.

"If you're ready, we'll get you signed out of here." He handed the purse to her, but kept the report in his possession.

Assured that she had recovered her poise, Deborah nodded. "Yes, I'm ready." She took the purse he held out to her.

After they had made the appointment, Zane took charge of the details of her discharge, accomplishing the whole procedure at the desk in record time. Deborah recognized that his forceful personality was one few people would argue with and the clerical worker he was dealing with was no exception.

"My car is parked outside."

"What about my car?" Deborah remembered with a start, stopping halfway to the exit door.

His hand gripped her elbow to propel her forward. "It's been towed to a garage for repairs. Tom has already handled the details so you don't need to be concerned about it." He pushed the door open and held it for her.

"But—" Deborah felt compelled to assert herself,

"it's my car. I have to notify my insurance company and—"

"I told you that it has already been done."

Deborah walked toward Zane's sleek, neutral-toned Lexus. She would have stopped without the hand on her elbow. Instead of feeling relieved by his announcement, she felt confused and suspicious.

"But why did you do it?" she demanded. "It wasn't any of your business."

"On the contrary"—Zane unlocked the passenger side and helped her into the seat—"the fact that you work for me made it my business. We all help in time of necessity. It's called teamwork."

"And you call the shots." But he closed the door on her faintly sarcastic response and Deborah doubted that he had heard her.

It was an unusual experience to have Zane behind the wheel. Usually she or Tom drove, depending on which of them Zane wanted to confer with at the time. But there was no mistaking that the hands on the steering wheel were very strong, very competent, and very much in control—just like the man.

During the first few minutes of the drive, Deborah studied his masculine profile, the rakish thickness of his jet black hair, and the steel blue of his eyes, which he kept on the road. Her arm began to throb, distracting her attention. She shifted its position on her lap to relieve the stress of the previous one. Her glance noticed the report on the seat between them.

"What time is it?" she asked suddenly.

"Where's your watch?" His quick glance noticed the bareness of her left wrist.

"I left it on the dresser this morning." In her haste to leave for the office, she had forgotten all about it.

"It's a few minutes before eleven."

"The meeting! We missed it," Deborah realized in a voice that revealed her own feelings of guilt and frustration. "You haven't had a chance to go over the report. The first few pages really should be retyped. I don't suppose there will be time—"

"The meeting was postponed."

"That's a relief." Deborah relaxed against the gray velour upholstery, and released a sigh that quivered through her nerves, easing their tautness.

"How is your arm?" With a sliding look that was both sharp and impersonal, his gaze ran over the bandage before moving back to the traffic.

Something clicked in her mind. Deborah had been puzzling over his presence. His show of concern was for totally selfish reasons. How severely was she going to be incapacitated by her injury? How much would it interfere with her ability to do her job? Anger splintered through her.

"Don't worry, Zane." Her voice dripped with sarcasm. "It's my left arm. Since I'm right-handed, I'm still able to take notes and function quite capably at the meeting."

"I told you it had been postponed, but I forgot to add one very important word: indefinitely. I'm taking you to your apartment," Zane announced.

She flashed him a surprised and wary look. "It isn't necessary. I'm able to work and I know how important this meeting is."

His sharp gaze caught and held hers at a stoplight. "I can manage quite well without you. Contrary to your opinion, your services as my assistant are not indispensable."

Stung by his dismissal of the need for her presence,

Deborah faced the front, her pride just a little bit hurt. "I never suggested that they were." *Maybe a little.* Everyone liked to be needed and Deborah didn't consider herself an exception. She liked to think that her contribution was important, but Zane Wilding made it clear that such a belief was a fallacy.

"My God, I suppose your feelings are hurt," he muttered in an impatient undertone and shot her a look. "I was merely trying to point out that we can survive without your presence today. The accident was a traumatic experience, not counting the injury to your arm. I'm offering you a day off—with pay."

Obviously he thought he was doing her a favor. How much more receptive she would have been if he had only said, "Somehow we'll make it through today without you," or at least implied she would be missed. But Zane Wilding never needed anybody, she remembered.

"Thank you." She ground out the polite phrase through gritted teeth and lapsed into a tense silence that didn't end until he had parked in front of her apartment. When he started to get out of the car, Deborah objected, "There isn't any need for you to walk me to the door. I can manage without your help."

There was a split second's hesitation before he shrugged and remained behind the wheel while she stepped onto the sidewalk. The car remained parked at the curb. The skin at the back of her neck prickled as Deborah walked up the flight of stairs to her apartment door. He was watching her, waiting to see that she made it inside. She fumbled in her purse for the key and finally managed to unlock the door, but she didn't reveal her awareness of the car as it pulled away from the curb.

When the door was closed behind her, Deborah was overwhelmed by a feeling of release. She trembled violently and blamed it on the aftershock of the accident. Dropping her purse on the sofa, she noticed the red stains on her dress. If she intended to get them out, she had to do something about them right away. Unbelting her dress, Deborah walked into the bathroom and paused at the sight of her reflection in the mirror.

No wonder Zane hadn't thought her capable of a day's work. Her mahogany hair was rumpled without any semblance of style or order. She didn't look like the picture of smooth efficiency. A sheen of pain made her eyes shimmer strangely, without their usual confident glow. Turning her head sideways, Deborah examined the nicks on her cheek, marks that were barely visible even now.

With vivid clarity, she remembered Zane asking whether her face would be scarred. The firm clasp of his fingers seemed to have left their sensual imprint on her chin. She could still feel them. Why would he care if she had been left with facial scars from the accident? She had worked for him nearly six months, but he was still very much a mystery to her in many ways. Deborah shook her head. Where was it written that she had to know everything there was to know about the man who signed her paycheck?

She stripped off her dress, taking care not to jar her injured arm, and washed out the bloodstains with cold water. Wearing just her underclothes, she walked into the bedroom, feeling enervated and tired by all that had happened. She slipped between the covers of the unmade bed and rested her head on the pillow to doze.

Deborah wakened in the midafternoon because of the throbbing pain in her arm. It made her restless and on edge. Donning a soft robe, she ventured into the kitchen. She knew she should eat, but the cold sandwich she fixed tasted like cotton in her mouth. Cradling her left arm in her lap, she tried to read, but the paperback tale didn't hold her interest. She began prowling the room, holding her throbbing left arm against her body. It was a long time since she had so much free time to kill. There was housework to be done, even in her small studio, but the way her arm felt, doing it would only aggravate her discomfort.

She was fixing a glass of iced tea when the doorbell rang. The sound startled her. It was barely five o'clock, not the hour when any of her friends might stop by to see her. She was so rarely at home lately that most of them had stopped calling. But Deborah had been so busy it hadn't mattered. A puzzled frown clouded her expression as she crossed the room to open the door.

"Tom!" She blinked in surprise at the brown-haired man standing on her threshold. "I didn't expect to see you. What are you doing here?" Remembering her manners, she opened the door wider. "Come in."

"I stopped by to see how you are." He walked into the apartment, mild eyes smiling at her.

"I'm fine . . . considering," Deborah qualified the statement with an offhand shrug. "I'm glad you came by. I was just pouring myself a glass of iced tea. Would you like some?"

"Sounds good." As she walked to the kitchen counter, he glanced around, taking in the modern decor. "You have a nice place."

"Thank you." She handed him a glass of tea and turned to retrieve her own.

Tom noticed the way she cradled her left arm in front of her to relieve the pressure. "How's that arm?" He sipped at his tea, studying her over the rim of his glass.

"It aches." It felt as if it were swollen twice its size, which of course it wasn't.

"Have you taken the pain pills the doctor prescribed for you?" He must have guessed that she was understating her discomfort because his gaze narrowed in quiet speculation.

"No."

"Why?"

"Because I don't believe in taking pills unless I absolutely have to. How will I know when I'm healed if it never hurts?" Deborah asked defensively. The phone rang and staved off a disagreement for the moment. Setting the glass of tea on the counter, she lifted the receiver of the wall phone. "Hello?"

"Deborah?"

The rich timbre of Zane Wilding's voice vibrated through her. Her heart skittered across her rib cage to create a funny sensation in the pit of her stomach. The way he said her name made it sound different, not quite belonging to her. Coming from him, it was always Ms. Holland more often than not, especially if there were other people around. There was something decidedly intimate in the use of her first name.

"Yes." Deborah forced the word out after a breathlessly long pause.

"Has Tom arrived yet?"

She darted a look at the man in question. "Yes."

"Let me speak to him."

She couldn't acknowledge the order. Instead she

shoved the receiver toward Tom and announced tightly, "It's for you."

As he took the phone from her, Deborah reached for her iced-tea glass, needing something in her hands to hide her trembling. Zane could have at least asked how she was, she thought bitterly and realized she was feeling sorry for herself.

Her back was to Tom, but she heard him say, "Her color is good but she says her arm is hurting her. It goes against her principles or something to take the pain pills the doctor prescribed . . . I'll tell her," Tom said in response to whatever Zane had said.

The statement made Deborah turn around, curious to know what message he was supposed to relay to her. After that Tom's responses became monosyllabic. Yet the way he kept looking at her gave Deborah the impression the conversation was still focused on her.

When Tom hung up the telephone, Deborah attempted a nonchalant tone. "What was that all about?"

"Zane said he didn't care what your principles were. You're supposed to take one of those pain pills. As a matter of fact, he made it a direct order." Tom smiled in a bemused way.

"Because it's a direct order from him, that's supposed to make a difference?" she mocked.

"Because it's a direct order, you are supposed to do what you always do—obey it without question," he replied half joking and half seriously. "Honestly, Deborah, it will help you rest and relax."

"Maybe." She abandoned her iced-tea glass and hugged her right arm protectively over her left. Unhappiness crept into her voice. "But don't pretend that *he* cares how I feel."

"If you had seen him after the hospital called this

morning, you wouldn't say that. Zane was frantic," he insisted gently.

"Sure," she agreed acidly. "The accident meant the meeting was postponed. He had to find out whether he was going to be forced to find someone to take my place. I'm not indispensable, Tom. He made that quite clear."

"None of us is indispensable—not even Zane. I think you took whatever he said too personally."

"If I did, I certainly can't blame him, can I?" Deborah laughed and it was a derisive sound. "Nothing with him is ever personal. He must be the original iceman—with all his feelings frozen inside."

Tom swirled the liquid in his glass and watched the tiny whirlpool of brown tea. "These last few years Zane has been almost like a monk, and suppressed nearly all of his emotions. He seems hard, I know. Don't be taken in by the facade, Deborah. He cares, but he's blocked all the outlets that might let it show."

Her head was tipped to the side in an attitude that was both skeptical and intrigued. *He cares* was the last phrase she would have attributed to Zane. And the comparison to a monk? Please. There was so much raw virility about him that she couldn't even imagine his taking a vow of celibacy.

"Are you trying to tell me that—" Deborah began in scoffing amusement.

But Tom interrupted, crossing the room to the sofa. "I don't have to tell you about his marriage. I'm sure your imagination is vivid enough. But when Zane took the vows 'for better or worse, in sickness and in health,' he meant them."

His words led Deborah into a mental maze, a labyrinth of thoughts that didn't offer a quick escape. She was conscious of Tom picking up her purse and exploring its contents, but it didn't really register in her mind. He crossed the room to stand in front of her.

"Open your mouth," he ordered. When she did, he placed a white pill on her tongue and handed her the glass of iced tea from the counter. "Drink."

She washed the pill down without realizing what she was doing. Tom had shown her a new facet to her employer's character. And Deborah wasn't sure it was one she wanted to explore.

"Will you feel like coming to work tomorrow morning?" Tom asked.

"Yes. I'd rather be working than sitting around here." Her reply was absent but truthful.

"Your car won't be fixed until Monday, so I'll pick you up. Around eight?"

"That's late."

"So? Enjoy the pampering and stop complaining," he teased.

Deborah smiled, as he intended her to do. "Eight o'clock, then. I wasn't really complaining."

"Have you eaten?"

"A sandwich. Stale."

He grimaced at that. Her opinion precisely. "There's a great seafood place down the street. Why don't I go bring us back something to eat?"

"Sounds great." Much better than trying to eat alone.

It was eight o'clock that evening before Tom finally left. It had been a very enjoyable evening, too. Tom was easy to talk to, and witty when he wanted to be. Not one word about business had been spoken, which was definitely a novelty. The pain in her arm had been reduced to a dull ache by the time Deborah crawled into bed shortly after he'd left. She immediately fell asleep.

Chapter Five

Tom was sitting on the corner of her desk, in the middle of telling a joke. "This fire-and-brimstone preacher finishes his sermon with a cry that all the liquor bottles in every house should be taken to the river and emptied into it. Then he gives a baleful look at the congregation. He gives them instructions to rise and open their hymnals to number 201—"

Deborah anticipated the punch line and began singing, "Shall We Gather at the River." They both broke into laughter.

"You've heard the joke before," he accused.

"No, honestly, I haven't," she said. "It was just so obvious."

"It was, wasn't it?" he agreed and they laughed again.

At the sound of the door opening, Deborah glanced up to see Zane walk in. It was almost two weeks since the accident and her arm had healed nicely. The only lingering aftereffect was the funny, curling sensation in the pit of her stomach when he appeared without prior warning. It was happening now. His impassive expression wiped the smile from her face.

"I hope the two of you got some serious work done in my absence," he remarked in a solemn tone.

Tom turned, smiling easily. "Hello, Zane. I was just telling Deborah a joke I'd heard." He was explaining their laughter but not defending it.

The explanation didn't soften Zane's expression when he stopped at her desk. "When you're completely recovered and get back to business, bring me the geological study on the Sand-Sea project."

His attitude riled Deborah's temper. As he turned away from her desk, she muttered, "I don't know where you lost your sense of humor, Mr. Wilding, but I wish you'd find it."

He paused, half turning to give her a sidelong look of lazy challenge. "Would you like to suggest a place where I might look for it, Ms. Holland?"

She had expected him to ignore her comment. For an instant, she hesitated. He was her employer, but a little voice goaded her with the reminder that he had asked for a suggestion. She lifted her chin a fraction of an inch to meet his gaze.

"Yes, I would." Deborah smiled with taunting sweetness. "Try hell. A lot of strange people end up there."

"I have a busy schedule. It's your job to fit these little side trips in, Ms. Holland." It was impossible, but there seemed to be a glint of amusement in those usually cold blue eyes.

Tom laughed, knowing her remark had been successfully countered. "What now, Deborah?"

A suitable retort escaped her, but Zane negated the need for one by speaking first. "Now she can bring me that study. We have a lot of business to get out of the way before I leave for California, so be prepared for a long day." With the warning issued, Zane walked to his desk to begin work.

"No rest for the wicked." Tom sighed and straightened from her desk. "You know where to find me if you need me."

Deborah gave him an answering nod but didn't verbally respond. His office was hidden away in the accounting section. Over the months, Deborah had learned that Tom Brookshire was something of a mathematical whiz, an expert in accounting and computers as well as a fairly accurate economic forecaster. Plus he held a law degree, although numbers were his particular fascination.

As Tom left, closing the door, Deborah sifted through the stacks of papers, reports and notes piled on her desk. She never seemed to make any headway when it came to clearing it, only in shifting the papers from one stack to another. Thank God for the Find function on her computer or she'd have to quit.

However, despite the disorganized appearance of her actual desktop, there was a system to it. She found the geological survey report almost immediately and carried it to his desk.

Zane barely looked up when she set it in front of him. "Get Dan Adams on the phone for me, Deborah."

Her heart did a little flip. He was using her first name almost all the time now, influenced by Tom's friendly ways. It had happened a half dozen times since the accident, usually when it was just the two of them in the office. Coming at unexpected times, like now, it did funny things to her, ruffling her composure and throwing her momentarily off balance.

Deborah nodded. Since Zane wasn't looking at her,

he didn't see it. "Was there anything else, Mr. Wilding?" she asked, her voice sounding controlled and businesslike. She hoped.

This close, she caught the lingering scent of chlorine that the soap hadn't washed away after his noon swim in the pool. Deborah had never taken him up on his offer to indulge in an hour of exercise and sun on her lunch break. But there were times when she envied his invigorated glow after one of those sessions.

Zane didn't immediately respond to her question, finishing the note he was jotting on the margin of a report. He combed his fingers through his black hair, making it gleam like rumpled silk before lifting his head.

"Have you finished transcribing those notes on the environmental impact study?" he questioned with an absent frown.

"Mrs. Haines is inputting them now."

"I want to see them as soon as she's done." It was a dismissal and Deborah returned to her desk.

The streetlights came on outside the window, signaling the approach of twilight. Deborah was seated in a straight chair in front of Zane's desk, taking down his rapid dictation. He stuck to the old ways, claiming that staring into a computer screen all day made his eyes cross.

Whatever. He actually got more work accomplished than anyone she'd ever known. And true to his prediction, it was turning out to be a marathon day. Tom had stuck his head in twenty minutes ago to say if there was nothing more, he was leaving. Zane had waved him away with barely a pause.

The rumblings of her empty stomach were growing louder. Surely, Deborah thought, he could hear them and get the message. Her fingers ached from gripping the pencil so tightly to keep up with his rapid pace. Her concentration was wavering after the long hours she had already put in. Deborah found herself unable to keep up with him.

"Slow down a minute," she complained. He paused until her pencil stopped its scratching on her notepad, then started again.

He'd barely got the next sentence out when the door burst open. "I knew I'd find the two of you t-together!" a hysterical voice screamed in accusation.

"Sylvia!" Zane was on his feet, glaring angrily at the wild-eyed blonde weaving into the room, before Deborah had even turned around.

"Don't sound s-so outraged!" his wife mocked in a slurring voice. "I've finally caught you. Don't think for one minute I'm taken in by this innocent l'il scene. I know you've been making love to her. But you heard me coming and—"

"That's enough, Sylvia!" His voice was an explosion of anger that made Deborah cringe involuntarily, an automatic reaction to a very loud noise.

But Sylvia Wilding must have been too numbed by alcohol to feel the reverberating shock waves of his anger. "You can't fool me!" she screamed in a nearly demented voice. "Just look at her face." She waved a limp hand toward Deborah. "Sh-she's not so good at controllin' her emotions. Her face is red as a beet."

It was true. Deborah could feel the scarlet heat staining her cheeks, but not for the reason his wife was implying, not because it was true, but because of the disturbing picture her mind had just painted of her locked in a passionate embrace with Zane.

"If Deborah's embarrassed, it's because she'd prefer not to witness you making a fool of yourself," Zane snapped.

"A fool? Me?" his wife began.

"Yes! Open your eyes, Sylvia, if you can see through the haze of booze," he added contemptuously. "Does it really look as if I've been chasing my assistant around my desk? Are either of us out of breath? Are our clothes messed up?"

His wife looked from one to the other. She seemed to crumple before Deborah's eyes into a sobbing, tragically pathetic creature.

"You may leave, Deborah," Zane issued the stiff order. When Deborah didn't immediately move to obey, he barked out, "Now!"

Normally she would have made an attempt at straightening her cluttered desk, but this time Deborah just set her pad and pencil on top of some papers and grabbed her purse from a bottom drawer.

All the while Sylvia Wilding kept sobbing over and over again. "I'm sorry, Zane. Forgive me. Please, forgive me."

But as Deborah walked out of the office, he made no move to comfort the crying woman. He was still standing rigidly behind his desk. Deborah felt that old surge of resentment at his callousness and slammed the door. He had about as much compassion as one of his computers.

Halfway down the corridor to the exit, Deborah realized that she didn't have her car keys. They were lying on her desk in the office where she'd left them that morning. She'd have to go back for them. It couldn't be helped.

Reentering the outer office, she crossed the darkened room to the door of Zane Wilding's private office. As she turned the knob to enter, she heard the voices inside and hesitated. Sylvia's crying had been reduced to occasional hiccupping sounds.

"I need a drink, Zane." She sounded frantic. "Don't you have any whiskey in this place?" There were noises that suggested she was searching the desks and cabinets for liquor.

"You aren't going to find Ethan in any bottle." His voice was broken, almost more shocking than if he had shouted. "If you keep drinking, it will kill you."

"But don't you see—that's what I want! I want to die!" His wife cried. "I want to be with my son again! I want to be with Ethan!"

"You don't know what you're saying. Come on. I'm taking you home." The fury in his harsh tone was severely checked.

Deborah hovered indecisively. Should she make her presence known or would it be better to wait in the shadows until they had left? She backed a step away from the door, biting her lip as she tried to decide.

"Don't touch me!" Sylvia screamed. "I can't stand it!"

There was a crash and the sound of glass breaking. An eerie cry of terror sent shivers down Deborah's spine. From inside the room, she heard Zane's muffled curse.

"Dammit, Sylvia. Look what you've done!" he muttered savagely.

"It hurts, Zane," his wife whimpered.

"I'm surprised you can feel anything." His dry retort was particularly cutting.

Overwhelmed by curiosity, Deborah couldn't stand to remain outside not knowing what had happened. She didn't care whether her presence was wanted or not. She opened the door and stopped just inside the room. Zane was wrapping a handkerchief around his wife's hand, the white linen showing the red stains of blood. Sylvia was watching with almost hypnotized horror.

His blue gaze slashed to Deborah, pinning her where she stood. "What are you doing here?"

"I left my car keys on the desk. What happened?" She stared at him with accusation in her eyes. In her mind, she blamed Zane indirectly for whatever had happened. If he hadn't treated his wife so roughly, she wouldn't have become so hysterical.

"My wife cut her hand on some broken glass. It isn't serious." He finished wrapping the handkerchief and attempted to put an arm around his wife's shoulders. "I'll take you home."

But Sylvia cringed away from him. "No."

His impatience was almost tangible. "Help me get my wife to the car, Deborah."

It was a request she could hardly refuse since his wife was making it so obvious that she wouldn't let him near her. Slinging her purse over her shoulder, Deborah walked forward to speak to the woman calmly.

"Why don't you come with me, Mrs. Wilding?" she suggested. "We'll take care of that hand."

A glazed pair of eyes blinked at her with the innocence of a baby. "A drink," she asked in a small voice. "I need a drink, too. Can I have one?"

"Later, after we've bandaged your hand." Maybe it wasn't fair to make a promise like that, but Deborah didn't care. At the moment it seemed no different from promising candy to a child, although she knew it was. "Come along now."

She curved an arm around the blonde's shoulders and Sylvia didn't resist, but meekly let herself be guided toward the door. The unsteadiness of her legs made the woman lean heavily against Deborah. Her breath reeked of cheap whiskey. It was so potent it almost gagged Deborah. Zane walked ahead of them to open the doors.

At the car, he unlocked a rear side door. Deborah had to almost physically lift his wife onto the rear passenger seat. Sylvia roused from her stupor long enough to look around her and take stock of the surroundings.

"Where are you taking me? What's happening?" The forlorn thread of her voice sounded frightened and lost.

"Ssh," Deborah soothed and slid into the seat beside her. She couldn't abandon Sylvia to Zane's ungentle care. "It's all right. We're just going someplace to take care of your hand."

Reassured, the blonde cuddled up to her like a baby seeking the comfort of her mother's arms. Deborah rocked her, aware of the clenched fists of the man standing beside the car, but she didn't acknowledge his presence with a look. The closing of the door was followed by the opening of the driver's door as Zane slid behind the wheel.

Not a word was exchanged between Deborah and Zane during the short drive to his condo. Out of Sylvia's unintelligible ramblings, Deborah was able to understand only a word or two here and there . . . *my baby, Ethan,* and *a drink.* The woman had obviously never recovered from the grief of losing her only child. It was a grief she should have shared with her husband, but considering who her husband was, Deborah understood why Sylvia was shouldering it alone, and why she had broken under the strain. She glared her silent condemnation at the man behind the wheel.

When the car was parked, Deborah tried to rouse the woman in her arms, without success. The interior light flared as Zane opened the rear door. The blonde was snoring, her mouth open and her eyes closed.

"Wake up, Mrs. Wilding. We're here." Deborah shook her gently.

"Leave her be. She's out cold." Zane didn't make any attempt to keep the sharp impatience out of his tone. "Move out of the way and I'll carry her in."

Disentangling herself from the woman's arms, Deborah slid out of the passenger seat, lying Sylvia down carefully as she did. She moved out of the way to stand on the sidewalk while Zane reached into the backseat to drag his wife's limp body out. He shifted her petite form into the cradle he'd made with his arms, and kicked the car door shut. Although Sylvia was a small woman, her semi-conscious state had to make her seem much heavier. But Zane strode up the sidewalk as if she weighed no more than a child. Deborah followed him, since it seemed the logical thing to do.

Zane paused beneath a lighted doorway and pushed a buzzer. Within seconds, the summons was answered by a gray-haired woman in a black dress that resembled a uniform. His housekeeper, Deborah guessed. The woman took one look at the blonde in his arms and immediately swung the door wide to admit them.

"Madelaine called. I'll phone her back and tell her Sylvia is here," the housekeeper stated.

There was an acknowledging nod from Zane. While the housekeeper scurried off into one of the rooms and closed the door, Zane carried his wife across the short entryway and up a flight of stairs. Deborah hesitated at the base of the stairs, wondering if she should go up to help. At that moment, the housekeeper came bustling past her to climb the stairs. Obviously she wouldn't be needed, so Deborah waited below.

After nearly twenty minutes, she was just about convinced they had forgotten she was down there waiting. Her stomach began growling hungrily again. She told herself not to complain. Her problems just didn't seem all that important compared to what she'd just seen. But oh, what she wouldn't give for a nice hot cup of coffee.

A footstep on the stairs spun her around. The housekeeper descended, her relatively unlined face an impassive mask that rivaled her employer's ability to conceal his thoughts.

"I phoned for a taxi. A cab is on its way to take you home," she informed Deborah.

Deborah stared at her wordlessly until she realized that she wasn't going to receive any thanks or expression of appreciation for her help in getting Mrs. Wilding home. She wasn't even going to be told how Sylvia was.

"I'll wait for it outside," she said and pivoted to cross the entryway to the door.

She was deeply upset by what she'd seen and how she'd been treated herself. The coolness of the night air had no effect on her overwrought state. Stalking like a caged tigress, she paced back and forth on a small square of sidewalk in front of the condominium. A few minutes later, a taxi pulled up in front. Deborah didn't wait for the driver to get out to open the passenger door, but climbed into the back unaided. She gave him the address of the office building and began rummaging through her purse for a mint. Anything to ward off starvation. The little plastic box was empty when she finally found it.

"Excuse me." She leaned forward to tap the driver on the shoulder. "Do you happen to have a mint? I know that sounds weird, but I could sure use one right now."

"Sure." He handed her back a roll of Livesavers. He glanced in the rearview mirror and watched the jerky, agitated movements as she ripped the silver foil and popped one out. "Let me guess. You had a fight with your fella, and you're going to go back and kiss and make up, so you want to freshen your breath."

"Wrong." She exhaled an irritated sigh. "I had a fight with my boss. Well, it was sort of a fight." Deborah sucked on the mint, feeling a little childish.

"What's the matter? Doesn't he pay you overtime?"

"Oh, he pays." Her voice was husky from her effort to calm down. "He just forgets to say thanks."

"I know the feeling, lady," the cab driver said, and made no further attempt to continue the conversation.

When they stopped in front of the office building, Deborah leaned forward to pay him.

"Naw. The fare's taken care of . . . and I'll add a generous tip for myself." He winked and climbed out to open her door. "Don't work too hard."

"I won't." She gave him a tense, absent smile as she stepped out of the cab.

Her car keys were still on her desk in the office. Pausing beneath a streetlight, Deborah searched her purse for the office keys to get into the locked building. She found them immediately and hurried up the sidewalk to the front entrance. Good thing she'd memorized the security code. She punched it in on the numbered pad and waited for the all-clear beep. Inside, her footsteps echoed hollowly through the empty corridor.

When she reached the private office, Deborah stopped inside the door to turn the light switch on. She started to cross over to her desk, but her glance strayed to the play of light on the broken pieces of glass scattered on the carpet. Since she was there, she decided that she might as well clean it up rather than leave it until morning.

Setting her purse aside, she walked over to Zane's desk and bent down to pick up the fragmentary remains of the crystal vase. Deborah started with the bigger chips, taking care not to cut her own hand on the sharp edges. The wastebasket stood in a corner. She emptied a handful of glass into it, then carried the basket over to where the rest of the broken glass lay. The crystal fragments made a faint ringing sound as she tossed them into the metal container.

The sound of the door opening startled her. Deborah straightened to whirl around, not certain whether she expected to confront a security guard or an intruder. But she certainly hadn't expected to see Zane. His piercing look, bothered her.

"What the hell are you doing here? How many times do I have to send you home before you get the message?" he snapped.

Of all the ungrateful, arrogant—Deborah closed her

mind to all the adjectives she could have used to describe him. "I stopped to get my car keys and decided to clean up this mess."

"Oh—"

She wasn't going to let him get another word out. Her simmering temper finally came to the boil. "And thank you very much, Deborah, for helping me with my wife. It was so thoughtful and considerate of you to ride with her." Her mocking singsong included all the simple words of gratitude he should have said. "I hope it wasn't too much trouble. You must be tired after the long day at work, Deborah. Why don't you go home and get some rest?" Deborah paused to take a breath and change to a sweetly demure voice. "I will do that, Mr. Wilding. In fact, I'll be leaving in just a few minutes."

He waited in grim silence as if expecting her tirade to continue.

"Are you through?" he challenged when it didn't.

"Is that all you can say?" She gazed at him in astonishment. Not a thing she'd said had struck home. Recognizing that it was hopeless to ever expect him to admit he was wrong, Deborah turned away and answered his question before he could respond to hers. "Yes, I'm through . . . for the time being anyway." She needed the release of doing something to vent all the negative energy her anger had generated. "But working for you, I'm sure there will be other occasions when I will lose my temper," she finished, tossing the ever smaller crystal fragments into the wastebasket.

"You're right. I didn't thank you for your help tonight and I should have," Zane began in a hard, tight voice, but he ultimately lost control. "Will you leave that damned glass be, and get off that floor? I'll clean it up myself!"

Deborah half turned but she didn't rise; her eyes were blazing. "Please," she prompted.

"What?" A dark frown gathered on his forehead. He seemed to be at a loss as to her meaning.

"*Please* leave the glass, and *please* get off the floor," she stressed with forceful emphasis.

"Oh, for God's sake." He turned his head to the side, muttering in exasperation. When he looked back at her, it was to issue a taut, "Please," with an insolence that was about as impolite as a person could get.

For a fleeting second, Deborah wondered if she were trying to teach manners to a jungle panther. The glitter in those eyes of his was actually menacing. Straightening, she brushed nervously at her skirt before again meeting his look.

"That's much better." Her smile was tense. "People generally react more favorably when other people are nice to them. Everyone needs a kind word now and then. Maybe if you had been a little kinder to your wife tonight instead of being so hard with her, she wouldn't have become so hysterical. She needs—"

One second, half the width of the room separated them. In the next, Deborah found that her shoulders were caught and she was being pulled against a wall of muscle. The impact made her catch her breath.

"She needs!" The mask had been removed from his features, revealing an anger that had been bottled up too long. "What about what *I* need? Ethan was my son, too!" A fiery anguish burned in his eyes as they searched her face, which he kept close to his. "Where was she when *I* needed her? Why did I have to be strong for both of us while she was protected and sedated from the reality of his death?"

"I didn't know," Deborah whispered. Never once had she considered the depth of his pain, but she saw it in his face. He looked like a wounded animal lashing out. His fingers were digging into her soft flesh, but she didn't cry out or struggle against his hold. "I'm sorry, Zane." And she meant it.

"It's always *her* needs, but there are things that I want, little things that should be so easy to provide." His low voice took on a different intensity that vibrated through Deborah's body. "A pair of eyes to look into that are clear and bright, instead of glazed by booze."

The blue force of his gaze was utterly compelling. Deborah was shaken by the impression that he could see deep inside her, all the way to her soul. The brilliance of his look seemed to blind her to all other sensations, including the hands that loosened their grip on her shoulders to glide down her backbone and mold her to his length.

"I want a body against mine that isn't limp from drinking for hours. I want it to be firm and alive." The husky murmurings of his voice seemed to awaken her flesh to the roaming caresses of his hands, exploring her waist, hips, and spine with sensual thoroughness.

She spread her fingers across his chest in mute protest to the reactions that were taking place inside her. The taut, muscled lines of his thighs were pressing against hers, inflaming her with their hardness. The heat coursing through her gave Deborah the feeling she was too weak to withstand this sensuous onslaught. Desires that had been dormant for so long—in both of them—were roaring back to life.

"And . . ." Zane paused. Her heartbeat quickened as his gaze lingered on her mouth. "I want to kiss lips that don't taste like alcohol."

His fingers touched the sleek bun at the back of her neck, then took apart its tidy smoothness. He held her head still, as if he expected resistance, while his mouth descended to claim her lips. He devoured them hungrily, savoring and exploring, plundering their softness. Deborah felt her appetite rising to the fever pitch of his. Common sense told her to stop, warning her of the danger of this much emotion, this much need.

A war waged inside her between flesh and spirit. Zane's overwhelming dominance of her nearly pushed the scales to the physical side, promising a wild, delirious joy. Her mind fought through the heady sensations to argue—after the joy would come bitterness.

He was *married*. To a deeply troubled woman. Their son was dead, but his memory would always bind Sylvia and Zane together. Deborah couldn't pick up the pieces of their shattered lives, not in a million years.

If only . . . If only . . . Never mind the *if onlys*, she told herself fiercely. Zane wasn't going to stop. Deborah realized this might be her only chance to keep this scene from reaching its climax—if that's what she wanted to do. No. It wasn't what she wanted.

"Zane, listen to me. If and when you're free— it won't be because of me. Do you understand what I'm saying?" She fought back the tremors that threatened to make her question weak. Her voice wasn't very strong, but its tone was level. "It isn't going to be one of my duties, like making coffee for you in the mornings."

She felt him grow rigid. It took all her control not

to wind her arms around his neck and encourage the embrace. But she knew her decision was the right one, even if it left her empty and aching inside.

Abruptly Zane released her and turned away. Her legs almost refused to function without the support of his, but she managed to remain standing. His back was to her. Deborah could see the harsh rhythm of his breathing as he struggled for control. She wanted to reach out to him, touch him, but she didn't dare. Bending his dark head, he rubbed the back of his neck in a gesture that was weary and a little dispirited.

"You'll have to forgive me for that." There was a trace of hoarseness in a voice that was otherwise level. "I forgot myself for a moment and remembered only that I was a man."

"No, you're just human . . . like the rest of us," Deborah offered quietly, because she, too, had nearly yielded to the sweet temptation of his arms.

"Good night, Ms. Holland." It was an icy dismissal.

But at least he hadn't told her to forget what had happened, Deborah thought as she picked up her purse and walked to the desk for her car keys. It would have been impossible to forget. Leaving the office for the darkness of the rest of the building, Deborah realized that she didn't regret what had happened. She knew now what Zane had been through and recognized the sheer loneliness of his existence without love and without passion. Zane was hard, yes, but he was also very human.

Chapter Six

"I'm crazy about the polka, aren't you?" Foster Darrow declared, his beefy face even redder than usual after the fast-stepping dance.

"I guess so." Deborah was out of breath and trying hard not to pant, after the unaccustomed exertion. The heat in her face warned her that her cheeks were flushed, too. She could feel tendrils of hair curling damply around her neck, having escaped the coil of hair atop her head. She was badly in need of a few minutes to get her breath and freshen up. "Would you excuse me, please?"

"Of course," the financier grinned.

Deborah angled away from the path that would have taken her to the table where Tom and Zane waited. She didn't care what business discussion went on in her absence. She would have been too exhausted to pay attention anyway.

Tonight's meeting was very important. Foster Darrow would tell Zane whether he would bankroll the latest LaCosta project. Most people thought big money decisions were made in large boardrooms or an attorney's office. That was only where the fine details were worked out. The committing of funds was more often done over, say, a lobster dinner and champagne. It was a lesson Deborah had learned very quickly.

In the luxurious powder room, Deborah sank onto one of the velvet-covered stools in front of the long vanity mirror. Her ribs ached from the bear-hugging of the heavyset financier. She reached for a tissue in the decorative holder and pressed it against her skin to absorb the thin film of sweat on her forehead, cheeks, and neck.

Her hair was a mess, little wisps sticking out all over the place. Sighing, Deborah began pulling out the bobby pins and shaking the long copper tresses free. One more polka and it would happen anyway, she reasoned, so why fight it? She took the small comb from her evening purse and arranged her hair into a semblance of a style.

The few minutes of inactivity slowed her heartbeat to a more normal rhythm. Deborah reapplied her lipstick and leaned back to survey the repair. Her mind flashed back to that first dinner with Foster Darrow so many months ago. His wife and daughter had been along that time.

After all these months of talks, dinners, cocktails, and endless negotiations, it was going to be settled tonight. She was nervous about the outcome. The project wouldn't necessarily fail without Darrow's financial backing, but they would have to wine and dine someone else and more time would be lost.

Zane was tense, too. Not that he showed it. But Deborah had gained valuable insight into her employer that night he fell apart. She no longer accepted what she saw on the surface, but kept looking for the man.

In critical situations, such as tonight, she'd discovered that he had a tendency to smile with just one side of his mouth. It was an action that always made him seem aloof—or like he didn't give a damn. She suspected that he really didn't. Zane rolled high for the thrill of gambling. He liked the danger, the excitement and the risks of big business. He had poured his whole life into it, because there was nothing left for him outside of it.

It was a sad fact. He had an empty marriage. Deborah didn't pity him, because he wasn't the kind of man a person would pity. Neither he nor Sylvia was to blame for what had happened. Deborah realized that. From the very little she had gleaned from Tom on her first encounter with the unbalanced side of Sylvia Wilding, it seemed that Zane's wife had never been emotionally stable. The loss of a child, their only child, had been more than she could take. Not even Zane's strength had been enough to help her through it. That wasn't his fault. It wasn't anybody's fault, which was probably the hardest thing to accept of all.

Zane's poignant declaration of his needs echoed back to her, as they had done many a night since the one when he had whispered them to her a month ago. Deborah remembered her disbelief at Tom's mention of his monklike existence. Zane's murmured yearnings had confirmed it, though. But his studliness was so at odds with vows of celibacy and fidelity, that she had continued to doubt. She was ashamed to admit— even to herself—that she had engaged in some discreet snooping before she was finally convinced.

His personal address book contained no phone numbers or names that weren't directly related to business or relatives. He'd handed her his personal bank statements for the past year to find any possible deductions his accountant might have missed. No flowers, no jewelry buys, nothing. Every source she checked revealed there weren't any women—on either a permanent or temporary basis.

Deborah gave herself a mental shake. She had promised herself she wouldn't think about things like that, especially his love life. He was her employer and he was still married . . . and that was the end of it. Zane had successfully managed to ignore the incident. He hadn't forgotten it, though. That was something she knew instinctively—and that there were times he watched her when he didn't think she knew.

Two women entered the powder room chatting noisily. At least they seemed noisy after the silence of her thoughts. Their intrusion served to remind her that it was time she went back to the table.

Rising from the stool, she smiled distantly at the two women and left the powder room. Deborah wound her way through the crowded lounge to the table where the three men sat. They didn't see her approach until she was standing beside her chair. Belatedly, all three attempted to stand, but she shook her head and told them to stay where they were.

"With your hair down like that, you look like a girl ready to abandon herself to another polka," Foster Darrow declared.

"It was simpler than trying to pin it up again," Deborah admitted, aware of the glance from the man next to her inspecting her changed appearance. The look was almost a physical touch, but she did her best to appear oblivious to it. "As for the polka, it'll have to wait. I'm really thirsty."

"Dancing does do that to ya," the financier agreed with a hearty laugh.

"Would you like a soft drink?" Zane leaned forward to ask the question. Deborah nearly jumped when she realized his hand was on the back of her chair. The accidental brush of his fingertips against the bare skin of her back sparked an immediate tingling of her flesh.

"No, this is fine," she insisted and reached for the watered-down gin and lime.

"It looks kinda flat. Want a swizzle stick?" The financier offered her one from the holder on the table and pointed it at her like a spear. "What's the matter with the men your age, Deborah? You're beautiful and smart, ya know. Some man should have dragged you home to his cave and married you a long time ago."

The hand had been removed from her chair. Deborah leaned back, striking a pose intended to appear casual and unconcerned.

"No cavemen for me, thanks. I guess I've never met a guy who put the thought of marriage in my mind." Not quite true. There had been one, but only one. Her gaze moved to Zane and moved just as quickly away from his veiled look. She leaned forward to take the swizzle stick and stirred her drink.

"Gotcha." Foster smiled. "You're doing fine on your own, so you don't actually need a man. You're happy with your life as it stands."

"I wouldn't go so far as to say that." Her natural honesty wouldn't permit it. "In the mornings when I have to wake up alone and fix my breakfast alone, and sit down at the table alone—well, that's the time when I'm lonely as hell."

As she spoke, Deborah finished stirring her drink and set it aside. She didn't really want it. The man sitting beside her probably hated the way it smelled, even if it was watered down. An inner force compelled her to look his way. She was trapped by a bright blue flame of understanding. It caught at her breath, stealing it from her.

She tried to deny the havoc his gaze was creating in her, and attempted to joke. "Of course, since I've been working for Zane, I haven't had time to sit around the breakfast table feeling sorry for myself."

There was that crooked smile, that slanted lift of his mouth. "No, you generally wait until you get to the office to have your coffee and Danish."

"Now you know my secret." Deborah laughed, but there was a tightness in her throat.

"Personally I can't eat when I first get up in the morning," Tom said and successfully broke the spell that had locked Deborah's gaze to Zane's. "I always have to wait a couple of hours."

"So do I," Foster agreed. "Now, my wife, she wakes up and immediately eats a gargantuan breakfast. I don't see how she does it."

The conversation digressed into a discussion of eating habits with Foster Darrow and Tom being the main participants. When Deborah agreed with Foster that bacon was too good for vegetarians, the financier guffawed and slapped the table. Then he excused himself, mopping his red face with a napkin first.

Tom darted her a conspiratorial grin. "Maybe I should go bribe the band *not* to play another polka." Like Deborah, he had guessed where Foster Darrow was going and for what purpose.

"I don't mind," she shrugged in resignation. "You know what they say—keep 'em happy. That's my job."

"Not really, Deborah. You don't have to schmooze

or drink or do anything you don't want to do." Zane's voice slashed apart the lighthearted atmosphere, its low, rumbling tone almost ominous. "Just say no. Darrow can be pretty demanding."

"I didn't mean that literally," she replied, just a little angry that he thought she was the type that would let herself be used in that way. "You should know that I'm capable of saying no."

Unconsciously Deborah had forced him to recall the night she'd rejected his advances. Even in the dimness of the lounge, she saw him grow pale at her reminder. His sensual mouth thinned. She had struck a raw nerve that hadn't healed for either of them, and she regretted her words.

"And you were right to do so," Zane snapped.

His usage of the past tense caused Deborah to dart a quick glance at Tom to see if he had caught it. Foster Darrow chose that moment to return to the table and Tom had already been distracted by his approach. Deborah couldn't tell if he'd heard Zane's slip.

As the financier stopped beside her chair, the dance band struck up yet another polka. "Woo hoo! They're playing our song, Deborah," the man joked.

To escape the table and the sudden tension between her and Zane, Deborah placed her hand in the one the financier proffered and rose to dance with him. She even managed a bright smile as she agreed, "So they are."

When the rambunctious dance ended and the financier escorted Deborah back to the table, Zane began to press for a decision. At first, Foster Darrow brushed off the mention of business during a social evening, regardless of its actual purpose. Deborah worried that Zane's timing was wrong, but within minutes the financier was enmeshed in the details of the project. He didn't even notice when the band played another polka.

Her concentration wavered and Deborah missed the point in the conversation when Foster actually said yes. The next thing she knew Zane was reaching in front of her to shake the financier's hand and clinch the deal. Dazed, it took her a few minutes to realize what had happened.

Elation at their victory was just surfacing as Zane got up from the chair. "It's been a long day, Foster. I still haven't adjusted to the change in time zones. I'm sure you'll understand if we call it a night. Tomorrow is going to be even busier, flying back and getting all the necessary papers drawn up."

"I agree. It is late." The financier stood.

Tom was already standing, which left only Deborah seated. Belatedly, she rose, too. A hand settled on the curve of her waist possessively. She didn't mind. Its warmth told her in advance that it belonged to Zane. Ostensibly his touch was innocent enough—to guide her from the lounge—but it sent a little pulse hammering in her throat. She was much too physically aware of him, all because of that one incident, and Deborah knew it had to stop.

"Good night, my polka princess." Foster Darrow clasped her hand in his pudgy fingers. "Be sure to have Zane bring you along the next time we meet."

"Of course," she murmured. "Good night."

The financier walked with them to the elevators in the hotel lobby. After a promise to be in touch within the next couple of days, he left and the elevator doors swished closed to carry them to their suite of rooms. In total silence they made the ride to their floor. Deborah was bewildered by the lack of even mild jubilation.

Zane unlocked the door to their suite. It rivaled a spacious apartment in size. Besides three private bedrooms, there was a living room and dining room combined and a kitchenette tucked in a small alcove. Deborah remembered one of the first business trips she'd taken with Zane, and her initial discovery that she was supposed to sleep in a bedroom in the same suite of rooms as Zane and Tom. At the time, she had wondered if she should request a private room on a different floor. All it took was one marathon session of paperwork that lasted nearly all night—complete with room service hamburgers and five laptops—for her to appreciate the advantages of staggering from one room into the next to fall into bed. Besides, neither Tom nor Zane was much of a night owl.

The hotel room door opened into a living room with luxurious furnishings and a thick carpet. Zane walked in and slipped the hotel key in his pants pocket. Deborah followed him, with Tom bringing up the rear. No one said a word.

"Why so silent?" Deborah finally burst out in disbelief. "Darrow said yes. Shouldn't we be celebrating or something? The way you two look, anyone would think he said no."

Zane didn't even acknowledge her comment with a glance, but Tom took the trouble to at least look at her blankly for an instant. Then a wide grin split his face.

"Shall we polka?"

It was such a ludicrous suggestion that Deborah could only stare at him in amazed confusion. Before she could protest, Tom was swinging her into his arms and swirling her around the room in a crazily exaggerated imitation of Foster Darrow, minus the loud accordions. His wild sense of humor—he seemed so mild-mannered most of the time—had Deborah reeling with laughter.

"Stop, please," she begged, laughing so hard that she could barely breathe. When he had twirled her to the front of the apricot-colored sofa, he stopped to let her collapse on the cushions. "You're insane, Tom," Deborah declared as she wiped the tears from her eyes.

"Didn't you enjoy the dance?" He assumed an expression of mock regret, but the mischievous twinkle in his eyes trumped it.

"You probably sounded like a herd of stampeding elephants to whoever has the room below us," Zane remarked dryly.

"How can you say that?" Tom chided. "My partner is as light on her feet as a ton of concrete."

"Thanks a lot," she protested and lifted the mane of copper hair away from her neck, letting the coolness of the air conditioning reach her damp skin.

"We're a little too matter-of-fact about Darrow's agreement," Tom said, sobering unexpectedly. "I guess Zane and I were thinking about all the work ahead of us, and everything that has to be put in motion now that we definitely have a commitment on the financing."

"You're right," Zane agreed. "So is Deborah. We should be celebrating. Since it's too late for room service, why don't you go down to the kitchen, Tom, and talk the night crew into making a platter of sandwiches and snacks. See if you can score a bottle of Dom Perignon while you're at it."

"Excellent suggestion," Tom said with alacrity.

"Here." Zane handed him some bills. "Just in case anyone needs persuading."

"Right." He started for the door. "I won't be long. Keep the party going until I get back!" With a cheery wave, he walked out of the hotel suite.

His departure exposed an undercurrent of electricity in the atmosphere that Deborah hadn't been aware of before. Now she felt it tingling along her nerve ends. The few seconds of silence that followed ticked loudly in her head. Her gaze swerved from the door to meet the unfathomable blue depths of Zane's eyes. He held her look for an instant, then turned to walk casually to an oak credenza along one wall of the living room.

"For once your outspokenness did some good," Zane commented. "If you hadn't said something about celebrating, do you know what we would be doing now?" He slid her a lazy, sidelong glance, accompanied by a half smile that turned all her insides topsy-turvy.

"No." She shook her head, wishing she didn't feel so wary.

"We would probably be sitting at that table"—he nodded in the direction of the polished oak table in the formal dining end of the room—"and mapping out the completion schedule for different phases of the project, discussing permits and a hundred other details. Instead we all get to kick back for an hour or so, get some rest, and be fresh to tackle everything in the morning on the flight home."

"I hadn't thought about it like that."

"No, you followed your instinct. It was the correct one."

Deborah heard something click before Zane turned

away from the credenza. He had taken several steps toward her before she heard the music and realized he had turned on the radio. By then he was standing in front of the sofa.

"Since Tom said to keep the party going until he returned, will you dance with me if I promise not to ask you to polka?" His joke took the seriousness out of his invitation.

What would he do if she said it was too dangerous to be in his arms, she wondered frantically. But how could she refuse when she had been the one to suggest they celebrate in the first place? No, Deborah knew she had to brazen her way through this moment as if she didn't care.

She forced out a laugh. "I'm holding you to that part about the polka. Anyway, sure. I'll dance with you."

Straightening from the sofa, she let herself glide smoothly into his arms, pretending a nonchalance she didn't feel. This time Zane didn't hold her at arm's length, but neither did he hold her close. Still, Deborah felt the erotic charge of the powerful body so close to her own. It became essential to talk and not let the romantic music weave a dangerous spell around her.

"Tom continually amazes me," she declared. "On the surface he seems so quiet, but he's really a lot of fun, too. I'm probably not telling you anything you don't know, right? You and Tom go back a ways, don't you?" Talking about Zane's good friend seemed safe enough.

"Yes." He ran his gaze over her brightly upturned face. "You really like him."

"Who doesn't?"

"Mind if I ask you a personal question?"

"I—I guess not."

"I'll get right to the point then. Are you and Tom having an affair?"

Deborah's first reaction was a startled, "What?" She followed it with an emphatic "No!"

"Is it so impossible?" His mouth quirked in a cynical line. "You're both unattached. You work together almost constantly. It would be natural for an attraction to spring up between you. Tom really admires you. I have the impression the feeling is mutual."

"Maybe so, but it's not what you seem to think," she said stiffly.

"But you aren't attracted to him?"

Her gaze was focused on the air beyond his shoulder. Feeling really steamed, she flashed an angry look at his face.

"If I was, would you suggest to him that he should sleep with me or something?" she accused.

Deborah couldn't ignore the nasty suspicion that Zane was trying to steer her to Tom to avoid her becoming romantically attracted to him. It was totally unfair since he was the one who had made the advance the previous time. She had never encouraged Zane to believe she found Tom sexually attractive. It angered her to think that Zane might believe she was yearning after him.

The humiliating thought made her attempt to twist angrily out of his arms. "That isn't what I meant at all!" Impatience surged through his clipped response as he immediately tightened his hold to keep her from escaping.

The pressure he applied got her back into his arms, close to his chest. The contact caught both of them off guard. Their dance steps ceased as Deborah's head was tipped back to let her startled gaze be captured by his possessive look. She was arched against his hard flesh and bone, stunned by his raw masculinity, and . . . ready for more.

"Zane." His name came from her lips in a voice that was half fearful and half wanting.

A muffled groan shuddered free of his throat as he lowered his head to savor the softness of her lips with his mouth. It was a slow, exploring process that melted her hesitancy. He coaxed her lips apart with very sensual skill.

Her hand left his shoulder to curve into the virile thickness of his midnight-black hair and force his head down so she could know the full possession of his kiss. She was crushed to him, male hands igniting flames of excitement on the soft curves they caressed. She felt his mouth moving over her face, demanding and relentless, tantalizing and seductive by turns. Deborah pressed her hips more firmly against his thrusting thighs—needing, wanting, aching with the same passion as his.

Not really thinking, Deborah didn't analyze the right or wrong of her actions. She was dominated by the pure sensual impact of the embrace. The potent, masculine smell of him enveloped her senses. His mouth, hands, and tongue made her whole body weak with desire.

Call it lust. The feeling was intense, almost consuming. Neither one heard the door being unlocked or opened. Tom's voice was cold water on the flaming embrace.

"The refreshments are served—" His announcement was abruptly broken off at the sight of them locked together, even as his words ripped them apart.

Deborah blushed scarlet under his shocked look. For a moment, nobody spoke or moved. Then Zane took a step forward, putting himself between Deborah and Tom.

"I hope you brought some champagne, Tom," he said in a remarkably even voice. "I think we all need a drink."

"Yes." Tom's voice was shaky at first, but gradually gained strength as he wheeled the serving cart into the room. "You betcha I have champagne. There's a tray of sandwiches here, too. Chicken salad, cheese, and ham. Tortilla chips and guacamole."

Deborah almost wished Tom had asked all the questions she knew were buzzing in his head, but he was taking his lead from Zane and pretending he hadn't seen anything out of the ordinary. *God,* she thought wildly, *they don't really expect me to eat or drink anything, do they?* But Zane was already taking a cocktail sandwich from the tray and biting into it while Tom popped the cork on the champagne bottle.

"What will you have, Deborah?" Zane asked, shooting her a meaningful glance to see if she had recovered.

At least he hadn't referred to her as Ms. Holland. Deborah thought she would have broken into hysterical laughter if he had. She made her way over to the serving cart draped with a white linen tablecloth. She remembered some old saying about chalk and cheese.

"Cheese, I guess." Her hand trembled slightly as she took the little larger-than-bite-sized sandwich from the plate. It tasted like chalk when she bit into it. Then Tom was putting a champagne glass in her hand. She briefly met his eyes and saw the flash of concern in his gaze before he looked away.

"Here's to the new project." Tom lifted his glass in a toast.

They all clinked their glasses together and Deborah tried hard not to let her gaze linger on Zane's strong, male hand and his oh-so-businesslike shirt cuff. It was harder, still, not to remember that same hand had been caressing and molding her hips to his, only moments ago. The devastating force of his touch was still vividly with her.

The next twenty minutes became a farce. Everyone talked about the project and the successful financing arrangements, but no one said a word about what was really on their minds. What remained unspoken filled the suite with a tension that scraped at Deborah's nerves.

Tom refilled his champagne glass and grimaced after taking a sip. "Bleaggh. This is gone flat."

"So has the party. We're all tired, so why don't we call it a night," Zane suggested.

"Yes." Deborah was quick to agree. "We have to be up early in the morning so we can pack and fly home." She set her glass down, catching out of the corner of her eye the look Tom divided between them. She didn't give his suspicions a chance to form as she turned and tossed a careless goodnight over her shoulder and walked directly to her private bedroom.

After closing the door, Deborah didn't bother to turn on the light. Instead she undressed in the darkness and slipped into her cotton nightgown. Tom's self-consciousness had been so obvious. She knew he had been wondering if she was going to sleep with Zane. She had no one to blame but herself for the direction his thoughts had taken. Deborah was well aware that she had been a very willing participant in the passionate embrace that Tom had walked in on. If he hadn't returned when he did, she had the uncomfortable feeling that she might have been even more embarrassed.

Where was her self-control? She had always been so levelheaded, almost never getting carried away by her emotions. That sure as hell didn't describe her behavior tonight. Zane Wilding was not only her employer but he was also a married man. What had possessed her?

As she climbed into bed, she heard the doors to the other bedrooms open and close. She stared at the ceiling. It wasn't going to be easy to sleep tonight, not the way her conscience was troubling her. Especially not knowing that Zane was in the next bedroom.

Her arms felt so empty. Turning onto her side, Deborah pulled the spare pillow to her and wrapped her arms around that. It was too soft, not at all like the hard, male torso she ached to hold. She closed her eyes tightly and a hot tear squeezed out through her lashes.

Chapter Seven

Room service arrived with three orders of a continental breakfast fifteen minutes after the wake-up call. Deborah took her coffee, juice and Danish into her bedroom to have while she finished her packing. Zane and Tom would have theirs at the table, but she wasn't ready to face them. Besides, she had noticed the faint shadows under her eyes when she'd put on her makeup, an obvious betrayal of her sleepless night. Secretly, she hoped the coffee and orange juice would have a reviving effect and chase away those shadows before anyone noticed them.

She drank her orange juice while she packed her cosmetics in their cute little bag. The coffee was still too hot so she ate half of the Danish and threw the rest in the wastebasket. She was folding her clothes and placing them in the suitcase with meticulous care in order to prolong the whole process of packing, when there was a knock at her door.

"Who is it?" She paused, feeling something flutter in her stomach.

"It's Tom. May I come in?"

Deborah hesitated only a second before responding with an offhand, "Of course." She heard the click of the latch, but she didn't turn around.

"I called downstairs for a bellboy," Tom said, walking into her room.

"You can help me close my suitcases in a minute. I'm almost finished." She continued with her packing, smoothing the material of a skirt she had just put into her suitcase.

"Deborah."

Something in his tone made her mentally brace herself. The muscles in her stomach knotted with tension as she held her breath. She wished fervently that Tom would leave.

"Yes?" Deborah tried desperately to appear casual as she gave him a brief glance over her shoulder before resuming the folding of her clothes.

He cleared his throat a little nervously. "I don't normally butt into anybody's private life," he began.

"Then don't start now," she retorted, much more sharply than she'd intended.

"This time it's different. It involves two people I care about a lot."

"Tom, don't." Deborah stopped pretending to fold the slip in her hands and clutched it tightly against her middle.

"I know this sounds like a line out of some old movie, but if I ever had a kid sister, I think she would have been like you. And I wouldn't be much of a big brother if I didn't warn her when I can see she's heading for trouble."

Her eyes were so dry they hurt. "Tom, honestly, I know you mean well and I'm flattered that you care about me, but I don't need a big brother. I—"

"Don't fall in love with Zane."

The blunt warning turned Deborah around. "I haven't." *Not yet anyway,* she qualified the thought.

"He'll never leave Sylvia. Not for you. Not for anybody." The sadness and firm conviction in his brown eyes reached out to her.

Deborah felt cold, icy cold inside and hopelessly empty. "I think I guessed that." Her voice wavered into a whisper.

"Don't get involved with him," Tom warned again. "His marriage to Sylvia will only tear both of you to pieces. You'll both be worse off than before."

"Yes," she swallowed the lump closing her throat. "I think I guessed that, too."

From the vicinity of the living room, there was the sound of someone knocking on the door to the hotel corridor. Zane called from another room. "Tom, that's the bellboy. Let him in."

"Right!" Tom shouted back, but paused to look at Deborah. "Are you okay?"

"I'm fine," she insisted. "I'm a big girl. I've weathered storms like this before. I can do it again."

"Chin up," he instructed with a lopsided smile and walked out of her room to answer the door.

The private Lear jet was streaking across the sky, too high to cast a shadow on the Grand Canyon as they flew across. Thunderheads billowed in the Rockies to the north, but the sky surrounding the jet was clear and the eastern horizon ahead was sapphire blue. The air was smooth. The only turbulence in the atmosphere was inside the plane.

Tom was seated at a desk in the customized interior

of the private jet, running numbers on his laptop. In a cushioned armchair, Deborah was editing a series of memos on another laptop, to be sent to the various department heads when they arrived at the corporate offices later on. Each reference to Mr. Wilding that appeared in the memo caused her pencil to hesitate on the paper. It was caused by the wincing of raw nerves.

"How are you coming with those memos?" Zane stood beside her chair.

Her head moved toward him, but not all the way, avoiding contact with his gaze. Deborah tried her professional voice. "I have two left." It worked. Good for her. "Did you want to brainstorm alternatives for the environmental impact report? I can finish these later."

She didn't immediately get a response as he turned the chair in front of her around so that it was angled toward hers instead of away. As he folded himself into it, she couldn't help noticing the absence of his suit jacket and tie. The white of his shirt was stretched across his chest, hinting at the rippling muscles that bunched beneath it. Her pulse skittered in an erratic tempo. Taking his action as an affirmative answer, Deborah flipped open her notepad and set it by the laptop, just in case he had ideas he wanted to sketch out.

"The efficient Ms. Holland." The grimness of his voice sounded awful. Her startled gaze lifted to meet the hard glitter of his eyes. "Hair pulled back in that prim bun. Crisp and collected. Butter wouldn't melt—"

"I wear my hair like this to keep it out of the way when I'm working," she began.

"It looks better loose," Zane interrupted, a muscle working in his jaw.

Oh God, she didn't want to know that. Taking a breath, Deborah glanced quickly down. He had leaned forward in the chair, which brought his face much too close.

"As for my tone of voice, I can't really help that. And I get to wear my hair the way I want to." She was assertive but she kept her gaze firmly downcast. "So. Let's concentrate on those alternatives."

"Deborah." His low voice carried a trace of exasperation along with a silent plea. But she refused to respond to the tug on her heartstrings. She wasn't that easy. Determinedly, she kept emotion out of her expression, aware of his searching gaze. At last, Zane let out a long sigh. She saw him flex his hands on his knees, then lace them together.

"Tom gave you a brotherly lecture this morning, didn't he?" Something in his voice said he knew the answer. Perhaps Tom had already admitted as much to him.

Deborah didn't see any point in denying it. "Yes, he did." She kept her tone very matter-of-fact.

"Tom is an intelligent, perceptive man. His counsel is always rock solid. I've rarely known him to be wrong. He never gives advice unless he knows what he's talking about."

Zane seemed to be hammering his point home. A numbness inched through her at the invisible blows. She managed a terse, "I believe that."

Keeping her gaze averted from his face, Deborah wished he would get to the point and quit torturing her with all this talk that she didn't know how to take. If he wanted to get a message across to her, why didn't he just come right out and say it?

As if reading her mind, Zane asked a husky question. "Are you going to take his advice?"

Stunned by his unexpected frank question, Deborah's gaze rose to his face. She couldn't answer him. She just couldn't.

His features became taut with the strain of control. "Stay away from me, Deborah . . . for both our sakes."

Before she could respond to that devastating command, he was swinging out of the chair and striding across the carpeted floor of the aircraft. Resentment flared through her. How dare he put the burden of that on her? She had never been the one to make the first move. She had never flirted with him or invited his advances. Why was it her responsibility to make sure it never happened again? She was *not* trying to lead him astray.

Tom intercepted her glare and sent her a quizzical look. Deborah quickly avoided it, pretending she hadn't seen it and stared at her laptop screen, not focusing on the memos she had been writing. She tried to bring her concentration back to the task, but she wasn't very successful.

Skimming the previous page of the report, Deborah checked to make sure she hadn't omitted any facts as she combined three department studies into one overall view. She flexed her shoulders and back tiredly and felt a prickling sensation along her spine. She guessed the cause, her sensitive radar signaling its awareness of Zane's gaze on her.

In a quick, sidelong glance, she took note of the figure behind the large oak desk. Zane was leaning back in his chair, making no pretense of working. A haunting grimness shadowed his features and the wintry steel of his eyes. The emotional strain of pretending there were no turbulent undercurrents between them was more than Deborah could take.

"Will you quit watching me?" she said with annoyance, fixing her frowning gaze on the notes on her desk.

"It's after five. You can finish drafting that report tomorrow. Go on home."

That dreaded coldness in his voice was back. It cut to the bone. Once she had worked until well after dark, but since that flight from California, Deborah began working banker's hours. No more late nights. No more slaving away until well after everyone else in the building had gone home. Only twice had she stayed late, and both times Tom had been there to act as a chaperone.

Deborah wanted to argue against Zane's order to leave, but she invariably lost those battles. Instead, she reached down to pick up the slim, feminine briefcase she had recently purchased.

"I'll finish this draft tonight at home." Snapping open the case, she arranged the papers and notes inside and put away her laptop.

"It isn't necessary." Zane rolled out of his chair with a leashed sort of fury, even though his voice was controlled. He walked to the small closet and removed her coat. "I'm not sending you home to work. You should be going out on a date."

He held her coat to help her into it. Deborah hesitated, then slipped her arms into the sleeves. "Maybe I should, but I don't happen to have a boyfriend or a lover to take me out."

It was a stiff, almost curt response. As he slid the

coat onto her shoulders, his hands paused and began a kneading caress that made all her defenses melt. Deborah closed her eyes to savor the feel of his touch. All her sexual and emotional frustrations surfaced with a powerful yearning to fall into his embrace.

"I think we're kidding ourselves," she declared in an aching whisper. "I should hand in my resignation and get as far away from you as possible."

"No." It was a choked protest.

At the ring of the phone, Deborah wrenched out of his hold to answer it, grabbing the receiver as if it were a lifeline. "Hello. Mr. Wilding's office." She heard the strained pitch of her voice, but there wasn't anything she could do about it now.

"Deborah?" her mother's voice responded. "Is that you?"

"Mom!" Her startled recognition was followed instantly by alarm. "Is something wrong?" Deborah had never known her mother to call her at work before, so her first thought was that there was some emergency.

"Yes. I haven't talked to you in ages." The maternal voice held a note of reproof. "Since you're always at the office working, I decided if I wanted to hear your voice, I'd have to call you there."

"Actually I was just leaving to go home to my apartment."

Her eyes strayed to Zane, but he had turned his back to her although Deborah knew he was listening. Would she have been on her way home if her mother had called a few minutes later? Somehow Deborah thought it was a question that she would never know the answer to. That charged minute when his hands had held her was gone forever.

"Do you have any idea how long it's been since I heard from you?" her mother asked.

"Didn't you get the check I sent you this month?"

"Oh, yes," her mother said, "I received the envelope from you with the check in it, but there wasn't even a scrawled note in it saying, 'I'm fine.'"

"I'm sorry, Mom, but I've been . . . very busy."

"Is something wrong, Deborah?" In the shrewd question there was concern.

"No, of course not," Deborah denied that quickly.

"I know there is, but you obviously feel you can't talk to me about it. You must be having man trouble. Well, I guess you're old enough to work out your own problems, especially personal ones, so don't worry. I won't pry."

"Thank you." Deborah didn't make any more of an admission than that.

"The main reason I called was to let you know that your brother Art has leave over Thanksgiving."

"Really? That's wonderful!" And her pleasure was genuine.

"Unfortunately I can't get any time off over the holidays, but I don't have to work the weekend before Thanksgiving. I thought we could have our family dinner on Sunday. Sarah and Barney can come then. Art plans to spend the Thanksgiving weekend with his girlfriend in Boston. Can you come?"

"I'm sure I can make it. It'll be so nice to see Art. What about Ronnie?" Deborah asked about her other brother, also in the air force.

"He couldn't get the time, but he has his fingers crossed for Christmas. I'd love to talk longer, Deborah, but since you are on your way home, I'm sure you don't want to stay around the office much longer in case your slave-driving boss finds you something else to do to keep you later."

"You are so right." Partly, anyway. "I'll be there the Saturday before so I can help you with dinner."

"If you patch up your differences with your man friend, bring him along."

"Don't count on that, Mom. See you."

"Take care."

As Deborah hung up the phone, she turned to find Zane watching her. "I take it one of your brothers is coming home. Or is Art an old boyfriend?"

"My brother. He has a furlough over Thanksgiving, so we're all getting together for a family dinner the Sunday before." She didn't know why she was telling him.

"The weekend after next."

"Yes." *So soon*, she thought.

"You can have the Friday before off."

"There's no need," Deborah started to protest.

"It'll give you time to pack whatever clothes and belongings you'll need for a month." Her mouth opened at the statement but Zane didn't give her a chance to ask where she would be going for a month—or why. "Instead of reporting back to work here on Monday morning, you can go directly to my country place. Here are the directions." He ripped off a sheet of paper from the scratch pad on his desk and crossed the room to hand it to her.

"Your country place?" Deborah looked at the directions blankly. "But why there?"

"Since my marriage, I always spend the holidays in the country. I don't see any reason to alter that tradition at this point in my life. Everything in this office will be transferred and we'll carry on our business as usual from there. A room is being prepared for you in the guest wing, since it's impractical for you to drive back and forth. It's as spacious as your apartment. You'll have maximum privacy while you're there." He paused in his explanation to cast a cool glance in her direction. "Meals will be provided. Any questions?"

"Not if you don't." The two of them under one roof for a month would be flirting with danger. Deborah knew it. Zane had to, as well. But if he was prepared to take the risk, she wasn't going to appear weak by running.

"Okay." He turned away and walked back to his desk. He never gave her another glance as he said, "Good night, then."

Tight-lipped, she didn't return the salutation as she gathered up her briefcase and purse and walked out of the office. This strictly-business routine was a farce. One of these days it was going to blow up in their faces. Deborah had the feeling the explosion wasn't very far away.

It was ten o'clock that evening before she quit working on the report she was compiling. It was a demanding task, even with a computer, to organize data from three sources into a comprehensive and highly detailed summary. When the document on the screen began to blur, Deborah knew she had worked too long. But it had kept her mind off more disturbing subjects—like her boss.

Tense from all that concentration, she filled the bathtub with hot water and scented bubbles. She had barely relaxed in the luxury of a leisurely bath when the telephone rang. Deborah listened to the first half dozen rings and tried to be the kind of person who could ignore the telephone. On the eighth ring, she gave up the attempt and sloshed out of the tub to dash to the kitchen wall phone. She didn't even stop to grab a towel, thankful she had closed the drapes previously.

"Hello?" She picked up the phone and waited for a response. When none came, she swore angrily at the unknown person who had hung up. "Damn!" But as she started to slam the receiver back on its hook, Zane's voice came over the line.

"Hello?"

The anger went out of her with a rush. "Yes."

"I didn't get an answer so I started to hang up, thinking you were gone," he stated.

"I was taking a bath," Deborah explained, a little of her pique returning. "The trail of bubbles dissolving on my carpet would prove that."

His sharp intake of breath came clearly over the line. "Dammit to hell, Deborah! Why did you have to say that?" Zane muttered.

"I wasn't trying to be provocative, *Mr.* Wilding." She gave him a taste of his own formality, paying him back for all the times he had squelched her and gotten all corporate. "Why did you call?"

"Did you work on that report this evening?" At her yes, Zane informed her that there were two points that he wanted covered in detail. He went over them briefly, and asked if she had any questions.

"No. I believe I've already gone over the specific areas you mentioned," she said, matching his crisp tone. "But I'll check to be certain. Is there anything else?"

His pause lasted no longer than a heartbeat. "No. Nothing."

"Then good night." It felt pretty good to be the one who dismissed him for a change. She heard his clipped goodbye just before the receiver settled onto its hook.

The evaporating bathwater had raised goose bumps on her skin, the scented bubbles drying and dissolving on her body. Shivering, Deborah hurried back to the bathroom. The water was only lukewarm. She rinsed the film of dried bubbles from her skin and toweled herself dry. There was nothing left to do but go to bed.

Chapter Eight

The directions Zane had given her were easy to follow. It was midmorning when she saw the black iron and red brick fences that marked the roadside boundary of his Connecticut estate. On one side of the road were pastures and the plowed ground of open fields. Beyond the grillwork barrier there was the rolling expanse of a lawn splattered with the bright autumn colors of fallen leaves.

Red brick pillars towered on either side of the entrance. The scrolled iron gates stood open, as if waiting for her. Deborah followed the road that led through the trees to end in a cul-de-sac driveway in front of a Colonial-era manor house. The sprawling two-storied house was built of red brick with white window and door casings. The front entrance was an impressive portico with white columns.

There was a narrow driveway branching off the cul-de-sac that apparently went to the rear of the house. Deborah debated whether she should take it, and decided instead to park in front of the house for the time being. She had barely stepped out of the car when the large white front door opened. A dark-haired woman in her late thirties stepped out. Dressed casually in slacks and sweater, she walked to the head of the short flight of steps leading to the porticoed entrance to greet Deborah.

"Hello. You must be Deborah Holland." The woman's smile was quick and ready, but there was a no-nonsense quality about her that earned Deborah's immediate approval. "I'm Madelaine Hayes."

Madelaine. Deborah remembered Zane mentioning that name, and always in connection with his wife. She climbed the steps and accepted the hand outstretched to greet her. Looking into the darkly intelligent eyes, Deborah had the feeling she was going to like this woman.

"Yes, I am. And I'm glad to finally meet you. Mr. Wilding has mentioned you many times."

"But you don't know exactly who I am." Madelaine Hayes guessed shrewdly.

"No," Deborah admitted with equal candor.

"I suppose you could say I do a lot of things around here that no one else can do. My main responsibility is to look after Mrs. Wilding. I'm a psychiatric nurse." She studied Deborah closely for a reaction to that announcement. When there wasn't one, she continued with hardly a break. "I also supervise the housekeeping, just to keep everything running smoothly for Zane."

Briefly Deborah wished she could refer to him with such casual familiarity, but there wasn't anything casual about their relationship. She preferred to change the subject rather than respond.

"Should I leave my car parked there or drive it around to the back?"

"Leave it there. Frank—my husband—can drive it around to the garage after he's carried your luggage in." Madelaine dismissed the need for Deborah to move the car with a shrug of her shoulders. Guessing that Deborah probably didn't know her husband's role, she explained, "Frank manages the farm for Zane. Come on. I'll take you inside and show you your room." She turned toward the door she had left standing open. "Did you have any trouble finding the place?"

"None at all. Mr. Wilding's directions were precise."

"They usually are. Do people call you Deborah or Debbie?"

"Deborah. I never got called Debbie, even when I was little." Deborah crossed the threshold into the formal entryway of the manor house.

She looked around her with interest. The marble floor was enhanced by the rich luster of the hardwood wainscoting. Instead of the clutter of antiques that Deborah had expected, the foyer and wide hallway were simply furnished. Nothing detracted from the restored beauty of the house.

"I didn't have a nickname either. But what would they have called me? Maddy?" Madelaine Hayes shuddered expressively.

A hand-carved, solid walnut door opened onto the foyer. Deborah turned toward the sound just as Zane stepped out. But he was a different Zane than she had seen at the office. Instead of the expensive suit and tie he usually wore, he had on a ribbed sweater and ripped-up, it's-the-weekend-and-I'm-going-to-relax jeans that hugged his muscular thighs. So blatantly virile, this new Zane had an immediate and devastating impact on her senses. He stopped abruptly when he saw her. His expressionless face brightened and she saw a flash of fire in his blue eyes. Much too quickly the look was gone.

"Hey. Got here safely, I see." He didn't actually seem to care all that much one way or another.

"Yes." Her heart gave a sickening lurch. It felt almost like Zane had slammed a door in her face.

"I was just taking Deborah to see her room," Madelaine explained. "I hope you aren't planning to put her to work until after she's had a cup of coffee and a chance to relax after that long drive. You and Tom can hold the fort for a little while."

Deborah envied the brunette's ease in asserting herself. True, she wasn't exactly meek herself, but she lacked Madelaine's capable ease. But obviously Madelaine had known Zane longer than she had. Plus she was married, which meant she didn't have the inner conflict of emotional attraction.

"Report in an hour—is that okay with you?" Zane made a show of consulting his watch.

"Sure," Deborah said. When in Rome, do as the Romans do: obey the emperor. She was really tempted to say it out loud.

"I won't let her get lost trying to find her way back to the study," Madelaine promised. "Do you want something?"

"Yes. Have Jessie bring us some fresh coffee." He started to turn to reenter the room he had just left when his wife's voice stopped him.

"Why wasn't I informed that a guest had arrived?" Sylvia spoke from the hallway, drawing all eyes to her.

A puzzled frown knit Deborah's forehead as she watched the petite blonde walk toward her. Sylvia Wilding held herself so stiffly, so erectly, putting one foot precisely in front of the other as if walking a tightrope, all the while facing straight ahead.

It wasn't until she heard Zane mutter under his breath to Madelaine, "Where the hell did she get the whiskey this time?" that Deborah realized the woman was drunk and trying very hard to not let it show.

"I don't know," Madelaine whispered back to him. "She must have some hidden that I haven't found yet."

"Welcome." Sylvia carefully walked to Deborah, ignoring her husband and Madelaine. "I'm sorry I wasn't here to greet you when you arrived."

"That's quite all right, Mrs. Wilding," Deborah assured her.

At the sound of her voice, uncertainty flickered across Sylvia's expression. "I have the feeling I should know you." She wore no makeup and there was a sickly yellowish cast to her skin. Her eyes, glazed with drink, darted to Zane. "I should know her, shouldn't I?"

"This is Deborah Holland, my assistant," he introduced them again.

"Oh. You aren't a guest then." She seemed to give up her pretense of sobriety and swayed unsteadily.

Madelaine was instantly at her side to put a supporting arm around her waist. Her attitude now was strictly professional. "I'll help Sylvia back to her room. Will you show Deborah where she will be staying?" she asked Zane.

"Yes." A nerve twitched near his eye, but it was the only indication that he wasn't pleased by the request. Without looking at her, he ordered, "This way," and started down the hallway.

Deborah had difficulty keeping up with his long strides, but she refused to ask him to slow down. Doors stood open along the way. She had a glimpse of a formal living room and a Tiffany lamp above a polished dining-room table. Zane made a right turn to guide her into a different wing of the rambling house.

"You have a beautiful home," Deborah remarked, liking what his swift pace allowed her to see.

"Fourteen years ago it was a home. Now it's just a house." His voice was hard and cold, rejecting her praise. He stopped and pushed open a door. "This will be your room while you're here." He stepped aside to let her walk in, but didn't follow her inside.

When Deborah realized that, she stopped and half turned. "Thank you for taking the time to—"

But he cut her off. "If you want some coffee, the kitchen is the second door after the right turn. I'll expect you in the study in one hour."

"Yessir!" Her temper flashed at his flint-hard attitude.

He didn't react, just walked away. After he'd gone, Deborah stood in the center of the room looking at the empty doorway. "Damn you!" The curse was barely a whisper.

Turning from the door, Deborah forced herself to look at the room. It was spacious, with a color theme of pale lavender and blue. Besides a double bed and dresser, there was a sofa, armchair, and a small desk. Near the window stood a small, circular table with two chairs. Of the two doors in the room led to a large bathroom, and the second was a walk-in closet.

"Hello." A man's voice called attention to his presence in the doorway. A tall, spare man smiled as he nodded to the suitcases he carried in his hands—her suitcases. "I would have knocked, but—"

"Come in. Let me help you." Deborah hurried forward to take one of the smaller cases he was juggling. "You must be Frank."

"That's right." He walked into the room and set her luggage on the floor. "I see Zane abandoned you to explore on your own."

"Yes." She liked the friendly, open expression on his thin face. No need to talk about dismal things with a nice man. She changed the subject. "This is a lovely room."

"The best we have. Zane insisted on that." His eyes flickered curiously and she realized she'd tensed up at the second mention of Zane's name.

"That was thoughtful of him." Deborah was stiff. She knew it, but she couldn't seem to make herself indifferent to the guy.

Frank Hayes tipped his head to the side in a studying manner. "We knew Zane had a new assistant, but he never mentioned you were . . . so pretty. To be perfectly honest, we were expecting someone with thick glasses and about forty more pounds." He grinned.

"I'm still pretty intelligent." She tried to respond to his humor.

"So. Did Zane give you a rundown on the layout of the house?" he asked, turning his attention to more serious matters.

"He told me where the kitchen was so I could get some coffee."

"The house is U-shaped and the hallway runs the full length of it upstairs and downstairs," Frank explained. "All the rooms open onto the hall. You'll get confused by the number of doors, but just keep opening them until you find the right room."

Yikes. That could get interesting.

"All the bedrooms are on the wing sides," he continued. "There are only two rooms on this side that are occupied. Yours and Jessie's. Jessie is our cook and takes care of the house, along with some day help. Madelaine and I have our bedroom in the other wing where she can be close to Sylvia. Naturally, Zane's room is on that side. So is Tom's."

"I see," she murmured.

"There's a courtyard inside the U, and a heated swimming pool beyond it that we keep open all year."

"But what about when it snows?" Deborah gazed at him incredulously.

"As I said, it's heated. It's a real hoot to go swimming when there's three feet of snow on the ground," he admitted.

"It must be," she agreed, intrigued by the idea.

"Be sure to try it while you're here." Frank started toward the door. "I'll be putting your car in the garage behind the house. You can't miss it. It's the only building behind the house."

"Thanks for bringing my luggage in."

He shrugged away her thanks. "See you at lunch."

Deborah adjusted quickly to her changed environment. Everything from the office—every file, report, and memo—had been transferred to the large study, in hard copies and disc files for the computers here. Before the first day was over, she had everything organized and at her fingertips. The study was large enough to hold desks for her, Zane, and Tom, with room left over.

Tom's presence helped to lighten the atmosphere, and the heavy workload helped assure that her attention wouldn't often get a chance to wander in other, dangerous directions. Everyone in the house, with the occasional exception of Sylvia Wilding, ate

together, which offered a further buffer between
Deborah and Zane.

By the time Thanksgiving morning dawned, Deborah had settled in so comfortably that it seemed as if
she had been at Zane's country house longer than
three days. Although it was a legal holiday, Deborah
worked in the morning—as did Zane and Tom.

The feast wasn't served until one o'clock. The
formal dining room table was set with the best crystal,
china, and flatware. The centerpiece was a fruit-filled
cornucopia. It was a lavish feast complete with stuffed
turkey, sweet potatoes, two kinds of vegetables, three
salads, and homemade rolls.

"Two Thanksgiving dinners in one year. You are
lucky, Deborah," Frank remarked as he took her plate
and passed it to Zane who was carving the turkey.

"Yes, I am."

"What's your family doing today?" Tom asked, helping himself to a cranberry-orange salad.

"My mother is working. My brother is visiting his girlfriend in Boston, and my sister is with her husband's
parents."

"I'm glad you're with us," Madelaine said. "Nobody
should have to spend the holidays alone."

"Do you prefer white or dark meat, Deborah?"
Zane asked the question. While in the company of
others, he adopted their habit of using her given
name, but his cool tone kept her at a distance just the
same.

"White, please."

"Ethan always wanted the drumstick. Remember,
Zane?" The thin but oddly melodic voice of Sylvia
Wilding, who hadn't spoken since she sat down at the
table, brought an instant silence into the room.

The carving blade hovered above the browned breast of the turkey. A muscle tightened in Zane's jaw as he resumed the carving. "Yes, I remember."

"Most little boys do like the drumstick best," she continued with a dreamlike expression in her haunted eyes. "Ethan never could eat it all, of course, but we always gave him one. Did I tell you I saw Anna Blackstone the other day, Zane? Her little girl, Susan, was the same age as Ethan. She's eighteen now. She's very pretty. You wouldn't recognize her."

"No, I probably wouldn't," he agreed without looking to the opposite end of the long table at the unhappy woman who was still his wife.

"Have some sweet potatoes, Sylvia." Madelaine attempted to divert the conversation.

Sylvia didn't even see the casserole dish that was offered to her. Deborah's heart twisted at the forlorn look that passed over the drawn features.

"Ethan would be eighteen if he was alive." Her watery eyes focused their pain on Frank Hayes, seated on Sylvia's left. "I miss him. I miss my baby." Her voice broke on the last word. As if in pain, she clasped her arms across her stomach and began to rock gently back and forth in her chair. "I miss my baby so," she whispered over and over, her voice growing softer each time until finally only her lips were moving.

Madelaine pushed her chair from the table. The grimly resigned look she cast at Zane indicated to Deborah that the incident was not unusual. Probably more the rule than the exception. The brunette excused herself from the table and walked to Sylvia's chair.

"Come with me, Sylvia." Madelaine took hold of the rocking shoulders and helped the small blonde up.

"I'll help you," Zane offered grimly, setting down the carving knife and fork.

But Madelaine shook her head in refusal. "It's better if you don't come, Zane."

His jaw tightened, but he didn't argue. Deborah gained the impression that Zane's presence somehow upset his wife. She remembered Sylvia's strident command that summer night long ago, that Zane was not to touch her.

In a low voice Frank told his wife, "If you need me, just call out." Madelaine nodded a mute acknowledgment as she guided Sylvia out of the dining room. Sylvia's lips continued their silent movement. She appeared to be in a trance.

Everyone's appetite seemed to vanish with Sylvia's departure. They went through the motions of eating, but no one did justice to the excellent fare before them, the incident casting a shadow on the feast of Thanksgiving. Afterward, Zane apologized to Jessie, the gray-haired cook.

"Ahyah, it couldn't be helped," she agreed in her hard New England drawl. "But it's just that many more meals you're going to be having of turkey stew and casserole and turkey sandwiches."

No one complained about that.

On Sunday of that Thanksgiving weekend, Deborah wandered into the informal morning room where everyone usually breakfasted. Only Madelaine was at the white table, sipping a cup of coffee.

"Good morning," she greeted Deborah with a quick smile.

"Good morning. Where is everyone?" Deborah sat

in one of the white matching chairs, facing the window that looked onto the courtyard.

"Frank went to church. Zane is swimming, Tom must still be in bed. Coffee?" She held the spout of an insulated coffeepot above an empty cup.

"Yes, thanks. How is Mrs. Wilding this morning?" She hadn't seen Sylvia since Thanksgiving Day.

"She's talking again, but her depression is so deep." Madelaine sighed. "It's pitiful."

"Yes," Deborah fully agreed, then mused, "It's unfortunate they didn't have more children."

"She would have been incapable of raising them. She can't even take care of herself."

"I understand, but it's sad. Maybe she would have gotten over Ethan's death if they had." In a way it hurt to say that, but it was on her mind so she said it.

"After Ethan was born, Sylvia couldn't have any more children. Frank was working for Zane then. He's told me how obsessive Sylvia was when it came to her son. She didn't want to let him out of her sight even as a baby. Zane had to force her to go out in the evenings without Ethan. It's a tragic irony that Sylvia was the one who was supposed to be watching Ethan when he drowned accidentally."

"Does she blame herself for what happened?"

"Yes, I suppose so." Madelaine shook her head, staring into the black surface of her coffee. "She had made Ethan her reason for living. When he died, I think she stopped caring about anything else."

"Even Zane," Deborah murmured.

"Yes, even Zane. A year after Ethan died, Zane tried to convince her that they should adopt a child. By then she had already started hitting the bottle. There wasn't any agency that would let them adopt a child when the mother was an alcoholic and probably bipolar. But Sylvia refused to discuss it with him. To this day, she won't even look at or talk to another child. She won't even acknowledge that they are in the same room."

"I suppose she thinks she would be betraying her son's memory if she let herself love—or even like— another child," Deborah suggested and sipped at her coffee.

"Possibly," Madelaine conceded. "She is an alcoholic, but her problems are much deeper than that. I really have to admire Zane for the way he's stood by Sylvia, never hating her for what she has done to herself and him." Her brown gaze slid to Deborah. "He is committed to her. You do know that?"

Stiffening, Deborah knew exactly what that look and that remark meant. "I've been warned about that before—by Tom, then Zane, and now you. Who's next? Frank?" Her question was tinged with amused bitterness. Obviously she wasn't very good at concealing her attraction to Zane.

"I hope you aren't going to pay any attention to those warnings," Madelaine's response was unexpected. "Zane needs someone like you. He can't keep living without loving anyone. And I . . . I don't think that look I see in your eyes every now and then is one-sided."

"Maybe not." Deborah's smile was jerky and wry. "But, as everyone has pointed out, there is no future in it."

"No one who is aware of the circumstances would condemn you or Zane for having an affair," Madelaine insisted. "As a matter of fact, every one of Zane's friends would approve of any woman who could bring happiness into his life. He deserves it, if anyone does."

"Yes. Although I've never pictured myself in the role of the 'other woman.'" Deborah wasn't able to meet Madelaine's gaze, but it was a relief to be able to discuss her feelings indirectly.

"Deborah"—Madelaine clasped her hand and squeezed it with comforting reassurance—"love is a blessing, not a sin. Knowing Zane, you wouldn't be the 'other woman.' You would be the only woman."

"I wish . . . " But Deborah couldn't find the words to express what she was feeling.

"I know." The brunette laughed to break the serious atmosphere. "You wish I would shut up so you could have some breakfast. There's bacon, eggs, and toast in the warming pans on the buffet. Help yourself." Pushing her chair away from the table, she stood up. "I'll even let you eat in peace without me chattering in your ear. I have to check on Sylvia. See you later."

Deborah sat for several minutes after Madelaine had left, digesting all that had been said before she bothered with breakfast.

Chapter Nine

"Frank and I are putting the Christmas tree up tonight. Would you like to help us decorate it, Deborah?" Madelaine passed her the platter of roast beef.

"I'd love to. It's been years since I've done that—not since I lived at home," she admitted.

"We want to get the house all decorated before the dinner party tomorrow night. It is the Christmas season, two weeks removed," the brunette reasoned. "You can help, too, Tom. We'll put you in charge of stringing the evergreen boughs and the holly."

"Not the mistletoe, though." Frank smiled at his wife. "That's strictly my department."

"Which reminds me, Zane," Madelaine glanced down the table at the man sitting at the head. "With all the activity going on tomorrow night, I don't think I should leave Sylvia alone. So I won't be able to act as your hostess for the party. Deborah can stand in for me."

Deborah stared at her for a frozen moment, stunned by the bomb that had fallen. Then she darted a wide-eyed look at Zane. He regarded her silently, a warm light in his clear blue eyes.

"Would you mind?" he asked quietly.

"I'll help out, if you like," she agreed.

"It's just an informal get-together of some of my friends," he explained, sensing her hesitancy.

"None of them is as formidable as the businessmen you've met, Deborah," Tom added, then winked, "and I can promise that none of them will ask you to polka."

"I like your friends already." She cast a laughing, sidelong glance at Zane. Her pulse quickened at the way he was looking at her, his gaze on the russet hair hanging loosely over her shoulders. When his look lingered on her smiling mouth, Deborah had to look away, and Frank provided the perfect excuse.

"Hey! It's snowing outside!"

Big, fat flakes drifted to the ground beyond the windowpanes. Most of the flakes melted, but a thin covering of white was beginning to form. An outside light provided a bright beam to illuminate the snowflakes against the gray-black backdrop of night.

"Our first snow. Maybe we'll have a white Christmas this year," Madelaine added hopefully. "Build a fire in the fireplace tonight, Frank."

An hour later, a fire was blazing and crackling over dry logs. Madelaine had put on a CD of Christmas carols to fill the living room with music. A tall, thick-needled pine tree towered in a metal stand in front of the paned windows that faced the cul-de-sac driveway. The tree lights, an old set with giant bulbs, were all strung and Frank was plugging them in to make sure they all worked. Garlands of fairy lights blinked on and off in perfect unison.

Madelaine stood back and clapped. Deborah had a garland of silver foil draped on her arms so she had to voice her approval.

"It's beautiful, Frank."

"Don't praise him too much or it will go to his head," Tom warned with a teasing grin.

"You get back to work arranging those boughs on the mantel," Madelaine ordered, waving him about his business. "We'll take care of the tree."

It took the three of them—Deborah, Madelaine and Frank—to wind the bright garland around the massive Christmas tree. Deborah's glance kept straying to the walnut doors. Zane was in the next room, working. Her enjoyment of the task would have been complete if he had been there helping them. There had been times in the past two weeks when Zane had betrayed so much with just a look. At times he even acted friendly toward her. But he had certainly done and said nothing to encourage all the foolish yearnings that had begun to besiege her.

"Here are the Christmas ornaments." Madelaine set two large boxes on a side table and opened them. "You two get started while I see how Sylvia is."

"I'll check on her for you, honey," Frank volunteered.

The brunette hesitated, then agreed, "All right." As he left the room, Deborah and Madelaine began hanging the brightly colored and decorated Christmas balls on the boughs of the tree. One box was soon emptied, but the second one went more slowly as they tried to find and fill in the empty patches. Deborah was stretching to reach a high branch without any ornament when she heard someone enter the room. She assumed it was Frank returning, since he'd been gone quite a while. She couldn't quite reach the branch. When she tried to make it that last quarter inch, she lost her balance. A steel band of muscle hooked itself around her waist to keep her from falling against the tree.

"You almost knocked the tree over." Zane's huskily amused voice came right beside her ear.

His arm had stayed around her waist. Deborah was certain her knees would have buckled if it hadn't been for his continuing support. Her cheeks were flushed with the excitement of his touch as she tried to look backward to his face. All she could see was the point of his chin.

"I need to be a few inches taller to reach the higher limbs," she offered as an explanation of her near accident.

"I'll hang that for you. Where do you want it?" His arm released her from his hold to take the Christmas ornament from her hand. She hadn't even been aware that she still had it.

"On that branch." Deborah pointed to the one. Zane reached it easily. With his height advantage, he could reach all of the places that neither she nor Madelaine had been able to reach. She took three more ornaments from the box. "Put this one on the branch just above the blue ball," she instructed.

There was a laughing glint in his dark blue eyes, but he didn't object. When it was hung, he held out his hand for the next one. She debated briefly with Madelaine whether the green one would look better near the red one or the orange.

"By the red one," Deborah decided finally, and conveyed the order to Zane.

"You like telling me what to do for a change, don't you?"

"I could get used to it," she sassed him.

His gaze caught and held hers for a breathtaking second, a charged message of awareness flashing between them. In the fireplace, a log burned through and collapsed in a shower of sparks. It broke the silent communication between them and Zane turned to the tree to hang the ornament.

"That's the last one," Madelaine announced. "Tinsel time. Come on, Tom. You can help."

He had finished arranging the nativity scene inside the garland of evergreen boughs and holly leaves woven along the edge of the fireplace mantel, and was sitting in a wing chair watching their efforts. At Madelaine's prompting, he rose to join them. She divided the packets of long silver foil among the four of them. They tossed it on the tree until it shimmered and gleamed in the multicolored blinking lights.

Stepping back, they all paused to admire the finished product. The mighty pine tree was bedecked in holiday finery, glittering and sparkling, just waiting for gifts to be stacked beneath it. Something brushed her hair and Deborah turned.

"You had tinsel in your hair." Zane held up the thin strip of foil to show her. With a glance she acknowledged its existence, before her gaze was compelled to return to his face.

Tom murmured something and Madelaine breathed a hurried, "Ssh."

Deborah saw Zane's gaze flicker upward and followed it to the sprig of mistletoe dangling above them.

"Got you just where I want you. . . "

As his murmuring voice hesitated, Deborah warned him, "Don't you dare call me Ms. Holland."

"Deborah," he finished, a light dancing in his eyes.

He lightly brushed his mouth over hers and Deborah felt him tremble. But Zane didn't increase the pressure of his kiss before he lifted his head. She wanted to cry out in frustration, but her expressive eyes said what her voice couldn't.

"Cocoa time." Frank returned to the room, carrying a large tray with five steaming mugs of hot chocolate balanced on its surface. "I stopped by the kitchen and persuaded Jessie to fix this for us. She even volunteered a plate of her Christmas cookies."

"You certainly timed it right," Madelaine declared and cleared the empty boxes off the side table so he could set the tray on it. "We just finished the tree."

"It looks great. I knew if I waited long enough you would have it all done." He grinned.

Taking a mug of cocoa and a cookie, Deborah curled up on the alpaca rug in front of the fireplace. Zane chose the chair that flanked the fireplace on her side, while Frank and Madelaine sat on the sofa that faced it. Tom remained standing, leaning a shoulder against the mantel and munching on a cookie.

"Does your family usually celebrate on Christmas or Christmas Eve?" Madelaine asked, directing her question at Deborah.

"On Christmas."

"I assume you're planning to go home for Christmas." Zane's curt statement held an undercurrent of challenge. Deborah reacted with prickles of defiance that she tried to disguise. She shifted her position on the rug to bring his chair into her view, tucking her feet beneath her to sit cross-legged.

"Yes, I am." Her hazel eyes coolly met his shuttered look noting the hard-grained lines of his face. He didn't have to like it.

"All right. Let's have the details," Zane said.

"My youngest brother, Ronnie, has leave to come home for the holidays. Since my mother had to work on Thanksgiving, she'll have Christmas day off."

"I should think so," someone murmured. Not Zane.

Deborah went on, "I know Christmas falls in the middle of the week this year, but it isn't a long drive from here to New Haven. I can leave on Christmas Eve and come back late Christmas Day. That's not going to interfere too much with your work schedule."

"I wasn't suggesting that you couldn't have the time off," he clipped out the response.

"Oh?" The way she said the one word made it clear that she doubted him.

"I was thinking of the heavy traffic."

"I'm a competent driver," Deborah insisted. His gaze slid to the small, red scar on her left arm. "That accident was not my fault."

"Accidents rarely are the victim's fault, but they get hurt just the same," Zane countered in a controlled voice.

"I'm willing to take the risk."

There was an impatient thinning of his mouth. "You always are. I don't think you ever listen to anyone."

"I don't know about that," Deborah said. "You told me to stay away from you and I have been." She saw the fiery blue glitter of his gaze arc toward her to remind her they weren't alone in the room. Her temper wouldn't be silenced by their quiet, onlooking faces. "I'm not saying anything they haven't guessed. They've warned me about you, too."

That was just a little too much for Zane. He got up and stood in front of her. "Why did you have to say that, Deborah? I don't understand you."

"Then leave me alone," she challenged him, her throat dry and aching. "I could definitely use less aggravation in my life."

Zane moved away and took three strides to the table where he set his cocoa mug on the tray. Deborah stared at the broad set of his shoulders. His back was to her. He was shutting her out again and denying the unspoken feelings that existed between them.

Madelaine was saying something, but Deborah couldn't hear the words above the deafening roar of her heartbeat. The CD player went on shuffle and an old tune played, Christmas rock-and-roll. Something about a blue Christmas. Zane turned his head to look at her. Something in the shadows of his blue eyes made her hyperaware of his emotional desperation.

The sharp breath she took went no farther than the lump in her throat. As if he regretted letting her have that little glimpse, the shutters came down to block out his thoughts. Zane abruptly turned aside.

"I have some work to finish up," he announced to signal his departure. Pausing, he sliced a look to Tom. "Where is that computer analysis of the year-end report for the Gillingham Company?"

"It's—never mind. I'll get it for you." Tom moved away from the fireplace to follow Zane out of the room.

The heat from the crackling fire warmed her back, but still Deborah shivered. She darted an uneasy look at the couple seated on the sofa. She uncrossed her feet to stand, staring down at the mug her nervous fingers clutched.

"I'm sorry if I embarrassed you," Deborah apologized. "I know I shouldn't have made such a scene, but—" What was her excuse? The turmoil of churning emotions made her restless and on edge.

"You don't have to apologize," Frank offered.

"I think you did the right thing," Madelaine added and ignored the shushing sound her husband made. "No, I mean it. You were right to force it out in the open, Deborah. It's time Zane stopped hiding it."

"Thanks for trying to make me feel better." Deborah appreciated their efforts, but there was only one person who could ease her torment and he had walked out of the room. She moved to the window by the Christmas tree where a heavy swirl of snowflakes whipped at the glass panes.

"Well? Zane may work all night if he wants," Frank declared, slapping his wife's knee as he pushed himself upright from the sofa. "But I'm going to get some sleep."

"It's been a long day for me, too," Madelaine agreed, rising to join him. "I'll check on Sylvia first, though."

Neither sleep nor the emptiness of her bedroom sounded inviting to Deborah. She was much too agitated and tense. She had an excess of energy that needed to be burned off, not bottled up by inactivity.

"Good night, Deborah," Madelaine said, and Frank echoed her words.

Snow, activity, and Frank sparked an idea. Deborah pivoted from the window. "Frank, do you remember what you said about swimming when there was snow on the ground? Would it be all right if I used the pool tonight?"

He stopped short, staring at her as if she'd lost her mind. "Alone? I don't think that would be wise. We're going to get a lot more snow. Could start tonight."

But Zane will chain me to the desk tomorrow so I can slave away for him, Deborah thought, but she didn't argue against his advice. "I guess you're right." She sighed in regret. "Good night." She walked over to pick up the tray of empty hot-chocolate mugs. "I'll take these to the kitchen and save Jessie a trip."

"Are you going to your room?" Frank asked.

"Yes." It didn't make any difference which empty room she prowled. She'd pace the floor in either so she might as well confine her restlessness to her own bedroom.

"We'd better switch off the tree lights then." He walked back to do it while Madelaine waited for him. Deborah left the room before they did.

No one was in the kitchen so Deborah washed up the cups rather than leave them for Jessie to do in the morning. Finally, she had no more reason to postpone going to her room.

The blankness of the television screen greeted her when she entered. It offered entertainment to while away the time, but it wasn't what she wanted. The small desk reminded Deborah that she owed her sister a letter, but she'd been sitting at a desk all day. The marble tub in the bathroom looked like a better way to relax. Deborah turned away from it with a sigh of dissatisfaction. The wide expanse of the double bed just made her nervous. The last thing she wanted to do was lie down.

A sharp knock at the door spun her around,

making her heart pound at the unexpected noise. Deborah swallowed hard and crossed the room to answer the summons. Zane stood in the hallway when she opened the door. Quicksilver tongues of fire raced through her veins.

"Frank said you wanted to go swimming." Wasting no time on preliminary greetings, Zane went straight to the point with a curt explanation of why he was there. "I wasn't sure you would take his advice about not swimming alone."

"So you had to come and check," she issued tightly, a thin thread of sarcasm lacing her words. "As you can see, I'm here. Satisfied?"

"Yes," he snapped. "It's better than wondering if you've cracked your head and are floating face down in the pool."

"I appreciate your concern for my welfare," Deborah mocked him. "How touching."

Anger blazed in his eyes, but his clenched jaw kept it back. "You have fifteen minutes to change and meet me at the rear entrance." Zane had barely issued the order before he walked away, leaving Deborah to gape after him.

When she recovered from her astonishment at his invitation, one minute had already gone by. She raced to change her clothes and make up for the lost time. Her warm robe offered a perfect covering for her tankini and would protect her from the elements, as well. Deborah slipped her feet into a pair of flat shoes and hurried down the hallway to the rear entrance. Zane was already standing there, waiting for her.

"I'm ready," she said in a voice that was slightly breathless from her haste.

There wasn't a response as Zane turned the knob of

the door that opened onto the courtyard. He switched on the flashlight he was carrying and its strong beam picked out the snow-covered path through the courtyard.

It was still and quiet outside, the falling snow making no sound as it coated the ground white. Since Zane had the flashlight he led the way and Deborah followed. It was pitch-black except for the light cast from the house windows.

"The pool was never intended to be used at night so there aren't any lights," Zane said to explain the blackness ahead of them, except for the falling white flakes. "There should be enough light reflected from the house for us to see."

It was a matter-of-fact statement. There was nothing in his tone or attitude that invited discussion. Deborah wasn't certain whether it was the coldness of the air penetrating her robe or his icy attitude that made her shiver. She noticed the sprinkling of snowflakes melting to crystal drops on his jet black hair. A cynical thought crossed her mind—how amazing that snow could melt on a man made of ice.

The flashlight beam shone on a strip of concrete that was free of snow, although it glistened wetly. Beyond it, a vaporous mist hovered on the surface of the pool, the heated water creating steam.

"Watch your step," Zane instructed. "The concrete deck around the pool is heated to keep ice from forming, but it'll be slippery from the melted snow."

His words of caution were indifferent and he didn't offer her the steadying support of his hand. Walking carefully, Deborah followed him onto the wet cement deck. He stopped in front of a small shed that housed the pool's filtering system.

"We can leave our clothes in here so they'll stay dry." He opened the door and propped the flashlight against the side of the building, its beam dimly illuminating the pool area.

Snowflakes flitted around him as Zane stripped off his sweater. The cold had begun to numb her fingers and they fumbled stiffly with the sash knotted around her robe. At least, Deborah blamed her clumsiness on the cold rather than her having to look at the rippling muscles of his shoulders and back. Without ceremony, Zane stepped out of the pants that covered his black swim trunks. Bundling his clothes and shoes together, he set them inside the small shed.

His sideways glance barely touched her before he took a step toward the pool and knifed soundlessly into the water. The concrete was warm beneath her bare feet, but Deborah felt the nipping chill on her exposed flesh. Shivers danced over her skin as she hurriedly folded her robe around her shoes and set them in the shed beside his clothes.

She walked to the pool's edge and hesitated. She didn't want to dive into the water until she knew where Zane was. He surfaced in the middle of the pool, his wet hair gleaming like black satin in the swirling white vapor. Facing her, he treaded water. Under his hooded regard, Deborah became conscious of the skimpiness of her two-piece flowered tankini.

"Quit posing before you freeze to death." His taunting voice annoyed her.

"I wasn't posing," she denied. "I didn't know where you were and I didn't want to jump in on top of you."

"You know where I am now."

Her teeth had begun to chatter from the cold;

otherwise Deborah would have said something cutting. Instead, she fluidly dived off the side, making a graceful entrance into the water, even if it lacked his athleticism. The heated water was a delicious shock to her chilled skin. Deborah surfaced not far from Zane, flinging her hair out of her face with a toss of her head and smoothing it backward with her hands.

"This is fabulous," she declared in amazed delight. "It's almost as warm as bathwater."

"You like it, do you?" A smile almost appeared as his look became gentle.

Her full appreciation of the experience was just beginning. She turned in the water, looking around her. While she was enveloped in warmth, everything outside the pool was wearing winter's white coat. The foglike mist floating above the surface of the water added to the magical wonder, creating a dreamlike quality to make the moment unique. Deborah turned her face to the black sky to let the snowflakes drop wetly on her lashes, nose and mouth.

"It is fantastic!" She was kind of repeating herself, but it didn't seem to matter. "No wonder you didn't bother to enclose the pool. This is sensational!"

The flashlight propped upward at the pool's side gave just enough light so that Deborah could see the snow frosting the bare branches of the shrubs and trees. Everything was being transformed to white with winter's breath while she was swimming in water as warm as summer.

"A lot of ski resorts have heated pools or hot springs for their guests."

"Yes, but they're for tourists and they would be crowded with people. This is private—with only the snow and the night sky and the mist." Deborah spoke softly, as if talking about intimate companions.

Zane abruptly changed the subject. "Do you want to make a few laps of the pool?"

Part of her wanted to tread water and marvel at the scene, but the energy within her demanded to be released. "All right."

She struck out for the far end of the pool with a strong but leisurely crawl. Zane kept pace beside her, shortening a stroke that could have easily outraced her. They covered the length of the pool four times before Deborah clung to the side in exhaustion. Zane was two lengths into the fifth lap before he realized she had stopped.

"You aren't quitting already, are you? We've just started." The glint in his eyes mocked her.

She had deliberately stopped at the shallow end where her feet could touch the bottom, but her fingers curled into the cement lip of the pool to keep her balance. She was winded from the four previous laps and wasn't about to try a fifth.

"You may have just begun, but I'm finished," Deborah countered in a voice breathless from her exertion.

A low chuckle came from his throat, but he didn't say any more. For a brief second, he straightened in the water, giving Deborah a glimpse of his powerful physique—the broad shoulders and narrow hips of a swimmer. Then he pushed forward for the opposite end of the pool. He disappeared into the mist.

Chapter Ten

Until her breath returned, Deborah drifted along the edge of the pool. Zane continued his laps across the pool's length while she was content to enjoy her surroundings. Snowflakes continued to whirl from the darkened sky and mix with the white steam rising from the heated water.

Staying close to the side of the pool, she began a slow backstroke. She was careful to avoid the center area where Zane was, not wanting to interfere with his swimming. The novelty of floating in warm water while all around her it snowed had not worn off. An enchanted spell had been cast.

"Keep your fingers together and cup your hands. You'll have a stronger stroke."

Zane's voice came out of the mist, startling her. Deborah stopped swimming and tried to come upright, not realizing she had left the shallow end and ventured into deep water. As her legs stretched for the bottom, she went under with a sputter of surprise. Immediately, she kicked for the surface and came up coughing. An arm went around her and Deborah clutched at the water-slick flesh of a muscled shoulder. With a powerful kick, Zane propelled her toward the side of the pool while she wiped her face and coughed out the water she had swallowed.

"Are you all right?" His arm remained curved around her middle.

"Yes." She nodded quickly and gulped in air.

The smoothness of the tile border was against her shoulder, but Deborah didn't remove the hand that circled his neck. Pushing wet strands of copper hair out of her eyes, she flashed him a smile of chagrin.

"I didn't realize the water was over my head there," she admitted.

"Obviously," Zane murmured.

While his arm continued to support her, his other hand gripped the edge of the pool to keep them at the side. Recovered from her accidental dunking, Deborah felt the first glimmer of silken awareness. Long, muscled thighs were floating against hers, masculine and firm in their contact. Her hip was drifting inside the cradle of his. The thin, wet material of her tankini top didn't lessen the sensation of her breast rubbing against the fine, wet hair on his chest.

Her eyes sought his face, sensual tension tightening her stomach. The brilliant blue of his gaze was watching the rapid pulse beating at the base of her throat. Slowly his eyes lifted to look into hers. They mirrored all the turbulent emotions that were quivering through Deborah.

The hand on her back tightened and it was all the invitation she needed to glide toward the strong, male outline of his mouth. When his lips parted to kiss hers, heat scorched through her that had nothing to do with the temperature of the water they floated in.

While her left hand clung to his neck, her right
curled into the wet, silken texture of his black hair.
Deborah wriggled and shaped her body to his hard
torso. The contact seared her with a longing for ful-
fillment that couldn't be denied. She ached to be a
part of him, her desire almost out of control.

"We're in water over our heads." His mouth moved
against her lips to speak the words, his voice husky
and rasping, betraying his aroused state.

"I don't care." If this was what drowning in love was
like, she wanted to go for it. A muscled leg eased its
way between hers to brace itself against the concrete
side of the pool below the water.

Deborah felt the muscles in his shoulders flex. His
mouth hardened on hers in a promise to return
before it pulled away.

"Hang on," he ordered and used the leverage of his
arm and leg to push away from the pool's side.

Automatically, Deborah linked her fingers together
behind his neck. The steel grip of his hand on her
waist kept her almost on top of him as he pulled her
along with him. The powerful stroke of one arm combined with the kick of his legs to carry both of them
toward the shallow end of the pool. Their eyes were
locked together.

Deborah knew she would trust herself anywhere with
this man. In his arms, she was safe. There was nothing
so insurmountable that they could not face and con-
quer together. He was not some god who would offer
her paradise. He was made of sinew and bone. Loving
him would be alternately heaven and hell, but Deborah
knew she could handle both.

When Zane stopped in shallower water, it lapped at
his shoulders. Her toes were barely able to scrape the

bottom. Not that it mattered. Deborah preferred to
hang onto him and have the strength of his body support her. It was impossible to get too close. Now both
of his hands were free, no longer needed to keep
them afloat. They pulled her buoyant weight firmly
inside the circle of his arms and pressed her curves to
his unyielding flesh.

His mouth was driving in its possession of her lips,
parting them to let the sensual probe of his tongue
fire her senses with its demanding claim. It raged
through her with primitive force, sending quivers of
joy deep into her soul. But Zane wasn't satisfied just
to stake his ownership of her mouth. He began brand-
ing her face and throat with kisses. Deborah returned
them with equal fervor, pressing her lips against his
skin, even though he tasted a little like chlorine.

Behind her neck, she felt his fingers tug at the knot
of one strap and untie the wet bow. His hands trailed
halfway down the sensitive skin over her spine to
unhook her top and free her breasts from their con-
finement. Deborah didn't even notice the top half of
her tankini floating aimlessly away from them. Her
senses were aflame with the sensation of her naked
breasts crushed to his bare, muscled chest.

Then his hands were gripping her waist and lifting
her weightless body partly out of the water, while his
mouth made an initial foray down the damp valley between her breasts. Her fingers clutched into the
bulging muscles of his shoulders to steady herself, her
nails digging into his flesh at the tantalizing brush of
his lips on a rosy nipple. Crystalline flakes of snow
melted on her face, bestowing her with nature's sweet
kisses.

The steel bands of his arms slid around her, one

circling her waist and the other curving under her bottom to mold the lower half of her body to the muscled tautness of his stomach. His licking tongue ignited a liquid fire that spread quickly through her veins, consuming her with a molten heat. Deborah shuddered with a wild need.

His hold loosened, letting her slide down to his level. He didn't miss the love-drunk look in her eyes. Her lips trembled for his kiss, but Zane denied her that satisfaction to rest his forehead against hers, closing his eyes. Her consolation was the caressing warmth of his heavy breath against her skin.

She savored the moment, letting her hands glide over the powerful muscles of his shoulders, and wander down to let her fingers curl into his springy chest hairs. Zane had claimed his ownership of her body. Now Deborah was claiming her right to his. Her touch produced a shudder that quivered through him. The circle of his arms grew smaller as he molded her more tightly against him and pressed his mouth to her cheekbone.

"Do you know what you're doing to me?" Zane breathed the sensual question into her ear.

"I . . . hope the same thing you are doing to me." Her whispered answer was equally revealing.

What little breath she had was taken from her as the hand at the small of her back slid under the elastic band of her tankini bottom, pushing it down. The wet material clung stubbornly to her skin, requiring the assistance of a second hand. Deborah floated free of his arms as the last barrier was banished to the pool. She treaded water several feet from where Zane stood. The darkness and the water hid her body from his eyes. Deborah felt a shameless twinge of regret. A

wanton part of her wanted him to look on her and be
pleased by her womanhood. They drifted closer, lessening the distance that separated them without elim-
inating it.

It was not an attempt to prolong the agony of wanting each other. Rather, it was a savoring of all that had
led up to the moment to come, when intimate discov-
eries would be made. There was no need to rush. The
anticipation was sweet and heady, an aphrodisiac to
the senses.

"I've wanted you for a long time, Deborah." He
moved closer, the strong, male lines of his face clearly
visible in the dim light. "Not just because you're a beautiful, exciting woman, although you are that." His voice
was a husky caress as warm as the water that sensually
caressed her naked form. "I've been tempted to make
love to a lot of women out of sheer sexual necessity. I
craved the satisfaction their bodies gave me, but not
anything else. I thought it would always be that way."

"Isn't it?" She wasn't trying to be provocative; her
voice was as huskily disturbed as his.

"You know it isn't," Zane insisted with a growl. "You
got under my skin. You with your pretty hair"—
his hand came out of the water to tug a long, wet
strand—"and those incredibly expressive eyes. Wow.
When you first came to work for me, I tried to ignore
you but you got to me. I tried, but I couldn't be indifferent to you. I should have realized it was a warning."

"I didn't recognize the danger signals either." Her
finger traced the sexy groove in his cheek near the
corner of his mouth. "Considering the way the sparks
flew when you rubbed me the wrong way, I should
have known what would happen when you rubbed me
the right way."

His hand slid to clasp her forearm. He kissed the inside of her elbow, then the small scar. "It wasn't until your accident that I realized what you meant to me. The hospital said you weren't badly hurt, but I had to see for myself. When I walked into that emergency room and you called me by my name, if the doctor hadn't been there I would have made love to you on the spot."

"Blood and all?" she said in surprise. "I don't remember that."

"Well, no. I would have restrained myself." His hand glided up her arm to caress her neck and the hollow of her throat.

"All I remember is you pointing out that my services were not indispensable," Deborah murmured, her breath catching as a finger teased the sensitive area near her ear.

"You were, though. It shook me to admit that. I had to send Tom over to see if you were okay that night because I didn't trust myself to be alone with you."

Zane's mouth seemed to grow jealous of the privileges his hands were enjoying and moved to continue the stimulating exploration of her neck and earlobe. Their bodies drifted against each other in the water.

"The night you got on my case for not responding to Sylvia's needs provoked me into showing how much I needed you. I came very close to insisting that taking care of me was part of your job—anything to have you."

"I didn't want you to stop that night," Deborah admitted, closing her eyes as his warm lips moved over her lashes. "The only reason I said that was because I was afraid of being the other woman in your life."

"The other woman." There was amusement in the

breath he exhaled. "You're the only real woman in my life. The only one." Zane briefly teased her lips, his white teeth tugging at the lower one for an instant. "When you and Tom were doing that ridiculous dance in the suite, I was overwhelmed with jealousy. The idea that you and he might be having an affair nearly drove me nuts. Just to see you laughing with him—"

She heard the remembered pain in his voice and quickly stopped him. "Tom is a great guy—wonderful and kind and gentle. But I was never attracted to him. Next to you, he . . ." Deborah laughed softly. "I'm not saying any more. You're too conceited."

"I am?" He bruised her lips with a kiss that soon hardened with passion.

With a faint moan, she wrapped her arms around him, wanting to get even closer to his maleness. She gloried in the strength that pulsated through his rock-hard body and the chest hair that was pleasantly rough against her bare breasts. She was excited by the taste of his tongue, the feel of his muscle, everything about him. Desire quivered through her.

Steam swirled around them, generated from the combination of their body heat and the warm water of the pool. Snow melted into crystal droplets on their skin and hair, but they were too engrossed in each other to notice it. Lips were busy kissing, teasing, and demanding while hands caressed, explored, and aroused willing flesh. Love was a hot flame that burned them together.

"Zane," Deborah whispered his name, loving him so intensely it was a pleasurable ache. Tears of boundless happiness were on her cheeks, mingling with the snow. "Why did you bother to tell me to stay away from you? Didn't you realize that it was already too late? Why did you waste all this time?"

"I'm married." He dragged out the words as if they were torture. There was a fierceness in the way his hands cupped her face as if he were afraid of losing her.

"Tell me something I don't know." She smiled, because it didn't make any difference. It seemed worse to pretend that it did.

"You don't understand," Zane insisted with a heavy sigh. "There are so many things I can't give you."

"I only want you. I'll be satisfied with that." Her voice trembled with strong undercurrents of emotion.

"Will you? I don't know that I'll be satisfied." His searching gaze probed deeply into her eyes. "I know there will come a time when I'll want to see our child at your breast." He lifted her to bend his head and kiss the swelling curve of her breast, cupping the underside with one hand. Deborah quivered as he straightened. "Would you want to have my child?"

"No." She swallowed the happy lump in her throat. "But I'd love to have your children. I want more than one."

She heard his sharp intake of breath before she was crushed hard inside his arms in an embrace that was brutal joy and aching regret. Deep shudders wracked his shoulders and Deborah tried to absorb his inner pain.

"So do I," Zane admitted in a quivering breath. "But I couldn't give them my name."

"You could give them your love. You would be their natural father. You could even legally adopt them," Deborah argued gently. "Don't put obstacles in our path to keep us apart. I'll just move them away."

"I couldn't stand it if people looked down on you, Deborah," he muttered.

"I couldn't stand it if you walked away from me— not after this. There has to be a way for us to be together." There was a desperate catch in her voice.

"We'll find one . . . because I can't let you go."

"You couldn't if you tried, because I wouldn't let you."

His mouth twisted wryly as he lifted his head. "I can't think straight when you are in my arms." He loosened his hold, but Deborah resisted.

"Don't think then," she protested.

"No. I need to figure this out." His hard jaw was set in a determined line.

"But—"

"Zane!" Tom's shout intruded on the moment. "There's a phone call for you. From California. It's important."

Together they turned in the direction of his voice. A flashlight beam zigzagged across the pool's surface until it found them. Deborah blinked and turned sharply away from the harsh glare, lifting a hand to shield out the spot of light.

"Better point that light in another direction, Tom," Zane warned. "The woman with me might not be embarrassed but I'll be jealous as hell of what you might see."

"Zane!" Deborah hissed.

Looking at the twin spots of pink in her cheeks, Zane laughed softly, "You shameless woman, you do have some sense of modesty." His teasing murmur was for her ears only.

"Sorry," Tom apologized after averting the flashlight. "Do you want to return the call a little later?"

"No. I'll take it." Turning again to Deborah, he ordered quietly, "You wait here a minute."

With effortless strokes, he swam to the edge of the pool. Shaking the hair out of his face, he levered himself out of the water onto the surrounding deck. His clean, male lines sent Deborah's heart thudding against her ribs as he walked to the shed where they had left their clothes. From inside, he pulled out a long beach towel and began wiping himself dry.

"You'd better go tell them I'll be there in a minute, Tom," he instructed, stepping into his pants.

"Right away." The flashlight was turned toward the house, its light outlining Tom's silhouette as he started across the courtyard. His footsteps made no sound in the snow, but the light kept getting smaller until it disappeared in the thickening snowfall. By the time the sound of a door closing echoed into the night, Zane had pulled his sweater on and was walking to the side of the pool, carrying the large beach towel.

"You can come out now." He waited at the ladder and Deborah swam to it.

Her toe touched the bottom rung when she remembered. "What about my bathing suit?"

There was a wicked glint in his blue eyes as he slanted her a smile. "It's too dark to find it now. We'll just have to wait until morning." He shook out the towel. "Come on. It's getting cold out here."

Grabbing hold of the ladder rail, Deborah climbed out of the pool. Immediately, the chill of the air's low temperature shivered over her bare flesh, the evaporating pool water cooling her skin even more. Before she could reach for the towel, Zane was swinging it behind her and wrapping it around her shoulders.

When he started to overlap the towel in front, his hands paused in their task. His gaze roamed up her leggy length to linger on the rise and fall of her breasts, firm and creamy smooth. Deborah trembled as much from the desire in his look as from the cold. At last his gaze trailed the last distance to her warm hazel eyes.

"God, you're beautiful, Deborah," Zane declared with a groan and tightly overlapped the beach towel to enclose her in a cocoon.

She gave a little cry of surprise as he unexpectedly picked her up and carried her to the shed. Without putting her down, he somehow managed to reach inside and retrieve her shoes and robe, adding them to his burden. Then he started for the house.

"What are you doing?" Deborah protested.

"I don't have the self-control to stand by and watch you dress. And I'm not leaving you out here so you can fall and crack your head," he told her flatly. His steady eyes challenged her to argue with him. He wouldn't listen to words and the towel was virtually a straitjacket. Also, they were already halfway across the courtyard. "Besides, you're cold." Zane voiced the last factor that had kept her silent. "There isn't any point wasting time getting dressed when I can have you inside where it's warm."

"You've thought of everything," she said, trying to keep her teeth from chattering.

He suddenly looked away, his expression turning grim. "Not everything." Deborah knew without asking that he was talking about their future and its uncertain outcome.

Entering the house through the rear door, Zane carried her all the way into her bedroom before setting her down. His hands gripped the sides of her arms, not allowing the towel to loosen. The brevity of his kiss was soft with regret.

"Go take a hot shower and get to bed," he told her and started to leave.

"Zane." Deborah abandoned her pride to ask, "Are you coming back?"

"No." He looked at her, noting the towel that had slipped off one shivering shoulder. "Not tonight. And not because I don't want to." He bent and kissed her bare shoulder before covering it with the towel.

"Then why?" She tried to sound casually interested and not as lonely as she felt.

"Maybe it's too late, but I have to consider the consequences of our actions—for your sake as well as my own." His hand stroked her cheek in a farewell caress as Deborah accepted his answer with stoic calm.

Then he was striding out of her room. Deborah refused to accept the possibility that she might lose him, that she might be allowed only a glimpse of happiness. After showering and slipping into her nightclothes, she went to bed and dreamed about Zane and falling snow.

The next morning, Deborah dressed and was about to leave her bedroom for the breakfast table when there was a knock at her door. Her heart gave a leap of excitement at the thought that it might be Zane and she rushed the last few steps to the door. Madelaine was in the hallway. There was a bright twinkle in her brown eyes.

"I think this is yours." She handed Deborah a wet bundle.

A scarlet heat suffused her face as she recognized her tankini. "Yes, it is," she admitted with a self-conscious laugh.

"Obviously Zane took you swimming last night." Then Madelaine could contain herself no longer and gave Deborah a quick smile. "Don't look so embarrassed. I'm a nurse, remember. Not much surprises me. Besides, I know you are going to make Zane very happy."

"If he'll let me," Deborah murmured and walked to the bathroom to hang the wet suit over the tub.

"He should have his head examined if he doesn't," the brunette retorted.

"Is breakfast ready yet?" Deborah changed the subject.

"Jessie was just setting the table. Sylvia's tray is ready so I'm going to take it up to her room before the food gets cold. I'll see you at the table." Madelaine waved as she walked out. "And keep your chin up. Zane knows a good thing when he sees it."

Deborah smiled faintly and dried her hands on a towel before leaving the bedroom for the sun-brightened morning room where the breakfast was served. Zane was standing at a window when she entered the room. Deborah paused, feeling her pulse accelerate. If he shut down again, she knew she could scream.

"Good morning." Her greeting was a deliberate attempt to draw his gaze.

He half turned to look at her. "Good morning." Nothing could conceal the warm light in his eyes. "I was just looking at the snow."

The world was white outside the window, but it wasn't the morning that Deborah was thinking about. It was last night. The same memory was reflected in his look.

"It's beautiful, isn't it?" she said.

Zane crossed the room to stand in front of her. His hand shaped itself to the side of her neck while his thumb drew lazy circles under her chin. It was a seductive caress to which she was all too susceptible.

"Breakfast is ready. And we have a lot of work to do today, Ms. Holland." The sensual look in his eyes mocked his own formality. Then his mouth was moving over her lips with a sweet intensity that was just about addictive. Deborah didn't mind. He took her hand and led her to the table, seating her in a chair next to his.

Work was exactly what he had in mind, but it was undertaken with a difference. Zane kept finding excuses to touch her—a hand caressing her shoulder or resting on the back of her waist while he studied the notes she was making. He smiled a lot, almost every time he looked at her. The obvious change in his behavior was noted by Tom.

"Swimming at night seems to cheer you up, Zane," he remarked at one point. "You should do it more often." His gentle look encompassed Deborah, signaling his approval of a relationship he had once counseled against.

At five o'clock, Zane glanced at his watch. "We'll quit for today." He began stacking the papers in front of him.

"Why so early?" Deborah frowned. Ever since the office had been transferred to the house, they had worked at least an hour longer.

"Have you forgotten? We're having a dinner party tonight. I thought you would want time to get ready."

She had forgotten. Too much had happened since

Madelaine had volunteered her as hostess. She spoke her first thought out loud, "What should I wear?"

"Don't tell me you don't have anything to wear," Zane mocked. "I bought you a closetful of dresses."

His reminder sidetracked her. "Hey, why did you buy me those gowns? I meant to ask. Were you ashamed of what I wore?" She remembered how her pride had been bruised by that incident.

"You'd be gorgeous in anything. I think I just delighted in showing you off." He shrugged.

"That's a diplomatic answer," Deborah responded with a trace of disappointment. "No wonder you're such a successful businessman."

Zane studied her for a long moment. "All right. The truth is I was defensive about you even then. I didn't want a bitch like Foster Darrow's wife or his daughter making snotty remarks about your clothes. I knew we'd be seeing a lot of them during the negotiations. I didn't want them to hurt you."

"Oh."

"You okay with that?"

"Yeah. I am."

"All right then." He gave her a huge smile. "Now, go make yourself more beautiful."

Chapter Eleven

Since the party was a pre-Christmas celebration, Deborah chose a velvet dress of kelly green. The silver filigree brooch was her grandmother's, a lovely piece of costume jewelry but with little antique value. She wore her auburn hair down, the way Zane liked it, and silver hoops in her ears.

There were butterflies in her stomach as she walked to the living room. The invited guests were Zane's friends. It was important that they like her, important to her if no one else. She tried to calm her jittery nerves with a deep breath. Inside the living room, she stopped as Zane swept her with a slow glance.

"How do I look?" Her self-confidence was definitely in short supply at the moment.

"Like the spirit of Christmas." His crooked smile was lightly teasing. He moved leisurely across the room and toyed with one of her russet curls. "You're beautiful, Deborah. Always."

The doorbell rang and the guests began arriving. Zane explained that his wife was not feeling well and everyone seemed to understand what he had left unsaid. Deborah was introduced as his assistant. No one questioned her position but she received a few curious glances, and speculating looks were exchanged between couples. Yet she wasn't made to feel uncomfortable—not by them.

With each passing hour, Zane became more and more aloof, speaking less, avoiding her eyes whenever she looked at him, and just generally shutting down. Deborah had the impression that she was somehow to blame. As the evening dragged on, she had to force the smile that curved her mouth and the responses to the small talk of the guests. When the front door closed on the last guest, her nerves were stretched as taut as piano wire.

The silence in the house was deafening as Zane walked past her to return to the living room. Deborah followed him, confused and angry. After switching off the tree lights, he walked to the fireplace and stirred the dying embers. A shower of sparks cascaded into the gray ashes. Deborah watched the silent death of the fire and knew she wasn't going to let hers end that way.

"What is it, Zane? What have I done wrong?" she demanded.

His back remained to her. He continued to stare at the banked fire, demonstrating impatience in the way he gripped the fireplace poker. "Nothing. You belonged tonight, Deborah." His voice seemed to come from some deep, dark place. "It felt right to have you by my side greeting the guests, right to have you sitting at the opposite end of the table from me, and right to walk our guests to the door. I wanted to choke every time I had to call you my assistant." He spun angrily. "But what else could I call you with my wife upstairs?"

"I am your assistant . . . unless you fired me in the last six hours," Deborah pointed out with relief.

"You know what I mean." He jammed the poker in its stand, metal clanging with the force of his action.

"Yes, I do." It was a consolation to her pride that Zane was bothered by her position. She moved slowly across the room to the fireplace and lifted her face to his. "But I've accepted it."

"Well, I haven't! And I won't!"

"What else can you do?" she reasoned quietly.

His eyes blazed over her face. With a groan, he gathered her into his arms and crushed her lips beneath his. His wild, desperate need tore at her heart. The raw emotion of his kiss enveloped her, making her weak because it echoed her feelings.

From another part of the house came a startled outcry, followed by a loud thumping. They broke apart, both looking toward the open doorway to the hall. Deborah cast a frowning glance toward Zane.

"What was that?"

"I don't know." His jaw tightened as he set Deborah away from him and started for the door.

Deborah hesitated only a second before she followed him, hurrying to keep up with his long strides. More sounds could be heard coming from the staircase . . . and voices . . . Madelaine's voice, then Frank's. The staircase was enclosed, except for the last short flight. As Deborah rounded the hall corner behind Zane, she saw Madelaine crouched beside a still figure on the landing. Sylvia Wilding had fallen down the steps. Zane rushed up the short flight to his wife's side.

"What happened?" He shot the question at Madelaine.

"I thought she was asleep and I stepped out of the room just for a moment. She slipped out while I was gone. Frank is calling an ambulance." She smoothed blond hair away from the forehead of the unconscious woman.

Zane bent over her, then shook his head in tired anger. "She's drunk."

"I know. I found a third of a bottle of rum in her room," Madelaine admitted. "It's probably what Jessie had left over from the eggnog."

"Why didn't she lock it up?" he demanded harshly.

"For all we know, Sylvia has a key to the cabinet. Or she used a crowbar." Madelaine straightened from her patient to glare at him. "Why don't you give up, Zane? You simply can't keep her here. You want her to have her own room, be free to come and go as she pleases, and not be locked in. You want her to live in a normal atmosphere, but Sylvia needs constant care and supervision. I can't give it to her. This isn't a controlled environment. Give up, Zane. She doesn't belong here any more."

There was a clatter of footsteps on the stairs and Frank came into view at the landing. "The ambulance is on its way."

"Is it necessary?" Zane questioned, without anger this time.

"I think she might have a concussion, maybe a cracked rib." The brunette nurse had regained her professional poise. "I'd rather be safe and have an ambulance take her to the hospital than drive her there ourselves."

By the time the wail of the ambulance sirens entered the driveway, Tom and Jessie had joined Deborah at the base of the stairs. As the attendants lifted Sylvia Wilding onto the stretcher, Zane glanced at Deborah.

"I'm going to the hospital with her," he said.

She nodded. "Of course."

"I'll come with you," Tom volunteered.

Zane hesitated, then gave in. Seconds later, Sylvia was being wheeled out by the attendants. Madelaine went along, too, but Frank stayed behind. The sirens wailed again as the ambulance drove away.

Deborah stayed awake until after midnight before she finally gave up the vigil and went to bed. Tom was at the breakfast table the next morning when she entered.

"Good morning. How is Sylvia?" she asked.

"A slight concussion and a lot of bruises. Other than that, she wasn't hurt. It's a miracle. Of sorts." He shrugged.

"It must have been late when you came back. I suppose Zane is still sleeping," Deborah guessed.

"He didn't come back with us."

"He stayed at the hospital with Sylvia?" Something in his tone made her phrase the sentence as a question.

"No."

"Where did he go?"

"I don't know." Tom shook his head and spread more jam on his toast.

"You must have an idea," she insisted.

"More than one, yes, but I'm not going to guess

where he is or what he's doing," he answered. "I deal in facts and statistics."

"Did . . . did he say when he'd be back?"

"No."

Without Zane to add to her workload, Deborah finished the backlog of papers, memos, and reports that had accumulated on her desk. It helped the day pass, but the evening dragged. No one was willing to venture a guess as to where Zane might be. Since no one else seemed to be worried, Deborah tried not to be either.

Zane wasn't at the breakfast table the next morning. She refused the pancakes and sausages Jessie brought and settled for juice and coffee instead. The others were still at the table eating when Deborah left to go to the study.

The doors were ajar. Deborah hesitated outside because they were always kept closed. She hurried inside to find Zane standing at a window looking out. He glanced over his shoulder when she entered, then turned to her.

"Welcome back." The words came out in an eager rush. "Where have you been?"

"With my wife." He gave Deborah a long look. "Sylvia stayed sober long enough to make the right decision."

"What do you mean?"

"She just signed herself into an excellent substance-abuse clinic. She'll have twenty-four-hour professional care, the best that money can buy, maybe the best in the country." Zane went back to staring out the window.

"I hope that it helps."

"The doctors aren't sure that she will ever get better. You can't just pour chemicals into your brain for years and stay the same. One way or another, she's going to be dealing with that for the rest of her life."

"What about you, Zane?"

He shrugged and focused on Deborah again, and gave her a look filled with sorrow. "I'm just numb. This was a long time coming. Now that it's happened, I—I have to make a different life. Without her."

Deborah nodded. His news was unexpected, but it was the best possible thing that could have happened for the two of them. Meaning Zane and Sylvia. Not her.

"Whatever I felt for her, Deborah—that died a long time ago. Our marriage has just been some words on a piece of paper for years now."

"It was a difficult decision for you." Deborah wanted to get close to him, but his attitude was keeping her at a distance, almost physically holding her away.

"Yesterday afternoon I had my attorney file for a divorce." Zane turned to look at her after he had issued the statement. "She's ready for that, too. Says we should have done it a long time ago." He heaved a sigh. "Our marriage was dead long before you came on the scene. We would have filed eventually, whether or not I ever met you. Her love for me was real enough, once upon a time."

"Once upon a time," Deborah said softly. "That's how fairy tales begin."

"Hmm. This one doesn't have a happy ending."

"Do you mean—"

"I'm talking about the end of my marriage. Circumstances being what they are, I can never walk completely away from her, or neglect my responsibility toward her."

"I understand."

"It just doesn't seem quite fair to you," Zane said •
quietly. "All the same, I *am* responsible for her—
there's no one else who cares about her. She needs
me and I have to be there when she does. She was the
mother of my son, and I can't just abandon her."

A tremulous smile curved Deborah's lips. "You
wouldn't be the man I love if you could, Zane."

Her honest response melted the ice in his heart forever. Zane started toward her and she met him
halfway.

"So knowing all that . . . do you still want to marry
me someday? Will you marry me, Deborah?"

"In a heartbeat," she whispered and went into his
arms.

Outside, the sun glistened on pure white drifts of
snow. Here and there bare, thin branches poked
through. But they would burst with new life in a few
short months, and fulfill every promise of the
coming spring.

Please read on
for an excerpt from the first in Janet Dailey's
brand new series, The Champions!

WHIRLWIND

Chapter One

Kingman, Arizona
Summer

Lexie Champion pulled off her sunglasses, wiped the lenses on the hem of her rumpled denim shirt, and slipped them into her pocket. Her eyes were gritty from the dusty desert wind that swept across the rodeo grounds, picking up the odors of manure, barbecue, popcorn, tobacco smoke, and diesel fumes—a mélange that, to Lexie, was as familiar as any air she'd ever breathed.

From the midway beyond the bleachers, her ears caught the music of a carousel. It blended with the bawl of cattle and the blare of the rodeo announcer's voice as the rodeo's opening ceremony began.

They'd driven most of the night to get here—she and the foreman, Ruben Diego, with four bucking bulls in the long gooseneck trailer. They'd arrived at the Mojave County Fairgrounds late last night and loosed the bulls down the chute into one of the holding pens. After giving their charges water and grain in rubber feed tubs, the two of them had crashed across the front and back seats of the heavy duty pickup for a few hours of sleep.

Now it was late in the day. The strains of the National Anthem from the arena told her that the rodeo, the centerpiece of Kingman's Andy Devine Days celebration, was about to get underway. The bull riding event would be last on the two-hour program. Before then, there should be time to relax, get some barbecue, maybe even change the clothes she'd driven and slept in. But Lexie was too wired to rest. All she wanted was to be right here, with her bulls. After the threatening message she'd received last week, she needed to know that the precious animals were safe.

Ruben had gone off to the midway for food and sodas. She'd told him there was no need to bring her anything, but he probably would. Ruben, a full-blooded member of the Tohono O'odham tribe, might be an employee of the Alamo Canyon Cattle Ranch, but he treated Lexie and her sister Tess as if they were his own daughters.

Alone for the moment, she leaned against the six-foot portable steel fence, resting a boot on one of the lower rungs as she gazed across the complex of pens and chutes. Here the rodeo bulls, trucked in by stock contractors like the Champion family, waited to be herded through the maze of chutes, rigged with a flank strap and bull rope, mounted, and set loose to buck.

Until the instant a rider's weight settled onto their

backs, most of the animals were calm. They were bred and raised to do one job—buck that annoying cowboy off into the dust. They knew what to expect and what to do. But at up to a ton in weight, with the agility of star athletes, they were amazingly powerful, incredibly dangerous. And in the arena, at any adrenaline-charged moment, the most amiable bull could turn murderous.

Nobody knew that better than Lexie.

Her thoughts flew back to the cryptic note she'd found tucked beneath the truck's windshield when she'd driven into Ajo for groceries last week. Written in crude block letters on a page torn from a yellow pad, it had been there when she'd come out of the store. Its simple message had sent a chill up her spine.

YOUR FAMILY OWES ME. ITS PAYBACK TIME.

Even the memory made her shiver. Had the message been a prank? Her first impulse had been to scan the parking lot for someone who might have left it. But she'd seen no one, not even a familiar vehicle. Impulsively, she'd crumpled the page and tossed it into a trash receptacle. If anybody was watching, she wanted them to know she wasn't scared.

Later, after realizing she'd destroyed evidence, Lexie had regretted the act. But nothing could erase the image of that message from her mind—the letters pressed hard into the yellow paper, as if in pure hatred. Why did this person think her family owed him—or her? And what did they mean by payback?

She'd told no one yet. Not her sister Tess or their

stepmother, Callie; not even Ruben. Why cause
worry over what was bound to be an empty threat?
But she wasn't about to leave her bulls if there was
any chance someone might harm them.

"Well, lookee here! Howdy, honey!" The slurring
voice made Lexie jump. The cowhand who'd crept
up behind her was dirty, unshaven, and, as her late
father would've said, as big as a barn door. His clothes
and breath reeked of cheap whiskey.

"You're a purty little thing with that long yellow
hair." He loomed over her. "I was thinkin' maybe
you're one o' them buckle bunnies. I got a buckle
right here if you want to see it." His dirty hand
tugged at the ordinary Western-style belt buckle and
unfastened it. "You'll like what I got underneath it
even better."

Until that moment, Lexie had merely been annoyed. She'd dealt with drunks at other rodeos. But
now a cold fear crept over her. She was alone out
here, where nobody could hear her scream over the
sounds of the rodeo. The man had her backed
against the fence, and he was big enough to easily
overpower her. There was a pistol under the front
seat of the truck, but it was parked in the lot reserved
for rigs, too far away to be of any use.

She glared up at the big man, trying not to show
fear. "I'm not a buckle bunny," she said. "And you're
drunk. I don't like drunks. Neither does my boyfriend. If you're smart, you'll leave before he gets
back here."

The boyfriend part was a lie, but it was the only
defense she had. Unfortunately, the way the man's
yellow-toothed grin widened told her it wasn't

enough. She'd told Ruben to take his time; but even if he were to show up now, the 150-pound foreman was pushing sixty. Without a weapon, he'd be no match for the hulking brute, and there was no one else in sight. Lexie was on her own.

Crouching against the steel fence, she prepared to defend herself. The big man was staggering drunk and appeared slow. A strike in a vital spot—his groin or his eyes—might disable him long enough for her to get away.

"C'mon, honey. You'll like it once we git started." He lunged for her, the move fast but awkward. Lexie had been poised to spring at him, boots kicking, fingers clawing; but her instincts took over. She dodged to one side as he lurched forward, stumbled over his own feet, and crashed full force into the tubular steel rails of the fence. Stunned, he grunted and staggered backward, blood flowing from his nose. His legs folded beneath him as he collapsed in the dust.

As the man curled onto his side, moaning and cradling his bloodied nose, Lexie whipped out her cell phone. She didn't have the number for fairgrounds security, but a 911 call should get some kind of help.

She was about to punch in the number when, from a short distance behind her, came the sound of . . . clapping.

Startled, she turned to see the rangy figure of a man striding toward her from around the far end of the fence. Moving fast, he came within speaking distance. "That was quite a show. Remind me never to tangle with Miss Lexie Champion."

It startled her again, hearing her name. But she

wasn't about to lower her guard. "I could've used some help," she said, glaring up at him. He was a shade under six feet tall, compactly muscled and dressed in weathered cowboy clothes. The only distinguishing feature of his outfit was the silver PBR prize buckle that fastened his belt. The man was a bull rider, evidently a good one, and he looked the part.

His grin widened. "If I'd shown up thirty seconds sooner, I'd have decked the bastard for you. But by the time I saw you, there was no need. I couldn't have done a better job myself." He swept off his battered Resistol hat and extended a hand. "Shane Tully. I took a chance on finding you here. It looks like I arrived just in time. If that jerk hadn't fallen against the fence, you'd have needed some help."

Lexie accepted the confident handshake. His palm was cool against her own, the skin as tough as boot leather. Shane Tully. The name rang a bell in her memory, albeit a faint one. He was a regular on the PBR circuit, his rank just moving into the top twenty. This year he was a serious contender for the finals in Las Vegas.

The man on the ground moaned and stirred. "Broke my friggin' nose," he muttered. "Need help . . ."

"Let's get you on your feet, pal." Handing Lexie his hat, Tully crouched behind him and worked his hands under the big man's arms. Some pushing and lifting got the drunk upright. Tully took a clean white handkerchief out of his pocket and laid it on the man's bleeding nose. "Keep it," he said. "This'll teach you not to make unwelcome advances to ladies. There's a first aid station on the midway, by the Ferris wheel. Can you make it that far on your own, or should we call security?"

The man swore under his breath and shuffled off, one hand clutching the handkerchief to his nose. Lexie kept her eyes on him until he'd gained a safe distance. Only then did she turn to face the bull rider.

She knew he probably wasn't here to compete. This rodeo was sanctioned by the Professional Rodeo Cowboys Association, or PRCA. The cowboys coming here would compete in bronc riding, calf roping, and other events including bull riding. In 1992, the leading bull riders had broken away from the PRCA and formed their own elite organization, the Professional Bull Riders, or PBR. Only the best could compete in their hugely popular events around the country. Membership, for both riders and bucking bulls, was by invitation only.

Which might have something to do with the reason Shane Tully had come to find her.

"You still haven't told me what you're doing here, Mr. Tully," she said, handing him the hat.

"It's Shane, and I can't say you've given me much of a chance."

He smiled with his mouth. His features struck Lexie as more rugged than handsome—deep-set brown eyes, a long jaw ending in a square chin, and a scar, like a thin slash with two stitch marks, running down his left cheek.

He had the look of a man who'd been through some rough times, but Lexie guessed that he wasn't much older than twenty-five or twenty-six. With a few notable exceptions, bull riding was a young man's sport. Older bodies couldn't take the punishment.

"I'm giving you a chance to tell me now." She folded her arms, waiting.

His gaze flickered past her, into the holding pen
where the four bulls milled like star athletes loosen-
ing up for the big game. Then his eyes, warmer now
with flecks of copper, met hers again. "I was in the
neighborhood," he said, "and I thought I'd stop by
and check out your bull, see how he bucks—maybe
give myself an edge if I happen to draw him later."

Lexie didn't have to ask which bull he was talking
about. That would be Whirlwind, the rankest bull
the Alamo Canyon Ranch had ever produced—the
bull that, after twenty-three times out of the chute,
had yet to be ridden to the eight-second whistle—
the bull that had just been selected to join the
PBR circuit.

More from Bestselling Author
JANET DAILEY

Books by Bestselling Author
Fern Michaels

___The Jury	0-8217-7878-1	$6.99US/$9.99CAN
___Sweet Revenge	0-8217-7879-X	$6.99US/$9.99CAN
___Lethal Justice	0-8217-7880-3	$6.99US/$9.99CAN
___Free Fall	0-8217-7881-1	$6.99US/$9.99CAN
___Fool Me Once	0-8217-8071-9	$7.99US/$10.99CAN
___Vegas Rich	0-8217-8112-X	$7.99US/$10.99CAN
___Hide and Seek	1-4201-0184-6	$6.99US/$9.99CAN
___Hokus Pokus	1-4201-0185-4	$6.99US/$9.99CAN
___Fast Track	1-4201-0186-2	$6.99US/$9.99CAN
___Collateral Damage	1-4201-0187-0	$6.99US/$9.99CAN
___Final Justice	1-4201-0188-9	$6.99US/$9.99CAN
___Up Close and Personal	0-8217-7956-7	$7.99US/$9.99CAN
___Under the Radar	1-4201-0683-X	$6.99US/$9.99CAN
___Razor Sharp	1-4201-0684-8	$7.99US/$10.99CAN
___Yesterday	1-4201-1494-8	$5.99US/$6.99CAN
___Vanishing Act	1-4201-0685-6	$7.99US/$10.99CAN
___Sara's Song	1-4201-1493-X	$5.99US/$6.99CAN
___Deadly Deals	1-4201-0686-4	$7.99US/$10.99CAN
___Game Over	1-4201-0687-2	$7.99US/$10.99CAN
___Sins of Omission	1-4201-1153-1	$7.99US/$10.99CAN
___Sins of the Flesh	1-4201-1154-X	$7.99US/$10.99CAN
___Cross Roads	1-4201-1192-2	$7.99US/$10.99CAN

Romantic Suspense from
Lisa Jackson

Absolute Fear	0-8217-7936-2	$7.99US/$9.99CAN
Afraid to Die	1-4201-1850-1	$7.99US/$9.99CAN
Almost Dead	0-8217-7579-0	$7.99US/$10.99CAN
Born to Die	1-4201-0278-8	$7.99US/$9.99CAN
Chosen to Die	1-4201-0277-X	$7.99US/$10.99CAN
Cold Blooded	1-4201-2581-8	$7.99US/$8.99CAN
Deep Freeze	0-8217-7296-1	$7.99US/$10.99CAN
Devious	1-4201-0275-3	$7.99US/$9.99CAN
Fatal Burn	0-8217-7577-4	$7.99US/$10.99CAN
Final Scream	0-8217-7712-2	$7.99US/$10.99CAN
Hot Blooded	1-4201-0678-3	$7.99US/$9.49CAN
If She Only Knew	1-4201-3241-5	$7.99US/$9.99CAN
Left to Die	1-4201-0276-1	$7.99US/$10.99CAN
Lost Souls	0-8217-7938-9	$7.99US/$10.99CAN
Malice	0-8217-7940-0	$7.99US/$10.99CAN
The Morning After	1-4201-3370-5	$7.99US/$9.99CAN
The Night Before	1-4201-3371-3	$7.99US/$9.99CAN
Ready to Die	1-4201-1851-X	$7.99US/$9.99CAN
Running Scared	1-4201-0182-X	$7.99US/$10.99CAN
See How She Dies	1-4201-2584-2	$7.99US/$8.99CAN
Shiver	0-8217-7578-2	$7.99US/$10.99CAN
Tell Me	1-4201-1854-4	$7.99US/$9.99CAN
Twice Kissed	0-8217-7944-3	$7.99US/$9.99CAN
Unspoken	1-4201-0093-9	$7.99US/$9.99CAN
Whispers	1-4201-5158-4	$7.99US/$9.99CAN
Wicked Game	1-4201-0338-5	$7.99US/$9.99CAN
Wicked Lies	1-4201-0339-3	$7.99US/$9.99CAN
Without Mercy	1-4201-0274-5	$7.99US/$10.99CAN
You Don't Want to Know	1-4201-1853-6	$7.99US/$9.99CAN

Available Wherever Books Are Sold!
Visit our website at **www.kensingtonbooks.com**

More by Bestselling Author

Lori Foster

Bad Boys to Go	0-7582-0552-X	$6.99US/$9.99CAN
I Love Bad Boys	0-7582-0135-4	$6.99US/$9.99CAN
I'm Your Santa	0-7582-2860-0	$6.99US/$9.99CAN
Jamie	0-8217-7514-6	$6.99US/$9.99CAN
Jingle Bell Rock	0-7582-0570-8	$6.99US/$9.99CAN
Jude's Law	0-8217-7802-1	$6.99US/$9.99CAN
Murphy's Law	0-8217-7803-X	$6.99US/$9.99CAN
Never Too Much	1-4201-0656-2	$6.99US/$8.49CAN
The Night Before Christmas	0-7582-1215-1	$6.99US/$9.99CAN
Perfect for the Beach	0-7582-0773-5	$6.99US/$9.99CAN
Say No to Joe?	0-8217-7512-X	$6.99US/$9.99CAN
Star Quality	0-7582-1008-6	$4.99US/$5.99CAN
Too Much Temptation	1-4201-0431-4	$6.99US/$9.99CAN
Truth or Dare	0-8217-8054-9	$4.99US/$6.99CAN
Unexpected	0-7582-0549-X	$6.99US/$9.99CAN
A Very Merry Christmas	0-7582-1541-X	$6.99US/$9.99CAN
When Bruce Met Cyn	0-8217-7513-8	$6.99US/$9.99CAN

Available Wherever Books Are Sold!

Check out our website at **www.kensingtonbooks.com**